TREASON OF
Sparta

Also by Christian Cameron

The Chivalry Series
The Ill-Made Knight
The Long Sword
The Green Count
The Sword of Justice
Hawkwood's Sword
The Emperor's Sword

The Tyrant Series
Tyrant
Tyrant: Storm of Arrows
Tyrant: Funeral Games
Tyrant: King of the Bosporus
Tyrant: Destroyer of Cities
Tyrant: Force of Kings

The Long War Series
Killer of Men
Marathon
Poseidon's Spear
The Great King
Salamis
Rage of Ares

Tom Swan
Tom Swan and the Head of St George Parts One–Six
Tom Swan and the Siege of Belgrade Parts One–Seven
Tom Swan and the Last Spartans Parts One–Five
Tom Swan and the Keys of Peter

The Commander Series
The New Achilles
The Last Greek

Other Novels
Washington and Caesar
Alexander: God of War

TREASON OF
Sparta

CHRISTIAN CAMERON

ORION

First published in Great Britain in 2023 by Orion Books,
an imprint of The Orion Publishing Group Ltd
Carmelite House, 50 Victoria Embankment
London EC4Y 0DZ

This edition first published in Great Britain in 2024

An Hachette UK Company

1 3 5 7 9 10 8 6 4 2

A CIP catalogue record for this book
is available from the British Library.

ISBN (MMP) 978 1 4091 9822 2
ISBN (eBook) 978 1 4091 9823 9
ISBN (Audio) 978 1 4091 9848 2

Typeset by Deltatype Ltd, Birkenhead, Merseyside

Printed in Great Britain by Clays Ltd, Elcograf S.p.A.

www.orionbooks.co.uk

For Giannis Kadaglou
Friend, comrade, researcher, hero.

Without you there would be no reenactment in Greece,
and none of these novels would feel right.

Glossary

I am an *amateur* Greek scholar. My definitions are my own, but taken from the LSJ or Routledge's *Handbook of Greek Mythology* or Smith's *Classical Dictionary*. On some military issues I have the temerity to disagree with the received wisdom on the subject. Also check my website at www.christiancameronauthor.com or the website https://plataea2022.com/ for more information and some helpful pictures.

Agoge The Laconian or Spartan training system. Sadly, almost all our information about this is much later, and may represent a sort of Spartan theme park established for rich Romans in a later era. Still, they did train some fine soldiers ...

Agon A contest. Also the root word of agony ...

Agora The central market of a Greek city.

Akinakes A Scythian short sword or long knife, also sometimes carried by Medes and Persians.

Andron The 'men's room' of a proper Greek house – where men have symposia. Recent research has cast real doubt as to the sexual exclusivity of the room, but the name sticks.

Apobatai The Chariot Warriors. In many towns – towns that hadn't used chariots in warfare for centuries, the *Apobatai* were the elite three hundred or so. In Athens, they competed in special events; in Thebes, they may have been the fore-runners of the Sacred Band. I have chosen to interpret them as possible elite military units.

Archon A city's senior official or, in some cases, one of three or four. A magnate.

Aspis/Aspides The Greek hoplite's shield. The *aspis* is about a yard in diameter, is deeply dished (up to six inches deep) and should weigh between eight and sixteen pounds.

Basilieus An aristocratic title from

a bygone era (at least in 500 BC) that means 'king' or 'lord'.

Bireme A warship rowed by two tiers of oars, as opposed to a *trireme*, which has three tiers.

Boule The council of a city, usually elected.

Chiton The standard tunic for most men, made by taking a single continuous piece of cloth and folding it in half, pinning the shoulders and open side. Can be made quite fitted by means of pleating. Often made of very fine quality material – usually wool, sometimes linen, especially in the upper classes. A full *chiton* was ankle length for men and women.

Chitoniskos A small *chiton*, usually just longer than modesty demanded – or not as long as modern modesty would demand! Worn by warriors and farmers, often heavily bloused and very full by warriors to pad their armour. Usually wool.

Chlamys A short cloak made by a rectangle of cloth roughly 60 by 90 inches – could also be worn as a **chiton** if folded and pinned a different way. Or slept under as a blanket.

Daidala Kithairon, the mountain that towered over Plataea, was the site of a remarkable fire festival, the *Daidala*, which was celebrated by the Plataeans on the summit of the mountain. In the usual ceremony, as mounted by the Plataeans in every seventh year, a wooden idol (*daidalon*) would be dressed in bridal robes and dragged on an ox-cart from Plataea to the top of the mountain, where it would be burned after appropriate rituals. In the *Great Daidala*, which was celebrated every forty-nine years, fourteen *daidala* from different Boeotian towns would be burned on a large wooden pyre heaped with brushwood, together with a cow and a bull that were sacrificed to Zeus and Hera. This huge pyre on the mountain top must have provided a most impressive spectacle; Pausanias remarks that he knew of no other flame that rose as high or could be seen from so far.

Daimon Literally a spirit, the *daimon* of combat might be adrenaline, and the *daimon* of philosophy might simply be native intelligence. Suffice it to say that very intelligent men – like Socrates – believed that god-sent spirits could infuse a man and influence his actions.

Daktyloi Literally digits or fingers, in common talk, 'inches' in the system of measurement. Systems for measurement differed from city to city. I have taken the liberty of using just one, the Athenian units of measurement.

Daric A gold coin of standard weight, minted in the Persian Empire. Coinage was relatively new in 480 BCE and standard weights and measures were a radical innovation. Cries of 'Persian Gold' usually meant that someone had been bribed by the Great King.

Despoina Female honorific, like 'Lady'

Diekplous A complex naval tactic about which some debate remains. In this book, the *Diekplous* or through stroke, is commenced with an attack by the ramming ship's bow (picture the two ships approaching bow to bow or head on) and cathead on the enemy oars. Oars were the most vulnerable part of a fighting ship, something very difficult to imagine unless you've rowed in a big boat and understand how lethal your own oars can be – to you! After the attacker crushed the enemy's oars, he passes, flank to flank, and then turns when astern, coming up easily (the defender is almost dead in the water) and ramming the enemy under the stern or counter as desired.

Diolkos The paved trackway that crossed the Corinthian isthmus, allowing ships to be transported from the Aegean to the Ionian Sea without circumnavigating the Peloponnese, saving time and shipwreck.

Doru/Dory A spear, about ten feet long, with a bronze butt spike and a spearhead.

Eleutheria Freedom.

Ephebe A young, free man of property. A young man in training to be a *hoplite*. Usually performing service to his city and, in ancient terms, at one of the two peaks of male beauty.

Ephor A member of the ruling council of Sparta, five magistrates with extensive powers, even over the two kings.

Epilektoi 'Chosen' or picked men. The best hoplites of any city, usually the best armoured and best trained.

Eromenos The 'beloved' in a same-sex pair in ancient Greece. Usually younger, about seventeen (but in Sparta up to thirty). This is a complex, almost dangerous subject in the modern world – were these pair-bonds about sex, or chivalric love, or just a 'brotherhood' of warriors? I suspect there were elements of all three. And to write about this period without discussing the *eromenos/erastes* bond would, I fear, be like putting all the warriors in steel armor instead of bronze ...

Erastes The 'lover' in a same-sex pair bond – the older man, a tried warrior, thirty to sixty years old.

Eudaimonia Literally 'well-spirited'. A feeling of extreme joy.

Exhedra The porch of the woman's quarters – in some cases, any porch over a farm's central courtyard.

Helot The 'race of slaves' of

Ancient Sparta – the conquered peoples who lived with the Spartiates and did all of their work so that they could concentrate entirely on making war and more Spartans.

Hetaera Literally a 'female companion'. In ancient Athens, a *Hetaera* was a courtesan, a highly skilled woman who provided sexual companionship as well as fashion, political advice, and music.

Himation A very large piece of rich, often embroidered wool, worn as an outer garment by wealthy citizen women or as a sole garment by older men, especially those in authority.

Hoplite A Greek upper-class warrior. Possession of a heavy spear, a helmet, and an *aspis* (see above) and income above the marginal lowest free class were all required to serve as a *hoplite*. Although much is made of the 'citizen soldier' of ancient Greece, it would be fairer to compare *hoplites* to medieval knights than to Roman legionnaires or modern National Guardsmen. Poorer citizens did serve, and sometimes as *hoplites* or marines – but in general, the front ranks were the preserve of upper class men who could afford the best training and the essential armour.

Hoplitodromos The *hoplite* race, or race in armour. Two *stades* with an *aspis* on your shoulder,

a helmet, and greaves in the early runs. I've run this race in armour. It is no picnic.

Hoplomachia A *hoplite* contest, or sparring match. Again, there is enormous debate as to when *hoplomachia* came into existence and how much training Greek *hoplites* received. One thing that they didn't do is drill like modern soldiers – there's no mention of it in all of Greek literature. However, they had highly evolved martial arts (see *Pankration*) and it is almost certain that *hoplomachia* was a term that referred to 'the martial art of fighting when fully equipped as a *hoplite*'.

Hoplomachos A participant in *hoplomachia*.

Hydria A ceramic water jar, sometimes beautifully decorated for temple use.

Hypozomata The tensioned rope connecting the stem and stern of a *trireme* and keeping the hull stiff.

Hypaspist Literally 'under the shield'. A squire or military servant – by the time of Arimnestos, the *hypaspist* was usually a younger man of the same class as the *hoplite*. (Thus different from the elite military unit of the time of Alexander the Great).

Kithara A stringed instrument of some complexity, with a hollow body as a soundboard.

Kline A couch.

Kopis The heavy, back-curved saber of the Greeks. Like a longer, heavier modern Kukri or Ghurka knife.

Kore A maiden or daughter.

Kubernetes The senior helmsman on a *trireme*.

Kykeon A welcome cup, which could be a simple as wine with grated cheese, or more complex. In the Iliad there's some suggestion that women know 'magic' versions.

Kylix A wide, shallow, handled bowl for drinking wine.

Logos Literally the 'word'. In pre-Socratic Greek philosophy the word is everything – the power beyond the gods.

Longche A six to seven foot throwing spear, also used for hunting. A *hoplite* might carry a pair of *longche*, or a single, longer and heavier *dory*.

Machaira A heavy sword or long knife.

Maenad The 'raving ones' – ecstatic female followers of Dionysus.

Mantis A seer or wizard.

Mastos A woman's breast. A *mastos* cup is shaped like a woman's breast with a rattle in the nipple – so when you drink, you lick the nipple and the rattle shows that you emptied the cup. I'll leave the rest to imagination …

Medimnoi A grain measure. Very roughly – thirty-five to a hundred pounds of grain.

Megaron A style of building with a roofed porch.

Metic A legally resident foreigner.

Mina Roughly a pound, in many ancient weighing systems across the Mediterranean.

Navarch An admiral.

Obol A small copper or bronze coin.

Oikia The household – all the family and all the slaves, and sometimes the animals and the farmland itself.

Opson Whatever spread, dip, or accompaniment an ancient Greek had with bread.

Pais A child. Sometimes a derogatory name for a slave.

Palaestra The exercise sands of the gymnasium.

Pankration The military martial art of the ancient Greeks – an unarmed combat system that bears more than a passing resemblance to modern MMA techniques, with a series of carefully structured blows and domination holds that is, by modern standards, very advanced. Also the basis of the Greeks sword and spear-based martial arts. Kicking, punching, wrestling, grappling, on the ground and standing, were all permitted.

Parasang A Persian unit of measurement, representing about five kilometers. An army was supposed to march four to five parasangs a day. Herodotus says the Parasang is equal to thirty stadia.

Pelte/Peltast The pelte is a

crescent or half-moon shaped shield usually made of wicker; the peltast is a lightly armed soldier carrying a pelte. Just to confuse us, later Peltasts carried small round shields ...

Pentekonter Fifty oared ships, about one third the size of a trireme, too small to stand in the line of battle but useful for trade and for piracy.

Petasos A broad brimmed sun hat, usually made of wool.

Peplos A short over-fold of cloth that women could wear as a hood or to cover the breasts.

Phalanx The full military potential of a town; the actual, formed body of men before a battle (all of the smaller groups for ed together made a *phalanx*). In this period, it would be a mistake to imagine a carefully drilled military machine. In modern scholarship there is much debate about 'when' the phalanx formed. In my opinion, the deep, cohesive phalanx of the hoplite was a development of warfare with Persia, and thus quite late, but I'm not a professional.

Phylarch A file leader – an officer commanding the four to sixteen men standing behind him in the *phalanx*. This term is probably anachronistic, but I needed something.

Polemarch The war leader.

Polis The city. The basis of all Greek political thought and expression, the government that was held to be more important – a higher good – than any individual or even family. To this day, when we talk about politics, we're talking about the 'things of our city'.

Porne A prostitute.

Porpax The bronze or leather band that encloses the forearm on a Greek *aspis*.

Proxenos Something like a modern consular officer, a citizen of one state who provided guest services and good council for another state. So, for example, Cimon son of Miltiades was proxenos for Sparta most of his life, even during the events of this volume.

Psiloi Light infantryman – usually slaves or adolescent freemen who, in this period, were not organised and seldom had any weapon beyond some rocks to throw.

Pyrrhiche The 'War Dance'. A line dance in armour done by all of the warriors, often very complex. There's reason to believe that the *Pyrrhiche* was the method by which the young were trained in basic martial arts and by which 'drill' was inculcated.

Pyxis A box, often circular, turned from wood or made of metal.

Rowers on a Trireme – *thalamite, zygite,* and *thranite,* the three 'layers' of rowers in a trireme from bottom to top. Given that everyone rowed naked and no one stopped to use a washroom, one can easily imagine why the lowest layer was considered the worst duty.

Rhapsode A master-poet, often a performer who told epic works like the *Iliad* from memory.

Satrap A Persian ruler of a province of the Persian Empire.

Saurauter The bronze spike on the back end of a Greek hoplite spear. Literally, the 'lizard killer,' which tells us a great deal about the boredom of military service.

Skeuophoros Literally a 'shield carrier', unlike the *hypaspist*, this is a slave or freed man who does camp work and carried the armour and baggage.

Sparabara The large wicker shield of the Persian and Mede elite infantry. Also the name of those soldiers.

Spolas Another name for a leather *corslet*, often used of the lion skin of Herakles.

Stade A measure of distance. An Athenian *stade* is about 185 meters.

Stasis In Greek, it means civil war, a terrible thought to all Greeks.

Strategos In Athens, the commander of one of the ten military tribes. Elsewhere, any senior Greek officer – sometimes the commanding General.

Synaspismos The closest order that *hoplites* could form – so close that the shields overlap, hence 'shield on shield'.

Taxis Any group but, in military terms, a company; I use it for sixty to three hundred men.

Taxiarchos A company commander; the officer in command of a taxis, which was not a standardized command. In modern Greek the expression 'Entaxi' still means 'in order' or 'okay.'

Tekne The craftspeople of Ancient Greece, highly skilled professionals with deep expertise.

Thetes The lowest free class – citizens with limited rights.

Thorax/Thorakes Chest or torso armour. In 500 BC, the best *thorakes* were made of bronze, mostly of the so-called 'bell' thorax variety. A few muscle corslets appear at the end of this period, gaining popularity into the 450s. Another style is the 'white' *thorax* seen to appear just as the Persian Wars begin – re-enactors call this the 'Tube and Yoke' corslet and some people call it (erroneously in my opinion) the linothorax. Some of them may have been made of linen – we'll never know – but the likelier material is Athenian leather, which was often tanned and finished with alum, thus being bright white. Yet another style was a tube and yoke of scale, which you can see in vase art. A scale corslet would have been the most expensive of all, and probably provided the best protection.

Thugater Daughter. Look at the word carefully and you'll see the 'daughter' in it ...

Trierarch The captain of a ship – sometimes just the owner or builder, sometimes the fighting captain.

Trireme The standard warship of the Persian Wars, a ship with three 'decks' or banks of oars, a crew of about two hundred including oarsmen, sailors and marines, and a heavy bronze ram. Early triremes focused on delivery of the maximum number of marines into massed boarding actions, but Athens, specifically, began to develop better rowing and ramming tactics. The modern reproduction 'Olympia' represents the best reconstruction research available on the military trireme. Triremes were not good sailors, and it was almost impossible to fight with the masts raised. They can carry only very limited cargo because they are lightly built and all the 'space' in the hull is filled with rowers.

Trihemiola The trihemiola is (apparently) a western Mediterranean design often associated with piracy; in terms of naval architecture it represented an attempt to combine some of the qualities of a sailing ship with rowing and combat abilities of the *trireme*. The ship sacrifices some rowers (and thus rowing speed and endurance) for permanent standing masts and a better steering rig. I have chosen to interpret them as fully decked, which would have made them heavier (and slower) but stiffer and much better for sea keeping.

Xiphos The Ancient Greek short, straight sword. Mostly leaf-bladed, and often pattern welded.

Zone A belt, often just rope or finely wrought cord, but could be a heavy bronze kidney belt for war.

Zygon/Zygos Related to the middle bank of oarsmen, above, it means 'the yoked ones' and implies the close relation of hoplites in combat; like yoked oxen. A rank of hoplites was 'yoked' and sometimes the term 'Yoked' (Zygos) was used for the whole hoplite class.

Names and Personages

On Apollo's Raven

Arminestos of Plataea, of *Raven*

Aten, his servant

Damon, son of Eneas, senior helmsman

Nicanor, second helmsman

Nestor, son of Dion and sailing master (Old Nestor)

Nestor, the sailor (Young Nestor)

Various Marines

Brasidas, Taxiarchos

Styges, the marine

Hector of Anarchos, the marine

Hipponax of Arminestos, the marine (sometimes captain of *Apollo's Serpent*)

Achilles of Simonides, the marine

Leander

Kassandros

Zephyrides

Heraklitus of Ephesus, son of Briseis and Artaphernes

Diodoros

Arios

Polymarchos of Croton

Alexanor

Archers

Ka, the Nubian archer

Vasilos, an older man from Magna Graecia

Nemet, a small Nubian

Myron, the former Helot

Phorbas, the former Helot

Oarsmen and Sailors
Poseidonos
Giorgos
Archelaus (later second helmsman)
Nicolos
Sikli
Kineas
Eugenios
Leon

Africans
Rigura, the King
Mera the cunning
Ole Llurin, the smith

The Ionian Squadron
Amaranth – Neoptolimos
Gad's Fortune – Parmenios
Apollo's Raven – Arimnestos
Nike's Wings – Damon
Apollo's Serpent – Hipponax
Theseus – Ion (cousin of Neoptolymos), a ship from Scyros
Black Raven – Moire
Amastris – Megakles
Arachne – Ephialtes of Naxos
Naiad – Theognis of Naxos

Athenian Ships and Captains
Parthenos – Ameinias of Pallene
Eumenes of Anagyrus
Horse Tamer – Xanthippus,
Athena Nike – Aristides
Ajax – Cimon, with Thekles as Marine captain. Cimon is an old friend, and one of the leading politicians of Athens, as well as being the son of Miltiades.
Dawn – Metiochus, brother of Cimon

Ionians
Anaxagoras of Clazomenaeu, Archilogos' friend
Briseis, wife of Arimnestos, former wife of the Satrap of Lydia, sometimes called 'Helen Reborn'

Archilogos of Ephesus, boyhood friend or Arimnestos, Briseis' brother, and leader of the new Ionian revolt

Alysia, a graduate of the school of Sappho, wife of an important Persian tax farmer

Cleis of Eresos, headmistress of the School of Sappho

Ataelus, son of Laertes, a pro-Persian Ionian

Thrasybulus the Samian, a pro-Persian captain

Theophilos of Lesbos, Archon of Mytilini

Dionysios his son, sometimes a marine on *Apollo's Raven*

Spartans and Peloponnesians

Pausanias, Navarch of the Allied Fleet and victor of the Battle of Plataea

Gorgo of Sparta (Queen and widow of Leonidas)

Demaratus, exiled King of Sparta and friend of Brasidas

Sparthius, friend and comrade of Arimnestos

Medon of Hermione, of *Revenge*

Corinthians

Lykon, son of Antinor, of *Penelope*

Philip, son of Sophokles, of Thrace and Corinth, of *Kore*

Adeimantus, son of Ocytus, Navarch of Corinth, of *Aphrodite*

Thracians

Katisa of the Melinditae

Brauron graduates

Thiale, Priestess of Artemis

Iris, wife of Hector

Heliodora, a young woman with blond hair (Hannah), daughter of Cleitus, wife of Hipponax

Athenians

Themistocles the cunning, hero of Salamis

Aristides the just, politician and warrior

Jocasta the wise, wife of Aristides

Cleitus of the Alcmaeonidae, formerly Arimnestos of Plataea's nemesis, now in an uneasy truce

Phrynicus, the playwright

Irene, his wife

Aeschylus, the poet

Pericles, an ephebe destined for greatness (age 20)

Aleitus, father of Euphonia, now-dead mother of Euphoria and wife of Arimnestos

Xanthippus, politician and captain

Socrates, a farmer

Gaia, his daughter, attending Sappho's school in Eresos.

Aegenetan

Polycritus, son of Crius, commands the trireme *Nike*

Plataeans

Euphoria, daughter of Arimnestos

Hermiogenes

Tirtaeus

Penelope

Eugenios, Briseis and Arimnestos' steward

Polymachos, an Olympic trainer of athletes

Persians and their allies

Xerxes, Great King of Persia

Ariabignes, son of Darius and brother of Xerxes, commanding the fleet aboard *Morbaal*

Theomestor son of Androdamas, Samian, of *Zoster*

Phylacus son of Histiaeus, Samian, commands *Paralamus*

Artemesia of Hallicanarsus

Artaphernes the Elder, first husband of Briseis and Satrap of Lydia

Artaphernes II, his son

Heraklitus son of Artaphernes and Briseis

Maskames, Persian Governor of Doriscus, the last Persian stronghold in Europe besides Byzantium

Cyrus the Persian, an Immortal

Darius, his younger brother, an Immortal

Aryanam, his friend, an Immortal

Prologue

Here we are again, friends! I promised you a hunt, and Thrace is the place to hunt. The game is better here than it ever was in my boyhood on Cithaeron, or in the hills of Attica. By Hera, there are still lions and bears here, and big deer fit for Artemis herself! We'll not be clubbing rabbits for our meals.

And since you've been kind enough to fill this two-handled cup to the brim with unwatered wine, and to have my *pais* bring it to me, I feel that you honour me. And what can I give you in return but a story?

Well. I am well known for my stories, I think. So set your hunting spears aside, fill your cups and place them by you, stretch out by the fire, and let's have a tale. Indeed, we'll have a circle of tales, will we not? For I am not the only voice speaking at our fire circle, and others will tell you of far-off places and other wars, other ships, other men and women, heroes and cowards and victory and defeat, and the gods who walk among men.

But tonight ...

There are some new faces here, so I'll remind you of how we got here. You may recall that at my daughter's wedding, I told you of the Long War, from my boyhood on the slopes of Mount Cithaeron, where my father was a great bronze-smith and my mother was a hard-drinking aristocrat, to the events of the modern age: the terrible defeat of the Greeks at Lade, the stunning victory of the Battle of Marathon, the tragedy of Thermopylae, the wasted victory of Artemisium and the desperate victory of Salamis. And finally, I told you of the day of the Rage of Ares, the greatest battle of our time, fought at my home town of Plataea between Mardonius leading the Great King of Persia's mighty army against us, the coalition of all the Greeks. Well, let's be honest – a coalition of Athens and Sparta, with some other cities trailing along with us. Too many gave earth and water to the Medes; Thebes, first and foremost.

But enough of us stood our ground and fought, and in the end, the Spartans and the Athenians defeated the Persians – aye, and the Megarans and Corinthians and some others. But we did a hard week's work and got it done, and a bloody harvest it was.

At my daughter's wedding feast, I ended my story by talking about the rebuilding, and that, my friends, is where I'll take up the tale tonight. I'll miss my daughter's friend with hair of fire, who blushes so freely and so brightly, and I'll miss my wife's soft hands reminding me to keep the story within the bounds of social acceptability. And perhaps I'll drink too much. These are times for wine, and friends.

And tomorrow we can run off our wine fumes and kill a boar.

But, as is so often the case, I've left my course.

It was the year after the supposed 'end' of the Long War to free Greece. It was the year that Timosthenes was *archon basileus* in Athens. It was the year my friend Astylos of Croton won every running event at Nemea and established himself as the greatest athlete of my generation. It was the year that I was *archon* in Plataea. It was the year in which the Spartan *strategos*, Pausanias, the victor of Plataea and Greece's greatest commander, rose high in the eyes of men, and thought himself the best man in Greece.

It was the year we thought to take the war to the Persians. At least, some of us thought so, as you will hear.

This is the story of that year.

Book One
Athens and Ionia

Perceiving that the Athenians were going to rebuild their walls, the Lacedaemonians sent an embassy to Athens. They would have themselves preferred to see neither her nor any other city in possession of a wall; though here they acted principally at the instigation of their allies, who were alarmed at the strength of [Athens'] newly acquired navy, and the valour which she had displayed in the war with the Medes. They begged her not only to abstain from building walls for herself, but also to join them in throwing down the walls that still held together of the [other] cities. The real meaning of their advice, the suspicion that it contained against the Athenians, was not proclaimed; it was urged that so the barbarian, in the event of a third invasion, would not have any strong place, such as he now had in Thebes, for his base of operations; and that Peloponnese would suffice for all as a base both for retreat and offence. After the Lacedaemonians had thus spoken, they were, on the advice of Themistocles, immediately dismissed by the Athenians, with the answer that ambassadors should be sent to Sparta to discuss the question. Themistocles told the Athenians to send him off with all speed to Lacedaemon, but not to despatch his colleagues as soon as they had selected them, but to wait until they had raised their wall to the height from which defence was possible. Meanwhile the whole population in the city was to labour at the wall, the Athenians, their wives and their children, sparing no edifice, private or public, which might be of any use to the work, but throwing all down.

Thucydides, *History of the Peloponnesian War* Book 1, Chapter 90

My story begins, as it so often has, with the spring trading fleets coming in from Sicily. By the spring of the year after Plataea, I owned four warships, all laid up in my own boat sheds just over the mountain from Plataea, and six round ships, varying in size from a small tub that could just carry a few hundred big amphorae of wine or olive oil to the new *Poseidon*, a slab-sided monster that could carry almost six thousand medimnoi of grain. I'd paid for her to be built to keep the Corinthian shipwrights in business over the winter, but I'd imagined that she might play a role in the grain trade with Aegypt, because I could guess that it would be a few years before the farmers of Attica and Boeotia had recovered.

I also had the *Leto*, who'd been all but rebuilt over the winter, so that she had shining new wood, golden in the spring sunlight, stark against the grey-brown of the older wood in her hull, and the *Io*. Hector, my adopted son, took the *Leto*, as he had in the year of Plataea, and Hipponax, my son by Gaia, took the *Io*, and they were away in the first blush of spring.

If you're not a sailor, listen. Greece is a country made by the gods for sailors, and not least because the land trails away into the sea in many directions, allowing a good captain to get off a beach in almost any wind. My sons were not taking such a foolish risk so early in the year; they could run down the Gulf of Corinth past Naupactus, all the way out into the Italian Sea, and never be so far from land that a man couldn't swim ashore. And then, a single day's sail, and they were in Croton, or one of the other Greek colony cities in Magna Graecia, and they could stay in with the coast around the toe of the boot and then for Syracusa on the first good wind.

They were joined by Leukas, who'd come over the mountains from Piraeus to take the big grain ship. He was the best of my captains, in any weather, now that Megakles and Moire had their own ships and their own business.

We loaded all three ships with whatever we could find to trade: hides, mostly, and some salt, and linen from the year before, and some loot; I remember loading one of the great tents that the Persians had left behind, and some Persian bows. It was an oddly jumbled cargo, but Leukas also had gold and silver to buy things we needed, and a long order list made up by half the citizens of Green Plataea – roof tiles and fabrics and statues and ironware.

And grain.

My sons were right sailor-men, and Leukas was the toughest helmsman afloat for all that he was a wild-haired Briton from the other end of the world. And the weather was surprisingly mild; indeed, we were in for one of the best summers any of us could remember.

And none of that kept me from worry, so that, every two or three days, I'd ride down to Prosili, our little port on the Gulf of Corinth, and look out over the flat blue sea and wonder where they were. And I made a dozen sacrifices to Poseidon in the first week alone, and more as the month drew on.

It was the new moon of Elaphebolion, as we reckon it in Boeotia, when they came sailing back across the gulf. A west wind wafted them all the way from Patras, and Hector bragged as he landed and kissed the beach that they hadn't touched the steering oars for two hundred stadia.

And there was Megakles, in a newly built *trireme*. It was the heavy Phoenician type, and had clearly been built to carry cargo, but his rowers filled the beach and he himself was proud of his ship.

He was full of news from the west: news of Sicily and Massalia, where Doola and Seckla had their warehouses. Why were a couple of Africans running a small trading empire in Gaul? That's another story you'll have to hear another night, my friends. Although, if you stay with me, you'll hear why it matters to this tale.

'In Patras they say the Spartans don't want to fight Persia any more,' Megakles said.

Hector, my adopted son, stopped embracing his own friends and came across the sand to me.

'It's true, Pater,' he said. 'I heard the same in Syracusa. They say the *ephors* want to send all the Ionians to colonise Italy. Or do we call it "Magna Graecia" now?'

6

I'm sorry to keep playing old tunes, but of course, this was what the Sparta First faction had wanted in the year of Plataea. What they'd always wanted – Ionia removed. I thought of what my wife, Briseis, who had once been queen of Ionia, might say.

I thought of what my brother-in-law and lifelong friend and enemy Archilogos might say.

And for the first time in many months, I wondered if the war with Persia was actually over.

Again, I have to digress.

At the same time that the Allied Greeks faced Mardonius and the Persian army at Plataea, the Allied Greek fleet, led by the King of Sparta, pressed eastwards into the maritime heart of the Persian empire – Ionia. Based first from Delos and then farther east, the Allied fleet was cautious at first, but in the end, at Mycale, we caught the Persian fleet and routed it at sea and then captured and burnt the Persian camp on land, and the Ionians, for the most part, liberated themselves on the spot.

Remember, friends, that Ionia is where the revolt against the Persians began. Remember that the Ionians *lost*, and were defeated, and had Satraps placed over their cities, so that they were forced to send contingents to fight us, the western Greeks. At Salamis, most of the best ships serving the Great King came from the Greek cities of Asia Minor.

And while I'd never say this to a crowd of Spartiates, the truth is that Mycale hurt the Great King a good deal more than Plataea. At Plataea he lost a great army; most of it was made up of his own fractious subjects, Medes and Indians and Aegyptians and Africans, and they were losses he could make up in an afternoon.

But at Salamis and Mycale, the Phoenicians were hammered, and the Ionians, in the end, changed sides, and suddenly the Great King *had no fleet*. Let me add that Sicily was not a different world, and the tyrant, Gelon, had just defeated the ships of Carthage, robbing the Phoenicians of their greatest allies and their most likely source of reinforcements.

In the aftermath of Mycale, the Spartan king, Leotychidas, kept most of the fleet together and went to the Dardanelles to cut the cables for the great pontoon bridge by which Xerxes, the Great King, kept sending reinforcements to Europe. But after that, he sailed home with the Spartan contingent, declaring the war to be over, while the Athenians attacked the Chersonese and took it, more by luck, if the truth be told, than by skill. Or so I've been told.

I wasn't there, but Moire was, in the *Black Raven*, with my sons. I'd gone home by then, to be a Plataean.

Enough of the world and war. Except you need to understand this. At Plataea, we saved the freedom of Greece. But at Salamis and Mycale, we ended the possibility of further Persian interference in our affairs – or so we thought. The Persian fleet was defeated, if not destroyed.

Ponder that while you drink your wine, and I'll go back to my story.

I left the beach with Megakles and Hector and Hipponax, and we rode back to my farm over the shoulders of the mountain on mules, far more sure-footed than horses on the steep trails, and we were in the old tower by nightfall. Achilles, my cousin, had given me back the farm after the battle. So many Plataeans had fallen in the great contest – the *agon*, as we called it – that there was better farmland and to spare all down the valley, available to any man with a strong stomach for burying the dead, or burning them. So we rode up the hill as we might have twenty years before, and into the yard of what had been my father's house, and Briseis came down to the yard dressed in a long, flowing Ionian-style *chiton* of transparent wool with a narrow edging of gold and purple. Briseis, dressed as a woman of Ionia, was not a sight commonly seen in Plataea, where women tended to a severe *peplos* with a long modest overfold. I remember her standing there in her purple and gold, the personification, if you will, of all our civilisation.

She welcomed my guests with wine and barley and cheese, and I was proud to see that although neither Hector nor Hipponax were the sons of her body, she embraced each before she kissed Megakles on the lips, which caused him to squirm in a way that made the rest of us laugh.

'You bring my sons home,' she said to me. 'What reward can I give you?'

I thought of my mother, drunk in her rooms, and my father, taking out his anger on his bronze, and I pondered how I, the Killer of Men, had come to have so much happiness in my life.

'I need no reward,' I said.

'Get a room!' Leukas leered. 'Enough domestic bliss.'

Briseis smiled her Ionian Aphrodite smile and led us into the hearth, where she made the matron's prayers before we set to a meal. She was a priestess of Aphrodite and she had a household shrine to Hera and Athena, and we made the rounds, so to speak. Briseis practised more piety than I was used to, but I liked it, and I loved her seriousness in ritual, her face turned to the rafters in invocation.

Leukas, Megakles and my sons took turns giving her the news from Sicily and the Peloponnese, and she nodded. Listen, friends: most Greek women are superb at managing a house or making a *kykeon*, but my wife had been a queen and could be again; and she was as good at politics as Aristides or Miltiades, and so she listened with a different ear.

That being said, we'd arrived at ways and means, you might say, and so she waited until they were all gone to our newly built guest quarters before she lay back on a *kline* and waved her hand.

'The Spartans don't want Ionia to thrive,' she said.

I nodded.

She poured herself a little wine and watered it.

'Do you know what they fear?' she asked me.

I shrugged. 'The modern world?' I asked.

There had been a time when I'd hated Sparta, but Gorgo and Sparthius had changed that for me. I now admired almost everything about Sparta, except their treatment of their helots and their cowardly, cautious ephors.

She smiled the smile women use when they see that men are not entirely fools.

'Exactly, my husband,' she said. 'They fear that Athens will rally the Ionians and make them strong.'

'Athens?' I asked. 'Athens is a burnt husk of itself without a working temple.'

'Now you sound like a Spartan,' she said. 'Athens has the mightiest fleet on Ocean, and Persia, however fast her Satraps rebuild, has nothing this evening to float on the sea. Athens can dictate almost any course she wants. Athens is also the last state standing with a merchant fleet, so she's going to control trade. She is about to be the richest city in the world. Athena must be pleased with her city.'

I nodded. I admit, when I recall these conversations, I'm probably adding together many such; certainly, Briseis and I discussed the future of our world, the world of Hipponax and Hector and her sons, too. So, allow me to misremember. Because the thing that I hadn't seen and she had, despite all my years as a pirate, was that Athens, not Sparta, now held the upper hand.

Regardless, what I do remember from that day was her view of the Spartans.

'They cannot allow Athens to lead. And as they see the phoenix rise from the ash,' she predicted, 'they will fear her more and more.' She looked out over our farm sadly. 'Come, husband. Sit by me. I am sad, because what I foresee is the diminution of my people. Athens will steal the art from Ionia and make herself great, and what will become of Miletus and Mytilini and Samos? Will we Aeolians and Ionians become satellites of Great Athens?'

I thought of her brother, my rival and friend Archilogos.

'Somehow I doubt that.'

'And yet Ionia is vulnerable,' she said. 'We need to be sure that Athens at least does not abandon the Ionians.'

'Do we?' I was probably running a hand over her thigh at that point.

She brushed my hand away. 'Yes, husband. We do. And let me remind you that we are in an open room with slaves and ten guests, and that perhaps your thoughts should be on packing for your trip to Athens.'

'Athens?'

'My dear,' she said. 'Did I forget to mention? Aristides has sent for you.'

It might have been simpler to mount a horse and ride to Athens. In the spring of the year after Plataea, I owned more horses than I'd ever owned; the Persians had left Boeotia rich in their abandoned horseflesh and I had a big Nissean, several fine Arabs, and a variety of decent small horses useful for work, as well as a dozen mules.

But Megakles wanted to get back to sea, and he was taking his cargo around to Piraeus via the *diolkos*, the stone road for ships. I chose to sail with him, and so, instead of riding a fine horse for Athens over Mount Cithaeron, I packed my best *himation* and some carefully chosen gifts on mules and went back to Prosili. I kissed my wife and we made sacrifices, and I was pleased to see that she was welcomed by the old priestess of Hera. Our temple was destroyed – our beautiful, if primitive, wooden Hera burnt by the barbarians – but someone's private votive statue stood behind the altar on an old table, and the priestess had survived, and we said the prayers. All over Greece that spring, people prayed in ruined temples and amid destruction, because the barbarians had savaged our holy places.

I did stop at Simon's new farm to ask him to look after my vines, and I mention this to show that in the year after the great battle, the Corvaxae were once again a single family. We'd made the spring sacrifices together, for the first time in a generation. We looked at our burnt houses and we worked together to rebuild.

I'm glad I stopped to visit him, because my mood was light riding over Cithaeron's seaward shoulder, and I was ready – if anyone is ready – to receive the bad news that was waiting for me there.

When I'd ridden down two days before, I'd ordered old Poseidonos, often my lead oarsman on the *Lydia* and now retired to the honourable post of watchman on my ship sheds, to haul out my warships for a spring drying. I had a mind to put the *Lydia* in the water. The old pirate in me suggested that, as we were still in a state of war against Persia, the whole Carian coast and the Aegyptian delta might be fruitful sources of income. I need to remind you, my friends, that in the aftermath of the Persian invasion, despite the loot of their camp, two campaigns of burning and looting by the Great King's army had left us poor and hungry. People *died* in the winter *after* we defeated Mardonius. We needed grain and we needed treasure.

When I returned from Plataea on that fine spring day, it was to find that one of my greatest loves had died over the winter.

The *Lydia* was too full of rot to be saved. Poor Poseidonos felt responsible, and he was drunk when I arrived, and a huddle of slaves, mostly Indians and Medes, cowered near the boat sheds, expecting my wrath.

I was too sad to be angry. I stood for a long time, looking at her upturned hull: the finest ship I'd ever sailed or rowed, the most perfect lines, produced by a genius shipwright at the very lowest ebb of my fortunes. The ship I'd had under my feet at Artemisium and Salamis and Mycale; the ship that I'd sailed right into the harbour of Carthage and out again.

When the *Lydia*, bright paint and vermilion sails, ran at her enemies, they panicked and fled. Her hull strakes and sail were known from Gades to Tyre.

And now, she'd rotted in twenty places. It was the teredo worm, and poor drying techniques, and I had only myself to blame, because after Mycale, in the hurry of trying to rebuild Plataea and work the soil, I'd allowed her to be badly stowed.

Leukas and Megakles came and stood with me, and after a while, I admit that I wept.

11

The next morning, as Megakles sailed for the diolkos, I decided to try and rebuild her. The diolkos was only a day's ride away, if that, and I knew that Megakles would be three days unloading his cargo, moving it across the isthmus, and getting his crew and hired slaves to drag the vessel. If you haven't seen the diolkos, it's a stone roadbed across the isthmus, with deep grooves cut in it that match exactly the wheel spacing of the great trucks that the slaves put under the bow, amidships, and stern of your ship. And then they haul it three miles across to the Aegean from the Gulf of Corinth. It's a miracle of good engineering, and very handy for rapid movement between two points that otherwise are ten to twelve days sailing or rowing apart.

At any rate, I spent the morning, stripped naked in the good spring sunshine, with twenty slaves and Leukas and Hector, prying away loose boards and looking at rotten tree nails. But the more we stripped her, the more damage we found, and not all of it was new.

The truth is that my beautiful *Lydia* had seen three oceans and put her beak in twenty foes, and she was too tired and old to do it again. Indeed, I began, looking at her timbers, to wonder how we'd survived Mycale. I thought that it might have been lucky that we'd spent most of the summer hauled up on beaches, or carrying messages.

But here's the point – and I've strayed a long road around, as is my wont. The *Lydia*'s death hit me like the death of a person. And it made me feel old. Her timbers were my timbers. She had made my fame; she was the basis of my reputation. Her rotten timbers were mine; the deep old cracks in her frame represented the ageing of my old bones.

I would soon reach my fortieth year. In Aegypt, men are accounted old at forty, and by all the gods and my ancestor Heracles, I'd had no reason to expect to live so long, as I'd thrown my body into every battle-rage in the Inner Sea and the Long War.

But tears and anger and sorrow accomplished nothing. So that night, I ordered a good salmon from the local fishermen; I gathered all my old crewmen who lived hard by, and sent to Plataea for my wife and any friends and former crew who happened to be about. And the next night, with Brasidas and Leukas and Megakles as my fellow priests of the cult of the good ship *Lydia*, with Poseidonos, Kineas, Briseis, Styges, Achilles and fifty others, we ate a feast, and then Megakles and I set her afire on the beach.

Just before I set her alight, Briseis stepped into the middle of the circle we'd made, and took the decorative panel from the front of the marine box over the bow. We'd already stripped the ram, cast in far-off Massalia from tin we'd traded ourselves, but Briseis took the beautifully carved timber, and she and Penelope carried it off the side.

Then we all watched her burn, drank our wine, and cried our tears.

Afterwards, we lay on our cloaks to sleep on the beach like weary pirates. I hugged Briseis. She was very gentle, and she held me in the darkness lit by the embers of my smouldering youth.

'I feel old,' I said.

She touched her lips to my mouth. 'Hush, my love. Persian mothers use your name to scare their children.'

I chuckled. 'I'm not sure that's a compliment,' I said.

She put her hand on mine and carried it to her belly. I thrilled at the touch, and my hand began to move.

'We are sleeping in the midst of your friends. On an open beach,' she said.

'You started it,' I accused.

She rested her hand on mine. 'I'm pregnant,' she said.

'What?' I asked.

Someone threw a sandal.

'A baby?' I asked, feeling suddenly younger and much, much happier. And then 'You shouldn't be sleeping out on a beach!'

'Don't be absurd, husband. I have born several babies and slept on innumerable beaches.'

I hugged her close. 'Bless you,' I said.

'Bless Lady Aphrodite, and Hera,' she murmured. 'Now do you feel better about your poor ship?'

'You and Penelope kept a souvenir?' I asked.

She laughed her throaty laugh. 'I wanted you to have something of her, when you build your new warship.'

'New warship?'

She laughed, and now her laugh said I was a fool. 'I may be a housewife in Plataea,' she said, 'but I do not think that I will remain so forever. Eh?' She smiled. 'And you, my lord and husband, are the very king of pirates. You will want a ship.'

I smiled at her in the darkness, because I knew she was right. I was not dead yet.

'I'll call her *Briseis*,' I said.

This, to a woman who'd never bridled at my going to war in a ship named for another woman.

'I think you should call her *Apollo's Raven*,' she said with an edge. 'Briseis is my name, not a ship's name.'

Right. Gulp.

Five days later, I was lying on a kline in the beautiful sympositastic space of Aristides' *andron*. A Persian slave served me wine, and Cleitus, once my dire foe, and Olympiodoros, who had commanded the *epilektoi* with me at Plataea, and Pericles, the young savant and competent spearman, and half a dozen other rich and powerful Athenians lay around me, and Cimon, Miltiades' son and almost my brother, lay beside me. Jocasta had joined us for a single cup of wine, something that would have been unseemly before the Persian invasion.

Aristides was very plainly dressed. Indeed, one of the many changes that war and siege had brought to Athens was a visible change in signs of wealth. I was the only man there wearing an embroidered himation of the old style. Once, we had worn the best of our wives' productions, and aristocratic women had (according to men) nothing better to do than weave a beautiful length of butter-soft wool and then spend a hundred evenings embroidering the surface with stars and dots – and, in my case, ravens.

The war had ended that. Every man present wore white, or off-white, undecorated in most cases except for a single stripe above the selvedge. In a country where everything had been destroyed, there was a certain equality that hadn't existed before. Or was it the phalanx of free men who had met the Thebans and won? And stormed the Persian camp? Regardless, the days of ostentatious display were gone in Athens.

Now, this may seem unimportant to you, but it spoke a great deal for the Athenians, that their richest men and women had decided not to flaunt their surviving wealth. They dressed more simply than Spartans, and their simple white clothes said, 'Our temples are burnt and our people are fighting to survive, and women have other tasks than adorning the clothes of the very rich.'

Clothing can speak very loudly. I was ashamed of my elaborate himation, although no one taxed me in any way.

Aristides rose to speak, and first he mixed us a bowl of wine, three waters to one wine, because we were going to discuss serious business. And then he poured a libation, and we all rose and sang a hymn to Demeter, because it was spring, and never before had any Greeks so valued the fecundity of the earth as we did that spring.

And then we settled, and Aristides raised the beautiful black *kylix*.

'We are meeting tonight to speak about the future of Athens,' he said. 'And with Athens, the future of Ionia.'

There was a low rumble of assent.

In moments, I wished I had Briseis on the couch by me, and not Cimon, although not for the usual reasons. She thought deeply and long about Ionia, and the truth was that the Athenians, like many good men, tended to see the world in ways defined by their own experience. Put another way, they wanted what was best for Athens, and they tended to define what was best for Ionia as what Ionia could do to benefit Athens.

Cimon and I were the closest the Ionians had to speakers at that meeting. Even Aristides seemed to believe the Ionians incapable of governing themselves, as if they had not been rich, independent cities for hundreds of years when Athens and Sparta were both smaller and weaker.

But the essential element of the symposium was a discussion of the role of Sparta. Let me remind you once again that not only had Sparta claimed the right to command by land, with her veteran warriors, but at sea, so that while Athens furnished more than half of the hulls for the Allied Fleet, Sparta almost always furnished the commander. Such remained the case that spring; Pausanias, the Spartan regent who'd led us at Plataea – and whom I knew to be a member of the Sparta First party – nonetheless had been proposed to command the Allied effort that year. Sparta intended to furnish eight ships and the commander, while Athens was expected to furnish sixty ships at least.

'And the worst of it,' Aristides said, 'is that while we would like to pursue an active war until Persia had neither fleet nor allies within reach of salt water, the Spartans intend to take as little action as possible.'

He looked around. We'd been at it long enough that all of us had consumed some wine, and most of us were both more relaxed and more garrulous. Cimon, who was the *proxenos* or representative of Sparta in Athens, wanted to speak, but it was not his turn.

Aristides looked at the wall hangings, which depicted Odysseus' return to his home, and Penelope weaving.

'Sparta does not want to further injure Persia,' he said quietly, as if he feared to be overheard, even here, in his own home on the slopes of the Acropolis in Athens. 'Sparta fears Athens more than she desires the freedom of Greece.'

I shrugged. 'That was true last year,' I said, and Aristides frowned, because I was speaking out of turn.

Cimon took the wine, and stood.

'As the proxenos of Sparta, it is my duty to remind you that Sparta has contributed as much as Athens.' He shrugged. 'As an Athenian, I admit that we had to drag them to fight at Plataea like old bullocks pulling a broken plough.'

I took the wine cup from his hand and drank some.

'My sons tell me that it's openly discussed in the Peloponnese that Sparta will require the Ionians to move to the west if Sparta is to remain part of the Coalition.'

Aristides smiled. 'We'll hear more of this when Themistocles returns from Sparta.'

I had wondered where the wily and sometimes dangerous Themistocles was. The architect of victory at Salamis, he was also perfectly capable of carrying on a conspiracy with three sides at the same time, and I didn't trust him. Aristides was a prig, and sometimes a prude, but he was also one of the best spear fighters in the world, and his sense of honesty and honour were as great or greater than that of the most punctilious Spartan. It was a matter of bitter irony to me that Themistocles, the epitome of the 'wily Athenian,' was well beloved in Sparta, whereas Aristides, the noblest Athenian, was more feared than loved there.

Perhaps men are more comfortable seeing their rivals and foes as caricatures than as men; perhaps it suited the ephors in Lacedaemon to negotiate with a man who reinforced their views of 'Decadent Athens'.

'Is Themistocles working on a new alliance agreement?' I asked.

Pericles smiled, as if I was a charming bumpkin. 'Not exactly,' he said.

Even Aristides looked ... tolerably duplicitous.

Cimon took the wine cup, drank, and handed it to the wine slave for more.

'Themistocles is in Sparta,' he said, 'reassuring the ephors that we will on no account rebuild our long walls.'

His words would have carried absolute conviction, except that when we'd landed at Piraeus from Megakles' well-found ship, I'd seen tens of thousands of Athenians of every class carrying stone – even column drums from the destroyed temples – and rubble from destroyed houses. Indeed, the hands of almost every aristocrat present betrayed the kind of dirt and wear and tear that men, even tough men, only experience moving stone. I had reason to know; I'd moved enough of it just clearing the floor of the old temple of Hera in Plataea.

'But you *are* rebuilding the long walls,' I said.

Cimon grinned. 'And *that's* why we didn't send Aristides.'

Aristides winced. Everyone else laughed, and in that laughter, my friends, you didn't need to be an oracle to hear the distant trumpets of Ares.

Cimon scratched his nose and looked at me.

'Once the long walls are complete we'll be safe from the Spartans,' he said. 'Only four weeks ago they threatened us – it was the night before Salamis all over again. They claim that our city is destroyed, that we should "relocate" ourselves. Indeed, there's a rumour that one of their fears is that we'll relocate and force the Ionians to sail with us.'

'How can any people so absolutely brave in the face of the storm of spears be so full of fear about issues of statesmanship and diplomacy?' I asked.

Cimon, who genuinely loved Sparta, was silent.

Aristides nodded slowly. 'Every system has flaws. Their ephors are both a strength and a weakness. In an emergency, the Spartans have the most conservative, and in some cases the least competent, leadership. Steady in normal times. Terrible when everything is change.'

I thought of my teacher, the philosopher Heraclitus.

'Everything is always change,' I said. 'Nothing ever stays the same.'

Aristides held his hands wide, like a priest. 'I hear Heraclitus in you, my friend. And while everything may always be in a state of change, it is not therefore absolutely evil that some old men try to keep things the same. Change for the sake of change is as inane as utter inaction.' He closed his hands. 'Despite which, in this instance, and for the last three years, I confess that I have found the views of the ephors duplicitous and cautious to the point of insanity.'

I nodded.

Aristides took the cup back from his slave with a slight nod of appreciation.

'Listen, friends. The long walls make us strong and safe from all our foes. And they will, I think, dissuade Sparta from making any grave errors about us. This is why I agreed to their rebuilding as the first priority, before even our houses and temples.'

He looked at Cimon.

'But when we are secure, we intend to prosecute the war. It is not over. They burnt our temples and our homes. They enslaved half the women of Ionia as sex slaves. We have defended ourselves nobly.'

Cimon began pounding our *kline*. 'Hear, hear!' he shouted, and all the rest of us joined in.

The effect of ten or twelve bowls of wine, eh? But listen, friends. Some of you were there. *We defeated the Great King.* Sometimes it was *still* hard for us to believe.

Pericles almost fell off his couch, he was clapping so hard, but he was young, and so was Olympiodoros.

Aristides held up the kylix for silence.

'Now we will take the war to them,' he said. 'We will begin with the liberation of the Ionian cities. We will fight to liberate those who want us – not, perhaps, every city, but we are not tyrants. If Halicarnassus wishes to remain subject to the Great King, we will not attack them unless they furnish ships to fight us.'

Music to my ears. My wife and brother-in-law would be delighted.

'I pledge three ships for that fleet,' I said.

Cimon shook his head. 'Best day's work my pater ever did, getting you the citizenship,' he said. 'I'm to have the command.'

'And what of Pausanias?' I asked.

Cimon nodded. 'He's a great man and an able commander,' he said. 'As long as he is willing to fight, we'll be fine.'

I sat back. 'My friends, let me make sure I have this aright. The war with the Medes is not over – we pledge ourselves to carry the war to them. But we're also prepared to fight the Spartans. We'll carry on this holy war under Spartan leadership, unless we find it unsatisfactory, in which case we'll do ... what? Sail off and make our own war?'

Cimon nodded. 'You know how much we can do.'

'I know how much we could do as pirates,' I said. 'And like you and Aristides, I've fought alongside Ionians. We need more of a strategy than you've proposed.'

Cimon nodded, and Pericles spoke up: the youngest, but already a voice in the councils of Athens. He looked around; he was a dignified youth and he knew that he needed our assent to speak, but everyone nodded.

'First, we take the Bosporus. It's a little like an extension of the Long Walls,' he said, waving one hand. He'd had a little too much wine, and he was slurring. 'We need the grain from the Euxine to feed all our people until Attica is fit to be farmed again. If we have the grain trade from the Euxine and we have long walls to our port, we're absolutely secure, and we can use our fleet wherever we want to help Lesbos or Chios.'

It made sense – the same sort of twisted sense that the Spartan ephors made.

'I suppose that to an Athenian, that's the appropriate way to proceed,' I said.

That shocked them.

'But if you are a man of Mytilini or Chios or Samos,' I said, 'It looks amazingly like Athens fortifying herself and then building an overseas empire for her own benefit.'

'If we aren't secure, no one is,' Aristides said.

'So might any Spartan ephor prate,' I said.

'I thought you just offered us three ships?' Cimon said.

'I did. I just want you to understand that I don't fully agree. Athens is safe. Why the Bosporus?'

'Because we have a democracy,' Aristides said. 'Because our people have been burnt out of their homes and starved on Salamis Island twice in two summers, and they want to know that they are secure and so is the food supply, or we will be voted no money to proceed.' He looked at me, and his smile was thin. 'And your Plataeans will want the Euxine grain as much as we Athenians.'

We did need the grain.

Ah. Democracy.

How soon one forgets.

Watered wine never gives me a hangover, so the next morning I was up early, riding down to Piraeus in search of a shipwright and a yard that would build me a beautiful trireme. Athens was building eight that spring, in eight different yards, and they were all fine vessels, but I was looking for something perfect.

It was a gods-blessed day, wandering from yard to yard, talking to workers and watching them cut and shape the timbers and the planks. Athenian ships – most ships, really – were built by laying planks to a form, or even a hole dug to shape in the ground, fitting them with biscuits, or billets, between the planks, just the way an *aspis* is made, really. When the planks are woven and pegged together, only then does the master builder put in an internal frame to strengthen the hull. Very small boats have almost no frame and the triremes need a huge internal cable – the *hypozomata* – kept taut by wedges, to keep them stiff and manoeuvrable, especially in a cross sea that can make a ship flex and its seams open.

When Themistocles used the money from the silver mines to build Athens a great war fleet, the shipwrights and designers of Athens had worked hard, and they had cut a great many corners. This might have made inferior ships, and indeed, the first ships of Athens' new fleet, copied from Phoenician models, were too heavy, designed to carry big marine contingents. But as they built more ships, faster, than any other yards in the world, they came up with new construction techniques and they began to experiment with designs intended to complement Athenian naval doctrine and the talents of their best captains. In effect, they began to build for speed, not strength, and manoeuvrability, not marine capacity.

I do go on, do I not? But the trireme is in my lifeblood, and I love them, and I love to watch them being built.

Sometimes, patience is rewarded. The last yard we visited that day was well over towards the old naval port of Phaleron, due south of Athens. Phaleron was more important before Themistocles rebuilt Piraeus; most of the Persian fleet had sheltered there in the days before Salamis. When they left, they burnt all the yards and naval stores, but two small yards had reopened in the rubble of the destruction. The first was producing fishing boats and stout small boats that would survive a night at sea.

The second yard was idle. But on the stocks, about half completed, sat a magnificent trireme, long and low and beautiful. Her planks had all been pinned together, and the ribs were laid lovingly, each one marked with charcoal. A single man was working, lifting a rib, shaving a little wood off, and putting it back. I watched him until he had the fit just the way he wanted it, and he walked forward to the next pair of ribs and began fiddling with the port side one of the pair.

I walked up.

He looked at me through the lattice of ship's timbers.

'Hello there,' I called out.

He waved at me. I saw the glint of his adze. It was polished like a sword blade. I'd never seen a man who polished the head of an adze.

'Beautiful ship,' I said.

'Nice of you to say so,' he said, and spat. He picked up a big wooden canteen and took a pull. 'Wine?'

I almost never say no to wine, so I took a pull. Blackstrap – the cheapest stuff you can buy, from the plain of Attica over towards Marathon. Dark as bull's blood, made yesterday by sweating slaves, and tastes of their sweat.

The thing is, friends, when you've had *no wine* for a while, you realise something. I learnt this lesson when I was a slave pulling an oar for Dagon.

There's *no bad wine*.

There's wine perhaps you'd rather not drink right now, because you can afford better. Sure.

But when you go without wine for a couple of years, you realise that the gulf between bad wine and good wine is nothing compared to the gulf between no wine and any wine.

There it is: all the wisdom of my whole life, in a few words. Drink up now.

Any road ...

'She's yours?' I said.

'Until one of my moneylenders comes for her hull,' he said. 'Maybe for building timber. Maybe firewood. Who knows? Those timbers are mostly seasoned oak. And those hull strakes are Attic pine, dried three years.'

'You selling?' I asked.

'Are you mocking me, sir?' he asked.

Now, I confess that I was dressed to look at ships, by which I mean I was wearing a chiton that Briseis would never have allowed out of the house, tied off with a *zone* made of old rope. The only sign of my status as a free man, much less a man of property, was a sea-knife with a carved bone grip that hung around my neck. No slave would own such a knife.

'Humour me,' I said.

He looked it over, as if he had never thought of selling.

'I was building it for the fleet,' he said. 'And then Themistocles told me that he didn't want my hull. Too light, too long.' He waved, as if the ship explained everything. 'They don't want the *tekne* to think. They want us to build to a pattern.'

Privately, I could see the point. If you'd seen the fleet back water on the morning of Salamis, you'd know that different hulls work differently and make it even harder for the various *trierarchs* to keep together.

'I'll buy her all found and ready to float,' I said. 'I can pay gold.'

My unnamed shipwright sat back against the timbers of his ship.

'Tartarus, brother, I'd have given you wine for nothing. I might even manage a sausage. You don't have to come it the nob.'

'Gold.' I reached into my purse, which I'd tied under my chiton, and hauled out a couple of Persian darics. 'Gold.'

His face changed, and for a moment, I thought he might cry.

'You're fucking serious,' he said.

'All found. How long?'

'I need to hire in help,' he said.

'That's all right,' I said. 'I need oarsmen and marines.' I paused and looked back. 'One question,' I said.

'You want to know my name?' he asked.

'Probably a good idea, ' I said. 'But why do you polish your adze?'

'Cuts with more precision,' he said.

'Damn,' I said.

The *agora* in Piraeus was as busy as it had ever been. Listen, friends – Themistocles built Piraeus. He found a sleepy fishing village and he made it the best port in the Inner Sea. The agora, the marketplace, has always been busy, but on that spring day in the year after the battle at Plataea, it looked as if every merchant in the world was there. There were Sicilians, and not just Megakles, although he was one of the first. There were Syrians and Carians and even Phoenicians. I suspect that if you looked carefully, you might have found a Persian who wasn't a slave.

I had a donkey. I'd had the donkey with me all day, for just this moment, and now I walked up and down the market, looking at what men had to sell, at who had money.

Most of the rich merchants with mixed cargoes congregated together on the seaward side – closest, I suppose, to their ships and the few breezes that might cool us, as if the breeze was the most valuable thing in the world. I stood with my donkey, watching them. Some were Corinthian, and some were from sandy Argos, and one little huddle around a table were from Croton, which men argued was the richest city in the world. And opposite them was a table held by six Aegyptians. They couldn't legally trade in Athens, but they had a *metic*, a kind of foreigner with a licence to trade – a man from Euboea.

The shadows were getting longer when I sat down on a stool.

One of the Aegyptians smiled at me and made a little brushing motion with his hand. The smile said, *I'm not a fool and I wasn't born yesterday*, and the brushing motion indicated that it was time that I moved on in case he had a real customer.

Sloppy-looking indigent as I was … possibly a bit of a hard case. One of the Aegyptians popped into their little trade tent and emerged wearing a sword.

I turned to the Euboean.

'I'd like to sell you something expensive.'

He looked at me, a measured stare. 'What do you have?' he said.

'A golden bowl big enough to bathe a baby in,' I said.

He smiled. 'My master doesn't buy stolen goods,' he said.

I sat back, ignoring the man with the sword and the man making the brushing motions.

'Is spear-won the same as stealing?' I asked lazily.

That got a chuckle. 'Spear-won?' he asked.

'I took it from the tent of Artaphernes,' I said. 'When we took the Persian camp, at Plataea.'

The Aegyptian making the brushing motion stopped.

'Get you gone,' he said.

'You really don't want a large golden bowl?' I asked.

He made a face. 'I don't want your scheme, your stupid prank, or whatever you plan, Greek. Just walk away.'

I looked at him. 'When I trade in Heraklea at the mouth of the Nile,' I said, 'Aegyptians are much more polite.'

He frowned, and the man with the sword walked up close, as if to threaten me.

It occurred to me that I could have taken it from him and killed him. Jutting your sword hilt at a man and thumping your chest is incredibly ineffective as a threat, but then, I actually wanted to sell the bowl.

So I took my donkey and rode back to Athens, where Jocasta made me wash and change for dinner.

In the morning, I put on a better chiton and good white sandals and a beautiful *chlamys*. I went and made some sacrifices, mostly of money, at the temple ruins of Poseidon in Piraeus and such. Then I took my donkey, along with Brasidas and Aten, my Aegyptian servant, to the agora.

I sat in the same seat and was treated like a different man. I've found this to be true so often that I try not to be angered any more – but honestly, the huge gold bowl had been on the donkey for two days and was just as good and just as solid.

We haggled for perhaps an hour. They offered wine, which I drank. Not bad, but over-watered.

In the end I got almost three quarters of what I'd guessed at the bowl's value – not bad, considering the market. And more than enough to pay for a trireme for a year.

We had some sacks of coins – indeed, you might well point out that I could just have given the shipwright the bowl, but I didn't. Any road, we had sacks, and they went on the donkey, who grunted and then gave a good bean-fed fart, perhaps commenting on men and their little ways.

I walked over to the officer of the archon basileus who controlled the market, and paid him for two days and an awning.

'What will you be selling?' he asked.

'Blood and fortune,' I said. 'I'm recruiting a crew.'

Brasidas wanted me to wait and recruit in Corinth, or even Hermione, where we could get Arcadians and Spartans, but Brasidas, for all of his Lacedaemonian reserve, still believed that all the men of the Peloponnese were superior to all of the men of Attica.

I didn't share his views. I knew perfectly well that Boeotian men were superior to both.

And you might well ask why I'd recruit new oarsmen, new deck crews, and new marines in Athens when I had so many of my old pirates settled around me in Plataea, but that was the point. I wasn't prepared to sacrifice my friends and comrades of twenty years of war. I wanted them safe at home with their families.

And anyway, they were all rebuilding.

I put a couple of planks from my new ship across a stack of empty oil amphorae, the big ones, and unfolded my camp seat. On the table I put my best *xiphos* – long and narrow, with a very heavy, square cross-section near the cross-hilt, and a broader point. The hilt was ivory, banded in gold; the pommel cap was a tiny shrine to Athena Nike, goddess of victory.

The ivory had a yellow tinge from years in my hand, and the blood that had flowed over it, polished almost white where I used it every day, practising my draw.

It lay on my best red-purple cloak, the one covered in small embroidered ravens. Euphoria had made it for me, ten years ago and more, and it was still one of the richest textiles I owned. It had a hole or two, lovingly repaired, but it was magnificent.

The cloak and the sword caught every eye in the agora.

I sat. Brasidas stood by me on one side, and Megakles stood on the other.

It took quite a while before we had our first bite. Men gathered, looked at us, and walked on.

I heard someone say, 'Arimnestos ... Plataea ...'

And then someone muttered, 'Pirate.'

'Miltiades ...'

'Lade ... Artemisium ...'

I started smiling.

Brasidas looked over the crowd.

'Some good-looking men there,' he said.

A tall man stepped forward, a crooked smile on his face. He glanced to the right and left and then walked straight to the table.

'*Xaire*,' he said, raising his hand in greeting. It was almost a salute.

'*Xaire*,' I said. 'How can I help you?'

The crooked smile didn't waver. 'I'm told you are recruiting,' he said.

I nodded. 'Yes. What can you do?'

He tilted his head to one side. 'I can kill Persians,' he said. 'You may not have seen me, but I've seen you.' He held out his right arm, and there was a deep cut, long healed, across the bicep. 'Artemisium.'

'Take the sword,' I said.

He put his hand on it, and his fingers closed on the hilt.

Brasidas nodded. 'Name?'

The man glanced at Brasidas and something passed between them.

'Leander, sir,' he said.

Aten wrote his name into a wax tablet.

'We'll get back to you,' I said.

If he was disappointed, he gave no sign. He nodded, and his hand moved – almost a salute.

As he moved away, Brasidas said, 'Give him credit. First man onto the deck.'

25

We all laughed. Now that Leander had come, they pressed forward, although the sword had its effect. About a third of the crowd simply walked away.

The next man up was too old to be a marine. He was over forty, and his eyes were as bright as stars, and he bounced a little even waiting at the table. His sword arm was criss-crossed with scars.

'Marine?' I asked.

He shrugged. 'I can do things that need doing,' he said.

Megakles leant over. 'Can you reef and steer?' he asked.

The man grinned. 'So I can, mate. Or use that little toy, if I have to.'

'Pick up the sword,' Brasidas said.

The man picked it up, gripped it the way a man would hold a hammer.

'Name?' I asked.

'I'm Nestor,' he said, 'and most of me mates call me "Old Nestor".'

'You don't seem so old to me.' I made a motion with my hand. 'Can you stand still, Nestor?'

He shrugged. 'I can ...'

I laughed. I liked him already.

Megakles handed him a bit of rope.

He tied a knot before Megakles could give him direction.

Megakles laughed. 'Take his name, Aten,' he said.

And so it went. They weren't all as clever as Old Nestor and Leander; there were some hard cases, some men demanding money, or begging.

It grew hot, and Aten went to get us an awning.

I looked up and there was Sittonax. He stood with his arms crossed, the least Greek-looking man I knew – tattoos, trousers. A gold torc worth about one third of a trireme.

I got up, walked around the table, and embraced him.

'You want to be a marine?' I asked.

He shook his head, a pained look on his Gaulish face. 'No,' he said. 'I might come along to see some fighting,' he added. 'I just wanted to introduce a friend.'

The man with him was almost, but not quite, as outlandish as Sittonax. He had blond hair, bright blond, worn long, and a chiton that had seen better days. And he had a lyre in a bag on his back.

'Diodoros,' Sittonax said. 'He's from – well, from beyond Gaul. No one here could say his name.'

Diodoros smiled. '*Xaire*,' he said. He hit the *chi* far too hard. He sounded like a barbarian.

'And you want me to take him?' I said.

Sittonax nodded. 'Yes. He can row, I suppose, or fight. He's a gentleman, like me. He wants to be a rhapsode.'

'A barbarian rhapsode,' I said.

Brasidas was moving his hand back and forth across his throat.

Sittonax smiled. 'I'm fairly certain I've killed enough men to crew a trireme in your service,' he said. 'Humour me.'

It's true, that to see Sittonax in action was to see Ares incarnate. I always found it a miracle that he'd lived this long.

'Aten!' I barked. 'Take this man's name.'

Then we picked up a dozen good Athenian oarsmen, all together with their rowing cushions and their back rests – proper oarsmen, with massive upper bodies and a certain leer that suggested that they were not to be trifled with.

They came in a clump, but they were so obviously the real thing that I signed them on the spot, and sent them to find friends.

'Not so many ships this early,' their leader said. He was a big brute – Kallimachos – and there was nothing *kalli* about him, except perhaps his muscles. 'Prize money?'

'Maybe,' I said.

'What's the split?' he asked, a knowing gleam in his eye.

'A fair split,' I said. 'Four shares – one for the ship, one for the officers, one for the deck crew and marines, one for the oarsmen.'

He grinned and showed his nine teeth. 'A few drachmas for me if I find you twenty more like me?'

'Did a jail break open?' I asked. 'Or are the brothels closed?'

We clasped hands and he was off to find more. Listen, friends! Professional oarsmen are like gold. They can row all day, and they can fight. I didn't bother to ask these men if they had weapons. Most oarsmen expect to get those from their ship, and anything they have, they sell as soon as the rowing season is over. They're not *nice*. But they can row. And before you think too little of them, remember that they won Salamis. Not us, the hoplites. And we all knew it.

We saw off an arrogant beggar, and then we had a short man who was almost as broad as he was tall. He was covered in tattoos, like a barbarian, but his Greek was smooth and native. He sounded Arcadian. He wore a faded red chiton and had an aspis.

Brasidas nodded. 'Pick up the sword,' he said.

The man reached out and took the sword as if grasping something precious – which, of course, it was. Almost without intending, he lifted the sword, his fingers wrapped lovingly around the hilt.

'Name?' Brasidas asked.

'Arios,' he said.

'We'll want the sword back,' I said.

He grinned.

I was no longer sitting at the table; I was standing by it, chatting with Sittonax, who was bragging of his various conquests. Listen, it may be the height of decorum among Athenians to never kiss and tell, but I gather it is different in Gaul.

On the other hand, a few years with Briseis and Jocasta and Gorgo and quite a few other women had rubbed off me the interest in hearing these tales. I was probably looking to escape when a big man with a long, sloping forehead and a jaw the size of a horse shoved through the crowd and pushed through the line. He was so big that no one tried to stop him, either. He was angry – angry enough that there was foam at the corners of his mouth. His eyes were wild – again, like an ill-used colt.

'Ares' dick!' he swore. 'You're gathering a crew without me?'

Truth be told, I would happily have gathered a crew without Leontos. He was the worst oarsman ever birthed; he broke more oars than a winter storm, and he fought with anyone put near his bench. On the other hand . . .

On the other hand, I was a little scared of him, although I'd never shown it, and he practically worshipped me, so imagine him loose on the deck of a Phoenician. I'd never even seen him take a wound – that's how terrifying he was. He took a great deal of special handling, even among the fractious bastards in the lower oar deck, but then . . .

But then, that's what it takes to command a warship, ain't it? Time, and thought, and experience, and knowledge of your people. In detail.

'Leontos,' I said, and put my arms around him.

Most of us called him Leon, and that was easier to roar in a fight. Sittonax shook his hand, and Brasidas came and put an arm around him, and then we had to buy him wine and let him sit behind the table with us, his head about two hands higher than mine.

Oh, I *can* say no to Leon. I just don't, unless I have to.

At any rate, Leon brought us another draft of right oarsmen, and they all insisted on lifting a big stone and tying knots to impress

Megakles, and then there were two men, one tall and the other less so.

The tall man looked as if he lived by a gymnasium, and the other man looked as if he lived next to a good taverna. Despite which, he looked fit and he had a look of keen intelligence that appealed to me.

'Marines?' I asked.

They were obviously hoplite-class men, from their good wool chitons to their sandals.

The tall one nodded. 'Yes, sir.'

'Ever served at sea?' Brasidas asked.

The tall man showed the scars on his arms – the scars you get in a close fight, where your armour can't protect you.

I looked at the smaller man.

He shrugged. 'Usually, I let him take the wounds,' he said.

I couldn't place their accents.

'Where are you from?'

'Corinth,' they chorused.

Not my favourite city, but I liked them both. Cheerful shipmates are a great improvement on dour shipmates.

'Names?' Leon barked.

'Zephyrides,' said the tall man.

'Because it's an ill wind . . .' the shorter man said. 'Never mind. I'm Kassandros.'

I pointed to the sword. 'Pick it up, please.'

They both gripped it correctly, and I saw their names written out and passed them down to the group waiting by the waterfront. By then, we had perhaps fifty oarsmen, maybe ten sailors, and six or seven marines.

The crowd was thinner. We'd set a standard – we weren't taking thin, desperate men as oarsmen or beggars, and word had gone out that we were paying hard coin. I'd have my oar banks filled in a couple of days.

A boy – or a very thin man – approached us. He was hesitant at first, hanging around the edge of the group of oarsmen. Many of them seemed to know him. Eventually, after we'd seated Leon, he came forward. He was an ephebe; he didn't have a beard.

'Deck crew,' he said. He took the sword correctly, and tied a number of knots. He had a funny habit of opening his mouth like a fish when he was concentrating.

'How old are you, boy?' Megakles asked.

'Not sure, sir,' the boy answered. 'At least sixteen.'

He was light enough to climb a mast, and I liked his cheerful face. 'Name?' I asked.

'Nestor,' he said.

'That'll be Young Nestor,' Megakles joked, and the name stuck.

I was ready to close up. Piraeus in late spring is hotter than the bronze disc of the sun, and I wanted to sit with my new people and drink some wine.

But another man walked up to the table. He was wearing a sailor's round cap and he had a big straw hat on his back.

'Can we help you, sir?' Leon said, sarcasm dripping from his huge mouth. Leon made a practice of attacking nearly everyone. Hard man to like.

The newcomer was older than me, about my height, and had a bit of a belly. On the other hand, the rest of him looked as solid as the old oak in my new ship's keel.

'Damon, son of Eneas,' he said. 'Second helm, *Blood of Ares*, prorates, *Athena Nike*. I'd like to be kubernetes – senior helm.'

Megakles raised an eyebrow. 'Got anyone from the *Athena Nike* can vouch for you?' he asked.

Half a dozen of our new oarsmen raised their hands.

'I can't promise you the rank,' I said. The kubernetes was, after the trierarch, the next in command. On many ships, he was actually the commander; in most Spartan and many Athenian ships, the trierarch was an aristocrat with less sea time than his greenest oarsman. 'Let's get to know each other. I saw the *Athena Nike* fight at Salamis. Why are you leaving her?'

Damon shrugged. 'She's been broken up,' he said. 'Worm, and rot.' He patted his gut. 'We're not getting any younger.'

'No, we are not, brother,' I said. 'Put him down.' I nodded to Aten.

I was boiling, and I felt a little like an egg on a griddle, and even Brasidas was miming drinking motions with his hands, when a man stepped up with a woman by his side.

He was a tough-looking man with a big smile. His arm was around the woman, who was young enough to be his daughter, open-faced and pretty, and with arm muscles like a *thranite*'s.

'Women on ships is unlucky!' Leon said.

The man smiled. 'Now, you wouldn't say that to your mother, would you, son?' he said.

Leon sat back, abashed.

The man leant forward, putting his hands on the table.

'I'm not looking for work. I'm looking for a fast passage east for me and my daughter. I've heard of you, Arimnestos of Plataea. Jocasta said I could trust you.'

'Jocasta sent you?' I asked. I was impressed with his handling of Leon – just the right touch, no hesitation.

He smiled. 'Yes, sir, she did.'

I looked around. 'I doubt we will leave harbour for a few days. Ship's not even finished.'

He nodded. 'Only ship headed east is a lubberly round ship with a Phoenician captain. He'll sell us both before we're out of sight of the Acropolis.'

I nodded. 'Where are you headed?'

He nodded. 'Lady Jocasta said you might touch at Lesbos or Chios.'

I got up and pointed at my stool for Aten to fold.

'Come and have a cup of wine,' I said. 'I do usually go that way.'

'I'm going to school,' the girl said. She didn't sound entirely thrilled by the notion.

'Sappho's school? In Eresos?' I asked.

She smiled. She wasn't shy. 'Yes,' she said.

'My wife went to school there,' I said. 'You'll like it. One of the most beautiful places on earth.' I nodded. 'Right. Aten, get their names.'

'I'm Gaia,' the young woman said. 'I promise we'll be good passengers. We always co-operate.'

'Socrates,' the man said. 'I build stuff.'

'Have you built a thirst?' I asked, and when Leon growled, I knew the work day was over.

I led my new mob to a taverna that looked like it needed business, and ordered wine for seventy.

It's good to have gold.

The next day, I ate a breakfast of hard bread and a little garlic in Jocasta's kitchen, collected Aten and Brasidas, and walked across the slopes of the Acropolis to the agora of Athens proper. It was not anywhere near as busy as the agora in Piraeus: a few farmers selling grain; a dozen young men practising for a play for the festival of Dionysus; and a group of young men sitting around the Royal Stoa, listening to Anaxagoras speak on the movement of celestial bodies – all very interesting if you like that sort of thing.

One of the listeners was built more like a pankrationist than a philosopher, and I watched him watching Anaxagoras with evident interest. Anaxagoras was Pericles' friend, an aristocrat from Clazomenae in Ionia. Although he was not directly a follower of my own teacher Heraclitus, I was aware that they had sprung from the same ocean, so to speak. Now he was discussing the size of the sun, which he insisted was closer to the earth than all other heavenly bodies except the moon.

He had a wizened winter apple and a small, round stone, and he was trying to convince his listeners that the eclipse, and the things visible during an eclipse, proved the size of the sun, which he said was as big as the entirety of the Inner Sea, or even larger.

The stocky man, the pankrationist, raised his hand.

'So you think the world is a sphere?' he said.

Anaxagoras shrugged. 'It seems the likeliest solution,' he said.

The man looked impressed. 'I've heard the world described as a wheel, or a circle,' he said.

Anaxagoras waved his hands in a vague circle. 'You know that sometimes, if the light is just right, we can see the shape of the earth as a shadow on the surface of the moon, whether by day or night,' he said.

The fighter nodded.

'And that shape is a circle,' Anaxagoras said.

'Absolutely,' the man said.

'And then, no matter where the moon is, the shape of earth is still a circle,' Anaxagoras said.

The man nodded.

Anaxagoras spoke again in his soft Ionian accent. 'You are a sailor, I think?'

'I'm a navigator,' the man said. 'Among other things.'

Anaxagoras held up his apple, reached into the dust, and put an ant on the apple. He rotated it in his hand.

'The horizon,' he said simply.

The man nodded. 'By Poseidon, sir – I've listened to a hundred sophists discourse on the clouds, the rain, and the gods. You're the first one who's ever had something intelligent to say. Thanks for the lesson.'

He turned away from the Royal Stoa and I stopped him.

'A navigator?' I asked.

He smiled. 'You're Arimnestos of Plataea,' he said pleasantly.

32

'You have the advantage of me,' I said.

'Proxenos of Athens. Rhamnus, actually.' He clasped my hand. 'I used to own a couple of trading ships. I lost them in the war.'

'Looking for work?' I asked.

He shrugged. 'Perhaps,' he said. 'I'm trying to raise capital to buy myself a ship.'

'How are you at the coast of Syria?' I asked.

He nodded slowly. 'I can pilot the coast of Syria – and Judea. Cyprus, too. I've been into Caria – I used to trade with Halicarnassus.'

I smiled. 'And if I could offer you a summer's cruise and a major profit?' I asked.

'Piracy?' he asked.

'I prefer the term "war",' I said. 'We're at war with the Great King.'

He grinned. 'Best offer of the day.'

I was late opening my table. But I took my time, laying my cloak over the table, putting my sword out. Leon came with a big stone; it weighed at least a talent, and I had a bit of a struggle getting it off the dust.

Megakles had two very different sizes of rope today.

'Gentlemen,' I said, 'we're not recruiting for the Argonauts. We need a hundred rowers and another dozen sailors.'

'We're going to be the first hull in the water,' Megakles said.

Leon grunted. 'I told my friends,' he said, jerking a thumb at a huddle of big men.

'You have friends?' I asked.

It was always a little dicey teasing Leon, but he was in a good mood today.

''Course I have friends,' he said, as if this was obvious to everyone.

His friends came forward, mostly young men with statue-like physiques. They lifted Leon's stone; one of them threw it to another.

'I see,' I put in.

Brasidas motioned to the next man, who proved to be a Sikeliot. He was delighted when Megakles spoke to him in Sikel, and he listened while Megakles spoke of Sicily. He had a scar across his face and he looked like a fighter, and he was cheerful, if a little slow to speak.

'Marine?' I asked.

He leant forward slightly. 'What's the pay?' he asked softly.

I told him: three drachmas a day for oarsmen, four for marines and five for deck crew. I told him the way shares would be divided.

He nodded. 'Deck crew,' he said. 'I have my own armour.'

Megakles handed him the two ropes of different sizes.

'Seize them together,' he said.

And then, when that was accomplished, he gave other directions, and the Sikeliot performed them all.

'Deck crew,' Megakles said.

'Name?' I asked.

'Archelaus,' he said. He looked to be as strong as the big oarsmen, too.

'Want to start earning today?' I asked.

'Yes, sir.'

I gave him directions to the yard at Phaleron.

'Take these men and report to the owner of the yard – Alexanor. He'll put you to work on the ship.'

'Aye, aye, sir.'

Ah, the pleasure of being a trierarch.

About noon, Cimon came with two other gentlemen. I didn't know them, and so he introduced them.

'Aristogeiton,' he said. 'His family were from Illyria, back before Pisistratus.'

We clasped hands. Aristogeiton looked like a scholar; he dressed simply, in the new style. He was round-headed and serious, with a certain dignity that can come with age.

'A pleasure, sir,' I said.

He inclined his head.

'Aristogeiton has been kind enough to support my trireme this year,' Cimon said. 'We heard that you were stealing all the best oarsmen and came down to investigate.'

Aristogeiton laughed. 'Cimon is afraid you have all the best oarsmen. I'm afraid I've invested in the wrong pirate.'

I glanced at the other man.

'If this is Aristogeiton, is this, then, Harmodius?'

Well, I thought it was funny. Brasidas laughed, too, but he's a very polite man. Aristogeiton gave me a look, as if he'd heard it all before.

The other man was taller, with sandy hair and a constant smile.

'Antenor,' he said. 'Mostly, I'm a farmer.' He was looking at the agora.

Cimon met my eye.

'You stole one of my officers,' he said.

Ah, just like a little band of brothers, that's us. I'd sailed under Cimon's father, Miltiades – the biggest pirate Athens has ever produced – and the apple doesn't fall far from the tree, I promise you.

'Damon, son of Eneas?' I asked.

'My second helmsman!' Cimon said.

I nodded. 'I didn't twist his arm. He wants to be kubernetes and I expect that he'll make the grade.'

Cimon stepped closer to me. 'Don't you think it might have been polite to ask me?'

Now, before I take this recollection any further, let me say that over the course of a dozen sea fights, Cimon and I have saved each other's lives a few times. I count him as more than an ally. A friend.

'I might have, if you'd been around,' I said softly. 'On the other hand, he's a free citizen of Athens, I believe.'

Cimon looked at me and looked away. 'Damn it ...'

I smiled. 'Cimon, if you want to keep him, make him an offer. I won't stop him – I can find another officer.'

Privately I thought, *if he wants to go, just let him go.*

I was watching the next candidate.

He was a big man, tall, heavily bearded, and he was blond. Blond men just aren't that common in Athens – Thrace is different.

'And you're going to have all the best marines,' Cimon muttered.

'So set up a table!' I said. 'Hells, Cimon, take part of my table and start recruiting for the *Athena Nike.*'

Cimon wanted to be angry at me, but good humour won out.

'See if I don't, he said. 'You need wine?'

'Always,' I agreed.

Back at my table, the big blond man was grinning as if being recruited was the most fun he'd ever had.

'Kalidion,' he said. 'I used to be called Dion, but some people added *Kali.*'

I laughed. It was no worse than my jokes.

'Marine, no doubt?' I asked.

He nodded. 'I have my own armour,' he said. 'And I can cook.'

Brasidas managed the smallest of smiles.

'I like men who come with extra skills,' I said.

Kalidion nodded. 'And I can read and write,' he said.

I pointed him to Aten.

'Put him down,' I said.

'That's all our marines,' Brasidas said. 'I'll start training them tomorrow.'

He took Kalidion and went off to find the others. They were easy to find; most of them were a head taller than the crowd, and Leander stuck out from fifty feet away.

In the time it took a man to deliver an entire court case, or less, Cimon had set up a table next to me. His timing was perfect; I was almost done. There were dozens, if not hundreds, of first-rate men left, and they might have grown anxious.

Cimon was a very rich man, and he announced that he'd be paying a bounty for every recruit.

I left before there was a riot.

I wandered down to Alexanor's yard with Aten carrying my stool behind me. I had grown too used to Aten – the perfect servant. I needed to let him go before I couldn't find my own chiton any more. But that was a problem for another day.

Alexanor now had more labour than he needed; I knew that as soon as I saw a pair of oarsmen sweeping the yard. Sweeping dirt is almost always an exercise in frustration, at the very least – usually an indication of over-employment.

I didn't really care. I'd got the golden bowl at the end of my spear, not the sweat of my brow.

The transformation in my trireme was incredible, though. Let me say, in my usual, discursive way, that most sailors – at least, the kind we'd hired as deck crew – were also carpenters and ship maintainers, and perfectly capable of building almost anything that could float. Now, under the direction of Damon and Alexanor, they were laying cross-timbers into the beautifully fitted ribs, and the shape of the rowing frame was starting to appear.

Most of the timbers were cut, and only needed precise fitting, and Alexanor appeared more than a little stressed, running from point to point. But the smell of fresh wood shavings and pine pitch was intoxication to an old pirate, and I stood there for as long as priestess dances for Artemis at Brauron, breathing in the new life of my new ship.

After a while, Alexanor came and stood by me. He still had the polished adze in his hand.

'How long?' I asked.

He made a face. 'I ... er ... um ... ordered ...' He looked around. 'All the cordage. Yes, I ordered the cordage this morning. Rope walks aren't busy now. You need a whole set of sailing tackle – need a mast, and mast has to be sized. Need oars. I was going to make them myself ...'

'That'd take too long,' I said.

'But that would take too long,' he agreed. 'So ... with your permission ... I'll just hire four oar-makers and have them work here?'

I called Megakles, who knew more about building ships than I ever would.

'Any advantage to fitting the oars to the rowers?' I asked.

He frowned. 'No,' he said. 'Terrible idea.'

Well, so much for innovation.

'Good, hire the oar-makers. How long?' I asked.

'All these people,' Alexanor said. He waved at the yard. 'And where are you getting sails?'

'All these people are *helping*,' I pointed out.

'I think she'll be ready to swim in seven days.'

'Seven days?' I asked. 'How about four days?'

'In four days, we celebrate the new festival of Artemis,' he said. 'No one will work that day.'

I rolled my eyes. 'What "new festival of Artemis"?' I asked. 'You Athenians and your endless festivals ...'

Jocasta leant over.

'Hold still,' she said.

There I was, the virtual pirate king of Athens, and I was holding Jocasta's wool, sitting in the old women's quarters on a balcony. I admit it was not unpleasant, with a cup of wine and Jocasta's company.

My hands were too hard and too full of little nicks and rough skin to be really good at holding her soft, long-fibre wool, but I swear she took a special pleasure in having me in the role.

'So why do we all have to take a day off for the Mounichia?' I asked.

'If your daughter were here, she'd be sure to tell you,' Jocasta said. 'Hold *still*.'

The next few days were, to be honest, delightful. Fitting out a ship – a good, handsome ship – is one of the joys in a sailor's life. It's work, but it takes in all the elements of a good party, including a little wine.

The men from the rope walks were happy to have the work. Of

course, the Persians had burnt all the rope walks, but they're not that hard to construct, and we started getting coils of beautiful brown-white hemp by the third day. The masts and spars came in, too – cut from the slopes of Parnassus, the boat sail mast only as tall as three tall men standing on one another's heads, the mainmast half as tall again. I put an inverted cone of bull's hide up the main mast; a man standing there can see a long way, at sea. Of course, the man had to get there, and that demands a monkey-like agility. But I had Aten, and I planned to recruit a few more boys just for the task.

The oar-makers came and sat on the ground in the yard, with spokeshaves and little saws and sharp knives. Oar wood was delivered in bundles of split-out boards, and they got to work, every oar made by hand. They were astoundingly fast; you could actually see an oar, a beautiful, slim, flexible oar, come out of the wood, as if it was just hidden inside that board and the oar-maker was releasing it.

And you might well ask what I was doing. Don't imagine that I was directing work in the yard; the old boat-builder shooed me along like a good housewife moving her husband out of the kitchen. But as he sent me gently on my way, he did mutter that I'd be needing sails, and that might be a tall order. This time I took the hint, and I walked up from the yard all the way to the agora in Athens – a good stiff walk, let me tell you. Going back and forth from the city to the port was restoring my leg muscles, at least. Any road, Cimon and Megakles agreed that the best sailmakers were up in Athens, so I walked up and found the men who wove sails. Boat sails are often boiled wool, sometimes foreign hemp – but the mainsail is a major piece of work, many gores wide in heavy linen canvas. Each gore or width of cloth is the work of many men or women for a week or more. A mainsail is an expensive item, and also a matter of pride.

I negotiated with three different outfits. Weaving interests me, and in Plataea, women do all the weaving, although in Athens you see more and more men in the trade, especially sails and nets ...

I'm off my story, as usual. So suffice it to say that I bargained with a man named Sicyon for a mainsail in new linen, with alternate stripes of red that was dyed in with a mixture of very expensive kermes and cheaper madder. It cost me heavily. It cost me more to have it in five days. Sicyon showed me around his shop, a pair of sheds on the slope opposite the Acropolis, with the biggest looms I'd seen.

Another day passed, and a coastal ship came in from Aegina. The captain said that the Aeginians were pulling their warships out of the sheds and drying the hulls, and that their fleet would be ready in nine days. A messenger boat came in from Hermione to say that the Spartans had held one of their many feasts, and that they were gathering their Peloponnesian allies. The *navarch* from Hermione wasn't a man I knew, but he knew me. While he praised the lines of my *Apollo's Raven* he told me that Pausanias, the victor of the battle of Plataea, would take command of the allied fleet.

Pausanias. Not my favourite Spartan. He was regent for Plaistarchos, and was himself a nephew of Leonidas, who fell at Thermopylae – an Agiad. Plaistarchos, of course, was the son of Leonidas and Gorgo. I knew that Gorgo had no great love for Pausanias, but saw him as a reasonable man. I knew him as an autocratic commander with a surprising streak of weakness for a prince of Sparta – jealous, a little vain, and perhaps bitter that Leonidas was remembered as a demigod and he, despite being the victor in the great contest, was not held in the same esteem.

We weren't friends.

More importantly, I knew from direct interactions with him that we didn't agree on strategy, on tactics, on the role of Greece or Athens. He belonged to the party in Sparta that was trying to maintain that the destruction of the city of Athens had destroyed their state. He certainly believed that all of the Ionians should be sent to colonies in Magna Graecia and Iberia.

I had to reason to believe that he'd avoid pressing the Great King too hard.

Now, to be fair, there were forces in Athens who felt the same. The big merchants had taken the last two years on the chin – trade with Aegypt and Syria and Tyre was at a standstill. Linen was expensive, and luxury items like glass from Aegypt were almost impossible to obtain. The value of spices was outrageous.

Athens needed trade. She needed an outlet for her ceramics and her tanned leather and her olive oil. Attacks on the Great King's fleet were only going to put all that farther away.

Or so it was argued, in the agora.

On the other hand, a free Ionia offered those same merchants a fantastic Asian market that could *only* trade with Athens; if the Ionians were at war with the Great King, all their trade would flow west.

That's where it all stood as Athens, with her desecrated temples and her broken agriculture, prepared to celebrate the first Great Mounichia.

Munychia is a tall hill that looks down on Piraeus and Salamis, too. It's the site of one of the oldest temples of Artemis – not, I admit, as old as Brauron or the sacred place on the Acropolis, but old enough to date back to the Trojan War.

And you'll recall that Hippolyta and Thiale, the senior priestesses from Brauron, had led all the girls of Athens in sacred dances on Salamis before the great battle there. Thiale had lifted her arms to the goddess as the Acropolis burned, and called down her curse and the curse of the immortal gods on the Persians and on Xerxes ... Thiale had been as much a leader of the Athenians as Themistocles or Aristides, and she was the high priestess of Artemis. And so, in the way that religion and politics blend together, the feast of Artemis of Munychia, in the middle of spring, became the feast of the commemoration of the suffering and death of the year of the Battle of Salamis. And that year was the first year it was celebrated, with a procession from the sacred place on the Acropolis all the way out of the gates and over to Munychia, and with all the ships that had been pulled from their ship sheds decorated with garlands. And hundreds of women and girls dressed as little bears and danced; they danced on the streets, and then groups of them came and danced on the decks of our ships, blessing our hulls and causing us to remember Salamis. You may recall that my pirates had shared a watchtower with the Brauron girls, or near enough, and my daughter Euphoria had been a leader among them. She and Heliodora, who was the best of the dancers and was now my daughter-in-law, had come over the mountains from Plataea to dance with the married women.

My soon-to-be passengers, Socrates and his daughter Gaia, came down to join us in the procession. Gaia was a Brauron girl, and she was dancing the bear dance at another yard. After we'd all walked to the temple with oars on our shoulders, and watched the sacred fire lit and the priestess summon the goddess, and then walked all the way back to the shipyard ... why, then the women came and danced for our new ship, and we ate a big tuna that had been roasted in clay, and drank some good cheap wine. All together, like the democrats we were. I could feel the anger in Sparta from the fire in the shipyard.

It was a good night, and a good feast.

And in the morning, we tapped at the *Apollo's Raven*'s hull to make sure the black pitch and the paint around her 'eye' was all dry. Then we put her on skids and ran her down the beach – two hundred men and a hundred women shouting and pulling on lines until her stern was awash. And then out into the waves on a glorious day, and launching a beautiful ship with a hundred chiton-clad women helping your men is like having an alliance with Naiads.

She floated, and two dozen oarsmen came aboard, the very best, led by old Poseidonos, who'd come across the mountains with the women, and Leon, who was not the best oarsman but couldn't be told 'no'. And with two helmsmen, a dozen oars, and four sailors, we crept around the headland into the harbour at Piraeus and warped her into a stone pier to put in her masts and rig the boat sail mast and the standing rigging. It's not much, on a trireme – nothing compared to the rigs on the bigger, deeper draught round ships we have now in the Euxine trade – but the rigging helps the hypozomata keep the ship stiff yet flexible. Rowing her round was probably the most dangerous thing I'd done in a long while; she was unfinished, floated high, had no ballast nor proper oar benches, and she rolled like a drunken *porne* showing her hips.

Poseidonos leapt off the ship and onto the pier like a much younger man, his shiny leather cushion dangling from his long oar.

'Sweet as a young girl,' he said.

I'd raised a daughter, and I winced.

'You mean, argumentative and prone to lying abed all day?' I asked.

The old oarsman laughed. 'Nah, I mean when they mean to be sweet, Trierarch.'

Our sailors went to work. I watched the boat sail mast go in; the yard crew knew their work, and then the new deck crew rigged her with black rope.

You'll recall that I'd ordered a set of sails – expensive sails – from one of the sailmakers in Athens. They weren't ready yet, mostly because Sicyon claimed he didn't have enough red dye to dye the linen and the wool. I walked over to his shop and told him to make them up in undyed wool. I was eager to get to sea.

He shook his head. 'Another day,' he begged.

I looked at the heavy, newly woven cloth, and imagined my red striped sails on some enemy's horizon, and I nodded and sat hard on my impatience.

At the other end of my stone pier, Cimon's beautiful *Ajax* came from drying to have her boat sail mast put in and her new ropes rigged. I met Cimon on the dock, watching for the *Athena Nike* under his hand.

'Sent for the rest of your pirates?' he asked.

'I have,' I said. 'My sons will be bringing them around. And Leukas and Moire.'

Cimon grinned. 'You have your own clan, just as my father predicted. Your sons as captains!'

He saw Damon giving an order aboard the *Apollo's Raven* and he glanced at me.

'And one of my best helmsmen,' he said.

I shrugged. 'When will you be ready for sea?'

'Sunrise the day after tomorrow,' Cimon said. 'I want to be at sea before Pausanias orders us not to go.'

Our eyes met. There were many things that it was best not to say aloud.

Between us, we could have fifteen ships.

'Syria?' I asked.

He spoke so quietly that it was difficult to hear him over the gulls and the squeak of the crane they used for the masts.

'Caria first,' he said. 'You look in on the Aeolians and I look in on the Ionians. Show the colour of our hulls, and see if we can rattle their Medizers and put some heart into their patriots.'

'And then Syria?' I asked.

'Yes!' he said. 'Unless you'd like to try the mouth of the Nile.'

I nodded. 'I was thinking Tyre,' I said.

He looked around for a moment. 'Are you mad? Of course you are. Tyre? You want to take fifteen Greek ships to the capital of the Phoenician fleet? The Great King's best naval base?'

'Bet you they aren't expecting us,' I said.

I had a last dinner with Aristides.

'Where are you bound?' he asked.

'If you don't know, you can't send a fast ship to find us,' I said.

Jocasta smiled primly. 'He's going to Lesbos,' she said. 'He's taking two of my friends – Socrates and Gaia.'

Aristides ate some more chicken and looked at me.

'You and Cimon are off to make trouble,' he said.

'Honestly, what I plan to make is money,' I said. 'But I'm open to admitting that I'll do some of my wife's business as well. In Ionia.'

Aristides swirled wine in his cup. 'You know the Spartans want the fleet to stay at Delos.'

I shrugged. 'Perhaps I won't be part of the allied fleet.'

Aristides shook his head.

I rolled over. It's hard to be emphatic on a *kline*; you are lying down, and you can't really wave your arms or be imposing. Maybe that's the whole point: lying in beds makes men less aggressive.

'We don't need an "allied fleet",' I said. 'The Great King is beaten. His ships are destroyed or in hiding. We don't need a cohesive strategy. We need fifty aggressive trierarchs to go over the horizon and make trouble until all the coastal cities see that they have no trade unless they join us.'

'And if the Phoenicians put their entire fleet in the water to hunt you down?' he asked.

I didn't tell him that I hoped to provoke that very reaction.

'We'll cross that bridge when we come to it,' I said. 'And maybe burn it behind us.'

Jocasta smiled. It's interesting, when you think of it; at some point, Jocasta and I had become allies against her husband on some matters of politics, and yet, she was absolutely the byword for modesty and obedience among Athenian matrons. Modest, obedient, absolutely pious, the perfect wife and mother. And she had some very strong views of her own.

Aristides didn't laugh.

'You and Cimon are leaving me to handle Pausanias,' he said.

I shrugged. 'He really doesn't like me,' I said. 'I'm doing you a favour.'

Aristides finished his wine in two gulps.

'I'd like to retire,' he said.

'Come and be a pirate instead,' I said. 'I seem to remember you on the beaches of Lesbos, the year before Lade.'

'A tempting offer,' Aristides admitted. He wasn't always a prude.

In the morning, I was at the beach before the sky was light.

So were my crew.

Oh, not everyone. Any new crew has some awkward sods: oarsmen who'd found a temporary companion the night before, or just the bottom of an amphora of wine, and couldn't be bothered to be awake. But the officers were good, and they had most of our people in ranks, with fires going and roast sausages. Any morning at Phaleron, you can find a dozen sausage-sellers with their little clay braziers; we'd brought them right down to the beach.

The *Apollo's Raven* was right there, too, hauled up stern first like a proper warship. All along her oar-strake, the top of the rowing frame, someone had painted black ravens of Apollo on the vermilion of the structure, and as the sun rose over Aegina, she was so beautiful that she made me tear up.

And her sails were magnificent, even tied down. The sail-makers were all there to see us off, too.

Euphoria came and gave me a hug.

'That's from my stepmother,' she said. 'I took the board from the *Lydia* and put it where Leukas told me to put it. With copper nails.'

'You are the best of daughters.'

'And I'd like fifty drachmas to buy something,' she said. 'And my husband is still four days away.'

I gave her five gold darics.

'Birthday present,' I said, kissing her head.

'The best of fathers,' she said. 'The kind with money.'

'Don't you have a husband for that now?' I asked.

She rolled her eyes. 'It felt good to dance the dances again,' she said. 'People talk about how bad it was when the Persians came ...'

She was watching the dawn breaking in magnificent colours to the east, towards Sounion.

'Yes,' I said.

You don't get to have so many good conversations with your young daughter that you want to give one up, even to launch a new warship. I was afire to get on with my ship, but just wise enough to kill my impatience and *listen*.

'But for me, they were great days,' she went on. 'Thiale made us into a regiment of Amazons. We were valued for everything we did, whether helping older people with food or doing the sacred dances. It was all an adventure.' She shrugged. 'Now the Persians are beaten and mostly, men want us to go back to our weaving.'

I didn't have much to say.

'We got used to being free,' she said.

All I could do was give her a hug.

'And the Mounichia brought it all back,' I said.

'Yes,' she said. 'Maybe Thiale and Hippolyta will effect some change. I don't know. I'm just not sure that being a wife and mother is all there is.' She looked out to sea. 'Men just sail away. It's ...'

'My daughter is a revolutionary,' I said, and raised my hands. 'So is my wife. I'm surrounded, and surrender.'

I made her laugh. But she meant what she said and I knew it. I'd

44

seen it in Briseis when she was very young – the revolt against the circumscribed life.

I didn't have a solution.

An hour later, we were afloat. Euphoria poured libations on the new bronze ram, and we took the *Apollo's Raven* off the beach and into the sea.

And two hours later we landed her, full of water, so that the *thalamites* in the lowest oar deck had their feet wet. A little disappointing, but normal for a new ship. Until the timbers swell a little, they leak.

And if you let the timbers get too soaked, they leak and they're heavy.

Why does anyone love them?

We had broken thole pins from awkward rowers. We had a set of broken ribs from an oarsman who'd missed his stroke and got his oar's butt in his chest, and we had some surly deckhands who'd discovered that the lines holding the anchor stones weren't tied to the deck ...

Good times.

And meanwhile, the mighty *Ajax* sailed rings around us and sent some not so good-natured jibes our way about a ship full of lubbers, and could they send us some actual oarsmen to train our thranites, and such jocularity.

An old ship with a worked up veteran crew.

Not for the first or last time, I doubted my wisdom in building new and hiring a crew when I had the very Argonauts themselves sitting around farming in Plataea; the more so when my daughter told me that most of them had headed for the ships as soon as Moire went to get the *Black Raven* back in the water.

But that die was cast.

I had a new ship, and a new crew with mostly new officers.

We beached, and started work on repairs.

You might think we were in a hurry, and we were. But you cannot hurry the formation of a crew, and Cimon, while he had his whole veteran crew on the *Ajax*, had nine other ships to crew. The recruitment table I had set up was going every day, and now a dozen other trierarchs were vying to get oarsmen.

Wages went up.

After the first day, and some repairs, I kept my ship at sea. I took us down the coast to a little village near Sounion that I had used before, in Salamis year. My oarsmen were less likely to ask me for higher wages, and frankly, I suspected that a few of them might be professional enough to take my money, run off in the night and sign on with some other, less demanding trierarch.

Well, unlike most nobly born Athenian captains, I've been an oarsman. I've heard the stories, and I have some notions of how to avoid being done brown, so to speak.

Mind you, a Greek fishing village of a few hundred souls is not an altogether dreary place, and I sent Leukas with a round ship full of wine, olive oil, spare oars and a dozen other sundries.

Three days' hard rowing and they were good. Five days and I was ready for sea; nothing shakes a crew down like actual rowing, day in and day out. I sent a boat to Piraeus to tell Cimon that I was ready, and he sent back by Moire, in the *Black Raven*.

In case none of you have twigged it yet, *Moire* is the colloquial word for 'Black'. Like Sekla and Ka and a dozen other fine men I know, Moire was from Africa, somewhere south of Aegypt. He'd held most of the ranks a man could hold, and now he was his own captain, but he'd already agreed to cruise with me that summer.

Leukas took over the *Amastris*, the former Corinthian that had given us so much legal trouble, and Megakles had the *Light of Apollo*, a captured trireme we took after Salamis and which had been repaired over the winter. The *Light of Apollo* looked Ionian, but we'd never know; Sekla had found her turtled and badly cut up in the shallow water off our beach at Salamis, and we hadn't reclaimed her until after the fight at Mycale.

And the last ship to come round the headland was my brother-in-law Archilogos in the *Lady Artemis*. With him, we had a nice little five-ship squadron, and then we had my two sons, each with a good round ship.

I was a little stunned when the men started coming down the beach. Sekla had told me, straight out, that he'd never go to war again, yet there he was, coming off the *Black Raven*. Alexandros had told me that he wanted to raise children and have a fine farm, and yet, there he was, captain of Moire's marines. Polymarchos was off with his athlete, becoming famous. He wasn't there, but his brother Alexanor was, as a marine, and there were Ka and Nemet with their little corps of helot archers – former helots, mind you.

Ka had with him a very tall man with a wispy beard. At first glance he looked a little old to be going to sea, but he shot a heavy bow. Ka had met him at the old shrine, and brought him along. He could sing, too, and his daughter was another amazing archer, but that's a story for another day.

In fact, my friends and former shipmates came on to the beach so fast, I wept. What better joy is there in life than having friends?

I turned away, and found Brasidas staring off into space, not meeting my eye, and just possibly fighting his own tears.

'Is Plataea empty?' I asked Moire.

He grinned. 'Pretty much,' he said.

Archilogos handed me a wooden case binding four wax tablets.

'I'm going to assume this is a love letter from my sister,' he said. 'Because otherwise I have to guess it's our marching orders for the liberation of Ionia.'

I made a face. 'Knowing your sister,' I said, 'which do you really think it is?'

Megakles snorted and turned away to shout an order. I hugged Hector and then Hipponax, and then Moire said, 'Really? My money is on orders for Ionia.'

Moire, who never jested.

Ouch.

And everyone laughed a long time. I certainly remember that.

Next day, Cimon met up with us off the point, and we sailed in two columns. We only sailed south around Sounion and then due east across the sound to Makronisos – barely a morning's pull. It's not an island where people live, these days; I think the Persians killed them all. But it made a fine rendezvous, and we brought our own sheep.

Socrates and Gaia, his daughter, were cautious at the campfires, and who wouldn't be, with a few hundred killers gathered for food, but they were cheerful and I promised them they'd be at Skala Eresos in two days at most. Then I walked around the campfires, made some bad jokes, shared too much wine, and gathered my captains and their officers and walked over to Cimon's beach across the headland.

He gave us more wine, and then we drew a big chart in the sand, marked it with shells and rocks, and led our captains through our plans.

I let Cimon do the talking. He speaks well; he is a true aristocrat.

'Friends, tomorrow we'll drop off the rim of the world and sail for Naxos. We'll pick up a ship there, if they're ready, and then sail north for Lesbos. We'll land at Eresos long enough to eat and drink and stretch our oarsmen's legs. then we'll work our way south, visiting the cities of Ionia, showing them the colour of our ships and waiting to see if there's anyone bold enough to join us.'

'What then?' shouted Cimon's brother, Metiochus.

Cimon smiled. 'When we're pulling up our anchor stones at Samos, I'll tell you.'

Silence. Torches snapped and burned and the stars shone down on us, and I thought of Cimon's father, Miltiades, and the shades of a dozen other men who should have been with us.

'But for those of you here for silver and glory,' Cimon said, 'let me remind you that we leave our own seas tomorrow. I believe that we're the first fleet on the water, and Arimnestos and I planned it that way. But we could find two hundred Phoenicians hulls-up on the horizon by midday tomorrow. Don't be sloppy. Row hard, practise hard, and be ready.'

See? A natural speaker. I'd have promised them loot.

Note that he hadn't said a word about patriotism, or the liberation of Ionia.

Midday the next day, we were struggling into the teeth of a wind, our oar benches fully manned and pulling like heroes, and we didn't make Naxos in a single day – or anything like it. We were three days to Naxos, and on the third day Cimon and I were hesitant to launch. For men like Sekla and me, who'd been past the Pillars of Heracles, it looked more like the Western Ocean than the Inner Sea. One of Cimon's triremes just barely avoided broaching on the beach when she launched. But we made the broad beaches of Naxos in rain and wind, and landed soaked to the skin.

Luckily, Ephialtes, our Naxian captive turned ally turned blood brother, came down to meet us. He had food and dry lodgings for three thousand oarsmen – a miracle he'd prepared with tents and the whole island helping. He launched his *Ariadne* the next morning into a beautiful sunlit day.

We turned our bows north and east, and ran on the wind, and no one touched an oar for two days and a night. Deep water sailing in spring is risky and could be deemed foolish, but we raised Psara, a tiny island west of Chios, at the dawn of the second day. Then

Eresos was only a day's sail away, and the great mountain of Lesbos came into sight almost immediately.

And we were lucky. We had our spring storm while we were in the enclosed slot between Andros and Kythnos. It would have been far harder in the open sea west of Lesbos. I know – I'd almost lost the *Black Raven* there years before.

Do I reminisce overmuch?

Regardless, we hadn't even scattered over the sea. We had fifteen ships with the *Ariadne* – fifteen ships who'd been together before, at Salamis and Artemisium and Mycale, too. We even had a simple signal book.

So when, at the end of a long day of blue water sailing, we saw the rock of Skala Eresos in front of us, and four big triremes hard against the coast, we didn't need to have a council. I brought my new *Apollo's Raven* alongside the *Ajax* under sail, and shouted, 'We can have them by night!'

Cimon waved. He already had his armour on.

Four ships. Three were obviously Phoenician; the fourth looked Ionian – lighter, smaller, faster. The ship's hull was brilliant, red and gold and blue, and painted on her bow was a winged figure.

The sun was setting in the west, behind us, and they should have been blinded. They should have relaxed, so deep in the Great King's Ocean.

Someone wasn't. Even as I watched, the brightly coloured Ionian trireme spun in her own length and raced away so fast that her ram bow raised a wave.

The three heavier ships were slower to react. They either didn't believe their smaller companion, or they had some of their rowers ashore.

I thought the latter.

I was at the head of my column, and I ordered Damon, at the helm, to take us north and west along the coast, as if we were pursuing the fleeing ship. He cheated the helm west, and Moire followed us, and Archilogos followed him.

My sons, in round ships, couldn't manoeuvre much. They just stood on.

Cimon's column went due north. Seen from above, we would have been like a woman raising her arms to the gods: I was the right arm, Cimon a longer left arm, and my sons were the head in the middle.

Aten was a veteran now, and he closed my good *thorax* around my middle and pinned it, and then clipped my greaves on my legs while we ran in on the Phoenicians. I had time to note that although I'd gained a surprising amount of new girth over the winter, I'd managed to lose some already. The thorax just barely closed. I needed exercise.

Aten didn't even raise an eyebrow, and yet I could feel his censure.

The Phoenicians suddenly woke up to their peril and began to man their ships. They were far too late.

And then, suddenly, all together, they beached. I watched their oarsmen scrambling ashore, their marines forming on the beach. I was quite close by then, and I knew the waters intimately. I knew that there was an old breakwater, as old as the Trojan War. I also knew that there was a narrow channel, just wide enough for a warship, on the south side of the rock.

I pointed to it, and Damon raised both eyebrows, but he didn't hesitate.

Aten handed me my beautiful, gold-inlaid Persian spear.

The oarsmen were still coming off their benches.

I ran forward, eyeing my marines, looking for Brasidas.

Ka stepped forward amidships and pointed silently. Ka is very dark-skinned – almost blue – and his arms and legs are exceptionally long. When he points like that, it is as if some god is telling you something.

He was pointing at a Phoenician. The man wore a long robe, like a Persian, and had a fine bronze scale armour on over it, and a helmet that looked like silver, or iron.

He had an axe in his hand, and a woman at his feet.

Now, the *Apollo's Raven* was not yet the ship the *Lydia* had been. But the oarsmen had found their feet, so to speak, and when Damon ordered them to drag their oars, they did. The ship slowed so fast I was thrown down to one knee.

We glided to a stop, about sixty feet off the beach, broadside on to the bows of the three Phoenicians. Their sterns were already pulled up above the tideline.

It's a huge and beautiful beach.

Behind me, the *Black Raven* was coming into the calm water behind the rock, and the *Lady Artemis* was right behind her, and off to my left, the *Ajax* was coming around the rock the other way.

The Phoenician raised his axe.

'Stop!' he roared.

Our ship rocked.

'Take your pirates back out to sea, or we kill everyone here and burn the town.'

He waved his axe.

The woman was Cleis, the great Sappho's descendant, and the mistress of her school. I knew her because she'd helped me before, and because she was Briseis' mentor. Her iron-grey hair spilled over the white of her Ionian chiton, and her shoulders were square and defiant even in the face of a squalid death.

I leant over the rail, looking at this fool. I say 'fool', because he must have been sent to put down rebellion and force the towns of Lesbos to stay allied to the Great King. Burning Eresos was absolutely not a way to accomplish that.

Anyway, it was a foolish threat. He'd never get it burnt before my marines massacred his.

But most important, his oarsmen weren't formed and ready to fight. They were drifting back, with many a glance over their shoulders.

'Ka?' I said.

But before Ka could move, the tall older man he'd brought aboard stepped up to the rail and drew. He had a Persian bow, a beautiful thing in blue and gold, and he drew it like a man shovelling sand. He bent first, and then rose, the bow coming up, and I could see through his chiton as the great shoulder muscles pulled the bow.

He had the setting sun at his back, and his target had to look into the sun.

The arrow hit him in the abdomen, and it went right through the bronze of his armour and up to the fletching in his guts.

'Uh,' said my new archer.

Ka grinned. 'Show-off,' he said.

'Take us in,' I ordered.

We had more than six hundred prisoners, mostly slaves. But we had other problems, as we discovered as soon as we were ashore.

Cleis, the woman who ran Sappho's school, was the perfection of cool dignity, despite having been manhandled and almost killed. Her iron-grey hair went in every direction, but her face was calm, and she smoothed her long chiton and looked at the Phoenician officer, who was dying fairly quickly on the sand.

'What a waste of a life,' she said. She looked at me. 'Arimnestos of Plataea, I believe.'

I bowed. She had more regality than most of the kings I've met.

'Yes, Despoina. My wife is Briseis of ...' I paused. Where was Briseis of, now? Plataea? Ionia? Miletus? Ephesus?

'I know Briseis,' she said. A small smile suggested that, despite war and peril, she found my marriage a matter of some small amusement. 'You've gone to war to get some peace?' she asked.

'Not at all,' I said. 'I'm here at Briseis' instruction.'

'And timely, too,' she admitted.

Behind me, Brasidas and all of my marines were 'organising' the Phoenician marines who'd surrendered.

She seemed unfazed as Leander bellowed 'Lie down on the sand!' at someone too stupid or too dazed to take direction. Arios took the man's arm and swept his leg with a foot-hook and dropped him, unharmed, on the sand.

Leander put a hand on the man's back.

'Told you to lie down, mate. You don't want us mistaking you for trouble.'

I thought of mentioning that the Phoenicians probably didn't have a word of Greek, but Brasidas and his people knew their business – our business.

Poseidonos had forty of my oarsmen in among the marines, 'helping' with their stretchers.

Cleis straightened the shoulder of her chiton. It was pinned with beautiful golden grasshopper pins, and two of them had been bent.

Ever the bronze-smith, I stepped up close.

'May I?' I asked, and started bending the soft gold back into shape.

Once I was very close, she said, 'The archon invited the Phoenicians in. He'll deny it, but I have ways of knowing things.' She looked at me, close enough to kiss. 'He was planning to take the town and make himself tyrant. Tonight.'

Ah, politics. And Greeks. Why do we mock the Thracians for their divisiveness when we're so damned good at it ourselves?

And the mistresses of Sappho's school ... I knew from Briseis how very effective the school was as a clearing house of essential information. Two hundred girls a year, from the best families in Ionia. Think of it, friends. Most girls have no say in choosing their husbands. They go to a stranger's house, and in Ionia, that man can be across the sea, far from home.

And then they may live shut into a woman's world, visiting other women, taking their slaves shopping ... Do we men really think that gossip and babies are the circumference of their world? I think not. And loyalties – old loyalties, to school friends and teachers – may weigh far more heavily that some mate chosen for your father's convenience.

Eh?

My point is that a thousand or more young women from the first families of the Ionian world sent letters and news to Cleis. When Briseis was the effective queen of Ionia, Cleis had been her best informant. And, of course, Briseis herself was part of the network.

Women. Men always forget them when the swords start to flash.

Heh.

All that went through my mind in an instant, and I stepped back, bowed, and looked for Brasidas.

He was standing quietly, his cloak covering his arms so that no one could see whether he had a weapon in his hand or not. He was watching Zephyrides and Kassandros and Kalidion as they rounded up oarsmen and made them sit in rows. The sun was setting; we could lose men in darkness.

I beckoned, and Brasidas came.

'Take ...' I met his eye so he could see how serious I was. 'Take Moire's marines, and Archilogos'. Tell them it's a crisis. Bring them to me at the double.'

'Yes, sir,' he said.

The *Black Raven* was already on the beach, and the *Lady Artemis* was landing, stern first, and so were the *Ajax* and the new *Athena Parthenos*.

'What will you do?' Cleis asked.

'I'll go up into the town to make sure it is secure,' I said.

'He has mercenaries,' Cleis said. 'A dozen men. Professionals.'

I waved at the beach.

She smiled. 'Point taken. Come to me when you have ... secured ... the town.'

I bowed again. In a way, it was like seeing Briseis as an older woman; her face was lined, and there was age in every feature, but the same square shoulders, elegant carriage, the same fire, the same determination.

Of course, running a school for aristocratic adolescents is probably not so different from commanding a pirate ship, either.

The Phoenicians weren't offering much resistance. Even in the long twilight of a spring night on Lesbos, they could see the archers at the rail of my ship, arrows on their bows.

And my oarsmen and marines, moving among them. And now, thanks to all the gods, Cimon was ashore, leaping into the surf with his marines and running up the darkening beach.

'What's happening?' he asked.

You know that feeling when there are too many people asking too many questions in the midst of what may be a crisis? It is like rage or frustration. And you can't let it get to you. Cimon was my friend, my peer, and had every right to ask.

I was just a little busy.

'Can you take charge of the beach?' I asked. 'I'm leaving you my oarsmen and marines, except Brasidas.'

Well, bless him, Cimon is not a man who needs details.

'Got it,' he said. 'Tekles!' he bellowed.

A big man came running up in beautiful armour – Cimon's captain of marines.

I turned.

'I need two men to escort the Despoina,' I called.

All of my marines were working, but my eye fell on Socrates and his daughter Gaia. I had him down as a tough man, and she looked strong and competent, and anyway, this was her destination.

'Socrates,' I said, 'would you and your daughter be kind enough to escort the Despoina up the beach and to her house?'

Socrates nodded. I pulled a spear out of the pile of weapons collected from the Phoenician marines, and a hooked *kopis*. I tossed them to Socrates, who dropped the sword-belt over his shoulder as if he'd done so a few thousand times.

'At your service, ma'am,' he said.

'Despoina, this young woman is here to join your school. This is her father. They'll see you safely up the hill.'

Cleis inclined her head like a queen.

'My thanks, sir,' she said. 'Good fortune, Arimnestos. Come and see me.'

I turned to find Brasidas with thirty marines and Ka and his archers. I could see half a dozen men I'd thought I was leaving behind – Styges, for one, and young Achilles. There were a lot of lonely young wives in Plataea.

'Poseidonos!' I called. 'Get me Leon and two more sailors, and some grapples.'

The old man saluted casually and called out some names.

'On me,' I said, and we plodded across the sand.

I know Eresos well. There's a seaside town, with Vigla, the old fortress, towering over it. Sappho's family ruled from Vigla, and her school is in the ancient fortress.

But the big town is inland almost ten stadia. It is one of the three real towns of Lesbos, with Methymna and Mytilini, and its people are fractious and tend to go with the Medes when offered a choice, while Methymna tends to side always with Athens in every conflict, and Mytilini shifts back and forth as the winds blow.

Archilogos joined me before we were across the sands.

'Where are we going with all my marines?' he asked.

'We're going to stop a *stasis* and probably prevent a massacre,' I said.

He nodded. 'I know Makar, the archon. He's a fool, and he thinks he's brilliant.'

'The very worst possible combination,' I said.

Archilogos glanced at me in the failing light, and stepped closer.

'It might be better for Ionia if he just ... died.'

The lights of Eresos proper were twinkling in the evening air, and I could smell jasmine on the breeze. Ten stadia isn't even an hour's walk, but as we went the moon came out and the last lines of pink faded from the western sky behind us, and suddenly the sky was full of stars.

'What are we doing?' Brasidas asked.

'Taking the city,' I said.

Archilogos nodded. 'If we're challenged, let me talk,' he said.

I put a hand on his shoulder. 'Why don't we just claim to be Phoenician mercenaries?' I asked.

He laughed. 'I forget what you're like,' he said.

The gates were closed. It wasn't a big town, but it had excellent walls: a *socle* of heavy stone, surmounted by a thick wall of mud brick.

'Halt!' bellowed a sentry. 'Who goes armed by our walls!'

In my best Tyrian-accented Greek, I called, 'You fucking sent for us!'

Archilogos just sounded like the Ionian he really was.

'Send for Makar!' he said.

Grumbling, the gate guard climbed down from his tower.

We called out several more times, mostly to make sure there wasn't another guard, and then Poseidonos, well along the wall, cast the first grapple. In two minutes, he and Leon were throwing ropes down.

Archilogos and Brasidas went over the wall.

I stayed with a dozen men.

It was a quarter of an hour before there was a stir in the gate tower.

'Who's there?' came a voice – deep, confident.

'Adon of Tyre. You asked us to come!'

The man leant over the wall. He had a purple cloak, and we could see that because he was flanked by two torch-bearers.

'Is that all the men you've brought?' he asked. 'I have a big town to handle.'

'Open the gate and we'll see what we can do,' I said.

He shook his head. 'And then I'll have a Persian garrison,' he said. 'That's not my intention. I'll be loyal, but I need some assurances first. You see ...'

Right next to me, the gate opened silently.

A man I didn't know was standing there. He was in armour. He raised his hands silently, as if surrendering.

Behind him were a dozen more men. And Brasidas.

Makar turned his head, as if he'd heard a noise.

'What the hells? You ...'

I thought quickly. I thought about a man who was selling his town to the Persians, but was prevaricating even with his new masters.

'Ka,' I said.

The arrows all hit him; the range was very short, and he was brilliantly illuminated.

Brasidas stepped forward.

'These are his bodyguard,' he said. 'They surrendered freely.'

'I want no part of this crap,' the man in the beautiful armour said. 'I'm Euboean. I'm not fighting for the Great King.'

Brasidas pushed past him. 'The town's ours. If you'll give me these men as guides, we can secure all the gates.'

'You trust them?'

'Two are Peloponnesian. None of them are Ionian. I'd say, hire the lot.' He pointed at the man behind him.

'Get it done,' I said.

Archilogos came out of the gate long enough to take the rest of the marines.

'Let me handle this,' he said.

And he was the right man to do it – a local, so to speak.

I found myself with nothing to do, so I went back to the beach with Ka.

Eresos had fallen to us with a single casualty – the would-be tyrant.

The Ionian revolt was under way.

I slept on the beach, rolled in my cloak. That's what comes of helping people revolt against their masters and then sending all your officers on missions – there's no one to find you a place to sleep. I couldn't find Aten; I couldn't find any of my people except Poseidonos, who – no surprise there – had an amphora of wine and a campfire. I sat with my new oarsmen, and eventually my new helmsman, and we told some tall tales. I expect I told some, although I can't remember, and then I put my head on my aspis and rolled in my cloak, just like the old days.

Except that when I was seventeen and learning to kill for my living, I didn't wake with every ligament aching and one of my hands so badly cramped that I couldn't hold my sword.

Apollo! I hadn't even fought. All I'd done was . . .

Well, all the normal things. Plus a twenty-stade walk.

In the light, I could see that we were in chaos; if a handful of Phoenicians or Carians had appeared off our beach, they could have had the lot of us. Bad discipline, bad planning, and mostly my fault. It's dashing and romantic to make up your assault as you go along, but it leaves no room for error or an orderly retreat.

As far as the eye could see, there were oarsmen lying on the beach, their bodies red in the light of the rising sun. It looked like the wrack of a battle – a disastrous defeat.

They were all going to need food, or this would get ugly and they'd go for the town.

I'd assumed Brasidas was in Eresos, but after a short wander among the campfires I found Alexandros, who had captained my marines for years and who was now with Moire. He woke his men, most of whom were sleeping in their armour. There was my cousin Achilles, looking very like a young man I once knew, and nursing a hard head.

Aten appeared with bread and cheese. He'd made the natural assumption that I'd sleep in Sappho's palace on Vigla. More fool me.

Hector appeared, rubbing his eyes, and in an hour I had food coming ashore from the round ships, and Cimon and Archilogos and I were watching the true sunrise over the mountains of eastern Lesbos and drinking hot tisanes. Or maybe wine. Warm wine and water with a little honey is quite good in the morning; add a little cardamom ...

'We need to get to Methymna and Mytilini before the Persians get a fleet here,' Archilogos said.

Cimon looked at me. 'Are we here to liberate Ionia or to make a profit?' he asked.

'You sound like your father,' I said.

Cimon smiled. When he smiled in just a particular way, he looked like his father; when he thought he was going to fool you, he looked like his mother.

'I'll take that as a compliment,' he said. 'I'm good either way. But tell me how you see this playing out.'

'I thought we'd land here, gather information, and have a meal,' I said. 'I hadn't expected an action and a city in revolt.'

Archilogos glanced at me, and I wondered if he knew more than I did. Had I been played? Was this the objective?

I shrugged. 'Regardless, friends, we can have our barley bread and eat it, too. Archilogos goes around to Mytilini. Cimon goes to Methymna – it's an ally of Athens. I put crews in these three triremes and recruit some local marines and officers. I know the town – there are good men here.'

Cimon rubbed his beard with his right hand.

'And ...?'

'And we rendezvous in three days, off Mytilini. In the harbour, if Archilogos puts up a signal.'

'Three bronze shields at my masthead,' he said. 'Or I'm standing off if the town's already taken.'

Cimon nodded. 'Methymna might contribute ships,' he said.

'Perfect,' I said. 'There's room for a few more.'

They were off the beach as soon as their oarsmen were fed. Chaos had become order, and there were lines of little clay braziers burning for five stadia, and men waiting for their rations. We bought a wagonload of bread – the barley of Lesbos is famous for good reason, and we all stuffed ourselves – and then they were away in the late morning sun, their oars flashing in unison. If you haven't been to sea, it's worth remembering that the rhythmic flash of oars can be seen far away – much farther than the hull, or even the mast. Sometimes you can see the pulsing light over the horizon, or through fog.

I borrowed a horse from Cleis and rode up into the main town, where I met with the *boule*, the properly appointed council of the town. None of them struck me as potential tyrants, or even very effective leaders, but they were steady and they promised their allegiance to the Allies, and I negotiated a treaty. I could only sign the treaty in the name of Plataea, of which I was an archon. You can still find a stone stele in Eresos proclaiming that the city and Green Plataea were to be allies against all foes for thirty years.

There's immortality for you, eh?

That took the morning, but it also got the word out to the aristocrats and the hoplite class, so that when my recruiting tables opened, there were dozens of men waiting, most with their arms. And the man at the front of the line was the man who'd commanded the would-be tyrant's bodyguard.

Brasidas nodded. 'Take him,' he said, in his laconic way.

'Ariston,' the man said. By daylight, he was of middle height; he looked sharp, and his eyes had the look.

'From Euboea?' I asked.

'Yes, sir,' he said.

'Ever heard of Eualcidas?' I asked.

He smiled. 'Yes, sir.'

I could see that he was as talkative as Brasidas.

'Are those your men?' I asked.

'Yes, sir.'

'And you'd like to keep them together?'

'Yes, sir. I recruited them, sir.'

I considered pointing out that we'd all almost killed one another the night before, and that he'd technically been on the other side, but that was the point – there were quite a few sides, that spring.

Brasidas tapped my arm.

'Very well. You and your people will be the marines on …'

I looked up at Megakles. He handed me a wax tablet.

'The *Adonis*,' he said. 'The other two are the *Morning Star* and the *Gad's Fortune*.' He gave a sniff like an old wife. 'Unless you want to change their names.'

Sailors do not like to change the names of ships.

'Who's Gad?' I asked. I thought I knew my Phoenician and Canaanite, but Gad wasn't a name I knew.

A crowd of hoplite farmers is not the Athenian agora full of philosophers. No one knew who Gad was.

I pointed at Aten. 'Go ask the prisoners who Gad is,' I said.

I went through a few local farm boys. They were technically hoplites and they all had the panoply, but none of them had ever been in a fight and I really didn't need their blood on my hands. But then there was a likely man – broad shoulders, bouncing with energy, even in his panoply.

He knew how to hold the sword, too.

'I can row,' he said. 'My uncle owns a small ship. I've rowed. I'm not proud.'

I liked that. 'Name?'

'Philippos,' he said.

'Marine, *Morning Star*,' I said.

'Thank you, sir.' Philippos had a cheerful air, and he grinned without servility and went to stand with the new marines.

I was lucky enough to pick up a few veteran oarsmen; all of them were local men stranded by the war – one a local firebrand who'd been ostracised for supporting the 'rebels'.

I have to remind you that in the eyes of the Great King and his officers, we were all rebels, but most especially the Ionians.

Anyway, I took him. He was as big as Leontos and had that look of absolute confidence that you often see in big, handsome men.

'Damysos,' he said.

We all laughed. Damysos was the fastest and smartest of the giants in the myths of the war between the gods and Giants.

'The *Morning Star*, Damysos,' I said. 'You'll be the stern thranite. Maybe a helmsman in time.'

He gave the casual wave of oarsmen everywhere; they don't salute and they seem to take pride in not being particularly military. He picked up his cushion and his pack. He had a *pelta* shield, three good javelins, and a kopis. A valuable man.

We were closing down the table, having picked up enough men to guarantee that the captured ships would be reliable, when there was a stir in the crowd. We had a crowd; with our glittering panoplies and foreign accents, we were probably the most exciting thing in Eresos in a decade.

The latecomer was running. He had greaves and a leather *spolas* and carried a spear, and he had his aspis on his back and another bag as well.

'Sorry!' he said. 'I overslept.'

He had dark brown hair, was deeply tanned, and looked as fit as Brasidas.

'I'm sure we can find someone to keep you awake,' I said. 'What's that on your back?'

'*Kithara*,' he said. 'I play.'

I pointed at one of my marines – the barbarian from far-off Germania.

'He wants to be a rhapsode. Perhaps the two of you should get together.'

No one thinks I'm as funny as I think I am.

'Name?' I asked.

'Sebastos, sir.'

'Welcome aboard. You go to the *Morning Star*.'

I turned back to find Aten had returned.

He whispered in my ear, 'Gad is their Hermes. God of fortune and luck and a little ... tricky.'

I beckoned to Megakles, who was recruiting deck crewmen out of the port's sailors and fishermen.

'If Gad and Hermes are the same god,' I said, 'can we call her *Hermes' Fortune*?'

Megakles frowned. 'I hate to see a name changed,' he said.

That was a no.

'Very well,' I said. '*Gad's Fortune* she remains. I note only that she wasn't especially fortunate for her former crew.'

After some food, I rode back down to the beach and then climbed Vigla. It is a tall hill, probably formed of some ancient volcano; it rises straight out of the sea and the top is relatively flat, as if it was formed by the gods to hold a fortress. Sappho's ancestors built on it, or so the locals say, back in the time of the Trojan War. You can still see the magnificent old walls built from stones too big for ten men to lift – proof that they were all heroes back then, some will tell you.

The road up to the gate is too steep to ride comfortably, so I walked up. It is a real effort on a hot day, but once at the top you step into a different world. There are olive trees in pots, and cats, and cool shade. The view from the walls is staggering, but the little palace is cool and pleasant, with arcades and colonnades in the local red-brown stone.

And girls and women. Sappho's school is in the palace, of course, and Cleis and her teachers had about two hundred students. There were a few men, but for the most part, it was a place for women, and I was met at the gate and escorted inside.

There were girls sitting under the trees, reading from scrolls. A girl was reciting verse, and another standing like a statue, watching all of the men on the beach far below, like busy ants. I watched, too. They were the former Phoenician oarsmen, loading on to the *Gad's Fortune* for a little sea trial with their new captain and deck crew.

The young woman glanced at me once and then went back to watching.

I heard women singing – a choir, in fact – and I wasn't sure I'd ever heard such a fine choir of women, except perhaps in Athens for the Panathenaea procession. Women's choirs were rare in those days.

My escort was a very serious young woman in a *chitoniskos*. I remained young enough, despite morning aches and pains, to find her chitoniskos very short indeed, but I could equally understand that in this climate, women, left to themselves, didn't need to be swathed in layers of linen.

And I could also see why men were escorted. Half the aristocrats in the Ionian Sea had their daughters here, and the women didn't need men ... leering. Or doing anything else.

'You are very famous here,' she said, a little breathless.

Fame is a funny thing. I guessed, in that moment, that this young woman would tell her grandchildren some day that she'd met Arimnestos, the killer of men. Or perhaps, here, on Vigla, I was Arimnestos, husband of the great Briseis. We are all many different people, I suspect. I'm aware that in my famous wife's story, I'm a bit player with a red sword.

I'm dithering. She led me to Cleis, who sat on a marble terrace, in a great armchair, looking out over the ocean.

'You look like Penelope, waiting for Odysseus,' I said.

She turned her head. 'I'm a trifle old to be Penelope,' she said. 'And I have never waited for a man in all my life.' Then she waved a hand. 'Don't mind me. All my girls are upset. There's flashing armour and young men and ... Goodness, in a moment I'll have them trooping down the hill to see the ships.'

'We'll be gone in a day,' I said.

'You think I'm an old prude,' she said, 'but I'm responsible for any girl who gets a round belly.'

'I understand,' I said.

'See that you do,' she snapped. And then she relented. 'I called you here to help you, not to give you orders.'

A slave brought me wine. Wine in mid-afternoon is a fine thing. This was honey-sweet and there were figs, almonds and cheese.

She laughed.

'Arimnestos! I see why Briseis loves you. You enjoy everything. Even my figs!'

I had my mouth full.

She looked out to sea while I chewed. I was hungry ...

'I'll stop being a barbarian,' I said.

'I'm glad you like honeyed almonds. Althea, a bowl of rose water for my guest.' Cleis looked at me. 'I can help you, and Briseis would want me to.'

I gave her a scroll tube. I hadn't opened it – I trusted my wife.

Cleis read it without a twitch on her face, and then she re-rolled the scroll and put it in the tube.

'I see,' she said.

I sipped my wine. 'I have not read that document.'

Cleis nodded and didn't offer it to me.

'Briseis says that you are going to liberate all of Ionia – not just the islands that came over to the Alliance after Mycale.'

I nodded.

She tapped the scroll tube on her teeth; I imagined that this was an old habit in a woman who read constantly.

'The Satraps of Lydia and Caria have been ordered to suppress the rebellion by any means necessary,' she said. 'I can give you a list that Artemisia of Halicarnassus sent to the Great King, of men she judged loyal to Persia.'

'Artemisia?' I said. 'Was she one of your girls?'

Cleis smiled. 'I have ways of speaking to her, and friends near to her. That was her, yesterday, you know. In the colourful ship.'

I nodded and sipped my wine. It was not the first time that the legendary lady of Halicarnassus had slipped through my fingers.

'Briseis says you mean to strike a blow that will ring through Ionia,' she said. 'Stopping that arse from making Eresos a tyranny is not such a blow.'

'I didn't imagine that it was,' I admitted.

She smiled. 'Ionia is divided,' she said, 'and a divided Ionia cannot furnish the Great King with enough ships to stop the Allies from sailing wherever they will. With determination and a great fleet, you could liberate even the mainland in a year or two.'

I nodded.

'But Briseis says that the Spartans don't want to liberate Ionia,' she went on, 'much less the mainland satrapies.'

I nodded again. 'It is the policy of the ephors that all of you should be sent west as colonists, since you are unable to defend yourselves.'

'Unable to defend ourselves?' she snapped. 'Sparta is some hill town full of shepherds. Do they cook their meat before they eat it?'

'They're fairly competent at war,' I said. 'It's a useful skill just now.'

She took a deep breath.

I raised a hand and interrupted. 'Despoina, I have fought for Ionia for twenty years. Ionians are like all Greeks – they'll fight among themselves for the sheer fun of it. I'm aware of the wonders of Ionian culture – I'm married to it. But the Spartans are not entirely incorrect. We, the Greeks of Attica and Boeotia and the Peloponnese, can only spend so much blood and treasure here. Athens seeks an empire. Sparta seeks to prevent Athens from having an empire. No one is really interested in a war against the Great King.'

Cleis snapped her fingers for more wine and sat back.

'So ...' she said. 'What do you plan?'

I wasn't sure that I wanted to tell her. I knew she had sources, but that game can always be played both ways. She was in an excellent position to betray me and my little fleet to her other friends, and I was a fool if I didn't think that Cleis had friends on both sides of the line.

'Briseis says you will do something that will set us on fire,' she said. 'We both know that sacking Sardis won't accomplish that. Do you agree?'

'Despoina, I was there the last time,' I said.

'Ah ...' She was surprised. 'I didn't know that.'

'I was with the Athenians,' I said.

I had the oddest feeling. I'd mentioned Eualcidas that morning to the Euboean, and now I was thinking of the fight at Sardis.

I wondered in the blink of an eye if I might end where I'd begun – full circle, dying on some battlefield in Ionia. Perhaps some young hero would come and retrieve my body.

To be honest, the thought made me smile, not frown.

'You really have seen Ionia at her worst,' Cleis said, breaking into my thoughts.

I shrugged. 'Perhaps.'

Cleis drank off her wine with the enthusiasm of a much younger woman.

'Listen, Arimnestos. I am accounted something of a seer – in this case, I think native intelligence is all that is required. You plan to surprise the Phoenicians at Tyre and burn their ships.'

I didn't disguise my surprise. I almost dropped my wine.

She smiled wickedly, reminding me of who she must have been fifty years earlier.

'It's simple,' she said. 'You seek to unite the Athenians and the Spartans – to rob the Spartans of any excuse for inaction, and to make it possible for the Ionians to rise. What would be more spectacular than an attack on the Great King's last fleet?'

I didn't try to hide my smile. Or rather, I did at first, and then I just gave in.

'Yes,' I said. 'I plan to burn the Phoenician fleet at Tyre.'

She sat forward. 'Now that would be something,' she said.

'So it would,' I agreed.

I had just betrayed my plan to a woman who could arrange for the Phoenicians to trap me and kill me, and I felt like a fool.

But she turned to face me, the sun on her face erasing years and reminding me of who she was. She smiled.

'I know a woman who can help you,' she said. 'A very remarkable woman.'

'One of your students?' I asked.

'In a manner of speaking,' she said. 'Her name is Alysia. Let me see if I can find her for you.'

'Find her?' I asked.

'She'll be somewhere on Cyprus,' the Despoina said. 'Give me a few days.'

I didn't give Alysia as much thought as I might have, because I had three new ships to integrate into my command, and a rendezvous coming up.

I did ask Cleis to help me find trierarchs. I wanted local men of property who could afford to keep their ships and who had some experience. She found them for me, and that way, they owed her a favour, and in a way, she owed me.

I felt like Miltiades. I fact, it occurred to me that I was becoming

Miltiades, and that was sobering. Besides, Cimon already had the job filled, except that he was, altogether, a much better man.

I met all three of them on the waterfront of Eresos, below Vigla. Parmenio was of middle height, blond, with aristocratic manners and a certain air of rakishness that decided me that he'd do. Helikaon was from one of Methymna's first families; he'd fought for the rebels at Lade, and then commanded an Ionian ship on the other side at Salamis.

'The moment we saw the centre give, we turned and ran,' he said. He smiled. 'If they hadn't put Medes on my foredeck I wouldn't even have stayed that long.'

He was soft-spoken, looked like a sailor, and his hair was blown every which way.

'I took a fishing boat out last night,' he said with a shrug of apology. 'I heard you were looking for captains and sailed around from Methymna. I haven't slept.'

My third captain was a short, sandy-haired man with dark brown eyes and a reputation as a good captain. He'd been trierarch of a military trireme for the Tyrant of Samos, and then for the rebels. We knew many of the same people. His name was Herakles, and he had relatives in the Aegyptian Delta and in Cyrene – a useful man to know and to have with us.

I put them into their new ships, and let them choose their own helmsmen, and we spent a long day rowing back and forth across the sea west of Lesbos. All the new oarsmen were the slaves out of the Phoenician ships, back at their oars. I offered them all my usual pirate's deal – row for food and wine for the summer, and I'd give them their freedom.

I've seldom known a man to refuse the offer.

Because of all this, we were a day late for the rendezvous off Mytilini, but I needn't have hurried. Archilogos had been successful, and had then taken three triremes from Mytilini and sailed for Ephesus, his home. Cimon and I waited a day, told each other a lot of tall tales of our shared past over wine on the same beaches we'd sat on during the Ionian Revolt, twenty years before, and then, when I'd begin to guess what Archilogos was about, I offered to run down to Ephesus and find him.

'If he's raising the whole coast, our little foray is wrecked,' Cimon said, and he had blood in his eye.

I thought about his anger while my people rowed the *Apollo's Raven* over to Ephesus to find our errant sheep.

I was worried – very worried – that our early spring element of surprise was already gone. If I could have stopped Archilogos from sailing into Ephesus I would have. Messengers could move overland, or by sea, and the news of our fleet might already be stirring the Phoenicians.

And it was becoming obvious to me that my wife had not entirely trusted me with her plans, and that in this case, Archilogos might be following his sister's orders, or their shared vision, and that I wasn't fully included.

It's very easy to grow angry at someone you love. Distance helps, and so does tension, and secrecy. I had all three, and in heaps. It doesn't excuse me, really.

But I was fuming by the time I reached Ephesus.

Archilogos had them manning ships. The council had already declared for the Alliance and they were looking for ways to participate without being too openly in revolt. If that seems cowardly, keep in mind that Ephesus, one of the homes of my youth and one of the richest cities in the world, is located just a few hundred stadia from Sardis, the virtual capital of western Persia, the seat of the most powerful western Satrap.

As all too often happens, I gave careful thought to the situation, tamped down all my anger and my suspicion, and went to see Archilogos ...

And it all exploded. Not my finest hour.

I think it was seeing that gate – that house. The house where I was a slave, first to Archilogos' father and then to Briseis. Ah, Hipponax. Ah, Briseis.

It was there that a number of tutors taught me to be a man; there that I learnt to kill. There that Heraclitus taught me to think, and be more than just a killer. There that I fell in love with Briseis.

So I was off my centre as soon as I walked through the gate, and when I saw Archilogos lying on a kline in a fine chiton, drinking pale golden wine from a golden kylix, I didn't even hesitate.

'Is this your rendezvous at Mytilini?' I shot at him.

'Would you like some wine, Ari?' he asked, and waved at a slave.

'We're paying several thousand oarsmen,' I said. 'We had a plan, if you remember.' I may already have been shouting.

'I have liberated two of the greatest cities in Ionia,' he said. 'We'll transform the shape of the war.'

'Not if the Phoenicians come and burn the harbour,' I said. 'You were supposed to nail down the allegiance of Mytilini and wait for us. Now the whole coast knows we have a fleet. I knew you Ionians were lazy—'

'Am I supposed to be offended?' he asked. 'And need you shout at me in my own house?'

'Are you ready to go to sea?' I asked.

He leant on one elbow. A slave had brought me a pretty silver cup full of wine.

'Ari,' he began, 'your plan is ...'

'Is what?' I asked.

'Unrealistic. Unnecessary. All of these towns will fall into our hands *now*.' He was almost pleading. 'We don't need another victory. That's what *you* want. But it's not what we need. Not what Ionia needs. All we have to do is show the flag and they'll all fall like ripe figs.'

'And then?' I asked. 'When the Persian fleet puts to sea?'

'The Alliance will crush it,' he said. 'Briseis says—'

'Not if it never sails east of Delos,' I said. 'Not if the Spartans fear the success of Athens more than they fear Persia.' I drank off my wine. 'I've had this argument with your sister. I know what Briseis says. And I know that she doesn't have a fleet.'

He shrugged. 'Too bad, Ari. I've made my decision. Why don't you sit down?'

A little thing. But he said it in the same tone he used to use when I was his slave.

'I can't sit down,' I said. 'I have a fleet waiting for me. A fleet of my friends, who are not rich Ionian fucks who have clean chitons and brilliant wine waiting for them at the end of every day. They're bad men with farms and wives and bills to pay, and I've promised them a victory and loot. Shall we come back and loot Ephesus?'

'Even for you, Ari, that's a foolish threat,' he began.

'Even for me?' I said quietly. I tossed him the wine cup and he caught it, because otherwise it would have hit him in the nose. 'I can't afford a diplomatic cruise up and down Ionia, showing the flag. If you wanted that, you should have said so. To Pausanias.'

'I did. He turned us down.' He shrugged.

'So you tricked me,' I said.

He shrugged. 'Have you lost by it?'

'I'm sailing in an hour,' I said. 'Come or don't.'

*

68

He didn't. I left the port of Ephesus, and my tired crew rowed us back into the teeth of the wind. They rowed all night, so that we were off the beach of Mytilini when the sun rose over the Olympus of Lesbos in the morning. They were tired and surly and, by the gods, so was I.

Cimon met me on the beach and heard my news grimly.

'I say we try,' I said.

'It was always insane,' he said.

'It's not much more insane now,' I said. 'We have the wind. We can outrun the news.'

Tyre was more than a hundred parasangs away – thirty-six hundred stadia.

Cimon shrugged. 'No guts, no glory,' he said. 'Let's try. We can always run to Cyprus if the Phoenicians are out.'

I nodded. 'My oarsmen need a day to rest,' I said. 'And I'd like the round ships full up with wine, oil and salt meat.'

'Agreed. Dawn tomorrow?'

We clasped hands, and I went up into the city of Mytilini, buying provisions.

I was still in a black mood when a beggar, or a dock-boy, came up behind me and tugged at my chlamys.

'Get away, *pais*,' I snapped.

'Are you Arimnestos of Plataea?' he asked.

He was a dirty thing, but not so small – a head shorter than me. Not a child.

'I am,' I said. 'What's it to you?'

'I have a message,' he said. 'From a lady.'

He handed me a scroll tube. Having that filthy adolescent hand me an ivory scroll tube was like finding a golden daric on an ash heap. His straw hat was so old and filthy that the sweat stains that adorned the brow had begun to turn black, and his hair was lank.

I reached inside my cloak and touched my sword hilt, just to be sure, and glanced around. I was drinking wine alone, at a seaside taverna; I'd eaten all the little fish they'd fried for me. I was thinking about Archilogos and Briseis, and regretting my attitude a little. Or, to be honest, I was regretting my anger, and then wallowing in it, and then regretting it ... Am I the only one who does this?

'What's your name, boy?' I asked.

He shrugged. 'Pais,' he said. *Boy*.

I nodded. A common slave name. I popped the scroll from the

tube. 'Scroll' was too formal a name. It was a few leaves of papyrus pasted together in a small sheet, no bigger than my hand.

Cleis bids me to meet with you. Follow the bearer.

I drank off my wine and waved down one of the taverna's slaves and sent him to my ship with a note of my own.

'I'm to follow you,' I said.

I was not particularly cautious; I trusted that anyone who used Cleis' name was not an outright enemy, even if the people plotting for the future of Ionia weren't exactly my favourites at that moment.

The boy weaved through the narrow streets of the dockside of Mytilini and then began the climb towards the acropolis, which is like an island of its own. We passed from a terrible neighbourhood of cold, dark tenements that leant like round ships in a gale, into a pleasant place with houses and chickens. 'Pais' turned into an alley and opened a gate. He vanished through, and I followed him.

I had one hand on my sword.

'Pais' crossed a pretty outdoor patio covered in seashell mosaic and went in the back of the house, through the kitchens, which were empty, fires doused. We ducked our heads for a low lintel, me watching like a man in a den of lions, and then we were in a big, long room where, I suspect, people usually ate.

He turned.

'I admit I've lied to you,' he said.

I drew my sword.

He pulled off his hat, and all his lank hair came with it, and underneath was a woman with strawberry blond hair and an impish smile that the 'boy' could never have worn.

'My name is Alysia,' she said. 'Cleis told me to find you. I gather you want news from Tyre?'

I stood, open-mouthed. How had I ever thought this beautiful woman was a boy?

Alysia began to laugh.

'My husband has just been to Sardis on business,' Alysia said.

Her slight stress on *husband* told me a great deal about what was and was not on offer, and indeed, even in wartime, most matrons would not be alone in an empty house with a man, much less a notorious man of violence.

I sheathed my sword and stepped away from her, to lean against the wall – the step away was deliberate, a message with body language that I meant no physical threat.

'What, may I ask, is your husband's business in Sardis?' I asked.

She smiled. 'We're factors for the Satrap,' she said. 'We farm his taxes and invest his profits.'

'Farming' taxes is a very Persian approach. You sell the whole tax base of an area to a single rich man, or a consortium, for a fixed sum – let's call it ten thousand gold darics for Lesbos. I pay the whole sum; there's the district taxes paid. Now I collect it from Lesbos. I can make an enormous profit, or I can be a patriot and protect people, like the little people. Or I can use it as a weapon, to crush my business rivals by demanding exorbitant sums from them.

Now, to be fair, the Persians have an inspection system as a sort of check on rapacious greed. The inspectors work in secret, and they come to your district and sort of ask around, looking to see if the tax-farmer is such a piece of work that he might cause a revolt.

Otherwise, they just collect money and get richer. It's a little like piracy, except on land and perfectly legal. Tax-farmers are the richest – and in some ways, most powerful – functionaries in the Persian empire.

'Is your husband loyal to the Great King?' I asked.

'My husband is extremely loyal ... to me,' she said, with a glance from under her eyelids that told me a good deal. 'I'm willing to work for the liberation of Ionia.'

I nodded. 'I'm interested in Tyre,' I said. 'And the coast of Syria.'

She smiled. She was very beautiful, with hair a colour almost never seen among Greeks, and a face that, if it wouldn't launch a thousand ships, might be said to be capable of launching some hundreds.

She reached into her bag – like any slave labourer, she wore a bag over her shoulder – and produced a pencil of charcoal; not a thing snatched from a fire, either, but the kind of shaped charcoal that artists use in the agora. She knelt with the fluidity of a dancer and began to sketch on the floor.

'Have you been to Tyre?' she asked.

'Never,' I said. 'For the last twenty years or so, the Phoenicians have all treated me as an enemy.'

'Who knows why?' she said dryly.

I grinned. She was easy to like.

I watched her sketching away. She was unafraid – unafraid of me, unafraid of being caught. Courage is probably the most beautiful attribute a person can have, and courage comes in many forms.

'This is the main city,' she said, sketching a triangle. Then she drew a line – the coast of Syria. The long, flat side of the triangle faced out to sea; one point aimed at the coast, one pointed north up the coast, and the third pointed south. Then she drew two half-circles, one each on the sides facing the coast. 'The Tyrians call it the "new city", because this city, on the mainland, is a thousand years older.' She drew a shaded rectangle on the coast.

That gave me pause.

'A thousand years?' I asked.

'The priests of Melqart say that the old city was settled two thousand years ago – more, really, but maths aren't my best thing and they always speak in their own festival dates.' She kept drawing, indicating the northern of her half-circles. 'This is the "Harbour of Sidon". It's called that because it faces north, up the coast, towards Sidon.'

I nodded.

'This is the "Harbour of Aegypt",' she said.

'Because it faces south, towards Aegypt,' I said.

'So glad you're paying attention. Off the southern point of the triangle, just here, there's a long string of rocks. Actually, almost islets – there are goats and sheep on a few. And a tower on this one, with a garrison.'

I nodded. The rocks trailed away south like a dagger pointed at Aegypt.

'All of the ship sheds are in the inner harbours,' she said. 'I don't think you can touch them.'

I rubbed my beard. I hadn't voiced it to Cimon, but I'd worried about that.

'Stone?'

'Stone, and very handsome, at that, with heavy doors of cedar and iron that would take a demon to burn through. But they have a heavy garrison – towers on the ends of the arms around the harbours, and archers.'

I nodded. 'Damn,' I said.

She looked up at me.

I half-knelt on the floor beside her. 'How do you know all this?'

'I've been seven times,' she said. 'It doesn't take the brain of Ares to know that sooner or later, the Greeks must knock Tyre out of the war.'

I laughed. I laughed so hard I ended up sitting on my arse beside her charcoal map.

'What's so funny?' she asked. Her fingers were black from the charcoal.

'It may not take the brain of Ares, mistress, but I can't get most of the Athenian, Spartan or Ionian commanders to see it.'

'I'm sure that I could convince them,' she said. Again, that flash of lowering eyes. Very effective.

I shook my head.

She stood up, dusting her hands.

'Here's the other thing I can tell you. The southern coast – that's what the Great King calls Phoenicia and Aegypt, right?'

In fact, I hadn't known that.

'The old Phoenician kingdom is divided into four – Sidon, Tyre, Arwad and Byblos. There's other cities that can raise fleets, but those are the greatest. Think of Tyre as Athens, and the others as Aegina.'

I nodded. All of this was news to me, and I was trying to take it all in and wondering how in a thousand hells in Tartarus I'd got through twenty years of war and never obtained all this intelligence.

Damn.

'All together, the cities, which include Naucratis in the Delta and some other Aegyptian cities, are called "The South Coast".' She was speaking slowly, and a flush had come over her. She was going to say something momentous, and she was very impressed with herself, and she enjoyed a little drama.

Very fetching, I must say.

More than fetching. I had a sort of spike of desire – the sort of thing that defeats marriage vows and blinds a man to consequence.

Luckily for my future survival, we were in the middle of a discussion of strategy, and military strategy is the very opposite of *eros*, at least to me. It reaches to the most rational part of my mind.

And I didn't think she was interested, anyway …

'So all these cities are the "South Coast" and Tyre is their Athens,' I said, mostly to indicate that I was following along.

She smiled, and reached into her bag again. She removed a scroll tube and handed it to me.

'A faithful copy of the Great King's sailing orders to his South Coast Naval District,' she said.

I rose to my feet, and went to the window, where there was better light.

The orders were written in Persian, by a scribe whose Median was better than his High Persian. The cuneiform was, thank the gods, the same I'd learnt as a boy in Ephesus, and cuneiform, because it is made with little shaped sticks, is always easy to read – every letter is always almost identical.

The problem was the dates.

The Great King, Lord of Lords by the grace of Ahura Mazda, says this thing: By the feast of Maidyozarem in the month of Truth, you will gather all your ships at Tyre to crush the rebels against our throne, and you will gather in the harbour of Tyre and await the directions of my loyal servant.

I could read it. I could understand most of it.

'When is Maidyozarem?' I asked. 'And what is the month of Truth?'

'You speak Persian?' she said, impressed.

'I grew up with it,' I said. 'But these months are new.'

She nodded. 'I'll find someone to ask,' she said. 'But I think it must be next month – the second after Nowruz.'

I was thinking.

I was thinking about fitting out the *Apollo's Raven*. I was thinking of how vulnerable she would have been during the fitting-out.

I was thinking of ships coming out of ship sheds, with a little rot in their hulls – of every shipwright in Tyre working on a hundred upturned hulls.

And then floating the finished hulls into the harbours.

And then putting in the masts and running gear ...

It had taken us a week for just one ship. I knew that Athens, which had an entire bureaucracy tuned to refit the fleet, expected to take almost three weeks to fit and launch one hundred and twenty triremes.

Let's say the 'South Coast' was as good. Even better, perhaps.

I stared at the document.

'Can you please find someone to confirm that "the month of Truth" is next month?' I asked.

'I can tell you the answer in a few hours,' she said.

I nodded. 'Meet you here?' I asked.

She looked thoughtful. 'I'd hate it if you were the kind of man who took my information and then sold me into slavery.'

74

I smiled. 'I think you'd make a terrible slave,' I said.

'Mmm,' she said. 'I'll send you a note about where to meet.'

Four hours later we were meeting in the courtyard of someone's home. It was a rich house, and there were slaves moving around, and the burble of voices and laughter, as if a party was going on in another courtyard nearby.

'Your house?' I asked.

Alysia shook her head. 'A friend's. That's my party you hear – I've just had too much wine and went to throw up.' She smiled brilliantly. 'I can confirm the date. And I have a further titbit, but I will only share it if you give me your word not to take a certain ship. It would bankrupt us.'

I nodded. 'Very well.'

She looked at me. There wasn't much light, and I thought that she was trying to read me, and I wondered what she'd been told about me, and what she believed.

'I'm Briseis' husband,' I said. 'Not just a sea brigand.'

'I don't know Briseis personally,' she said, 'but she and my husband are not friends.'

Ahhh. Not all about me, then.

She inhaled deeply. 'All right, here we go.' Her voice wasn't steady. 'We got a ... How do I explain this? An order for hard currency. From the Satrap. Today, from Sardis, but for Sidon, asking for specie to be transported there immediately, to arrive in two weeks. To pay the shipwrights.'

Perfect.

'Almost too good,' I said.

'The Persians are too big and too well organised to use their own messenger service as a deception,' she said.

'I agree,' I said, 'but your husband is a Persian tax-farmer and you want me to make sure your cargo of specie is not intercepted between here and Sidon. I see lots of room for you to lie and play me.'

She shrugged. 'Sure,' she admitted. 'But then, I assume you'd come back here and kill me.'

I nodded. And I was Miltiades.

'No,' I said. 'I'd sell you into slavery.'

She winced.

'Just so we understand each other,' I said. 'Nothing personal. Strictly business.'

'I was starting to like you,' she said.

'You are the best intelligence source I've met in this part of the war,' I said. 'Pardon me if I *have* to know that you are straight.'

'I may need to go and throw up,' she said. 'I'm not used to being threatened. You may go.'

And there I was, dismissed.

That was fine.

In the morning, as our oarsmen loaded on to our ships and the good citizens of Mytilini breathed a long sigh of relief, I found Cimon.

'Walk with me,' I said.

'Certainly, Pater,' he said with an odd smile, and suddenly I knew why.

Miltiades had always said 'Walk with me.' Sometimes on this very beach.

We walked south along the beach and I outlined the source, the quality of the intelligence, the substance, and how I planned to use it.

'That woman deserves a statue in the agora, if this works,' he said.

'But you agree?' I asked.

Cimon slapped me on the back. 'Brother,' he said, 'this is the best news so far. I believe, now.'

I nodded. 'So do I.'

'You didn't believe before?' he asked, astounded.

'I believe in Moira. And Tyche. I believe that if you do your part, the gods will do theirs. So yes – I came out here on a wing and a prayer, hoping that we'd get a little luck.' I shrugged.

He laughed. 'And that's why Aristides won't let you do our strategic planning,' he said. 'You and I know there's Fortuna involved, but Aristides ...'

We smiled, embraced, and jogged off towards our ships.

We went south, but we navigated a roundabout course, one meant to confuse watchers and keep out of the sight of the Great King's agents. You might think that was impossible with a fleet of twenty ships, including those we'd picked up from Lesbos, but we sailed down the *west* coast of Chios, stopping for mutton and wine at Mesta. My son Hector ran an errand for me and came back with three donkey loads, and we touched up our supplies of grain and salt fish. Then back south and west to Myconos, where we found a dozen merchants out of Athens, and no news of Pausanias or the

Allied fleet putting to sea. After a day of rest, Sekla had a little luck, and found a merchant who traded into the Nile Delta. He gave us his route in exchange for two hundred drachmas in silver, paid on the barrel. We paid it and Sekla's informant gave us a detailed sailing instruction, including some descriptions of islands, and even a dozen little pictures carved into the wax of a pair of tablets.

I knew most of the route, and so did Sekla. There was a part in the middle we'd never done before, and I suspected very few other ships had tried it. But none of the trierarchs made a fuss, and Cimon simply gave a shrug. We went to the temple and made sacrifices, and then we gave our sailors and oarsmen another night of sleep, through which I admit I fretted, took too many walks, and drank too much. Then we were away south on a sweet wind that saved our oarsmen a great deal of rowing. We had a long day, from sunrise straight through the night, with the worried oarsmen pissing over the side and being careful with the water, watching the command deck and the helmsman and whispering. I could hear Poseidonos reassuring the poor bastards, but they weren't used to my navigation, and they weren't the veterans who'd been to the Hesperides and Gaul and out through the Pillars of Heracles.

It's very lonely in command. I'm sure other men have noted this, and it's nothing new, but out in the very middle of the Inner Sea, under a wheel of stars, even with a fair wind and a following sea, without so much as the notch of an island all around the wheel of the sky, it is very easy to doubt your wisdom.

Listen, I've become a fairly competent navigator. But remember that I didn't really go to sea until I was Archilogos' slave. Most fisherman use the sea from the age of ten years or so, and they know the wheel of stars and the smell of the surf. I came late to the knowledge, and Paramanos was my first teacher, and then Sekla and Megakles, who was under my lee, about half a stade away, tempting me to signal him.

Of course, I had doubts. Myconos to Astypalaia, which Athenians call Chora, is more than six hundred stadia by my dead reckoning. And we hadn't seen a sign of land since we sunk Amorgos astern.

Still, hundreds of other captains with less experience than I had made this route work, and I had brilliant stars and a fine wind.

The problem with command is that you worry anyway. Nineteen ships behind me in two long lines, sailing along, and if I missed my measure, we'd run aground and be broken for firewood in five hideous minutes, because we were running fast in the dark, in a world where most captains either beached for the night or laid to.

I poured a cup of wine and poured it out to Paramanos, and another for Poseidon.

I prayed.

Damon, my new helmsman, stood by me in the darkness without complaint. His wake was near perfect; I went astern a few times to check it, just to make sure that some secret change of tide or current wasn't ruining my dead reckoning. You really don't want to hit an island in the dark.

Nestor, son of Dion, came aft, and turned our sandglass, and marked the time on a wax tablet, and I sent him forward to throw a line and mark the log. These were techniques that the Greeks had learnt from the Phoenicians, or rather, that we'd learnt when we were Dagon's slaves – the secrets that the Phoenicians and the Carthaginians used in long navigation, allowing them to at least guess at their speed and drift. And I had an advantage they lacked – a little geometry with Pythagoras' daughter, Dano. And geometry allows you to calculate the third side of a triangle if you know the first two and some of the angles. Even if you have to guess at the sides, the rate of drift in a light breeze, and the rate of your travel through the water … Even if you have to guess the angle of the wind against your ship (not so difficult, with a bit of old linen in your hand), your answers give you an approximation.

I'd learnt it all years ago. I'd practised it out on the western Ocean and brought my ships through alive, all the way to Alba, west of Gaul.

So when my prayers to Poseidon were done, and Nestor had brought me the results of heaving the log, I did my calculations, found them reassuring, and went forward among the whispering oarsmen. I went to my command post in times of combat – the platform where the mainmast was mounted – and I called out, loud and clear.

'Listen up, lads!'

Brasidas muttered something.

I ignored him. 'I hear whispering like a wind across the bow – I know you're worried. There's nothing about this you need to worry about. We'll be on a beach in six hours. When the sun rises, you'll see the mountains of Astypalaia, dead ahead over the bow, and we'll be drinking some new wine before the sun is directly overhead.'

Poseidonos made a circle with his thumb and forefinger – a sailor's indication that I'd struck the gong.

I went aft to the helm and ran all my calculations again.

Because ...

Rosy-fingered dawn – and never was there a happier phrase – touched the eastern horizon; the chilly grey of the wolf's tail was driven into the darkness, and Aurora herself came up. East was east, the sun was in the right part of the sky, and south-by-east was my course. There, not quite over the ram of the bow and the marine box, were the five peaks and twin islands of Astypalaia. My dead reckoning had been out by a very small but noticeable amount, and we had to make a slight turn, which Damon did without an order, bless him. He corrected our course as the sun rose so that the oarsmen, craning their heads round, never saw that I'd been off by a bit.

Of course, in an ocean, *a bit* becomes *quite a bit* very quickly. But dead reckoning is an approximation, and you are a fool if you expect otherwise.

By midday, we were indeed enjoying the very limited pleasures of a fishing village with perhaps five hundred inhabitants. We probably drank all the wine on the island, and we bought a boatload of salt fish.

I had a long conference with Cimon and Megakles and Sekla in a 'wine shop' that was really just a waterfront house built of baked clay brick and whitewashed; it had four tables. Regardless, it was the only wine shop, and we sat there. I'm hoping you'll laugh, because the elite of the Athenian navy, so to speak, were crammed into six old wooden benches, and the owner was terrified of us.

I digress. We looked at the next few legs, because from here on, we were at the mercy of our purchased navigations, which were nothing but a series of island names and tiny pictures. I wanted as much light for navigation as I could get, so we left the beach long before darkness, to the utter disgruntlement of the oarsmen. They were further put out that with a perfectly good breeze and the mast already raised, we used oars as we crept along the coast.

I had only my wax tablets after this.

I aimed the ship south and east again, with the setting sun in the west as my guide. I aimed for the tiny islet of Syma, a single peak sixty stadia away and still visible. In fact, it was almost exactly as described, which raised my heart.

Three hours later, as full darkness was falling and the moon was rising, we were skirting Syma, having passed between the Dog Rocks exactly as Sekla's pilot had reported; 'two small spires of rock about three stadia apart.' An accurate description.

South and east of Syma we passed Plakida, just keeping her in sight on the port side, as our merchant had advised.

And then darkness fell, and we were back under the wheel of stars.

Sailors are odd cattle. Apparently, because I'd done it all the night before, they had no further concerns. While I kept my command deck for the second night running, my head pounding with fatigue, Old Nestor in the steering harness amidships, my oarsmen snored away without a care in the world. I had the odd temptation to wake them all and tell them that tonight, I was heading for an island I'd never seen before, with nothing but dead reckoning to measure, and the word of a man only Sekla had met.

He had said somewhere around two hundred and fifty stadia. We had a fine wind blowing almost straight over the stern, and we had both sails rigged. The ship was as steady as a trireme with a narrow entry and a ram bow could be in the middle of the Inner Sea, hurtling along on a starlit night.

I sent Damon into the bow, and then I woke Brasidas and had the marines stand watches, listening for surf, watching for anything . . . anything at all.

Brasidas poured me a cup of wine and handed it to me without any words.

Old Nestor smiled. 'I'd take some of that,' he said.

I gave him half the cup. 'It's just his Laconian way of telling me that I'm fretting and I should calm down,' I said.

Brasidas smiled.

Eventually I managed three hours of sleep, and I woke to Leander shaking my shoulder.

'First light,' he said.

I sat up.

It was an odd dawn, with the promise of rain: clouds off to the east, and the smell of water in the air.

There wasn't much to be seen for some time, which didn't prevent the marines on watch – Zephyrides and Kassandros – from talking constantly. Actually, it was mostly Kassandros, watching gulls.

Old Nestor gave me the steering oars and stretched.

'Getting too old for this,' he said. 'You do a lot of deep green navigation, eh, sir?'

I shrugged. 'On this trip we're taking some risks.'

'A big blow would scatter the fleet and wreck us,' he said. 'No offence.'

I nodded and poured him some water from the jug that the boy had left.

'We can't afford for anyone in the Great King's employ to see us,' I said.

Nestor nodded. 'Fair,' he said. 'I can take the steering back.'

I was just out of the rig when Kassandros hailed.

'Land!' he shouted. 'Like a wall, all the way south.'

I ran forward along the amidships catwalk and climbed over the marine box into the bow, touching the timber from the old *Lydia* for luck as I went.

There was the island, as predicted.

'Best two hundred drachmas I've ever spent,' I muttered.

We were east of Crete, north of Aegypt, and we'd hit a long, narrow island in the middle of nowhere. I'd never been here; we were not on any trade route. All the big ships hit Crete; the little fishing vessels crept from island to island, and Carpathus, if that was the island's name, was off the tracks. I'd coasted it twice before, however, heading for Cyprus back in the Ionian Rebellion, which made this part nostalgic. I'd coasted the southern beaches, but this time I touched at Saria, the spur at the northernmost tip, a small island. There was a deep cleft in the island – no beach to speak of, but space for twenty triremes and three round ships to drop their stones and heave to. We cooked a meal on our sea stoves and ate. The round ships boomed us water out of their holds; we shared out sausage skins of sesame seed and honey.

And then we turned east. Due east, for Cyprus. Eighteen hundred stadia of blue water sailing, give or take. Nobody runs a line out over the stern to measure these things, eh?

It wasn't nearly as terrifying; it was merely hard. For one thing, the coast of Asia came into sight early, the great mountains of Caria poking up over the horizon to the north. But the shipping would all be in with the coast, and we were out here, where no one would notice us … I hoped.

Rain came up from astern, and the wind rose, and we lost sight of any other ships except Moire's *Black Raven*, which we could see from time to time when there were gaps in the rain. South of us was Africa – the Nile Delta and all the fascination that held for me. I still wanted to go into the Red Sea and find out where the good iron came from, south of Aegypt, and now I had an excellent route into the Delta without having to touch at Crete.

And I was remembering how much I loved to be at sea.

Day dawned on our second day out from Carpathus, and the rain let up. We were all soaked, even with the awnings up over the oarsmen, and we rolled them back, dried the ship, baled her dry, and rowed, because when the last rain died, so did the wind.

We rowed all day, and as we rowed, we picked up our friends. We had never lost the *Black Raven*, as I've said; but before midday we had the *Ajax* in sight, and we found the rest fairly quickly. I had to pray no one had run in with the land, but sadly, our ship out of Naxos had done just that, checking his navigation when he was alone in the rain.

He hailed me and owned up, and I had to shrug it off. One sighting of one warship. That shouldn't have alerted the Great King's navarch.

Should it?

Sunset of the second day out from Carpathus, and we were deep in the empty triangle between Crete, Cyprus and the Nile Delta. The rain had pushed us farther south; now we were running along without even a line of mountains on our north.

Nothing. Nothing out to the rim of the world in any direction.

'Tomorrow dawn should see Paphus Rock,' I said with more confidence than I felt.

But I was wrong.

Diodoros was in the bow, singing softly to himself. He had an excellent voice, and he was singing something – a scene from the *Iliad*, I assumed, because Ajax the Greater was in it, but not something I knew. That was no surprise; as a well-travelled man, I already knew that there were ten or more versions: local heroes emphasised or turned into traitors; Achilles made a milksop, a comic figure, a coward ...

Sebastos sat with him, curled into the curve of the bow, playing on his kithara, which I suspected was a beast to keep tuned on the sea. They played well, and then ...

Diodoros looked out over the bow, stiffened and pointed wordlessly.

I was watching them because of the singing. It's probably all that saved us.

'Hard to starboard,' I said. I picked up a stick I'd used to practise my cuts early in the night and tapped Poseidonos, none too gently. 'Oars! Awake!'

The old giant was awake instantly.

So was Leon, who sat opposite him – the senior thranite.

'Awaken all the oars!' I yelled.

Damon, my helmsman, was leaning so far out that I feared he might go over the side, trying to turn the ship.

I ran forward.

Waves show oddly in the dark. If conditions are just right, the wave-tops almost glow with a light of their own; it can be quite eerie.

About ten ship's lengths off the bow, there was a line of surf.

'Sails down!' I roared.

Old Nestor was awake, a knife in his hand. I gave him a nod and he slashed the heavy cordage that held the yard aloft and was tied off to the port-side rail.

The yard crashed to the deck, waking any laggard rowers. But it saved us; even as I cut the same line on the boat-sail mast forward, the yard's tip went over the side. The mass of the sail dragged like a sea-anchor, and we were turning rapidly to starboard, as fast or faster than the oars could have carried us.

'Lantern in the stern!' I roared.

Fire aboard a trireme is a very carefully managed thing. In my ships, the firepots for food and emergency light were kept amidships – two big, heavy iron pots with forged covers. Leander probed one and lit an oil lamp, and dashed aft, even as Dion began shouting in his deep voice for the ship astern of us, Moire's *Black Raven*, to turn.

A big signal lamp went up the swan's head on the stern.

Off to port, a voice roared, 'Hard to port!' in Athenian Greek.

As soon as I knew that the port column of ships was warned, I turned to the other problem – namely, that now we were being sucked into the breakers and we had no way on us any more. The surf seemed to be right next to us; I swear I could feel the spray on my cheek.

Rocks. A line of rocks like an ugly fence, marching away into the darkness.

I cut the mainmast yard away myself, and the whole of the *Apollo's Raven* seemed to bounce, a bird ready to take wing.

'Oars out!' roared Poseidonos.

A surprising number of oars came off their notches and out. Oars are stored inboard. In a veteran ship – and, thanks to the gods, ours was in this respect – the oarsmen cross their oars inside the hull, so that the blades are barely out of the thole pins and the butts, or handholds, are tucked under the opposite bench.

It means that in a crisis, the oar can be taken up and fed out of the oar-port in seconds – even faster for the top-deck thranites.

'Give way, all!' Poseidonos bellowed.

It was ragged, but not so ragged that anyone missed their stroke or got the butt of an oar in his teeth.

This is where your veterans count. This is where everything is details and heartbeats.

Like Megaros, a steady man, thranite port side, waiting patiently to push his oar out, waiting for the pull so that he wouldn't foul anyone else, as calm and steady as a good hoplite in a battle line.

Like Leon, his anger leashed, pulling like any other two men.

Like Cleontos, a very young fisherman from Eresos, cutting the boat-sail yard free *after tying a pair of spare oars to it.* Because that way, we'd find it easily, and the oars would float. An amazing piece of crisis thought, given the situation.

In three strokes of the oars, we had some way on us.

After the fourth, Dion roared, 'She steers!'

And he turned us to starboard again.

For three strokes, it was touch-and-go. I considered the obvious: order the port-side rowers to check, or even back, water, and we'd turn in our own length.

But not if they made a mistake.

We were perhaps half a stade off the rocks, and any error and we would strike. We might not sink, but once you get into a tide race amid rocks, even with brilliant oarsmen, it's very hard to claw off.

By Artemis, my friends.

For three strokes, it was all in the balance. I couldn't see any gain. I wondered if Dion had been too optimistic in claiming that he had steerage way.

But then I saw the stars move at the bow; I could see the bow moving ...

I looked out to port. The stars were there, innocent, glowing against the vast blue-black of the night sky, but below them, the waves lashed on the ugly broken teeth of a coast.

Where in Tartarus was I? How wrong had I been?

The stern was perceptively pulling away from the surf.

I found that I hadn't been breathing. I took a deep breath, and the air shuddered in my throat and I wanted to shout, to dance, to kiss Briseis on her lovely neck ...

I wasn't going to die.

When you get right down to it, it's a miracle that I'm still alive. I've gone spear to spear and helmet to helmet a hundred times. I've been through a dozen storms at sea. I've ridden a dismasted trireme, been sea-lashed out of sight of land in the western ocean ...

Fortuna. Tyche. Moira. Call it what you will ...

I'd survived again.

I leant out to starboard and watched Moire get the *Black Raven* around. The next in line, the *Ariadne*, was making her turn with two stadia to spare. Just visible in the moonlight, another ship, possibly *Gad's Fortune*, had her oars out and her sails already down.

Brasidas came back along the deck and handed me a canteen full of wine.

'That woke me up,' he said.

We had to lie to until morning, our fleet a huddle of ships, oars in, anchors down, with a dozen men on every ship watching the coast.

Morning broke, grey and dull, and as the light grew, the sun refused to appear – a leaden day, heavy with moisture that refused to fall.

The sea was flat and dull.

I really had no idea where I was, and the growing light did nothing to help me. When it was light enough that I couldn't wreck us, I got under way, and we re-formed our two columns. First we went inshore and fished up our boat-sail mast and our mainmast – a nasty process that took us hours, with a dozen swimmers in the water.

Cimon went north, and Moire went south, and both of them returned about midday. We were trying to manage the great flapping, soaking mass of our mainsail, which was like a gigantic dead jellyfish on the surface of the water, and kept trying to slip away and sink. Finally, we stretched it between us and the *Ariadne* and we folded it away.

Every time another ship came close enough, I shouted my apologies. There's nothing else to do in such situations. I admit I've seen some fools pretend various things, but really, when you make a mistake, it's best to just own up.

Megakles came over, his ship stern to stern with mine, and watched the coast.

'South coast of Cyprus,' he said. 'I couldn't tell you just where.'

'I screwed up,' I said.

He shrugged. 'Eh,' he said. 'A little more wind, a little less wind ...' He looked at me. 'Sailing at night is very risky. You are used to being the darling of the gods and we all almost paid for it.'

He stepped up close. 'Cimon won't take you on because he needs you, and Sekla worships you.' He held up his hands to show he meant no harm. 'But I helped teach you to be a captain, so I'm here to say ...' He looked away, and then back, so that his brown eyes were locked with mine. 'That was fucking stupid.'

Well, well. There I was, with more than forty years, and I was like a god in war, and men trusted my words in almost every situation.

So let's thank the real gods that I still had friends who would tell me these things.

Of course, my first reaction was anger. Anger at Megakles, for telling me what I had known since the first breaker appeared off the bow – that this was truly my fault. That I was rushing headlong when that level of haste was too dangerous. I knew who was to blame, and that made Megakles' comments even harder to listen to.

I turned away, lest I lash out. I walked to the rail and looked out to sea.

And then, thanks to Athena, perhaps, whispering in my ear, I said, 'I know.'

Megakles nodded sharply. 'Good,' he said.

He didn't stay to mollify me or make me feel better. He nodded again, his face set like stone, and he leapt back aboard his own ship and fell back to his place in the line.

We had the sail aboard, and I was considering my nautical sins, when Cimon came back.

'Kourion, just down the coast,' he called. 'No Persian garrison, and the council will let us land.'

I let him lead us along the coast, rowing slowly so as not to tire our oarsmen. And we landed on a broad beach, leaving two ships out as guards – more to keep the Cypriotes from leaving than to prevent any sudden attack.

We gave our people a day and a night. We paid hard silver for meat and cheese and wine and oil and fresh-baked bread, because a good meal makes all the difference when you are going into action.

We were five hundred stadia from Tyre, which was south-east of us, straight downwind, twenty hours away.

Like most things in war, our attack on Tyre was going to be a nice mixture of luck and skill.

The beach at Kourion was mostly pebbles, smooth as old linen, kind against unsandalled feet. There were wine shops up in the town, but they would have prying ears. The beach was ours – there wasn't a stranger on it.

More importantly, we'd told our oarsmen to expect action in the morning, and they'd had a big meal. And while we didn't tell them the target, there was an obvious one – Amathus, the Persian royal capital of Cyprus, just a half a day's rowing along the coast. They went off to spend their drachmas and tell their tales, and we settled down to plan – twenty captains and twenty helmsmen, and a dozen marine officers. A big crowd, but in a show like this, having all your people know what you are doing is much more important than perfect secrecy.

We had a good fire; even though Africa was just over my shoulder, it was cool on that beach. Aten moved around the circle with a dozen other servants, making sure that men had wine. There was a low murmur of talk, and some grumbling.

'Good evening,' I said. The fire snapped and crackled, and they fell silent. 'The target is Tyre.'

That brought me absolute silence – a quiet so profound that someone in town shouted drunkenly 'Artemis' tits!' and the sound carried right among us.

I smiled. 'I'll take that as an omen of good fortune,' I said.

In Ephesus, where I grew to manhood, people used to touch the goddess's breasts for luck.

I had drawn a picture in the sand, based on Alysia's description.

'Anyone been to Tyre?' I asked.

Ephialtes raised his hand. Helikaon stepped forward, and Parmenio. 'Describe it?' I asked.

Helikaon looked around, but the others deferred to him. He was a handsome man, for all that his hair went in every direction and looked like the nest of some deranged bird. He had a fine sword, which I'd noticed before – short, like a Spartan sword, in a fine red sheath. It was strapped high in his armpit for a quick draw, the way I wore mine. The way he wore it spoke of years of experience, and the hilt was good African ivory, slightly yellowed with age, with a band of fine gold on the pommel.

'Before the war, I traded on the Phoenician coast,' he said. He knelt in the firelight. 'The drawing is correct. This line is the coast – the old city is here, and warehouses all along here.'

I had drawn Alysia's triangle, with the long side facing out to sea, so to speak, and he cut indented beaches into the two short sides for the harbours.

'I've only been to the Harbour of Sidon,' he said. 'The southern harbour was military only, and there were a lot of rules about entering it. I had to have a special permit even to trade there. The law is that only Tyrian hulls can trade from Tyre.' He shrugged. 'There are ship sheds here, all along the northern harbour, and sixty more on the south side, or so I'm told. The prevailing wind is from the southwest this time of year. It's a bad coast to be caught against. That's why Tyre is so important – there aren't many harbours.'

He glanced at me for approval and I nodded.

'We need luck,' I said. 'And the aid of the gods. My intention is to aim a little south of Tyre, perhaps as far south as Akko. We make our landfall at last light and come up on Tyre in the dawn.'

Megakles raised an eyebrow. 'Five hundred stadia of open water and you think that you can raise Akko on demand?' he asked.

His unstated comment was '*after last night's little performance?*'

'Can you?' I asked.

We looked at each other.

Parmenio raised his hand. 'I can,' he said. 'I've made this run before, in a round ship. With less room for error than we have here.' He spoke with confidence.

I wanted to believe him. I really wanted to believe him.

I didn't know him well, and I looked him over. Tall, blond, with pale blue eyes – not anyone's picture of an Ionian. He spoke softly, but he wasn't soft.

Well, confidence is a blessing. He was confident.

'You lead, then,' I said.

Cimon pointed his cornel-wood walking stick at the drawing.

'Let's say we pull it off. We are coming up from the south on the morning breeze as the sun rises. What then?'

'Your call, son of Miltiades,' I said. 'What do you think?'

He threw his scarlet cloak back over his shoulder, and tapped the sand with his stick.

'If the gods favour us,' he said 'the ships will be in the outer harbours, or here, along the mainland beach, refitting. If the gods are against us, they're all still in their ship sheds, ignoring the Great King's orders. And if the gods hate us, they're all fitted out and crewed, two hundred to our twenty.'

Cimon and I had already made our plans, so I knew what he'd say.

'As soon as we can see, we'll know,' Cimon said. 'If they have their boat-sail masts in, they're rigged, and we're fucked. We put our helms over, pick up the coast wind, raise our mainsails and run. No fighting, no nothing.'

'We'll lose all the wages of our oarsmen!' Herakles of Methymna said.

'You'll be alive to recoup your losses another time,' Cimon snapped. 'If the Phoenicians are ready for us, we run. With an hour's head start, we'll outrun them. But listen well, my friends. No one takes their mainmast down until I signal. You'll need your mainsail to win this race.'

Many heads nodded.

'If they are still in their sheds,' he went on, 'then the harbours are at our mercy, if we're fast. We'll have to be fast – we know that they have harbour defences and marines and archers.' He looked at me.

'Then we're cutting out any merchant that's at anchor,' I said. 'That is to say, Cimon and his column are cutting out merchants. My column is watching.'

'And everyone shares,' Cimon said. 'Those who capture and those who watch.'

'If we aren't threatened, we take everything in the harbours,' I said. 'We put the most valuable cargoes in a couple of round ships, and burn the rest.'

People nodded.

'When we're seriously threatened, we run. Sidon can't send a squadron south if the wind's blowing from the south-west. If there's no Phoenician fleet in the roads, odds are no one can get to us.'

'I like that option,' Herakles said.

'Trouble is ...' Cimon smiled like a fox. 'Trouble is that we're patriots, not pirates. We want to hurt the Phoenician fleet, not just harm their commerce.'

'If their ships are still snug in stone sheds, there's not much we can do,' I added.

'So,' Cimon said, 'option three. The gods love us, and the

Phoenician fleet is out in the roads and harbours, but their masts aren't in and their crews and running tackle are ashore.'

The fire crackled. Aten asked Cimon if he wanted more wine. He took it and drank deeply before continuing to outline his plan.

'Then it is no holds barred – the final match. A huge risk. If I signal "general engagement", every ship grapples an enemy and sinks it. And then another, and then another. If you sink three, you will have the praise of all Greece. Sink four, and you're a hero. Sink five, and you are with the gods.'

I spoke up. 'Sink five and tow one away, and the gods are with you.'

Men laughed.

'Not much profit in that option,' Herakles said.

'Your children will never again be troubled by the Great King,' Cimon said. 'Isn't that a profit?'

After most of the captains were gone, I made a long eye contact with Cimon – like a lover looking for an assignation, as he quipped at the time. I waited out his so-called sense of humour.

'There's going to be a rich merchant anchored out,' I said. 'A round ship, Greek built. She's not to be looted. We take her, and then we let her go out of sight of land.'

Cimon drank off his wine. 'No need to tell me twice,' he said.

Moire, Sekla and Ameinias of Pallene, trierarch of the *Parthenos* and a veteran of Salamis, stayed with Parmenios when the others were gone, and with Megakles and Damon, laid out the courses by star sightings they took with straight sticks on the beach. Cimon and I worked out the orders of sailing and the loading.

To reach the coast of Syria at Akko, we needed about twenty hours, if the wind didn't change.

So many ifs.

Twenty hours sailing in the darkness – the very thing that had almost killed us the night before.

If we left our beach at dawn, we'd reach the coast of Syria about four hours before dawn the next day.

Worst case, we'd be slower than our expected cruising speed under sail, and we'd arrive off the coast in broad daylight, and messengers would ride.

It was all a risk, and Megakles shrugged.

'We have to land in the darkness,' he said. 'I don't see any other choice. But we have a few hours of extra time. How about, midnight tomorrow night, we shorten sail and row?'

That seemed a sensible way to handle the risk. *And* it meant that our sails would be down if the dawn caught us still out at sea.

'Excellent idea,' I said.

Cimon agreed.

'Dawn,' I said.

We loaded our ships in the dark: twenty low, black shapes, bows out into the low waves. The oarsmen went aboard in orderly rows and sat, careful not to tip the hulls. The smell of fried fish and olive oil filled the air from the early breakfast we'd all eaten – almost four thousand men on one long beach.

My son Hipponax and my foster-son Hector were dressed as marines now. The round ships would stay here, under their usual commercial captains. If we didn't return in three days, they had a series of rendezvous for which to aim, retreating back north into Ionia.

I'm sure you are all eagerly awaiting my description of the raid, but I have to explain why using round ships for resupply is so difficult.

Oared ships and round ships only share one point of sail – when the wind is almost dead astern. As soon as the wind shifts to the aft quarter, the round ship has an advantage. Place the wind side-on, blowing over the rails, and the round ship wallows on, albeit not so speedily, but the oared ship has to take down its sail and row.

Now place the wind anywhere forward of amidships, and the world changes again. The oared ships row steadily on, making say, twenty stadia an hour. But the sailing round ships can no longer go forward at all. They have to make long boards – long passages across the wind – turning as sharply as the round tubs can manage and coming back, sometimes travelling ten stadia north and another ten south just to make two or three east, for example. And in some winds, they can't make any progress at all.

And in a calm, the round ship floats, trapped in a circle of its own filth. The oared ship makes its steady progress.

So while it was innovative and vital for sea-dogs like Miltiades and Cimon to use round ships as supply ships – after all, they held fifty times as much cargo as an oared ship, and had very little crew to consume food – despite the utility, we usually had to plot alternative courses for them. In this case, sailing from Cyprus into Tyre was to sail into what is, to all intents, the world's deepest bay, and ran the risk that they wouldn't get out again until high summer, if ever.

So we sent them north, and we had to carry all the food and water we'd have for three to five days. All the old captains knew what this meant: just two years before, Sekla and I had raided Samos, and we'd endured three days with almost no water to escape the Red King's wrath.

No one ever talks about food and water. In Homer it's always helmet to helmet, the fighting, the blood. I promise you, my friends – war is about food and water. The rest is a mere matter of rowing.

Where was I?

Ah. The dawn. An ugly dawn – another leaden day, with no bright sunlight to raise a man's heart. But the waves were almost flat and the wind was just as we wanted it, cool and fresh out of the mountains of Cyprus. We whispered away, our sedate pace barely raising bow waves. And on that morning, my *Apollo's Raven* was in the middle of the right-hand column. Parmenio's ship, *Gad's Fortune*, led the column with Moire's *Black Raven* second and Ephialtes' *Ariadne* third.

Have you ever seen a squadron of ships in line ahead? It raises the heart. You know what Sappho said. And I'm sure she was praising some lover, but I think that she was wrong – a squadron of warships is the loveliest thing.

And there we were, sailing out on the wine-dark sea. Twenty ships against the whole might of the Great King.

Or, looked at another way, twenty veteran ships against the remnant of whatever we hadn't killed at Artemisium and Salamis and Mycale.

I grinned. I sacrificed a goat on the beach – a spurt of blood and a favourable omen. Then I threw a silver cup and a dozen good pearls into the sea off the beach, for Poseidon and his lovely daughters, and we were away.

The day passed slowly. Twice we sighted ships, their sails nicking the horizon to the south. They were traders out early in the season, trying to be the first into the Nile Delta, or running a cargo of cedar out of Sidon, slanting away on the opposite tack. Both ships vanished as soon as they sighted us. Any merchant worthy of the name would run the moment he saw twenty warships.

But none of them were placed to run south and east.

Midday saw a weather change, and a wind change.

In an hour, the wind was blowing over the starboard bow and we were rowing. The wind was a light breeze. It held no rain, and we rowed easily, making good time over calm seas. At that speed, we could row with just two thirds of our people, and let a third rest. We'd had days to work up; our people had hard hands.

Now they earned their drachmas.

In late afternoon, the wind began to increase. It was coming off Africa, far to the south – hot off the sultry sands, and carrying a few grains of sand along. Not like autumn, but still, enough to sting your back and hurt your eyes. The deck crews rigged the awnings, and we rowed on, in to rising seas.

The worst of it was that we were rowing south and east, and the wind was coming from south and west, almost broadside to us. Triremes are marvellous ships, and their design is tried and tested, but there's one thing none of them excel at, and that's crossing a rising sea, with the waves coming at the long side of a narrow ship that can be a might top-heavy at the best of times.

I sent my marines below, all the way to the lowest rowing tier – the thalamites. I needed to keep all my weight low, and I was lucky in my marines. Arios and Philippos immediately took oars and began to row, which won them praise from all the oarsmen. Marines generally behaved as if they were a race apart, and it was good for the oarsmen's morale to see them row.

The Inner Sea doesn't get a long rising swell like the Western Ocean does, but we had some waves. Every tenth or twelfth rolled into the lower oar ports, soaking the rowers and putting water in the bilges. It wasn't dangerous – yet – but it was uncomfortable.

I scratched a stay and whistled for the wind to change, and made another prayer to Poseidon and threw a gold spoon I'd got from the spoils at Plataea over the side.

Poseidon is one of the less responsive gods, I find.

The wind continued to rise, and it brought more sand.

Still, I could see eight of my ten ships, and four of Cimon's. I wasn't afraid yet; we were still making good time, and we were, by my count, halfway there, or more. The new worry was that, in addition to the sheer danger of the cross-sea, we were making leeway. That's a fancy nautical way of saying that our nearly keelless ships were being pushed sideways almost as fast as we were rowing.

It was almost as if Parmenio could read my mind, because fifteen minutes after I came to that conclusion, he turned three points to starboard, almost due south. He was guessing that we were making a lot of leeway, and he was doing the nautical equivalent of what a boy does, when he aims ahead of a running rabbit with his rock. Or rather, imagine that you are swimming a river with a swift current, and you want to land in a particular place on the opposite bank. If you swim directly for your chosen landing, you'll be moved downstream, yes? So you aim upstream of your target.

Parmenio's turn had another happy consequence. We were now taking the waves a quarter off the bow, rather than broadside on. Everything improved, including morale.

But the calculations of our distance travelled became very difficult indeed. I had Damon throw the log while I took the steering oars, feeling my long, narrow ship shudder under the pressure of the waves. This was her worst point of sailing or rowing, except taking waves broadside. Her narrow entry and deep ram, vital for warfare, were against her here, so that every wave wanted to push us off our chosen course.

My shoulders were taking a bruising from fighting the steering oars. And we were still taking water.

Giorgos, formerly one of my oarsmen and now a trusted deckhand with good armour and a steady sense of humour, came and took the steering oars. I drank a little wine and water and went amidships to look for the rest of the fleet. The sun came and went through the clouds, spray and blown sand. An odd day, and when, later, the sun began to set, it set red as blood and huge on the western horizon.

But as the sun set in the west, we were still together. My ship, perhaps the narrowest, was struggling the hardest, and we'd fallen astern of the *Amastris* and the *Light of Apollo* so that we were last, by a dozen ship's lengths. And as night fell, all the captains spaced out, both fore and aft and side to side, because no one liked to run afoul of another ship in the dark.

But despite losing ground, I could see my squadron, and I could see a gleam of red from Cimon's *Ajax* and blue from his brother, Metiochus's lovely ship, *Dawn*. I was satisfied, or as satisfied as a man can be when his beautiful ship is behaving badly and taking water, when the weather is turning bad and everything is going wrong.

Darkness fell and the wind rose.

It wasn't even a storm. I've seen far worse, and so had many of my people.

It was just bad enough to wreck our plans, and maybe wreck our ship. An hour after full dark we lost sight of the stern lamps on the *Amastris*, and before the hourglass turned again, we lost the *Light of Apollo*.

We were alone in the dark on the great ocean, and our oarsmen were getting tired. We had the wind on our starboard bow, and we needed to row to keep it there. We had water in the bilges, and we had six sailors at the slide-pumps. All the marines who weren't rowing were baling and hurling the water over the side.

We had to keep rowing, because as the wind and the wave height rose, we were in more peril. If we stopped rowing, we'd turn broadside to the waves, and if we did, they'd roll us over or just push us down.

Here's the measure of our fear.

I've mentioned that every trireme is held together by a heavy cable of woven ropes that runs down the middle of the ship. The twisted cable is called the hypozomata and it keeps the ship stiff, but allows it to flex in heavy seas.

That night, I could hear it move. The ship would go over a wave and stretch the cable as the wave came amidships, and for an instant the bow and stern were in the air. And then we'd go into the trough, and the bow and stern would fold slightly, and the hypozomata would relax like an arm muscle, or an unstrung bow. And then we'd go up the wave and it would stretch and make a snapping moan.

A terrible sound. Because sooner or later, the joints of the ship would stop bending, and some would break. And we'd spit out the oakum between the main seams and take on water.

Poseidon. I needed a miracle. *And it wasn't even a storm.* This is hard to explain to those who do not keep the sea, but you can die in weather that would scarcely trouble a farmer in Boeotia.

I took all the rest of my pearls and put them in my old cow-horn cup. It wasn't made of gold, but then, the Earth-Shaker would know that I loved that cup. Leonidas of Sparta had drunk wine from that cup. So had Paramanos. So had Lydia. And Gaiana. And almost all my friends, my lovers, and even a few enemies.

I poured it full of my last pearls, and hurled it into the black night and the roaring waves.

Below me, Poseidonos roared out the stroke, and we pulled forward. I had two decks rowing, and we didn't have to go fast – we just had to keep the bow up to the waves.

I'd done this before.

I knew that the night always ends, if you keep rowing.

But after an hour, the wind rose again, and I had to commit my reserves and order all three decks to row.

We weren't winning.

I went down and rowed for a while, taking Poseidonos' place. I noted that every one of the marines was rowing, and I loved them. I also noted that my sailors were also rowing. I could see a handful of my veteran oarsmen – Sikli, and Leon and other men – their backs lit by a flickering oil lamp hung from the rowing frame, not because it was necessary but because it was good for morale.

On, and on.

I almost felt as if I was rowing for Dagon. If you haven't been sitting here and following this story, I was a slave for Carthage for a while. I rowed as a slave for some years. Dagon was the trierarch, and a worse man I've never met. I've had some enemies, but for the most part, they've been men like other men. I've gone sword to sword with Cyrus of Persia, and I couldn't ever hate him. A far more honest man than I'll ever be. But Dagon was bad to the core of his heart and bones, rotten like an old apple tree. He liked to hurt us – he enjoyed breaking our bodies.

And that's what the sea could be like, too. I rowed in Poseidonos' place, and I felt as if I was rowing for Dagon. I hope that does it justice.

I rowed as long as I could – perhaps two hours. I felt weak when I gave the oar back to Poseidonos, but he grinned.

'You can pull an oar,' he said. 'Now talk to the boys.'

He was right.

I walked, bent over, along the narrow catwalk between the thranites. I touched each man on the shoulder and spoke to those whose faces seemed to need a response.

'Three more hours,' I said.

I made that up. I had no idea how long we had to go until morning. No idea where we were. I just lied.

'Three more hours, friends,' I said.

Then I dropped down the short ladder to the *zygites'* deck.

'Three more hours,' I said, walking along the planks. Because of the hull shape, it was even closer and narrower here. And damper. I could smell the bilge. In a heavy pull like this, men had to piss from their benches. You don't want the details, right? You row naked ...

Right.

I watched the rowing frame bend as we topped another great roller, and winced.

'Three more hours,' I said.

I got all the way to the stern and then I dropped down to the thalamites. The lowest of the low – the worst oarsmen, men being punished, men who weren't strong enough for the upper oar looms.

All my marines were now rowing with the lowest ranked men. It brought tears to my eyes. There was Brasidas, pulling without even a grunt. There was Leander, and Arios, Zephyrides and Kassandros, Diodoros and Sebastos, and big Kalidion. Ka was pulling an oar, and so was Nemet, his rail-thin body moving as if he was made of muscle – which, of course, he was.

'Three hours,' I said.

After Nemet, I could see that the bilges were overflowing. Looking down, I could see the hull flex, and I could see water coming in.

But we weren't done yet.

I went back on deck, up to the command platform a little above the marines' catwalk.

Forward, all I could see was darkness.

Aft, the same.

I found Old Nestor and sent him forward to cast the log, and then I stood in the sandy rain and calculated. I'd never before had the experience of doing geometry that made my heart race with fear.

No stars. Nothing to sight.

I worked it twice and got the same answer both times.

'We're going fast,' I said. 'Cast again, this time over the starboard side.'

'Aye, Navarch,' he said, and went back forward.

He came back with his rope and his log and his calculations, and told me his answers.

We were rowing into a wind. We were rowing *fast* into the wind, and I couldn't measure the drift, but it had to be fast.

I went aft to the helm, and altered course. Immediately, the ship was easier, as we put the bow into the waves.

Fifteen minutes later, the wind turned, coming from almost due south.

I turned again, putting the bow into the wind, Damon grunting.

But I prayed. Literally.

'I sing to Poseidon, the Great God, mover of the earth and the sea, god of the deep who is also Lord of Helicon and wide Aegae. A two-fold office the gods allotted you, Earth-Shaker, tamer of horses and saviour of ships!'

And the wind howled. There was a spurt of sand, like I was breathing wet desert. The ship shuddered.

And then ...

The wind ...

Fell.

Suddenly, we were rowing in a calmer sea with longer, lower swells. It was a sudden transition, and we went up a long wave and never seemed to come down. The rowers were at the catch, and Poseidonos was singing the hymn, and most of the oarsmen knew it. They roared the hymn as the oars lashed out into the dark water and the bow cut it, and we were flying into calmer water.

It was raining – not a hard rain, but a light rain, as the wind fell away to be a zephyr from the west.

We were saved.

Except that it was still dark, and we had no idea where we were, or where the rest of the fleet might be.

But my oarsmen were singing, and by the gods, we weren't finished yet.

There's an old song in Boeotia of our hero Orion. In the war of the Titans, Orion fought alongside Hera and Zeus, and in one of the early battles he fought alone, surrounded by foes, into the night, alone against a hundred Titans, and his mighty spear slew them, and with every blow he cried 'Day will come again!'

So when my oarsmen were done singing the hymn to Poseidon, I roared out, 'Day will come again!'

And they roared back.

By the gods. The *Argo* never had such a crew.

About an hour before dawn, the rain lightened, and stars began to appear. I knew the constellations as soon as I had a patch of sky bigger than my hand, and after a consultation with Damon and Old Nestor, I ordered the ship to turn to port, several points. I was now heading in with the coast of Syria, or so I hoped. Remember that we should have reached somewhere close to Akko just after the middle of the night.

The sun rises in the east, and that morning it rose, pink and beautiful, on a new world with a calm sea and a nice southerly breeze, a true *Notos* without the sand. It was so gentle that it didn't raise a whitecap.

And there was the coast, spreading along before us.

As soon as the word spread, men cried aloud, or laughed, or grunted. I ordered the rowing rate slackened, and gave everyone a rest. We turned broadside to the gentle breeze and floated, rocking gently, while I went up the lines that held my mainmast. I was not as spry as I had once been, and climbing a rope took time and all my concentration. Aten could have been up and down twice in the time it took me to go up once, but I had to see for myself.

You may remember that I'd put a wood-and-leather bucket, a sort of nest, at the top of my mainmast. And you'll pardon me if I explain a little more of Dano's geometry to you, or that of her father Pythagoras. But from the deck of a trireme, where you stand about twice the height of a man above the water, you can see about seven stadia, but if you're looking at a ship with masts ten times the height of a man, you can see them almost twenty stadia away. And if you can climb to the height of your own mast ...

Well, you can see farther. I've never had the time to test it, but my little experiments on the coast of Gaul suggest you can see thirty stadia or more, depending on weather and clouds and wave heights.

I rolled into the leather cone, already a little queasy. At deck level, we were rolling gently. Up here, the mainmast was moving through a long arc, and I'm not my best at heights, let me say.

Despite that, what I saw raised my heart a little.

Off to the south, I could see a smudge of smoke. By Poseidon, I could even smell it: the charcoal burning smell of thousands of women starting their day and making food; of bakery ovens baking bread. And something else.

I watched for a while, and it seemed to me that I could see the loom of land there – a promontory. My first thought was that I was looking at Tyre, the island off the coast, but as the sun rose, I was more and more certain that I was looking at a long promontory stretching out from the land.

No idea where I was. Not my coastline.

But if that was the bad news, there was good news to balance it. Because even as I watched, the western horizon began to lighten as the sun rose farther out to sea. It lit the bare poles of ships – not just one or two, but six ships. That they were triremes became obvious very quickly – the placement of the masts, the fact that their hulls remained invisible.

The longer you spend at sea, the better you become at identifying other ships at long distances. It's a little like spotting your best friend in the agora, or your wife among other women at the well-head. You can't say exactly what it is about that shape that's definitely Briseis, but you know her from fifty paces away, in a crowd of women, all wearing wool veils.

'I can see the *Black Raven*,' I called down. 'And the *Ajax*. And the *Athena Nike*.'

The closest in was a puzzle. I didn't know her well, but the more I looked, the more certain I was that I was looking at the *Gad's Fortune*.

'Turn to starboard. Cruising speed. Another point, there. Very well – hold that heading.'

I called all these commands down to the deck until we were pointed straight at the ship I took to be the *Gad's Fortune*. Then I grabbed the mainstay that held the mast to the deck, wrapped my legs around it for good measure, and slid down, burning the backs of my legs in my enthusiasm to get on to the deck.

I was fairly confident in my identification, but just after I got to the deck it occurred to me that I was running down on a Phoenician trireme and taking for granted that she wasn't an enemy. My mast was still up, and my marines weren't armed.

And that's how disaster strikes you.

It was a useful lesson, but not one, thank the gods, for which I had to pay that day. Because five stadia later we had her hull up and turning towards us – the *Gad's Fortune* in all truth, and Parmenio leaning out from the amidships rail to yell a greeting. In minutes we were stern to stern on the gentle swell, a dozen cursing deck crewmen poling us off while Parmenio leapt aboard my ship.

'Where are we?' I asked by way of greeting.

'That's Zeus Point,' Parmenio said. 'And that's Mount Carmel – and there's Shikmona, that the Phoenicians call Efa.'

'So we're south of Akko,' I said.

Parmenio shrugged. 'Well south,' he said. 'It was always a risky passage. I'm sorry ...'

'Don't be,' I said. 'A brilliant piece of navigation. How far, do you guess, to Tyre?'

'Two hundred stadia?' He shrugged again and looked pained. 'I'm sorry, Navarch. But we're too far south and it'll take all day ...'

'Except that we have the wind in our favour,' I said. 'Follow me.'

'Yes, sir,' he said, and we clasped hands, and he leapt back onto his own stern.

It was not yet quite dawn. And if I could just make out the coast of Syria – or perhaps this was Judea – there was little chance they could count our masts.

'About ship,' I ordered.

We only had two decks rowing, and they responded like heroes, for men who'd rowed all night. We turned end for end in less time than it would take to sing an epitaph, and then I raised a bronze shield and a red flag on my stern: *Follow me.*

'Mainsail,' I ordered.

The deck crew got the sail aloft, and Aten climbed the mast to watch the coast. The mast had gone up quickly enough, and the breeze strengthened slightly. Almost directly astern – a trifle over the port quarter.

'Make her tight, there,' Old Nestor called as the mainsail belied out, hiding Aten high above us. 'Tight! Haul!'

Suddenly we were flying.

'Oars in!' I roared, because Poseidonos seemed to be asleep.

He turned and looked at me sheepishly.

The ship heeled slightly as the breeze freshened, as if Poseidon, having punished us all night, chose now to make it up to us.

'Cast for me, Nestor,' I begged.

I took the steering oars to feel her under my hands and to give Damon a rest.

He showed me his result. We were making something like twenty-five stadia an hour, allowing for all sorts of errors of calculation.

Eight hours to Tyre.

Broad daylight.

I turned to Damon, who was rubbing his shoulders.

'What do you think of the weather?' I asked.

He looked aft. 'More wind out of Africa,' he said. 'A three- or four-day blow.'

'What do you think of running out to sea and lying to until morning?' I asked.

He shrugged. 'If it blows, we'll be in Caria in the morning,' he said.

So. Now or never.

And I agreed. Last night had been a taste of heavy weather. Spring could be beautiful or brutal in the eastern seas.

I cheated the helm west, standing a little farther out to sea, and gradually edging towards Cimon's *Ajax*. I came up with him after about two hours of sailing, and by the time we were running alongside, side by side, I could see at least three more sails on the western horizon, and maybe five. It was an odd, bright day and the horizon was the same colour as the sea.

When I could see him, I went up on my port-side rail, wrapped an arm in the rigging, and leant out. I still had to roar as if we were in a storm.

'Today or never!' I called.

Cimon nodded and pointed at my signal, still visible on the stern, and he nodded emphatically.

That was our command conference.

Another hour, and the *Ariadne* emerged from the horizon and fell into line. She brought with her the two other captures from Lesbos, and now we had nine ships, and at least one more out to the west.

As the sun climbed in the sky, I ordered Old Nestor to slacken sail and brail up. We were very fast on this point of sail, but not everyone was, and I wanted a squadron, not eleven individual ships.

The *Gad's Fortune* came into line behind me, and the *Black Raven*, and Megakles in the *Light of Apollo*. Cimon had the *Ajax* and his brother Metiochus followed him in the *Dawn* and then Ameinias in the *Parthenos*. The *Ariadne* was coming to join with the Lesbians. I thought that I could just make out Lykon in the *Penelope*, well ahead of us; his gilded stern swan glittered ten stadia away.

As the sun reached the middle of the sky, we came up with Lykon, and he fell in to the shorter column, behind the *Ajax*. I thought we might have two more on the horizon, but we had more than a dozen ships, and we were an hour from combat.

I stripped naked. 'Get my armour and my best chiton,' I called to Aten. 'And oil.'

I turned to Young Nestor, who was on deck. 'Give me a rope over the stern,' I said.

I dived over the side from the bow and swam easily as the ship passed me. Men waved out of the oar ports and the rowing frame as they passed, and I caught the trailing rope and hauled myself up the side, dripping like a Triton. Aten had a linen towel. I used a strigil to oil myself like an athlete, and then I put on my best chiton, red, embroidered all over with ravens and sunbursts.

Aten clipped my greaves to my legs and then combed out my hair.

There wasn't as much of it as there once had been, and I laughed.

There was a lot of hair in that wooden comb.

I used it to comb my beard while Aten pinned my bronze thorax closed. I was happy to see there was a little less of me than there had been at Lesbos. Then he held my sword-belt over my head until I liked the way it hung, tight up into my armpit, the hilt protruding slightly. I drew it, performing one of the shorter Lacedaemonian *Pyrrhiche* forms to train men to draw their swords and return them in combat.

Aten had become quite adept. I could remember when he'd shaken with fear on the morning we fought off the coast of Attica – only two summers before. Now he was almost as tall as I was, and he had his own armour.

Hector and Hipponax came up, looking like gods in bronze. Like me, they wore full panoply – thigh armour, shoulder pieces. Ship fights aren't like land fights. They are short and sharp, and you may have to fight by yourself.

Looking down the deck, I could see Brasidas and Leander, Arios, Zephyrides, Kalidion and Kassandros and Sebastos, all armed, and then the deck crew, most of whom had more and better panoplies than rich hoplites in Athens. Giorgos wore all bronze, and so did Old Nestor. I was thinking of mocking him for his white beard, but I'd noticed, when I combed mine, that grey hairs were coming out in the comb, and I thought perhaps I should keep my views to myself.

And there was my 'new' archer, Vasilos, who was older than I was, stretching his shoulders, and Ka and Nemet, rolling knuckle-bones for who got the 'honour' of climbing the mast to shoot down from the little nest.

I waved to Ka, and he came aft.

'Go up the boat-sail mast,' I said.

'Mainmast is taller, boss,' he said.

I shook my head. 'It's coming down in half an hour,' I said.

He nodded. 'Sure,' he agreed.

And just before I ordered us to turn east, towards the land that was almost invisible to starboard, I ordered our mainmast down and stowed. We turned slightly more due north, so that the wind was dead aft. The mast came down as sweetly as a baby laid in a cradle, and I had the pleasure of watching the operation repeated all along the two columns.

Now we were long black hulls that stood only the height of a man off the sea – low and dark.

'Turn to starboard,' I said. 'There. That's your heading.'

I sang the hymn to Poseidon quietly, and made a sacrifice over the stern, and when I turned back, I could see the coast of Syria as plainly as the nose on my face.

Just over the port bow, I could see an island, and a smudge of smoke, and a low line beyond.

Before I was sure, I heard the whoop of joy from the next ship behind me, and there was Parmenio, waving.

So it really was Tyre.

I called all my marines and deck crew together amidships, so that they didn't throw off the rowers.

'Here we go,' I said. 'If we have to run, I want all of you out of your armour and ready to relieve oar stations. Otherwise, listen for Brasidas or me. I want to take one with us – the rest we burn. Ka?'

'Ready,' he said, and pointed aft, to where three of his former helots had lit a line of firepots, all clay. We had a dozen.

'Amidships is the best target,' I said. 'If a ship is empty, we go alongside and you take torches and set her alight by hand. If she's manned, we use the firepots. Clear?'

Brasidas looked bored.

No one else did.

I've no doubt said this before, but battle has a strange way of changing time. By Artemis, even hunting does this. Surely you have felt it – three hours of waiting in a hide for a deer to walk down your trail passes like three days, and then you are standing over the cooling carcass of your kill, your spear in your hand, and you can't even fully remember how those last seconds passed.

After a night that had lasted an eternity, and a day of sweet sailing and relative boredom, we turned in for the coast of Phoenicia, and Tyre was twenty stadia away. And the waiting seemed the worst of all – armoured and ready, and Tyre was creeping over the horizon, too far away to see if there were ships in the channel behind the island, or whether they had their masts in.

Half an hour, and no change. The sun went down behind us, halfway down the sky. By luck and good planning, it would be low enough to blind a sentry on the walls as we closed.

Luck and good planning.

And then, suddenly we could see that the inner harbours and the channel between island and mainland were crowded with ships – dozens of ships, hundreds – and most of them were low to the water and didn't have a mast in. We closed, our hearts high, and we could see that the enemy ships rode well out of the water. They were newly launched, without stores aboard.

I laughed. I drank off some wine with Brasidas and hurled the cup into the sea. At this rate, I was going to be drinking wine from my bare hands.

I didn't care. There was Tyre.

I went down on to the catwalk of the top section of the rowing rig, where I could lean down and be heard by all my oarsmen.

'All the fish are in the barrel,' I called. 'There's going to be a lot of finicky manoeuvres in a tight harbour. Listen for orders. We won't wear you out, but we will change direction. Attention to your orders and we'll all be heroes.'

Just a murmur and a growl.

'And rich,' I added.

I altered course slightly, cheating a little further south. I wanted to come in at the southern end of the channel that ran behind 'New Tyre'.

Time seemed to speed up. It always does, the sands of Chronos' hourglass swirling, running faster.

I could make out individual ships. We were opening the bay behind the island now, and we were south of the island and the mainland warehouses. We were visible to anyone who looked out to sea.

Too late to turn back now.

Cimon raised the two bronze shields on his stern: *General Engagement*.

All the way. We were going for the whole prize.

Our two columns were well closed up, each ship about half a ship length back from the one behind it. They were like a battering ram headed for the south end of the Tyrian harbour. The closer we got, the more obvious was their degree of preparation – there were ships being fitted out before our eyes. In the southern, or Aegyptian, harbour, I could see cranes like those at Piraeus swaying a mast into a trireme that was alongside a stone pier. I could see open ship sheds ...

Too close to waste time on the 'Harbour of Aegypt'. Suddenly everything was going to happen at battle speed ...

Unless ...

An idea began to form in my head.

We could see a big trireme, a heavy ship, dead ahead. She was anchored well out, and already had her mainmast aboard and her boat-sail mast up, but if there was a crew aboard, we didn't see them.

'Pass her by,' I said to Damon, and he tapped his steering oars and we swept past, rowing steadily.

Then another big trireme, and a third, and a fourth, all anchored in a line. If I was going to take a ship, one of these would have been perfect, but unfortunately, the beginning of the action wasn't the time to start towing a hulk.

We passed them by, leaving them for the last ships.

On the beach, just a stade away, people were *cheering*.

There were people cheering on the pier in the naval harbour, too. *Why in all the cold hells were people cheering?*

I had to ignore them. The cruising speed of good oarsmen on rotation is about twenty stadia an hour – a little faster than a good distance runner. You seem to be moving quite slowly ...

Until you're in a close-packed enemy harbour.

We were sliding into the deepest part of the outer harbour. I could see the bottom, only perhaps ten or twelve paces deep, and rocky. I chose my first target at random. It seemed to me that they had fitted out their warships and then sent them to the outer fringe of the harbour to wait in the water, and that the inner harbours held the most vulnerable ships.

I threw caution to the winds. The cheering suggested that they still had no idea who we were – that, or Phoenicians have a different way of showing aggression than Greeks.

'There's our prey,' I said to Damon. 'Turn into the Harbour of Aegypt.'

Right into the lion's den.

The harbour entrance was only about a hundred paces wide, and there were fifty ships waiting to get their masts and oars. They were all about the same, except for a big round ship in the midst of them, low in the water.

'Her,' I said.

There were men aboard – they were waving. Someone on the headland, fifty paces away, was shouting in Phoenician Aramaic. Not one of my languages.

'Lay us alongside,' I said.

To Brasidas, I said, 'Cut her cables and set her afire.'

He smiled. 'Fire,' he said, in his Laconian drawl.

Damon laid us alongside with a gentle scrape down the side, the Phoenician sailors aboard the round ship cursing and yelling. I know a sailor's curses when I hear them.

Brasidas gave the word, and Leander and Hipponax leapt together. The sailors on the round ship never knew they were in a fight. Brasidas, a merciful man, threw them overboard, and then came back to the rail.

'Pitch and spars!' he called.

'Fire,' I called back, and he waved.

Diodoros threw a torch down the main hatchway, and Arios dropped one aft. The other marines fired the sails and rigging, and they all piled back aboard and we cut her loose.

The southerly wind was a light breeze inside the arms of the inner harbour.

'Hard to starboard,' I said to Damon.

The rowers were ready; the oars shot out and we were turning, turning away from our deadly companion.

We backed water at Old Nestor's command and then shot forward. I could see a low hull, long and lean – a big ship, as big as the *Gad's Fortune* or even longer. We ran through the anchored hulks, my archers putting fire arrows and firepots into them, and then we went alongside the big trireme, a heavy ship in the Corinthian style, meant to carry a lot of marines. Just possibly a capture.

The round ship was a roaring titan of fire, and she'd run into three other ships, and they were moving together on the light breeze, a column of fire rising like a morning sacrifice on Cithaeron.

Consternation on the pier and on the headlands, and still not a single archer.

Again my boys leapt on to the enemy deck. This one was completely deserted, and they fired her without opposition and came back aboard, unexpended spirit making them a little too sharp.

There was a line of fires across the harbour, and the round ship was now the centre of an inferno that was burning so hot that we could feel the heat where we were.

'Take us out,' I said. 'About ship.'

We rotated end for end in place as the long trireme burned, and then we ran free, almost brushing the northern headland as we left the Harbour of Aegypt. Aside from a scorch mark on the port bow, we were unscathed.

And there were fires burning all across the harbour, a chaos of fire. I counted forty ships afire, and I'm sure there were more.

'Let's get some treasure,' I said to Damon, and he grinned, his teeth shining in the sun.

I had time. I told Old Nestor to keep the rowers slow, and we pulled at a restful pace north, looking at the chaos and the burning ships.

I was making this up as I went, but when the *Ajax* came out of the smoke behind me, I knew I wasn't the only old pirate left on the seas.

We'd listened to what Parmenio had said. The south harbour for warships . . .

The northern harbour, the Harbour of Sidon, for trade.

We rowed north, and I drank water and handed some to the marines.

Hipponax grinned. 'Aren't they going to fight?'

'Thank the gods for their *hubris*,' I said. 'If we don't have to fight, all the better.'

We rowed far enough along the island to open the northern harbour, and we could see into it. It wasn't crammed with ships – too early in the season. But there were a dozen merchants of all sizes – a sweet little round ship, the kind that could carry perhaps six hundred transport amphorae, or more, in her holds, and still take a nice cargo of linen. There were bigger ships in the harbour, but this one appealed to me, both as an owner and because she looked to me as if she was in the Aegypt trade, and low in the water – not unloaded.

'Take me that ship,' I said.

For the third time, my marines went over the side. The deck crew were Aegyptian, because I understood their surrender, and Aten went with Brasidas to ensure their compliance.

'Tell them to set sail and follow us out,' I called.

I left them with Leander and Arios to make sure they complied, and two of my armoured sailors to make sure the ship was handled well.

We turned again. The *Ajax* had a big grain ship and another, smaller ship already. There were finally soldiers on the wharves, and arrows began to fall on us. But we picked up an Ionian loaded with Phoenician goods, and made him rue that he hadn't sailed that morning. I left Zephyrides and Kassandros and two more sailors with them, and we followed the *Dawn* out of the Harbour of Sidon.

The whole reach of the inner road was full of smoke.

It was like a dream.

I turned to Hipponax, who was steering to give Damon a rest.

'Look at that,' I said, or something equally banal. 'They'll never forget this.'

'Tyre is finished,' Hector said.

I shook my head. 'They'll rebuild,' I said. 'They're tough. But I'm guessing that they believed their own crap that we couldn't sail east of Delos. Surprise! We can. And Tyre will never send their full complement of ships *anywhere* again. They'll have to defend all this.'

The stolen merchants turned north of the open sea. I hadn't seen Alysia's ship – or rather her husband's. Perhaps someone else had snapped her up, or perhaps she was somewhere else entirely.

We lingered in the smoke, our eyes watering. I confess it – I was looking for a fight.

Cimon formed up on me, and then the *Gad's Fortune* came up, and the *Black Raven*.

I couldn't see much through the smoke, especially south. But I knew that there was weather coming, and the afternoon was getting on.

I laid out the signal for retreat.

There was shouting in the smoke, and I saw the flash of oars before I saw the ship.

And it wasn't one of ours.

The Phoenician came out of the smoke and then there were six of them, all together, in a well-formed line except the last, closest to me, who had to leave his line to get around the burning wreck of a merchant that was drifting down the channel on the brisk south wind.

You always think you want a fight, right up until you realise what a stupid notion that was. Now I had a fight – we'd caught a lion by the tail.

There were more behind the first six. Three more ...

'Starboard,' I called to Hipponax. He was still in the steering rig. 'Beak to beak.'

'Aye, Pater.'

We aimed as straight as an arrow at the end Phoenician, the one who'd turned to get out of the way of the burning ship.

Nemet scurried up the boat-sail mast.

The Phoenician was coming around.

'Now, my lads!' I called down to the rowing decks. 'All you've got.'

To Hipponax I said, 'Put us between the wreck and the Phoenician, and go for their bow. The cathead. Strike ...'

Far too late, they realised that we weren't one of theirs – that we were in earnest. Their captain was good. He turned in place to get his bow on my bow, and I missed the perfection of Harpagos. We didn't do his little trick of ramming the enemy cathead. Hipponax was too inexperienced, and he aimed too far aft, still compensating for his turn to pass the burning ship. It was so close to our own port side that we were no doubt scorching our paint.

But we didn't need to have a perfect strike. We went down their side after slamming into their ram, so that both ships shuddered, and they still had oars in the water when ours were already in. We did them little enough damage and shot by, having crushed perhaps a dozen oars on their starboard side.

Naturally, in the way of things, they turned sharply to starboard, because the side we'd swept was in chaos and the port side was still rowing.

But the hand of the gods was there. As they turned, they struck the burning wreck as we vanished, having threaded the needle between them, and I slapped Hipponax on the shoulder.

'Drag the oars,' I called to Poseidonos.

We slowed.

'Hard to starboard,' I said. 'Put the oars over hard. Port-side oars, back!'

We turned in place. It seemed slow ...

The *Ajax* was locked, broadside to broadside with a Levantine trireme, and I could see the marines fighting above the heads of the oarsmen. The *Ajax* was on the far side of the enemy ship, so her flank was turned to me. An easy kill.

But I doubted that Cimon would thank me. I suspected he had his capture planned, and I had my oarsmen row soft, headed east towards the mainland beach, invisible in the smoke of a hundred burning ships.

We got around the stern of the *Ajax*'s foe, and there was another Phoenician, just backing water after going bow to bow with the *Amastris*.

'Ramming speed!' I bellowed.

And then we saw what the *Apollo's Raven* was made of. She leapt like a cat's pounce – slow crawl to ramming speed in two ship's lengths. Our ram crunched into the naked flank of the Phoenician, the beam reinforcing the ramp riding up over the upper rail and then forcing it down. We could hear the screams of the oarsmen and the explosive cracks as the beams of the rowing frame shattered. Our bow pressed her down, and she tipped and began to fill.

'Back oars!' I roared.

Poseidonos ordered them to reverse on their benches, and then we felt the drag.

The ram was caught.

'Pull!' Poseidonos cried.

The oars beat the water to a froth.

The big Phoenician was sinking, and our stern was starting to rise – I could feel it in my feet. By the gods, we were going to be sunk by our first kill.

And then there was a gentle *pop* underwater, and we slid free, the stern coming down with a slap and we drifted a few paces.

'Water coming in the bow,' Ka called.

I cursed.

Militarily, we'd won a clear victory, and even if we all died here, we'd done the damage we'd come to do. But I had not planned to sacrifice myself or my ship and crew, and now I cursed myself for wanting a fight. Fighting is chancy – people can die.

'Back water,' I ordered.

My rowers were already reversed, and with the bow damaged, it was possible that backing water was going to be our best point of rowing.

I ran forward, wishing that I hadn't sent Old Nestor away.

And there was *another* Phoenician. He came out of the smoke in the middle of the channel, and made for us, but we were backing water at a steady rate.

To the east, the *Gad's Fortune* was already turning, and the *Amastris* had made another kill.

The *Ajax* was turning end for end.

'Time to go,' I said.

I raised the signal for retreat just as the two ships from Lesbos and the Naxian *Ariadne* appeared to the west, close to the island of Tyre.

The *Dawn* was backing water the way I was. Of course, we'd all done it at Artemisium – done it for stadia. Cimon's brother probably thought it was a tactic I was using.

Then the *Parthenos* emerged from the smoke to the east, also backing water. The *Ariadne* ran down at ramming speed, slowed, and turned in place …and began backing water. It was a pretty manoeuvre, but it was not the rapid retreat I wanted.

And still my Phoenician was stalking me, as if he knew my bow was damaged.

I called to Brasidas.

'We need to take him,' I said. 'Grapple and board.'

'Of course,' he said.

I ran back to Hipponax. 'I need you to pretend to go bow to bow,' I said. 'But just shave down her side. Do you want me to do it?'

Hipponax looked at Damon. Damon looked at me. Then my son gave me one of those looks sons give fathers.

I'm all grown-up and I can do this for myself.

I wanted Damon at the steering oar. Or better yet, I wanted it to be me. If the Phoenician caught us dead on our damaged bow, we'd sink on the spot. I was willing to wager a krater of solid gold against a seashell that we'd lost our bronze ram.

But then, sooner or later, they have to be men. And they have to be confident, and lead others, and believe that they can do things.

I've heard that supposedly great men rarely have great sons, and I think this is the heart of it – some men can't let go.

'Damon, command the oarsmen,' I said. 'We need to get our oars in at the last possible heartbeat.'

'Sir,' he said.

'Hipponax …'

'I've got it, Pater.'

I nodded. 'Very well.'

I picked up my favourite spear and went forward to where the marines waited amidships. Sailors knelt with grapples ready, and the marines were kneeling in two ranks.

An arrow came off the Phoenician.

And then Nemet began to loose from the boat-sail mast. He had two quivers, and he said afterwards that he emptied both of them as we closed, all in the last seventy paces or so. We didn't charge the enemy ship; we merely slowed our retreat and let him catch us. But that had its own dangers as our line matched our speed, and suddenly we were bringing on another engagement, with more Phoenician ships coming out of the smoke.

We were out in the channel by then, rowing in among more completed warships, already four stadia north of Tyre, with a patchwork of warehouses and waterfront dives visible on our port side, on the mainland.

We were backing down a line of completed ships, and my eye was caught by a pretty *trihemiola*. It's a bastard rig, much favoured in the western parts of the Inner Sea – a trireme with a slightly more robust build and permanent standing masts. A sort of compromise.

It was love at first sight. She was probably Carthaginian, or even Sicilian ...

North of us, the coastline of Asia stretched away, and the open sea beckoned to the west. To the south, there was fire and smoke, and possibly a storm brewing over the Nile Delta.

Hipponax left it very late, touching the oars a little.

Nemet shot and shot.

And some of his arrows were going home.

The last seconds were a blur. In five heartbeats, the Phoenician tried to make a hard turn to starboard, and my son tried to turn a little to port and then back to starboard.

But one of Nemet's arrows went into the enemy helmsman, and he died atop his starboard-side oar. Their ship tilted, turning too sharply for their speed, and our ram-less bow slammed into their port-side bow with a sickening crunch. We all fell, and Nemet was thrown from the boat-sail mast and all the way over the side of the enemy ship, flung a full fifty paces into the water.

Now all of our marines had expected a long-side engagement, and we were in the wrong place, and we rose and ran forward. The enemy archers were shooting, but our archers shot them flat in a few arrows. Sebastos took an arrow through his foot below the greave and went down, but the rest of us went over the bow.

She was sinking. My beautiful *Apollo's Raven*'s bow was crushed.

She wouldn't sink fast. But now we had to take the Phoenician, or die trying.

I wasn't in front. I had Brasidas and Hector in front of me, and they were the first on the enemy deck, going into the rowing frame.

Phoenician oarsmen are mostly slaves.

Thank the gods.

I looked down at a thranite in the bow, and he looked terrified, but not dangerous. I put a foot on the rowing frame and made the leap for the amidships catwalk, a dance I'd danced twenty times before. I landed, made sure of the three oarsmen behind me, then saw in a glance that as Brasidas and Hector went forward towards the command deck, the enemy marines were behind us, in their armoured box over the bow, just turning to come back at us.

An archer loosed at me, perhaps fifteen feet away. I took his arrow on my aspis and it exploded, the spray of splinters in my throat and shoulders.

I killed a Phoenician as he tried to get his balance, and I kicked his dying body into his mate, sweeping my spear like a broom at head height, punching with my aspis. I caught the edge of his aspis with mine, and pushed it down and got in close, and then I ignored him and threw my precious gold-inlaid spear into the man behind him.

Never get attached to a spear.

The man on the other side of my aspis tried to push with his upper body. I rolled his shield down and stabbed him in the neck, overhand, with the sword I'd just drawn from under my arm – high to low, the blade following the line of my thumb over the top of the shield I'd just frozen in a vulnerable place with my own.

Arrows sprouted like new growth in springtime, and the next two fell, one with Ka's black arrow *and* my gold-inlaid spear. They fell over the side and vanished into the bright azure sea. Then Kassandros locked his aspis to mine and took a spear on it, and Giorgos rifled his long spear between us and took another, hitting the man so hard in the helmet that he fell like a sacrificial ox.

There were only four of them remaining, and they were brave enough, but when two thirds of your marine contingent dies in twenty beats of your heart, you hesitate. They pressed forward, not with determination but with Phoenician fatalism, and they died for it. The biggest one tried to press my shield down, as I'd killed his mate. My deadly xiphos licked out like an adder striking, under his shield, cutting one thigh and biting deeply into another. I could see his eyes in the eye-slits of his helmet – they were green, and deep. He set his shoulders and didn't know that he was already dead until the power left his legs and he fell, his eyes still alight with war fury.

And then I was breathing like a bellows and there was no pressure on my back, and I turned.

Brasidas had cleared the enemy command deck.

'Take command!' I called to him. It was all a matter of timing. 'Get Nemet out of the water!'

I jumped back aboard the *Apollo's Raven*. She was going down by the bow, but slowly.

Men in the bow were up to their knees in water.

'Listen to me!' I roared, pulling my helmet off. My hands hurt; my aspis shoulder was burning. I had no idea if I'd taken a wound.

No time.

'Listen up!' I roared. 'We can't take this ship home!'

I ran aft, almost tripping headlong over one of the many lines from our mainmast.

But the benches were still reversed ...

The plan came together in my head as I reached the command platform.

'Damon!' I called. 'They have to row! I know she's heavy and sinking. Twenty strokes!'

I ran to the stern as I heard the first orders from under my feet.

I pointed at the trihemiola, rocking gently on the waves, five hundred paces aft.

'Put the stern into her side,' I said.

Hipponax couldn't see over the rising swan's breast of the stern, so I gave him a heading by laying a spear on the deck in front of him.

We were under way. I could feel it.

The *Ajax* had the retreat order flying, and we had nine ships in line abreast. They didn't know I was sinking, and now the Phoenicians were coming after us like wolves. Wolves are cautious until they're sure they have the upper hand.

They came on, and we retreated.

'Water's gaining,' Poseidonos shouted.

'Pumps!' I yelled, but of course, most of my marines were gone, and half my sailors. I regretted my early captures. Never take prizes until the fighting is done – a mistake I've made before and would make again, but one I don't recommend.

'The thalamites can't row!' Poseidonos called.

I looked down, and the water was rising, and the poor bastards were so well disciplined that they were sitting in the rising water.

'On deck!' I called. 'Thalamites! Come up! Come on!'

As they came on deck, I put them to work on the pumps, simple wooden devices that shot water over the side. Too much water. Frankly, it was as much to give them something to do as because it would save us.

Ten were on deck, then twenty, then thirty. They would have made us top-heavy, except that all that water was already ballast.

My beautiful *Apollo's Raven* was dying, but she was game, and we were backing, the mid-deck zygites and the upper-deck thranites pulling like heroes. I could see Leon's oar bending with every mighty stroke, and Poseidonos' on the other side, as if they alone would get us home.

I ordered all the thalamites with no pumps to come aft, and the bow rose a little. Not much, but it might buy us a little time.

I got up on the rail and looked aft. We were less than two hundred paces from the trihemiola.

I jumped down and moved the spear.

'Just thus,' I said.

Hipponax moved, perfectly aligning the ship. It was so hard to turn that he grunted.

'She's a slug,' he said.

My poor *Apollo's Raven.*

I looked down.

There was a lot of water there, and I suspected that the damage we'd taken in the open ocean had come home to roost, so to speak. My beautiful ship was opening at the seams.

A hundred paces.

Seventy-five paces.

'Listen up!' I called, my voice already hoarse. 'We're changing ships. We're going to ram a ship stern-first. Giorgos leads the sailors – put grapples in her and bind her fast. Then the thalamites go over the side and go straight to their benches on the new ship. Then the zygites, and then the thranites. Marines last. Got that?'

I hoped that they had it.

Hector made a face. 'What if there's a crew aboard?'

That was the last thing I heard before we struck – a gentle bump, as the way had been coming off us for ten strokes as the *Apollo's Raven* began to settle.

I was the first. I leapt, landed on her rowing frame forward, and then leapt again for her main deck and made it.

The benches were empty, and so was the command platform. Aft, where there was a full deck over the rowers, I saw two men and a woman. They were ... very surprised. But not so surprised that they wanted to be dead or slaves, and all three dropped over the side into the water as I ran to the helm.

She was anchored bow and stern. There was no way I could fetch the stones aboard and make it off before the Phoenicians came up with me.

I took my sword and started sawing away at the aft anchor cable, even as Giorgos went for the bow, and my thalamites were going obediently into the lower rowing deck.

She smelled of new wood. The deck under my feet gleamed like ivory, and the rowing frame was cedar.

We had a little more luck, because as the thalamites and marines crowded aft of an almost empty *Apollo's Raven* they pushed the stern down and the bow out of the water, but by then, many of the seams were going, and she was going down. By the time that Hipponax and Hector were the last two men aboard, the nearest Phoenician was only half a stade away and the deck was awash.

Hector said something.

Hipponax was getting free of the steering rig.

Hector ran aft, one lone figure of bronze who appeared to be running on water. In fact, I knew that the buoyancy of the wood would keep her at the surface for hours, until it became waterlogged.

Hector ran to the bow, and found the long strip of painted wood from the *Lydia*. He tore it loose and ran back, waving it like a prize. He gave his brother a hand, and Hipponax made it over the side, and then Hector was on the deck, and Giorgos and I began to show the flexibility of the trihemiola.

We didn't have an oar to put in the water. They were all right where they ought to have been – stored amidships, lengthwise between the benches. A mere quarter of an hour to serve out.

Giorgos and one of the boys climbed the mainmast shrouds, and with two flicks of their knives they cut the yarn holding the sails against the yards.

The mainsail came down with a whisper and a rustle, and I belayed it, alone, moving as fast as I could.

The same wind that had fought us all night, the wind that was blowing the smoke in our faces, now filled the trihemiola's mainsail.

We began to gather way, even as Damon and Hipponax threw themselves at the widely separate steering oars – a different arrangement. Everything was different. We were barely controlling chaos, living one heartbeat at a time, but my people were aboard. The lead Phoenician was perhaps ten ship's lengths away, and her archers were loosing with the wind behind them. Thanks to the gods, we had the high sweep of our stern timbers between us and the archers.

The archery was odd, though, as if the enemy archers didn't want to hit us ...

I can be slow. I realised that I was seeing our capture, with Brasidas on the command deck, and Nemet loosing arrows to make the other Phoenicians believe they were allies.

Brasidas had promised the rowers their freedom, of course.

They just weren't the best rowers, and they weren't going as quickly as I would have liked.

But they were moving, and the wolves behind were closing in on me.

Our sail was full and drawing. Giorgos and two other men got to the forward mast, a mast a little bigger than on a trireme, and they dropped the foresail and it filled.

A distinctly better motion, as if pressing her bow down made all the difference.

Well, every ship is different.

To my port and starboard, there were our ships, still backing oars, but all of them were getting their mainmasts up. Cimon raised a signal and every ship began to turn in place – port-side oars going all out, starboard-side oars dragging.

The Phoenicians went to ramming speed just as Brasidas came up abreast of us.

'Hello!' he called. He was smiling.

I waved and leant out to watch the Phoenician dead astern. I was hoping ... hoping ...

I whispered another little prayer.

And she struck the wreck of the *Apollo's Raven*. She was awash, her rowing structure a palm's breadth under the water, and remember, our boat-sail mast snapped and threw Nemet when we broke our bow.

Nothing to show.

The *Apollo's Raven* was dead, but she took one more enemy with her. The Phoenician's ram ripped into the sinking oar-rig and tangled. Their rigging all came down, and they were unprepared, and ...

The south wind filled our sails and we turned for the open sea.

Book Two

Cyprus and Ionia

SPRING, 478 BCE

With Pausanias sailed the Athenians with thirty ships, and a number of other allies. They made an expedition against Cyprus ... and afterwards went to Byzantium.

Thucydides, Book 1 94.1

Spring was passing when we came on to the beaches at Delos and found the Allied fleet there, engaging in the usual Greek political bickering that always seemed to precede even the most routine action.

I wasn't ready to deal with Aristides yet, much less Pausanias. I went ashore with Cimon and our captains, and we made our sacrifices for victory, and we bought stores of wine and oil and grain from the temporary agora that a dozen merchants had set up. Delos isn't a very big island, and it seemed to me that we couldn't stay long, but there were already organised camps springing up, with tents made of boat sails, and timber brought from the mainland.

I won't say that no one noticed us. Aristides sent for me, but Cimon and I walked into a temporary taverna built of linen canvas, old hides and piles of amphorae, and we had our slaves bring us seats.

It was beautiful. Spring in the Inner Sea is always an event. Everything dry and dead suddenly bursts into life, and there are flowers where you'd swear there was only gravel and volcanic rock, and the lambs frisk about. I've been to places like Alba and Gaul and Latinium, where it seems to be green all year around, but in Ionia, on the islands, it is as if life leaps full-blown from arid waste. Demeter's daughter comes to us, and there are thousands of tiny flowers everywhere.

'We might as well tell him where we are,' I said.

There were forty men in the taverna – mostly prosperous men, marine officers and captains. It was the most expensive place with the best wine. Not a good place to hide.

Cimon grunted, and as if we'd summoned him by Hecate's magic, Aristides came in, with Pericles at his heels, a dozen hoplites attending him. Aristides was a handsome man, but despite being Athens' greatest soldier, he looked like a farmer with financial woes, in a cloak somewhere between pale blue and rose that had once probably been a dark red. The hem was frayed.

'A whisper tells me that you all didn't go to the Ionian cities,' he said.

'We did, too,' Cimon said.

Aristides looked at me.

I shrugged. 'We raided Tyre,' I said.

Aristides sat there for a moment.

Around us, the conversations of forty Greek aristocrats died away.

'You raided Tyre,' he said.

'Someone had to,' Cimon said. In my opinion, one of the best Laconian lines ever delivered.

Aristides sat back, considering the two of us.

'You took ... what – twenty ships? And you kicked the hornets' nest?'

I smiled. I liked Aristides, as you know, even when he was being a prig. Today, he'd come instead of the Spartan commander, to chew on us about unlicensed piracy in Ionian waters. I knew what he thought we'd done.

He'd come himself, so that we wouldn't get into a fight with the Spartan. Give him that much.

So instead of getting angry, or shouting, or just getting up and walking back to my ship, I leant back as far as my folding stool would allow, searching for the tent-pole holding the hide roof, hoping I could ease my shoulders against it.

'We *burnt* the hornets' nest,' I said.

Aristides looked back and forth between us.

'We took seven triremes,' Cimon said.

'We burnt another fifty,' I added. 'Perhaps twice that.'

Aristides shook his head. 'You ...' He was, for once, at a loss for words.

I let myself smile, and Cimon was grinning.

'The war at sea is over,' Cimon said. 'I'll wager a talent of gold against a mina of silver that the Phoenicians don't put a fleet to sea except to cover their convoys ... not for ten years.'

'Apollo!' Aristides said. Not a man given to taking the god's names in vain, he shook his head. 'You are serious.'

'We are serious,' I said. 'Listen, Aristides. Remember the forward strategy? Remember the last Olympics but one? Themistocles and

Cimon and I argued that we should take the fleet and destroy the Persian naval bases.'

Aristides managed a smile. 'We had no idea what we were facing,' he said. 'But I remember that.'

I nodded. 'Well,' I said, 'five years late, we did it. Perhaps the Great King can patch something together out of his loyal Ionian cities. Halicarnassus still has a fleet, and perhaps the rubble of Miletus can raise a few ships. But Archilogos is in Ephesus, and Lesbos and Chios are in our hands. We just set fire to the Great King's beard at Tyre.'

Aristides was still looking back and forth, as if expecting one of us to reveal a joke, or a lie.

'If you factor in the thrashing that the Sicilians gave to Carthage,' I said, 'I would guess that Athens now has the only major fleet on the face of the Inner Sea.'

Aristides blinked. 'How many ships do you believe you burnt?' he asked.

So, over some wine, we told him the story. The tavern-keeper was an honest scoundrel and brought us some oil-fried shrimps and some bread. Then we were using almond hulls as ships and puddles of oil on the big trestle table to represent the land, and we re-fought the whole action. Lykon of Corinth came over and joined in, and Moire. By the time we were done, most of our captains were clustered around, shouting out their own roles in the fighting.

Aristides was quiet through the entire performance. Only after the laconic Moire had explained how he came to take a Phoenician trireme fully rigged, and Brasidas another, sailing it home, did he sit back, waving his hand over his wine cup to indicate that he wanted no more.

'This changes everything,' he said.

'Because we can all go home?' Lykon asked.

'Because now we can drive the Persians right out of Europe. Free all of the Ionian cities.' Aristides looked as if he was far away. As if, until that moment, he'd never believed in the forward strategy.

Maybe he hadn't. In his heart, he was a hoplite, not a navarch.

But young Pericles was so excited that he looked fit to burst. Pericles was no longer an aristocratic boy. He was an ephebe, but a big, powerful one – eighteen years old, with a growing beard and an aura of command that I suspected was going to make him more dangerous than his father Xanthippus or any of his Alcmaeonid uncles.

'We can take it all,' he said.

'Do not ...' Aristides said. 'Do not say such things.'

But young Pericles' eyes were so bright that he might have been one of the gods.

'No,' he said. 'No, we can take it all. We can rescue the Ionian Greeks, our own cousins, from their subjugation, and we can make them into a league that will withstand the Phoenicians and the Aegyptians, the Carthaginians and the Persians.'

Aristides' mouth trembled with anger. 'Restrain yourself, young man. Or you will gain us conflict with Sparta and no such sea empire as you imagine.'

'Sparta is the past,' Pericles said, as if Apollo was speaking directly to him.

I hated to throw cold water on a fire I had started myself, but Pericles, for all his spirit, was wrong.

'Pericles,' I said, 'when this war started, you were not yet born or conceived. When this war started, we took Sardis and burnt the temples.'

'I know,' Pericles said, all injured adolescence. 'I know all that.'

'Apparently not,' I said. 'Because when the Long War started, we had most of the ships and all of Ionia on our side, *and the Persians came and took it all*. It has taken us your entire life to *get back to where we started*.'

Aristides looked at me. I knew that look – the look he gave me when he occasionally remembered that I was more than a sword-arm and a spear.

If Aristides was surprised, Pausanias was infuriated.

'You just sailed off ...' he spat.

I've said this before. Pausanias had somehow missed the parts of the *agoge* that made Spartiates immune to the sort of pettiness that the rest of us are prone to. Spartans are complicated people. They have many flaws, not least of which is their habit of commanding their slaves, which leads them to imagine that other people are also slaves. They commit more hubris than any other group of men.

But in one thing, they are like the gods – their system of training makes them better than mere men. They do not easily anger or take offence. They speak little, and when they do speak, they do so with humour and with clarity.

The truth, I think, is that most of us are afraid, at least some of the time. Afraid we will be found wanting. Afraid we are not as good as other men. Afraid that we will be dominated. Afraid that we will have to fight.

The brutality of the agoge appears to relieve the Spartiates of all of that, at the cost of many other things. I do not approve – indeed, it would be hubris of my own to believe that I could approve or disapprove of another people's system of government.

This is my long-winded way of saying that the best of the Spartans enjoyed a godlike security in themselves that was almost impossible to ruffle. And somehow, Pausanias, their commander, hadn't got it. He gave voice to anger and tempers that no other Spartiate would have allowed himself. Perhaps that was at the centre of the drama we were about to see played out.

'You just sailed off . . .' he said again.

I've never liked Pausanias, and he was very much on the other side of almost everything I stood for. He was Queen Gorgo's enemy, he was a leader of the Sparta First faction, and he'd argued vehemently that Sparta should defend the Isthmus of Corinth and abandon Athens. On the other hand, he'd obeyed his government and marched into Boeotia, and he had won the battle of Plataea, although it was not won by generalship, I promise you.

It was won by spears and shields, not by generals.

And I was not a product of the Spartan agoge, or anything like it. I was a bronze-smith's son from Plataea.

So I shrugged and barked a laugh. On purpose.

'You arrogant puppy!' he yelled. 'You just sailed off on your own, never thinking—'

Cimon laughed.

Pausanias grew redder and redder.

'Never thinking?' I offered.

Aristides glared at me and put his hand on my shoulder.

We were standing in front of the great Temple of Hera on Delos. The Spartan ships were beached on the south-west of the island, and Spartans have always been partial to Hera, I suppose.

'Did you give a thought to our strategy? Did you misunderstand that I was the commander of the Allied fleet?' He pulled his cloak around him. 'All of you foreigners are insubordinate, but this is the limit.'

Again, I shrugged. 'We won,' I said. 'I believe that is its own justi-fication.'

'I have a difficult time imagining a strategy that is improved by sitting on your arse here at Delos,' Cimon said, 'or worsened by the destruction of the enemy fleet.'

'I will decide ...' Pausanias said. He was regaining his temper; he wasn't weak by any means, merely ... curiously vulnerable, for a Spartiate of the royal family. He looked at me. 'I will decide what our strategy will be. I do not enjoy having my choices dictated to me by arrogant upstarts.'

'Ever been to sea before, sir?' I asked in mock respect. 'I've been fighting this war at sea since the year we burnt Sardis.'

'It is difficult to imagine a Spartan navarch,' Cimon said, helpfully. 'I mean, without an Athenian to put a little spine in him.' He smiled more broadly. 'Could you explain what "upstart" means in this context?'

Pausanias turned slowly. 'I can have you arrested. I am the Strategos of the Greek Allies. You will obey. In future, you will not take any action without my permission. Do I make myself clear? I am the victor of Plataea and I will decide on the strategy of the Greeks.'

Cimon spat thoughtfully and said nothing.

Aristides looked at me and then looked away.

I considered a great many responses, and then decided that I didn't need to be angry. Indeed, I knew full well that I was provoking Pausanias because he was an arse and deserved it. But I needed to stop.

I bowed. And walked away.

Cimon came with me, and a little later, Aristides.

'You're welcome,' I said.

Aristides shook his head.

Cimon smiled bitterly. 'Night before last, at Naxos, we predicted all of this,' he said.

It was true. We'd sat on the beach and wagered each other whether we were punished for attacking Tyre.

Of course, we'd been watching our oarsmen divide up the spoils from our take. We'd shared everything, down to the last ostrich egg. We'd taken seven merchant ships, one of them stuffed with Aegyptian treasure.

Captains got much bigger shares, but most of us had used our shares to buy in the captured ships at a pre-set value. We had new ships, and we promoted new captains.

In truth, by the time we landed at Delos, we were a quarter of the ships on the beaches. We could have made a great deal of trouble.

But at least we never expected any thanks. And to be fair, we'd made a small fortune in loot. No one needed to call us heroes. We'd done Greece a service, but at a profit.

It still rankled. Still does. I account the raid on Tyre one of the most brilliant actions of my career, and no one even remembers it.

If you think about it, the Greeks are unkind to all their victors. Look at what happened to Themistocles, and to Pausanias, too, although in his case, he cut the caper. But still ... we're not easy on our heroes. Maybe it is in our national character.

Bah, let's have a little more wine, here.

The next days passed in a blur, and I'm not at all sure that I have the order correct. The things that stand out are twofold – that Pausanias dismissed most of our ships and sent them home, and that I discovered that Briseis' son, Heraklitus, was serving as a marine on Helikaon's ship. If I say that both of these were of equal import, I suspect I will have a great deal of explaining to do.

Perhaps Heraklitus is the easier to discuss. He was Briseis' son by Aristagoras, or so the world thought. I had been at the edge of death in the great harbour of Carthage when Briseis told me that Heraklitus was my son, and I barely knew him. He had grown to manhood in a household that served the Great King, and where I was thought of as a dangerous slave who'd escaped to be a criminal and a pirate.

We'd almost crossed spears on the beach of Mycale, although to be fair, he was largely responsible for saving his mother from the Red King, but you have heard all my stories and you know that one.

We had spoken perhaps two or three hundred words in our lives. Briseis had cautioned me to be wary of him. In truth, I didn't even know if he knew or suspected that he was my son. After all, he looked enough like me that Cimon smiled every time he saw the boy.

I know that Archilogos had spoken to him on my behalf, a year before.

And Heraklitus might have spent the summer winning his fortune with his spear. It's a family tradition, and he was fast the way I used to be fast, and arrogant the way ... never mind. He might have been merely an excellent marine among many brave and excellent men.

But Pausanias wouldn't have us. That is, he had almost forty ships from the Peloponnese and he was determined not to cede any pre-eminence to Athens or her allies, so he only accepted a total of forty more ships. Only thirty from Athens – a handful from Aegina and Euboea.

The rest he referred to as 'pirates' in a speech to the Alliance council, and he ordered them home. When the ships from Lesbos protested, he told them, to their faces, that all of the Ionian cities should be disestablished and their citizens sent to Sicily to found new cities. I knew this was his private belief, but to hear it stated outright in council was chilling. It was the pathway to another kind of war, and we all knew it.

'You are not members of the Alliance,' he said. 'You have no status with us save as supplicants. And it is a foolish risk by these seasonal pirates to allow you the means of making war.'

That was me – a seasonal pirate.

Listen. In the late spring of the year after Plataea, Pausanias was the most famous man in the Greek world – indeed, perhaps in all of the world. He was of the Royal House of Sparta; he was the victor of the battle of Plataea.

So why, you might ask yourself, was this great man – possibly the greatest in the Hellenic world – behaving like a petty tyrant? It's a good question. From secure old age, I think Pausanias let success and a little power and fame go to his head. He wasn't trained for it.

But on his road to Hades, he had help. As you'll hear, if you sit and drink wine with me.

Regardless ... in that summer, he did as he pleased, and no one stood against him.

Well ... almost no one.

When he was done speaking, Aristides rose. Aristides would have made a better Spartan than Pausanias – he was grave, dignified, absolutely just, and almost impossible to move to mere emotion. He could be an awful prig, but he was very good at leadership. And he, too, had led thousands to victory at Plataea.

He rose, and received the homage of silence. We were in the old theatre at Delos, and the sound carried magnificently, but they were silent for Aristides.

'Friends,' he said, 'the Lacedaemonians have the right, from ancient times, to appoint the leader of any army or navy of all the Greeks, and Pausanias has the right to command. He may direct the fleet as he pleases, although it is possible that *sending ships home* is a little beyond his powers. However, it would seem to me better to listen to the strategos explain why his strategy is better suited to eighty triremes than say, ninety or one hundred. Are we perhaps too many to fit on a given beach?'

Pausanias rose. 'It is too many because I say that it is too many,' he said. 'I have no need to explain myself. Obey, or go home, Athenian.'

Wrong tone. Wrong everything. Greeks do everything by consensus. It's very difficult to give orders to Greeks – even Spartans.

I rose. Pausanias glared.

I smiled. 'I don't believe that you can send me home, Pausanias.'

He didn't rise. But his face grew red.

'I am the archon of Plataea this year,' I went on. 'My ship is crewed with Plataeans. I believe that it is beyond even the machinations of the wily Lacedaemonians to claim that Plataea was somehow not part of the Allies, when we fought the Medes at *Plataea*.'

I got a laugh from the gathered men. That laugh hurt Pausanias – he knew his standing had just been lowered.

'And as for the term *seasonal pirate* ...' I began, and Aristides gave me a look that implored my silence.

'I was a pirate in these waters when you were stealing food in the agoge, Pausanias,' I said, but I made myself smile when I said it.

I sat down amid general applause, and laughter.

My smile was false. Even then, even as a man who was no friend of Pausanias', I wondered, 'Why is this man acting like this?' And I couldn't work it out.

An hour later, Sparthius came to my ship – my best friend among the Spartan peers. I was sitting in the shade of an awning stretched from her port-side oar gallery, and I rose, clasped his hand, and Aten poured him wine.

Bulis had always been the talkative, friendly one, and Sparthius the silent one. But Bulis had died with an arrow in his eye at Plataea, and now it was left to Sparthius to speak to me.

'Are you here as a herald for Pausanias?' I asked. I pointed him to a folding stool.

He smiled. 'Perhaps,' he said. 'This wine is very good.'

I'll try not to bore you all with my little triumphs, but we had three ships out of Tyre with holds full of wine, and we were selling it in two locations on the beaches. And sailors are very free with their money, when there's wine involved. Eh?

I asked about his wife and sons, and Bulis' wife and sons. Bulis' wife was an old friend of mine, or rather, a plain-spoken acquaintance. Sparthius and I chatted away for as long as a priest might say the dawn service in the temple of Olympian Zeus, and he asked after Briseis, and I told him about Hipponax and Hector.

He put his hands on his knees and met my eyes.

'Pausanias does not love you, brother,' he said.

I nodded.

'He will allow you to stay with the fleet,' he continued, 'but the others must go. Understand – there is conflict, even in the heart of the Vale of Sparta.' He looked away.

'Conflict?' I asked.

Sparthius met my eyes again. His were golden brown and deep and honest.

'You know that it is not the place of any Spartiate to speak ill of our mother country,' he said.

'Sparthius, you speak in riddles like the priests of Apollo. Indeed, I might wonder if you'd just been breathing the vapours in the temple.' I leant back.

He smiled.

'Do you mean that Pausanias' decisions to send thirty ships home is unpopular with the ephors?' I asked.

He looked away. 'I am only here to ask that you not provoke Pausanias in council.'

I leant forward. 'Sparthius,' I said, 'ask yourself why Pausanias is so easy to provoke.'

I held my cup out to Aten for more wine. I was definitely drinking too much, but Delos is a dull place with too many priests. The whole island was beginning to smell like the Olympics – that is to say, flowers and piss. Fifteen thousand men on one tiny island too rocky to dig a proper latrine ... I leave the rest to your imagination.

I leant to put my back against the hull of my new trihemiola. It was vibrating, because the oarsmen were scraping the hull clean and applying a new coat of black pitch. We'd taken her unfinished, and, as it proved, we didn't do a good job of pitching her hull the first time, which cost me time later, as you'll hear.

When you want to have a conversation with a Lacedaemonian – a peer, that is – you still have to do most of the talking. They just sit, looking thoughtful and polite.

So I had a go.

'Pausanias is the leader of the party that wanted to see Athens destroyed,' I said.

Sparthius shrugged. 'Athens *was* destroyed' he said laconically. Unsaid, 'Look where that got us.'

'And now they are rebuilding Athens,' I said.

I waited, leaving my comment in the air. When the Persians burnt Athens in Salamis year, many among the Peloponnesians had said that Athens no longer existed as a polity. Themistocles had corrected them by offering to take the Athenian fleet over to the Persians.

Well, not exactly, but very like.

And the next summer, when the Persians came again under Mardonius, Plaistarchos, the Spartan king who was too young to exercise command – the king for whom Pausanias was regent – came to Athens and tried to insinuate the same thing. Gorgo, wife to Leonidas, who'd died at Thermopylae – Gorgo, my best friend in Sparta ... Gorgo had undermined Pausanias, so that instead of abandoning Athens, the young king swore to support Athens.

See? Greeks. It's a wonder we get anything done, and the habit of Greeks in calling the Thracians treacherous is remarkable in its insolence. The Spartans, especially the most conservative among them, had been trying to arrange the collapse of Athens for fifty years.

But there was another party in Sparta – the party of Leonidas. Leonidas and all his lineage – and his brilliant wife – wanted Sparta to look outwards, not inwards, for glory. Leonidas had seen Athens as an ally, nor was he the first of his line to feel that way, and he died to prove that many Spartans had horizons wider than the Vale of Sparta itself. Gorgo had kept his party alive – Gorgo and men like Bulis and Sparthius. Plaistarchos should have inherited the party from his father. But Pausanias, who also should have been part of the outward-looking party, was instead the de facto leader of the Sparta First faction, those who wanted Sparta to be pre-eminent, but isolated from the rest of the world. The faction that supported the destruction of Athens again and again.

Sparthius smiled a bitter, thin-lipped smile.

'New walls,' he said in his Laconian way.

'Apollo,' I swore.

You may recall that when I started this story, I mentioned that the Athenians were building new walls around the city and planning long walls all the way to the sea at Piraeus, because Phaleron was too small for their new fleet, and because Themistocles, who had great vision, whatever his other shortcomings, saw in the port of Piraeus a fortress and a city more important than Athens herself.

Say what you will about Themistocles ... he planned brilliantly.

'This is about the new walls?' I asked.

Sparthius spread his hands. 'The ephors asked that they not be rebuilt,' he said. The way he held his hands said, *I recognise that it's a ridiculous request, but what can you do?*

Because, let's be honest, friends – the new walls weren't built to stop the Persians.

The new walls were built to stop Sparta. With a complete city wall, Athens was virtually impregnable against Sparta's lamentable siege capability. And with long walls to the sea, Athens would be virtually impregnable against a land army.

'So ...' I said. 'Athens built her new harbour and her long walls, and Sparta can no longer trust Athens. She sends Pausanias out ... not to command, but to limit Athens.'

Sparthius spread his hands again. 'We have convinced Pausanias that it is to everyone's benefit to take Cyprus from the Great King,' he said.

That's a damned long speech, for a Spartan.

'Because otherwise he was going to sit here at Delos?' I asked.

Sparthius shook his head. No Spartiate would speak ill of another, but if you spent enough time with them, you got to understand their elliptical ways of voicing criticism.

'If you would avoid provoking him,' Sparthius said, 'we might sail off and do some good.'

'With eighty ships,' I said.

'Eighty-one,' he said. And rose to his feet. 'Good wine. Perhaps I'll come back.'

A flash of his red cloak, and Sparthius was gone.

The Athenians worked it out among themselves. Cimon stayed, and so did Metiochus but Ameinias went home with the *Parthenos*. The Athenians sent eight ships home, and I sent the men of Methymna and Eresos and Mytilini home. Their captains bought their ships outright, and Aristides met with them quietly and promised them that the Allies would admit the Ionian Greeks to the Alliance as soon as it could be arranged, but they were bitter and angry.

Our Naxian ship, the *Ariadne*, was already home or near enough, and they sailed off with some treasure and a promise from Aristides.

Megakles took the *Apollo* back to Sicily with a cargo of spices we'd taken off the Tyrians, and Moire took the *Black Raven* to the Isthmus and then back to Prosili in the shadow of old Cithaeron.

I saw them all off with a heavy heart, but if the seas were free of Persians and Phoenicians, then it was time for trade. The two commodities we specialised in, wine from Gaul and tin, were in high demand. Moire was going to get a cargo of hides and anything else he could scrape together at Corinth and he was going to Massalia.

Sekla took command of our larger round ship, with Hector as his helmsman and first mate, and sailed away for Aegypt. Leukas sailed with Moire, intending to put the *Poseidon* on the seas and take her round the Chersonese into the Euxine for a big cargo of grain.

We were sailors. If Pausanias didn't want men like Sekla and Leukas, they had much better ways of spending their sailing season.

Hector and Hipponax sailed away with Sekla, and I had room for a couple of young marines aboard the new *Apollo's Raven*. My captured trihemiola had no name that we could find, and she was so new that her owners hadn't finished fitting her out; her sides weren't covered in pitch yet, for example. So we put the long, decorated board from the *Lydia* at the little break where her standing deck rose above the oar deck, a unique feature to the trihemiola, just at the mainmast. It fitted neatly there, and the oarsmen tended to touch it for luck as they passed.

I kept most of my oarsmen, and I had room for almost twenty marines – that's what those big decks aft of the mainmast are for. So I kept all of mine and added my young cousin Achilles and Briseis' son, Heraklitus. Brasidas said that he was polite and kept to himself, which is high praise from a Spartan.

If I had views on what kind of fleet would send captains like Leukas and Moire home, I kept them to myself.

We met, as a council, one more time before we sailed, and Pausanias announced that we would take Cyprus. He was quite confident that with eighty ships and our marines we could take the Persian capital of the island, a place called Amathus.

I didn't mention that I'd used Amathus as the feint for our raid on Tyre. I did say that I suspected that the city would be on its guard.

We sailed the next day. We didn't attempt anything daring. The Peloponnesian navarchs didn't do a great deal of blue water navigation, so we ran down the coast of Naxos and camped there, and had an easy day in beautiful weather to Ios. Then we had a long day, two hundred stadia and more, going due south into a haze and then rain, and we fetched up on the coast of Crete.

I spent the easy days learning to handle my new ship. She had a tendency to pull hard to port, which made steering very tiring, and she took on water in any kind of sea, which was annoying. I was finding it difficult to love her, with her strange rig and her two big masts, but when we had the wind with us, she handled well enough, pulling off to port. She was better under sail than any trireme I'd ever handled.

But it was exhausting to stand at one of her steering oars, hour after hour, as the whole weight of the ship seemed to want to move her bow to port. And as we crossed to Crete, she took on enough water to cause me serious worry. I wished that I had some old salt like Megakles to hold my hand. Damon looked at the steering oars and the odd wake several times and shook his head.

'Something in the stern, right along the keel,' he said. 'I can't get at it.'

I agreed, after I got soaking wet and filthy in the nice mixture of various foul things you find in a ship's bilge, even a new ship. I got filthy, trying to work my hand into the area that seemed to leak. I swam in the sea for an hour to get clean.

So when the fleet beached east of Knossos, I sent a boat to Cimon saying that I needed a repair. I took my ship into Knossos, or rather, the harbour of Heracles there, a few dozen stadia from the city. I found a shipwright happy enough to take her and we beached her just west of the city. The shipwright dug out a section of the beach with forty slaves and made her a little harbour all of her own, and then pulled her in, stern first. I'd never seen that done before and I was impressed.

In a quarter of an hour, both the hard pull to port and the leak were explained – she had a hand's breadth of wood warped away from her stern. It was almost like sabotage – a piece of wood so bad that it was almost intentional. I smiled to think that somewhere in Ionia, some Greek patriot had set this little trap for the Persian or Phoenician crew.

My shipwright took the whole strake out and replaced it in six hours, using good oak tree nails to pin the whole thing. He commented to me about how differently the ship was constructed.

'Where's she from?' he asked.

I shrugged. 'I took her from the Phoenicians,' I said.

He nodded thoughtfully. 'I wonder if she's from Rhodos,' he said. 'I've heard they're playing around with decked warships. But look here. You know ships, I take it?'

I admitted that I had known as ship or two.

'The timbers are heavier than I'd expect,' he said. 'And she's put together with tree nails like these. Almost as if he'd assembled the frame and then put the planks on, the way you'd build a house.'

Interesting, if not earth-shaking. I filed that away, paid him in stolen gold, and my oarsmen put her back in the water. As soon as I had her out to sea, I could tell that the steering difficulty was gone, and so were the odd pull to port and the leak.

Suddenly she was a sound and weatherly ship, and Damon and I shared a grin – a grin that grew on the Nestors, old and young, and Poseidonos and a dozen other veterans over the next day. After we rejoined the fleet, we re-stowed her hold. She had a hold aft of the mainmast that took more cargo than most triremes, at the loss of about sixteen oarsmen from a proper trireme.

She also had a keel of oak, a single piece of wood that ran from bow to stern and went about a hand's breadth into the water. This was much more keel than a trireme had, and was going to make beaching on gravel a challenge, but it seemed to have miraculous properties when it came to sailing with the wind somewhat abeam.

I picked up a pair of long boats, because if she was going to have to anchor it would have to be far enough out that she wouldn't drag her anchor and run ashore on a breeze.

Pausanias sent me a messenger to tell me that leaving the fleet without his consent was forbidden, and if I did it again he'd treat me as a deserter.

I got in one of my new boats and had myself rowed down the beach to Pausanias' ship, the *Rage of Ares*. I went up the beach, nearly tripping in the soft sand, and found the great man at a big campfire built of driftwood.

I waited courteously, just within his peripheral vision, until he turned.

'Plataean,' he said. That's what he always called me.

'Pausanias,' I said.

'Say your piece,' he said, obviously weary.

'I came to apologise,' I said.

That took the wind out of his mainsail.

'Apologise?' he asked.

'I told Cimon and Aristides that I had to repair my ship. I'm sorry I didn't inform you. We were taking water.' I nodded.

He looked at me, trying to read me. The men of Lacedaemon seldom lie, and they don't expect it in others. Pausanias was sometimes deceptive, however, and I knew he suspected me. I couldn't decide whether to protest my innocence or just stand my ground. If you are wondering why I apologised, try being in a state of near war with your commander for a week or so ...

'Thank you,' he said, with a slight bow of his head. 'I hadn't realised. In future, send such requests directly to me.'

'Yes, sir,' I said.

Listen, I can be a good subordinate. You cannot lead if you cannot follow. I wanted him to see that I wasn't going to try to eat his bread.

'I suppose that I have to offer you a cup of wine,' he said, with a slight smile.

'You don't have to ...'

'And then all of my people will talk to you, Plataean. And they will ask you for stories, and you'll tell them, and they'll all love you.' He glared at me. 'I find it tiresome.'

Learn to tell a good story, I thought.

I also thought that the supreme commander of the Allied Fleet looked a good deal more tired and unhappy than he had any reason to be.

'I'll just go and drink my own wine,' I said.

Pausanias smiled bitterly. 'And I'll be a poor host, and the gods will spit on me. I'll endure your stories, Plataean.'

His helots served me wine, and I found myself standing in the firelight with twenty Spartiates, veterans of Plataea and a dozen other fights.

Spartans are good company, at least if you play by their rules. They are unfailingly polite, and if you can ignore the terrible way they deal with their slaves, they are as fine a group of gentlemen as you'll ever hope to meet. I mean, if you happen to be a bronze-smith, their casual contempt for all the tekne, the craftspeople, may pall after a bit. And their absolute adherence to a set of assertions that may be debatable to others can also be annoying or just dull. There's a tendency among Spartiates to have as much disdain for intellectual pursuits as for craftsmen.

I'm hardly a philosopher, but I'm interested in ideas. Even tactical ideas tend to provoke a Spartan. It's as if they're aware that they live inside a set of bounds that are themselves open to challenge, and they resent them.

Right, so, if you avoid all that contention and don't challenge them on their laws or treatment of slaves or their government …

They're good men.

As I've said before, I'm not impressed by Sparta. I believe that they've come up with a society that sacrifices far too much to get a fairly slim margin of favour in wartime.

And you may well complain that I own slaves, and I'm no better than they. I'm almost positive that this is true in some absolute, moral sense – Heraclitus would agree. But at a pragmatic level, my slaves, and most other slaves in Boeotia, are the chance effects of raids and war and financial collapse, and most of them will be free within their own lives. I've been a slave twice.

What I was not was a racial slave. And the Messenians, the helots, are enslaved by the shapes of their noses and the height of their foreheads. They can never be free. And therein lies the evil. Sparta pretends to be brave, but at the heart of it is a stain of cowardice – they are afraid of their slaves. They maintain that racial slavery by brute force. They have secret police informers and execution squads. Every Spartan boy is taught that the helots are the 'first enemy'. And half the time when the Spartans are supposed to send a contingent, they have to stay home because they fear some uprising. They make up great stories about religion to cover their fear of their slaves, but at the heart of it …

All of this is directly relevant to the story I'm telling, but on that night, at that campfire, it was relevant because while I'm fond of particular Spartans like Sparthius, I'm very much on edge with groups of them.

Sparthius came up to me and introduced me around, but half the men present knew me from the days before the fight at Plataea. Diokles, a big man who'd been in my mess group for a while, came up and took my hand.

'This old man repaired my greave for me,' he said. 'Just to prove that he was not only a better fighter, but also better at being humble.'

The Spartans all laughed.

'And then you all outran me,' I said.

Pausanias smiled. I'm not sure that, until then, I'd ever seen him smile, except in the moments after the victory at Plataea, in Mardonius' tent, where he'd grinned like an Olympic victor.

'Were you competing to be humble, Plataean?' he asked. 'It sounds like you.'

Sparthius laughed. 'Bulis called him on it, and he stopped being an arse.'

'He did, too,' I said. 'And yet, I really did fix Diokles' greave.'

They all laughed as if I'd said something really funny.

Conversation became more general, and the Spartans were discussing omens, seers, and Pausanias' request for a *mantis*. They were discussing the performance of their seer at Plataea and wondering if the fleet could find a mantis as effective.

I didn't enter in. I had nothing useful to add. I have certainly seen remarkable things from seers – I was learning from Aristides to perform the rites and read the entrails myself. And yet, even though I'd seen Teisemenos in action, seen his reading of entrails and other signs and listened to his almost magical appreciation of the complexities of the real world and the dream world, I still felt in my heart that Plataea was won by small farmers with spears, crouching behind their aspides and refusing to run. Perhaps because of Heraclitus, I was unhappy with the idea that events in the world were preordained and all that implied. Perhaps I was just too practical to be a priest.

Spartans are very religious – almost fatalistic. And they do like a good seer.

Euryanax, Pausanias' cousin and one of his senior officers, wanted the great seer Teisemenos sent for.

And in stating this aloud, Euryanax exposed the rift in the heart of the Spartan force. All I had to do was listen. Sparthius tried to amuse me, to limit my ability to hear what was, in effect, a family quarrel, but I can listen to two things at once. Anyone who's ever been a slave learns to do this.

Euryanax wanted the best battle-seer in the world to come out to Cyprus, because Euryanax wanted to win victories and defeat Persians. It was clear from his whole demeanour that he took this seriously.

But there was another man, a senior Spartiate, a little older than me, named Telekos – another cousin of the kings, and a Eurypontid, I believe. If you want an examination of the Spartan royal houses, bring more wine – it's not simple. There are two houses, the Agiads and the Eurypontids, named after two descendants of Heracles, my own ancestor. Leonidas and Pausanias were both Agiads. Demaratus, who we met in Persia, and Leotychidas, who commanded the fleet with Xanthippus of Athens at Mycale, were Eurypontids.

Got all that?

Telekos belittled Euryanax.

'Aren't you tired of pouring out Sparta's treasury for these useless Ionians?' he asked. 'Thieves and liars. And the Athenians are as Ionian as the Lesbians or the Chians. If we can't enslave them all, let's leave them to rot.'

Euryanax shrugged. 'Why?' he asked.

'The Great King is not now, and never has been, any threat to Sparta!' Telekos said with great authority. 'If Leonidas had not flouted the legal requirements of the ephors, none of this would ever have happened. We don't need a battle-seer. We only need to sail up and down, doing nothing, until the Athenians lose interest in war and return to trade, their natural condition.'

'How are you dealing with your son?' Sparthius asked. He meant Heraklitus. He was trying to distract me.

'So far, he's just another marine,' I said cheerfully.

The cheer was a lie. It wasn't that simple, and we both knew it. Heraklitus and I were wandering towards a collision. I'd guessed that he'd guessed that he was my son. Like a man aware that his beautiful wife may be sleeping with his best friend, he was not really interested in facing that reality, and he was avoiding it. Also, like that same man with the beautiful wife, he couldn't leave it alone.

I loved Sparthius, and I wanted to talk with him because I didn't like the changes I'd seen in him since the death of Bulis. He was withdrawn, cautious, closed.

But I was interested to hear this Telekos, because I felt as if I was listening to the Spartan ephors themselves. I'd met them, remember. Six deadly old men.

Euryanax was speaking even as Sparthius asked about my son. I didn't catch it all, but I caught when he said, 'What is excellent! Don't you want to go spear to spear with the Great King's best? We were bred like good hunting dogs for this contest.'

'We are helping Athens to achieve an empire,' Telekos said. 'We are dying so that their lowest class can rule the future of Greece and free our helots.'

That got a stir out of everyone at the fire. As I've said, just mention freeing the helots and they all become automatons.

Euryanax was a good soldier, but he was also a good thinker. He smiled, raised an eyebrow, and raised his wine cup.

'It's always a kill shot, claiming someone will try to free the helots,' he said. 'But what I think you fear, Telekos, is the constant work of gaining and then ruling a spear-won empire. It would imply change. But despite what the ephors like to say, Lacedaemon has changed before and it will change again. The rules of the Olympics change. The rules of the agoge change. War with Persia will change the way we conduct war. We can rule the change, or we can be ruled by it. And when you speak of the little men of Athens, do you mean Themistocles? Aristides? Cimon? They are men the way we are men.'

'No,' Telekos said. 'We are Spartiates and they are not. There is no comparison. We are strongest and best. Let them obey us.'

'Telekos, if we followed your path, the world would forget that Sparta even existed.' Euryanax drank off his wine.

Telekos shrugged. 'I would be happy to return to Lacedaemon and forget that the world exists, in revenge. I don't need so much as one olive from outside.'

'And yet, don't you think that in a few years, someone with a large army and a new innovation might come and take us?' Euryanax asked.

Telekos smiled as if he'd gained the upper hand. 'Even if that did happen, which I doubt, it would be preferable to helping Athens build the engine of our destruction. And even if we fall, we'd fall as Lacedaemon, not some bastard thing.'

I smiled. Sparthius had become caught up in the debate and had stopped trying to distract me. Telekos saw my smile and resented it. Truly, I've got into more trouble smiling than frowning.

'You find us funny, foreigner?' he asked.

'Yes,' I said, earning no friends.

Pausanias, of all men, came to my aid.

'That is no tone to take with a guest,' he said. 'And Arimnestos is behaving like any man would, watching his host have a fight with his spouse.'

He looked at me. And I met his eyes and smiled a different smile – a sort of 'if you would have it so, I'll play along' smile.

Telekos was not feeling obedient.

'I insist on knowing why this foreigner finds me funny,' he said.

'Walk away,' said Sparthius. 'I'll calm him.'

I spread my hands, and then raised one, in the manner of Greek orators.

'You debate like Athenians,' I said. 'You speak of lofty ideals, both of you – of things that would be estimable, whether you choose to go home, or to conquer the Great King.'

Well, that's not what they expected.

'But it seems to me that the truth is that you men of Lacedaemon have chosen to move on Cyprus because it aids your allies and colonies in Crete. It does nothing to liberate the Ionians, because you fear that they will be allies of Athens. You are here because Athens rebuilt their walls. So that while you debate two ideals, in fact, you perform a convenient fiction. Like any Greek.'

Silence.

Pausanias turned, and his eyes tried to bore holes in my head.

'Are you saying we lie?' he asked.

I shrugged. 'The Persians – the real Persians – never lie. They don't even prevaricate. They speak the truth. And they say, "All Greeks are liars."' I paused, considering what I was about to say, but the daemon was on me, or Athena had had enough of Pausanias and was whispering in my ear. 'They don't say, "All the Greeks lie except the men of Sparta."'

Sparthius frowned.

But damn him, Pausanias smiled.

'You see far, Plataean,' he said. 'And you are more like us than you admit to yourself.'

Euryanax turned towards me, and his face was as red in the fire-light as his cloak by day.

'You think we are here only for self-interest?' he spat. 'You should hear what some proposed we do!'

'Hush,' Pausanias said. 'Keep home arguments at home.'

Curiously, when I stepped out of the firelight, it was Telekos who followed me.

'Foreigner,' he said.

I turned, ready to fight.

He was just a shape against the firelight.

'I like your blunt talk,' he said. 'And I think we are allies, not enemies. It is the lying that I hate, not the . . . ' He moved a hand. 'If they get their way, and we gain a spear-won empire, we will not be ourselves. Look – they are ready to lie and scheme already, and we have not landed a hoplite on Cyprus.'

Honestly, I didn't know what to say. I still don't. They are complex men, like any men, the Spartiates.

Have you ever been in a heated argument, and realised full well that there was honour to the other side, as well as your own? *Of course* Telekos had a point. He was right ... and wrong.

Later, at my own beach fire, I told the whole tale to Brasidas.

He drank off some wine and stared into the embers of the fire.

'I think that you are asking me, as a Spartan, to explain,' he said.

'Perhaps,' I said. 'Or perhaps I just needed to tell it out – to play it again, like a good hymn heard at the temple that you whistle on your way home.'

'I'd prefer the latter,' he said. 'Because I'm not a Spartan any more. I am a man of Plataea.'

'Of course,' I said, fearing I'd offended him.

He touched my arm. 'No, listen. You know that the Plataean phalanx is no match for a Spartan phalanx?'

'Yes,' I said, and perhaps I bit it off. I am a proud Plataean. I don't like to concede second place.

He nodded. 'I thought that was the measure of a man – of a system. The better man can kill the worse.'

I nodded. Brasidas was suddenly fluent.

'But this is what makes me a Plataean ...' He paused, and glanced at me. 'I don't believe that any more. I believe that many men are of great value. Perhaps some are better, but treating them as if they are better makes for jealousy and bad feeling. And the wagon-maker and the bronze-smith are men of worth. The great warrior is only in his place on the battlefield because of the bronze-smith and the wagon-maker. Yes, Plataea has a few worthless sods, but let us be honest – there are worthless sods even in a Spartiate mess group, just not as many. I would *rather* live in Plataea. So when you relate to me a debate among Spartiates, men of the royal families ...' He shrugged. 'They sound to me like privileged foreigners debating an unreal world. I am painfully aware that my former motherland almost failed to come to fight at Plataea. Such selfishness ...'

He got up – greatly moved.

'I'm ...' I started to say, and he was walking. He went about twenty paces and stopped and looked up at the blanket of stars ...

Leander, one of my new marines, had been listening quietly. He looked up.

'I've never heard him say so many words all together,' he said.

Brasidas was still within earshot.

I nodded.

'It's an effect of Plataean citizenship,' I said. 'We're all pretty talkative.'

The next morning we put to sea and formed in four big squadrons. Like the good Plataean I am, I followed the Athenians. I found myself arrayed in Aristides' squadron, and we rowed across the wind in a fairly neat line and watched the Corinthians and the Hermionians and the ships crewed out of Lacedaemon itself struggle to maintain formation in a crosswind.

We rowed as far as Carpathus, completing a giant circle for me and for Cimon and Lykon and a handful of others, and landed there. The next day we took a different and much less daring route, rowing north-east to Rhodos and then coasting Asia. landing on empty beaches and eating our sparse supplies because we had no round ships to support us. When we were off the coast of Pamphylia, the Athenians decided to launch a raid – we were, after all, at war with the Great King. We landed near Sise and pillaged a fortified town, took anything worth taking and burnt the place. The Spartans affected to find us all barbarous, but they ate the sheep we provided them fast enough.

Ever wonder why almost every good-sized town on the Inner Sea is set five or six stadia back from the water?

Bastards like me, that's why. Never be close enough to the sea that someone in a black ship can land before you can call out your militia.

We had to row again the next day. My oarsmen were loud in condemning the lubberly fools who made them row all day instead of sailing across the blue water, and they were happy to tell all the other oarsmen on the cold beach at night how they'd *just done this* but better and faster.

I didn't tell them to hold their tongues. Why would I? We were fighting a war at sea like Spartans – with cautious approaches and limited knowledge of navigation.

To Cimon's immense disgust, Pausanias didn't even attempt to prevent the Lycian coasters from running down to Cyprus to warn them. Any guilt I might have felt for my threats against Amathus was dispelled by the knowledge that most of the fishing fleet of Sise had gone to warn the Great King's officers that there was a Greek fleet on the way.

And that's why, when we arrived off Amathus a week later after some of the slowest rowing in Greek history, I was unsurprised to see the gates shut in our faces and a strong garrison on the walls. Pausanias summoned the place to surrender and got a snappy reply from the governor, to the effect that we were all rebels against the justice of the Great King and if we'd surrender to him, he'd see to it that the King of Kings was merciful.

There was worse to come.

We built camps on the beach with the usual banter about being the Greeks at Troy. Some of the camp was built too close to the waterline, with the expected results. Our second day in the camp, the wind blew off Africa to the south, with sand and heat and bigger waves ...

And we had to build a new camp. There was grumbling. There was more grumbling when we found that the Great King's soldiers, most of whom were Aegyptian, had filled in one of our wells during the night because the Peloponnesians hadn't set a good enough watch. Reduced to just one water source, we seemed fine for a day ...

I've done all this before. I knew we were in trouble as soon as I knew we had only one well. I took my new ship, tentatively called the *Apollo's Raven* even though I've never had much time for the God of the Lyre and the Golden Bow, and I ran down the coast to Kourion and loaded my bilges with sealed amphorae of water. I may have loaded twenty or thirty big jars of wine, too.

About three hours each way.

I returned to the scene I'd expected. Because what happens in the first day when there's not enough water is that most men don't know they haven't had enough water. They grow angry, and then they grow tired. And then, sometimes, they grow even angrier.

We – and I mean the Athenians here – were closest to the well. Cimon's marines had found it when we landed, and secured it – about three stadia in front of us. We'd extended our camp in that direction and we had a guard of marines on it at all times.

That meant that the Peloponnesian oarsmen were walking six or seven stadia to get a drink of water. Most of them had canteens, but not all. Sailors are used to having two hundred amphorae of clean, fresh water in the hold, available to all.

I landed, shared out some fresh water with my division, and saw the swirl of a handful of scarlet cloaks coming along the beach. I knew it was Pausanias, and I knew he was angry.

Aristides came out of his awning at the edge of the palisade. Most of the Athenians were veterans of a dozen sea campaigns. They used the mainsails of their ships as big communal tents and the boat sail, the smaller one, as the officer's tents, both run over spare spars. The Athenians had cooking stoves and charcoal.

Some of the Peloponnesians did, too. But not all.

Pausanias walked right up to me. He had a staff in his hand. I was vaguely aware that it was a symbol of his authority, given by the ephors, the six old men who wanted to pretend that they, and not the kings, controlled Sparta.

I should have thought that one through. It's like a cunning riddle someone tells in a taverna after the oil lamps go out. I had all the clues and I wasn't seeing it.

'When we spoke the other night,' he said, his voice tight, 'did you imagine because I guested you at my fire that you could then flout my authority?'

'No,' I said. I think I even added, 'Sir.'

He nodded. 'I have the right to order you seized and beaten,' he said. 'You have disobeyed a direct order.'

'Shall we do this in private?' I asked.

'No, Plataean,' he said. 'I think it's time you learnt who is commander here.'

I nodded. 'I'm aware that you are the commander,' I said, keeping my temper firmly in check.

Aristides was coming. He'd save me. Or save Pausanias.

'But you disobeyed my direct order not to leave the fleet without my permission.'

'I didn't leave the fleet,' I said. 'Sir.' I looked around. No Sparthius – not even Telekos or Euryanax. Not one Spartiate I knew. And they did look like they meant to take me and beat me.

'You rowed away!' he said, his temper slipping.

'I went down the coast for water,' I said. 'And I came back. My hold is full of fresh water.'

'You disobeyed!'

'No,' I said, 'I used my own initiative to do something you should have known to do yourself.'

'So now you shout my failure—'

'I asked you to do this in private,' I said.

145

He nodded. 'Very well. Seize him.'

Aristides said, 'That would be a terrible mistake.'

Pausanias was in control of himself, I'll give him that. He turned to the Athenian commander.

'This is not a public assembly,' he said. 'Nor are you involved in any way. Good day to you, Aristides.'

Aristides the Just could be a prig – he was an uncommonly difficult man at times. But he was as stubborn as a mule when it came to justice.

'This man is under my command,' he said. 'You cannot punish him without my permission. And honestly, Pausanias, if you punish a trierarch for fetching water, when you didn't punish the Peloponnesian marines for sleeping on watch—'

'They weren't Spartans,' Pausanias said, and then shook his head. Better men than Pausanias have been tricked into debate by Aristides' tone. He's a master at making you debate when you hadn't planned to discuss anything. 'That makes no difference. The Plataean disobeyed me—'

'I didn't,' I said.

'. . . and I'll see him punished.'

By then, Brasidas and all of my marines were gathering a spear's length away.

Cimon's marines were coming down the beach.

This was going to be ugly.

Let's pause for a moment, here on the edge of violence, and ask, why is Pausanias being like this? At his campfire the other night, he was . . . very like a good commander.

I don't have an answer. I'm just telling the story.

Aristides took a step forward, placing himself between me and Pausanias.

'You cannot legally punish this man,' he said. 'You have to ask me to punish him.'

Because I was very close, I heard what he said. He said, 'By Zeus, father of gods, don't misplay this, Pausanias. Leave it to me.'

Zeus, father of gods. Zeus, to whom kings and tyrants and all those in authority pray for good decisions.

Pausanias was losing his hard-won control of his anger. His mouth was twitching, and his grasp on his *skutali*, his staff of authority, had become a death grip.

But like a brave man fighting a tide of enemies, he didn't surrender to his temper.

Nor did he glance at Cimon's marines or mine.

He straightened, and tossed a salute with his staff.

'Very well, Navarch. See to it.' He turned and began to stride away.

Aristides turned to me. 'You are dismissed from the fleet,' he said, his voice level.

I choked. Anger rose to blind me – rage. The indignity. The unfairness. The blemish on my reputation.

On the other hand, that other part of me – the part that is a commander, that reasons, that loves Heraclitus – that part flew above my rage, measuring. Admiring Pausanias a little, because he'd found a middle way and not broken his fleet in two.

Had I disobeyed? I'd never intended any such thing.

Had I intended to make Pausanias look bad?

Well. There you have it, friends. I had. And that's bad for discipline, isn't it?

All that in the blink of an eye, and still the irrational rage choked me like the black dust of death.

Cimon, close by me, said, 'Aristides, if he goes, I go!'

I turned on him, and unfairly, perhaps, vented my rage.

'Don't be an arse!' I spat. And then, with more control, 'Don't make this worse than it already is.'

Cimon couldn't have looked more shocked if I'd bitten him.

He actually stepped back, as if I'd landed a blow.

'I'll go,' I said. I turned to Brasidas. 'Summon all hands. Load the ship.'

Men began to edge away.

My oarsmen were muttering.

'Stow it!' I roared. 'Pick up your cushions and your sea bags. We sail in two hours.'

Aristides made a beckoning sign and walked off down the beach towards his tent. I made sure my armour was back aboard, and then walked out through the gentle surf around the bow of my ship, the way any captain does, looking for damage. I used the time to calm myself.

Then I made my way along the seashore, five ships, to Aristides' new ship, the *Athena Promachos*. I walked up the sand and found Cimon and Aristides alone.

'I had to,' Aristides said.

'I know,' I said. 'Cimon, I'm sorry.'

Cimon looked at me for a moment and then handed me a small cup of wine.

'Apology accepted,' he said tersely.

'Why before all the gods did you not ask us?' Aristides asked me. 'Ask me? Ask Pausanias?'

I nodded and looked at my sandals. 'I find him overbearing, and I wanted him to see what a real commander would do,' I said.

'You wanted to rub his nose in it,' Cimon said, nodding. 'He's impossible.'

'He's not impossible,' Aristides said. 'He's here under conflicting orders and he's never conducted a sea campaign. And he doesn't trust us, and we're the only people who know how to fight at sea or conduct a siege.'

'Conflicting orders?' Cimon asked.

'It's a low fence to clear, if Athenians are judged the masters of sieges,' I said.

I thought of the Persian siege mound at Miletus.

I was all about offending people that day.

'Be that as it may,' Aristides said, 'we've conducted more sieges than Pausanias.'

'Conflicting orders?' Cimon asked again, a little louder. He was still angry. I couldn't blame him.

Aristides swirled the wine in his cup.

I shrugged. 'I think the ephors want Sparta out of the war altogether, and the kings want glory,' I said.

Cimon nodded. 'I see.'

Aristides set his jaw, looked out to sea, opened his mouth to speak, closed it, swirled his wine, and looked at me.

'Speak your mind,' I said. 'I'm the one leaving in disgrace, not you.'

'I'll have you back in a month. Two weeks, if you insist.' Aristides was gentle. A good man and a good friend.

I nodded. 'Aristides, I acknowledge that I was in the wrong,' I said. 'Thanks for getting me out of it. If he'd beaten me, men would have died.'

Aristides looked away, and swirled his wine. 'I considered letting it happen,' he said. 'For everyone's good.'

Cimon went red.

I hadn't sat down. But I stiffened in shock.

'What?'

'It would have been the end of Pausanias' command,' Aristides said. 'I suspect that in a few days, the Lacedaemonians would have gone home. Absolutely the best course for everyone concerned.'

'Because we'd have control of the siege?' Cimon asked.

Aristides looked out to sea again. 'That, and other things,' he said. 'But . . .'

I understood Aristides. 'But that would have been morally wrong,' I said. 'And innocent men would have died.'

'Yes,' he said.

'Like Pausanias,' I said.

He nodded slowly. 'Yes,' he said.

I took a deep breath. 'How do you feel about me sailing for Ionia?' I asked.

Aristides drank some wine. And finally, his eyes met mine.

'I will not ask or tell you to go to Ionia,' he said. 'But I might privately pray to the gods that you go to Ionia. I might wonder if it was time for your wife to go to her native country.'

Cimon raised his chin, a man taking in a great many things in one moment.

'Oh,' he said. 'Zeus, Aristides. You are playing a dangerous game, for a man called "the Just".'

'We're playing some serious games here,' I said, a little bitter. 'All of us.'

Aristides nodded. 'Just because they are foolish, do not think they are not deadly,' he said. 'Sparta has deeply divided councils and some evil councillors. But Sparta is not . . . unique . . . in that respect.'

I pressed him, but he drank off his wine.

'You should get to sea,' he said. 'It grows dark. Here are my dispatches for the Assembly, and this for the Boule.'

I walked a stade with Cimon.

'I'm missing something,' he said.

'As am I,' I said. 'There's a . . . malevolence here that I don't understand.'

Cimon met my eyes. 'Exactly.' He looked away. 'Damn it! I like the Spartans.'

I shrugged, because mostly I didn't, but I'd spent enough time making an arse of myself and offending my friends. So instead of railing against Sparta, I said, 'I'll be gone a while, I expect. Don't get killed. I'm sorry I bit at you.'

'Just don't do it again,' he said, more like his father than was quite right. 'None of us like to look bad in front of the boys, eh?'

I nodded. It was true – a sad truth of command. Was that Pausanias' problem? That he feared 'looking bad' too much?

Cimon looked at me, his jaw set – still a little angry.

'What does Aristides think you are going to do in Ionia?' he asked.

I looked back, where Aristides the Just stood alone at the bow of his ship, making his evening prayer.

'Rally it,' I said. 'For Athens.'

Cimon looked at me. And then back at Aristides.

'Fuck,' he said. 'So this is it. I should be with you.'

I clasped his hand. 'Nope,' I said. 'You should be here, looking innocent.'

That made him smile. I thanked the gods.

We sailed after sunset but while there was still light in the sky – another old pirate tactic. I wasn't after prey, however. I just ghosted along the coast of Cyprus, heading west, rounded the great headland of Akrotiri, and landed on the first good beach for the night.

I spent a good deal of time thinking about what Aristides was hiding. He was a terrible liar – a man almost honest enough to be a Persian.

So he really only lied by omission.

He knew – or thought he knew – something bad.

And he clearly felt sorry for Pausanias. Pity, even ... pity for the heroic, victorious royal regent of the mightiest military state in Greece. Honestly? I understood. When Pausanias wasn't being a fool or a tyrant, he seemed like an excellent man.

I fell asleep and dreamt of Briseis shrieking at me. Not a pretty dream. She turned into a bear and ran.

I used to have that dream ... Briseis and I have been separated many times, and I fear ... I fear ...

I feared that she would leave me. Even then, I still feared it. I had taken the queen of Ionia and made her a farm wife in Boeotia. And now Aristides wanted me to take her back to her kingdom. I lay under my cloak, tossing and turning on the surprisingly cool sand, and I thought about my son Heraklitus, about Briseis, about Ionia. About Sappho's school, and all those women who were patriots for an idea that had never really been a country – Ionia. And Archilogos.

Eventually I fell asleep.

The next day we sailed into Kourion and I purchased stores. I paid out twenty drachmas a man, most of the silver I had aboard that wasn't loot, and let the oarsmen and sailors and marines have a night on shore. They were angry and felt that I'd been abused – fair. But they would have a hard time holding on to ill usage while they did whatever men do with a pocket full of silver in a dockside.

So we had some hard heads and probably some red faces when we rowed away on the dawn breeze the next morning. A young oarsman had a woman's scarf wrapped around his loins and no other clothing, and was much mocked, but as I pointed out, he'd probably had more fun than most. His name was Kephalos, and he did indeed have a big head.

I sweated the wine out of them for two hours, and I pointed the bow north and west and raised first the boat sail and then the mainsail. I was learning the rig on my new ship, and I spent most of the next two days and nights on deck, taking the steering oars as often as I wanted, watching the clouds over Asia, and learning how the *Apollo's Raven* behaved under sail. She'd been a bit of a pig under oars. The upper decking weighed more than a trireme's superstructure, and we had about twenty fewer oarsmen to push the extra weight through the water. My old *Lydia* had been the same type of ship – a trihemiola – but she'd been built of lighter wood and she hadn't been fully decked. This ship took some getting used to, and she wasn't going to be the fastest under oars. On the other hand, we had almost double the marines of a trireme, and six archers. And we could always make sail.

'I think we need new tactics,' I said to Brasidas.

He nodded thoughtfully. 'Boarding, rather than ramming,' he said.

'A true ship-splitting ram could bring down the mainmast,' I said. 'And that might sink us.'

So we discussed possibilities – oar strikes with the ram to force another ship to turn. We still wanted to strike bow first, amidships, so that our marines could go in cleanly. With Brasidas and sixteen marines, much less our armed sailors, we should be more than a match for any ship on the seas.

When we rowed, which we did every day, Poseidonos drilled his oarsmen on all of the basics and some special manoeuvres: getting their oars in and out in perfect unison, as fast as one of Father Zeus's thunderbolts; dipping all together on the first stroke, not the third

– even very good ships sometimes struggled with the first strokes, and lost valuable time that way; switching directions, so that an oarsmen raised his oar, ducked under it, and sat on the opposite side, pulling backwards. It was a dangerous manoeuvre, because a man could get an oar in the head or in the gut and take a real injury, even be killed, and almost certainly end up with broken ribs.

Three days to Rhodos, and scarcely a grumble for being out in the Great Green so long. We made a pier-side landing at Rhodos, and I bought provisions and again gave my people a night.

I sat alone in a good place, with white walls and slaves who weren't beaten, drinking a good wine and thinking about my wife and Ionia and Pausanias and Sparta and Aristides ...

And there was Heraklitus. Not in my thoughts – I mean, standing right in front of me.

'Trierarch,' he said formally.

I made myself smile. '*Here we go*,' I thought.

'Please sit down,' I said.

He looked at the seat. He was wearing a very good chiton, such as only Ionians wear now, embroidered with flowers and acanthus leaves, with a double-woven hem. He was tall and strong and I found him a little dull.

I thought he was going to refuse to sit, but then he did so with a touch of adolescent gawkiness. A slave came over, smiled a slave's smile, and offered him wine, which he accepted.

'Are you my father?' he blurted.

I drank some of my wine, thinking of Aristides swirling his wine in his cup. Understanding that he knew something that he *didn't want to be true*.

'Yes,' I said.

Some things you say vanish into the wind and are never heard again.

Some things, once said, are set in stone – a road taken, a die cast. They echo down the years and carry a weight of consequence.

We sat in silence for a threatening length of time.

'Drink your wine,' I said.

He looked away and then back at me.

'You never ...'

I sat back. 'I never anything,' I said. 'I was in the middle of a ship fight in Carthage when your mother told me. You were already an ephebe, a soldier for the Great King. Why would I come and present myself to you?'

'And my mother?' he asked. His anger was revealed.

'What about your mother?' I asked.

'Whoring her way to power with any man who had a strong spear-arm?' he asked.

I thought of fetching him a slap, but didn't. Instead, I tilted my head to one side. And pointed at the slave girl who had attended us.

'You think she's available?' I asked.

Heraklitus looked shocked. 'She's ...'

'She's a slave in a dockside tavern,' I said. 'Can we agree that we could both buy her if we wanted to?'

He blinked. I think I shocked him – good old Arimnestos, corrupter of the youth.

'Yes,' he croaked. And then, stronger, 'I don't want to.'

I laughed. 'Not my point. Does she have any choice about who she lies down with?'

'She's a slave,' my son said.

I have learnt a thing or two since I was his age.

I swirled my wine and drank some.

'You mean my mother didn't choose her partners.' He bit off each word.

I shrugged. 'I think your mother chose a great deal. She used the weapons that came to hand. She used them well. And because she used them well, I'm going to put her back on the throne of Ionia.'

'Ionia doesn't have a throne,' he said, as cocky as someone I remembered.

'It will, when Briseis sits in it,' I said.

He looked at the slave girl. And back at me.

'I don't know you,' he said. 'Why did you disobey the Spartan general? Why did you let him punish you? Why did we run away?'

I poured more wine and inhaled the good resin smell of the torches around us.

'I was wrong,' I said. 'I should have asked permission to go and get water. I could explain more, but I'd only be telling you what a fool your father can be.'

'But you are the great killer! And you *let* yourself be humiliated.'

I nodded slowly. 'If I'd made a fight of it ... if I'd killed Pausanias, let's say ... how many men would have died on that beach? Good, brave men, dedicated to fighting the Persians?'

He didn't look impressed. 'It stuck in my gullet to see you humiliated.'

I pointed at the girl. She was mostly naked – or rather, she wore a chitoniskos that covered her genitals and was open at the sides. On the other hand, she was clean and neat and had some dignity. I waved her over and ordered another pitcher of wine. She smiled her slave's smile. I gave her a silver four-drachma piece for her own, and the smile got real.

She walked away.

'Tell me, Heraklitus,' I said. 'Does she know I was humiliated?'

He made a face. 'No,' he said. 'That's stupid. How would she know?'

'Hmm,' I said. 'Really, how would anyone know? I mean, I'll be honest. I was enraged. My rage lasted a little less than an hour. Sometime in the next three weeks, someone will do something as stupid, or even stupider, and no one will remember what happened to me. In two months it will be a matter for humour. In a year, Cimon will tell a story about it. In two years, I'll tell a story about it. Rage is pretty worthless, and humiliation is something we feel, not something tangible that happens.'

He nodded, but he nodded like a young man being told something he absolutely does not believe.

'You sound old and wise,' he said.

' I learnt it from Heraclitus,' I said.

'Mater's teacher,' he said.

'My teacher,' I said.

'Did she sleep with him, too?' he asked. He shook his head. 'No, no, I won't make a scene. But you tolerate her, and I had to grow to manhood with men … men …' He looked away, and I could tell he was blushing. 'She never behaved like other women. She never hid herself away, she never shied from public notice, she never mourned …'

I began to understand the size of the boil I had to lance. Interesting, how we think we're the centre of the universe. I'd thought that my son would either need me or hate me – it was going to be about me.

It wasn't about me at all. He had no problem, in his head, with being the son of a famous pirate and killer.

His problem was Briseis. He didn't understand his mother.

Well, that gave us something in common. And later … when I lay down to sleep, I suddenly wondered if my own mother had a story of her own. And why my father hadn't been much at telling it.

That was a new thought. I didn't like it much.

I walked Heraklitus back to the ship and I slept like a young child. In the morning we were away, rowing into the wind one day and sailing other days. We landed on tiny Astypalaia and then we crossed to Naxos. I'd made my decision. I left a note for Ephialtes, and sent a long, carefully written apology to Archilogos by means of a merchant bound for Ephesus.

I went back to sea, racing for Athens.

I dropped Aristides' dispatches in Athens after a mere nine days at sea and took his letter to Jocasta with my own hands. I introduced my young marine. Jocasta gave me one glance and raised an eyebrow a fraction, which I took to mean that she could count years and also knew who Heraklitus resembled.

And then I borrowed two of the great Cimon's horses and rode for Plataea as if the Furies were behind me.

Somewhere in the starlit skies of the Aegean I'd made my choice. Briseis was not a bird to be caged. She was going back to Ionia, because she could rally people who wouldn't even speak to me. And on another level, because she wanted it, and there was no reason she shouldn't have her way. I suppose what I'd realised on the beach or shortly after was that all of this new, second Ionian revolt was tied to my fear that I'd lose Briseis to her other life, and ... and ...

Perhaps Heraklitus untied my knot when he presented his own.

I shook my head and let it go. Pure selfishness, really.

I rode over the path to Erythres, thinking old thoughts. It always made me happy to go home. I loved the moment when I reached the height of the pass and I could see into Boeotia.

'Where are we going?' my son asked.

I'd halted my horse and dismounted for the last, steepest climb, and now I was standing where we'd found the dead slave boy, all those years before. I could see the cart ruts, and the deep cuts in the stone where the ancients had made lanes for their chariots, or so the priests said.

That was the day I'd met Tiraeus, now a prosperous smith with his own forge. So in a way, that boy hadn't died in vain. Or maybe that's a false argument.

'We're going to the family altar,' I said. 'We're going to talk to the gods.'

High on Cithaeron, just below the peak, there's an ash altar. It's very old, and underneath it, if you are a busy adolescent with nothing better to do than dig in ash, you can find a big stone. It's not worked stone, but an uncut rock the size of a boat. And someone has carved letters into it. They are the old letters, the way they were made in my great-grandfather's time.

It says Cithaeron.

Heraclitus – my teacher, not my son – used to discourse on origins. Indeed, he was a great examiner of origins, and he might have been held to be a great blasphemer, because he was suspicious of the origins of the gods, or at least the stories we tell about those origins. He noted, for example, that the mighty Artemis of Ephesus was almost a completely different goddess from the Thracian Artemis, the gentler Ionian Artemis, the darker and more complicated Attic goddess. And he posited that there were very different worships, once, and that as the peoples spread over the earth their understandings of the goddess changed. And those changes interested him extremely.

I am now a better travelled man than Heraclitus, and I admit that his theory still seems sound to me. The farther I travel, the more points of view I see and hear ...

Never mind. I wander off my course again. What I mean is that I suspect that my ancestors worshipped the god of the mountain, not Zeus on Olympus. They'd never been to Olympus. Why would they know or care? They had their own mighty mountain with its own mighty storms and lightning bolts, their own legends and tales.

That's what I think.

And sometimes, in my mind, I still pray to old Cithaeron. Because Zeus seems a little high and mighty for me, but my mountain is where I have hunted deer, played, eaten and drunk wine, killed outlaws and made love to my wife. Few sights on this earth move me like the bold outline of Cithaeron rising before me.

And that ash altar is my family's altar. We are descendents of Heracles, sure, but I've never been a priest of Heracles and I wouldn't start now. I have progressed through all the mysteries of the priesthood of Hephaestus, because I was born and bred a bronze-smith, not an archon, and Hermes and Hephaestus are the only gods that make working men priests.

Honestly, if I could pick and choose my gods, I'm very partial to Artemis. I feel she's touched my life over and over again. I was healed and saved from degradation by priests of Artemis in Asia as a boy.

I was educated as a philosopher in the portico of her temple. The priestesses of Brauron were, I think, the salvation of all the people trapped on Salamis, with their observances, their dances, and their insistence that we might survive. They kept the idea of 'Athens' alive in her darkest hour.

And of course, Artemis is my daughter's goddess. She went to Brauron. She danced the dances and was a 'little bear'. Now, because she has been reared as an aristocrat, she will probably grow to be a priestess, which would please my drunken aristocratic mother more than any of you can imagine.

Apollo has touched my life, too, but I've always been suspicious of the God of the Golden Lyre and of rhetoric and poetry. I suspect he's as twisted as Hermes. And he hasn't really done me a great many favours, but then, why would any god do a man favours? Eh?

Right. The story. My point is, our altar – the family altar – is to Cithaeron. I've made sacrifice there to Zeus and other gods – it's an open-air altar, and at least in Boeotia that means you can direct your sacrifice as you will. But it's Cithaeron. And it's ours.

Of course, my son had never seen it. And to be fair, he didn't seem too impressed, but then, why would a gentleman from Ephesus be impressed by a pile of rocks and rain-swept ash in the woods at the top of a wild mountain?

I was moved just standing there. Little things stood out to me, things that told me of the passage of time. I could see the little shelter that Leukas and I had run up, the night before we went to the Greek army at Plataea. The roof of pine branches and leaves had survived the winter surprisingly well.

I could see where I'd lit a larger fire, that night, and spoken to all of my dead, asking their forgiveness.

I could see signs of other visits. I had been at war with my cousins for some time, but the great battle had finished the process of reunification. The jeweller polishes stones by turning them in a drum of other stones – that's my family.

I built a small fire.

'Do you hunt?' I asked my son.

'Anything,' he replied in a tone that didn't prove he was very good at hunting.

'Do you think you could get us two rabbits?' I asked.

'I'll kill a deer!' he said.

'We don't need a deer,' I said. 'And I'm not going to spend two days with no good water while I dry deer meat. No waste. Kill some rabbits.'

He nodded and ran off with his spear. The fact that he neither stripped naked nor left his spear behind didn't suggest that he'd caught a lot of rabbits in his time, but youth makes its own way.

I prayed a little, sang a hymn, and laid a fire. Then I propped up the sagging structure Leukas and I had built, and, as Heraklitus wasn't back, I took my horse and rode down to the spring and filled our canteens. I bathed, to be clean for the god, and it was damn cold.

When I returned, he hadn't. So I picketed the horses against the coming of night – there are wolves on the mountain. I got them enough fodder to keep them happy. The Corvaxae haven't usually been so prosperous as to ride horses to the summit, and there wasn't much grass except close to the campsite and the altar, but I ranged around and collected some.

Still no son.

It occurred to me that he might have got lost on the flank of the mountain. In which case, he'd spend a cold night, and I'd spend a hungry one.

The sun began to dip, and I sat in my little shelter, watching my unlit shelter. After a while, a pair of rabbits appeared in the clearing and began eating the sweet grass that seems to be created by the passing of many human feet.

Ever notice the habit rabbits have of looking at you with just one eye? The larger rabbit looked at me for a long time.

I shrugged. 'If I kill you, he'll think I have no confidence in him,' I said.

Well, I got no answer, but after a time, the rabbits ate their fill and loped away.

Deep in twilight, I sounded my horn. I almost always carry mine. It's small, dyed red, and easy to use, and I blew three loud calls. It amused me that if my cousins were out in their grape arbours, they might hear my horn on the mountain and know me, twenty stadia away.

I lit my fire.

I was rewarded in a quarter of an hour with the sound of many branches breaking, and then, at the edge of true night, by my son coming into the clearing.

He had two rabbits, and he was wearing his chiton as a wrap around his waist.

'I lost my spear,' he said. He was annoyed.

I wasn't. I was deeply pleased. 'Well done,' I said.

That surprised him.

'The god only gives you animals if you are worthy,' I said.

His look was, if not disdainful, at least fairly derisive.

'Oh?' he asked. 'I tore my chiton.'

He looked as if he was going to say more.

I shook my head. 'Humour a bumpkin from Boeotia,' I said. 'Go and wash at the spring.'

An hour later, we were eating roast rabbit. The bones, hide, and fat were wrapped in a bloody bundle on the ash altar, and I lit that fire from mine, and we prayed together.

When we'd sung a hymn to Zeus, I said, 'Cithaeron, this is my son, who you do not know. Thanks for letting him hunt on the mountain. Keep him safe and bring him home.'

Simple stuff. Cithaeron is not a complicated god.

The next day we rode down the paths I'd hunted as a boy. We took our time, and I may have told my son a lot of lies about my youth, mixed with some misplaced wisdom and even some truths.

I do like to talk about myself. And I was thinking a great many things, including that I was past forty and still alive.

We were most of the way down the flank of the mountain, and we came to the rise and dip where I'd fought the bandits. I was almost the same age then as Heraklitus was now, and I stopped and said a prayer for all of them, and then we went over the rise.

And the hair stood up on my neck.

For there, in the little dip, stood my son's spear, thrust upright into the gravel of the road.

I plucked it out and held it for a moment – a fine weapon, of course, because Archilogos could afford the best. I handed it to him.

'Now you should be exceptionally careful of this weapon,' I said.

'Why?' he asked, in the perpetual whine of the young.

'Because a god has touched it,' I said.

He shook his head. 'Pater, you are a respectable man – a brilliant warrior. Famous. And yet you prattle about the gods as if they were all around us.'

'Yes,' I said. 'I do.'

Take that, Brasidas. I can be Laconian, too.

★

At the base of the mountain, we passed the shrine to Leitos. I touched the shield and Styges emerged from the house. It was no longer a hut, but a good, stone-built guest house. Styges was the priest now, but he had another life. He was an honoured man and beginning to have political power in Plataea, and he lived in the town, fifteen stadia away. But I knew he came to the guest house frequently.

'There's a Thessalian here,' he said, as if I hadn't been away all spring. 'Not a bad sort. Seen a little too much. Cup of wine?'

I dismounted.

'Who's the sprig?' Styges asked.

'My son,' I said.

Styges smiled, his rare, genuine smile. 'Yes,' he agreed. 'How was the spring campaign?' He handed me wine.

I smiled. 'We bounced the Phoenicians at Tyre,' I said.

He grinned. 'I heard. Leukas came through and told many a tall tale.'

Just for a moment, I was going back in time. I think it is the shrine. It's an old beehive-shaped stone tomb from the time of the Trojan War – it seems timeless. It is supposedly the tomb of the only Plataean to go to Troy, and he came home and died of old age, which makes him a winner in my notions of war. Since anyone can remember, there's been a priest, usually some old soldier who keeps the place and talks to other old soldiers who need someone to drink with.

It's a timeless place, as I say.

And I had sat here talking with Styges, when he was younger than my son, and wore kohl on his eyes for his lover, Idomeneus, who was a Cretan, and probably killed more men than Hades. To see Idomeneus leap on to an enemy deck was to see the god of war come to life, but without cowardice or pity.

And now Styges was himself a notable warrior, tall and strong and broad-shouldered – considerably larger than Idomeneus had ever been.

Things change. People change.

Styges smiled. 'You, sir, are wool-gathering.'

I nodded. 'We burnt the Phoenician fleet,' I said again. 'It was glorious.'

'I wish that I'd been there,' Styges said.

'Bored with bronze shaping?' I asked.

He looked away. 'No,' he said. 'But I wouldn't mind shipping as a marine for the summer.'

'You know you are always welcome,' I said.

Styges nodded gravely.

Heraklitus looked bored. When Styges went in to fetch his kit, he asked me, 'Who is he?'

'A hero,' I said.

My son rolled his eyes. 'You insist that you live in a world of heroes and gods,' he said.

I nodded. 'Yes,' I agreed.

I could tell that he was growing fractious. I knew the cause, and I knew that he was looking to pick a fight to make himself feel ... not better, but different. I was young, once.

'You want to talk about your mother,' I said.

'I most certainly do not,' he said.

'I promise that you do,' I said.

Styges came out. I put his aspis and armour on my donkey and gave him a hand up to ride double with me – my borrowed horse could bear double for a few stadia, mostly downhill.

We started out, picking our way across the stream.

'About your mother,' I said.

Heraklitus turned his head away. Then he looked back at me with all the anger of the young.

'Not now!' he spat.

Styges laughed softly against my neck.

'He has a problem with Briseis?' he asked.

'Too many lovers and husbands,' I said.

'Young people are often rigorous moralists,' Styges said.

'I swear to you, Pater, I will turn around and ride back to Athens.'

Heraklitus was red in the face and his horse was fidgeting in a dangerous manner, because her rider was giving so many conflictual signals.

Styges chuckled against my back.

Heraklitus rode up alongside me.

'I can't believe you'd discuss this in front of a stranger!' he shouted. 'He will laugh at us!'

'So you want to protect your mother's reputation?' I asked.

'Pater!' he spat. 'Why are you doing this?'

'An excellent question,' I said. 'Let's stop for a moment.'

I let Styges down, and then slid down myself. I let my son have the height advantage.

'Do you remember Styges at Mycale?' I asked.

Heraklitus, like many youths, didn't have much in the way of observational skills. Only now did he really look at Styges. He turned up his face.

'Oh. You are one of my father's marines.'

Styges smiled gently. I began to wonder if I'd done this wrong. Styges could get angry, and then things would go badly, and his smile was not a loving smile.

'I am sometimes one of your father's marines,' he said.

Heraklitus made a face. 'That doesn't entitle a stranger to be present while I discuss my mother,' he said.

I nodded. 'My son, I mean no offence, but if any one of the three of us is a stranger, it is you. Styges is one of my closest friends – virtually my brother. I have known him from childhood. I doubt if I have three secrets from him.'

That stung Heraklitus. His horse backed. The horse's ears went back, too.

I was going to speak a warning, but Styges glided forward and took the bridle in one hand and began to calm the horse.

'Dismount,' he said.

Heraklitus rolled off gracefully.

The horse eased immediately.

Styges spoke up. Remember, too, that almost every day, he spoke to skittish veterans and injured men.

'I was sold as a slave when I was very young,' he said. 'I was trained as a sex slave. And sold as one. No one rescued me.' He shrugged, his voice calm, even, unhurried. 'One of my owners was a good man who made me into something better. Later I met your father, and your mother.'

He turned slowly until he faced Heraklitus.

'We are more than the sum of our parts, young man,' he went on. 'We are what we are allowed, and then what we choose. You are blaming your mother for a life she lived in a different world. You lack the life experience to have earned the right to judge.' He rubbed the mare's nose and gave her a kiss. 'In fact, perhaps we never earn the right to judge.' He looked at the horse. 'You are anxious and upset, because your relations with your mother are strained. The horse understands that as well as I do, so don't trouble to deny it.'

Heraklitus walked away into the woods beside the road. He walked off blindly, and I heard him trip over a branch and not even curse. But then, I suspected he was angry, humiliated, and perhaps weeping.

'More wine?' I asked Styges.

'Always,' he said, reaching for my canteen.

I have had several houses in Plataea. My cousin burnt my father's house. Later, after we rebuilt the tower, I gave it to that branch of the family as a peace offering. When I came home from Gaul and Alba and my adventures in the tin trade, I built a fine house in the city, inside the walls. The Persians destroyed it, down to rubble. It was a beautiful house with paintings I commissioned myself. Jocasta complimented me on it, and I take that as high praise, but the truth is that it was the house I built for Briseis.

My third house, I have mentioned. In that year after the great battle, it was liveable, but still being built, and everything smelt of powdered stone and fresh wood. The hearth in the kitchens didn't draw properly through the roof-hole and there weren't interior steps to the women's quarters yet – not that Briseis was ever the woman to confine herself.

Naturally, she'd taken over the best room. She had four weaving frames set up. When we'd all come in from our sacrifices of home-coming in the courtyard, and drunk off a welcome cup of kykeon, Briseis led us inside and showed off her weaving, a proper Greek matron showing her productivity.

She'd woven me a cloak – a magnificent cloak, in the Ionian style, dark red, with ravens and suns. She had it still suspended on the frame, and she glanced at it with quiet satisfaction.

Briseis. Even now it is difficult for me to do her justice. How many women, in their own lifetimes, are referred to as Helen of Troy reborn? I confess, she was a raven-haired Helen, but at forty, or near enough, she was as beautiful as a spring day, as calm as the sea at midsummer. The dangerous variability of youth had given way to an almost rock-like steadiness.

I had come to realise that she was difficult for some people to like, mostly because she was a terrible mirror on other women's lives. She was beautiful, she was a successful matron, with three surviving children, she could weave like Ariadne – indeed, she could do all the things women were supposed to do, and she could do them expertly. She ruled my household without apparent strain or effort. My soldiers mostly admired her, and even slaves tended to develop affection for her because she was absolutely fair.

I think the reason so many people hated her was that she could do all these things, and yet seemed to care very little for them. What she enjoyed was the exercise of political power, and it was as if the gods had forgotten to tell her that political power was the arena of men, and men alone. She had a special genius for exploiting divisions, for putting her finger on the exact person who could exercise influence, for understanding exactly what effect a word or gesture would have.

Her enemies, and they were many, claimed that she used sex to accomplish her aims. I suspect that this had happened from time to time – her charisma was such that she could change a meeting by entering a room – but she was far more effective than a single attractive woman could ever be. She had powers, and when she chose to use them, she could move the world.

It is sometimes difficult for a man to be married to a woman who is in many respects greater than he. But I promise you, it wasn't that difficult. You will recall that I had been angry when I realised that she and Archilogos had different plans than Cimon and I. On the other hand, because I strive to be an honest man, I also understood by the time I stood in my own house in Plataea, and the barley was ankle high in the fields outside, that Briseis had been correct on every point. The Alliance was deeply threatened, and the freedom of Ionia was, in fact, the real struggle.

Heh. One of the real struggles.

I suppose I could have stormed about and made trouble. But I left that to my son by Briseis, who entered my house ready for war and walked about with the storm clouds clear on his face.

A Persian slave took Heraklitus off to his guest room, and Briseis offered wine and a couch to Styges.

'No, no, mistress,' he said. 'I'm away. I have town business.'

I embraced him and let him go.

'I didn't expect you this summer,' Briseis said. She was ... cool. Her eyes held some caution that I didn't like.

'I'm not back for long,' I said. 'The cloak is magnificent.'

'I do a good thing now and then. I enjoy weaving – I get most of my best thinking done when I weave.' She smiled.

I smiled back. 'I'm here to take you to Ionia,' I said. It just seemed simpler to get it out of the way.

Ever since I'd decided, back off Naxos, I had had nightmares – dreams in which she was gone, and I lived alone, or I lived in a barracks. It was all very clear to me where this could lead, and I feared, deeply feared, that these were the sort of dreams the gods send to men to warn them.

She was standing by her loom, half turned away from me. She had raised a hand – I think she merely meant to stroke the wool.

I saw the tension in her hand, the very slight intake of breath.

She turned slowly.

'What?' she breathed.

'I'm here to take you to Ephesus, or Mytilini. Or Eresos. Wherever you like.'

She came towards me.

'It has become clear that you and Archilogos were correct,' I said. 'The only hope of the Greek Alliance is that Ionia be restored to freedom, and united. With a fleet to support Athens. Sparta—'

'Sparta is not interested in Ionian independence,' Briseis said. 'And it may be worse than that.'

I had sat on one of the kline, the dining couches along the walls. Now I leant back on the fresco of Artemis hunting a stag – really excellent work, by a friend of Phrynicus the playwright.

'We all know that now,' I said. 'Pausanias is leading a force that is laying siege to Amathus on Cyprus.'

'I know,' she said. She smiled a little.

I knew that smile. It meant trouble for someone.

'Aristides is a fool for following Pausanias,' she said.

'Will you ever come back to Plataea?' I asked.

She turned and looked at me, and I looked at her.

'I am your wife,' she said. 'I did not take these vows lightly.'

'But ...?' I said.

She shrugged, turned away, real anger on her face. That scarcely ever happened.

'Once this begins,' she said, 'it will not be swift, and it will not be easy.'

Bodies say a good deal, even in trained people. She was stiff with anger ... and something else. She was not coming to my couch.

So I got up and walked to her, and put my arms around her.

She stiffened a little ...

And then relaxed. She had so much presence, as a person, that I always thought of her as tall, but in truth her head was just a little higher than my chin.

'I'll buy a house on Lesbos, then,' I said.

She turned in my arms and looked up at me.

'Achilles, you will just surrender your life to mine?'

I looked at her for a long time – long enough that our steward Eugenios came to the door of the great room, paused, and walked away as silently as he could.

'I expect you'll need me around to kill the odd rival,' I said. 'Or perhaps just to sulk in my tent.'

'You never sulk,' she said. 'It is without doubt your best feature.'

'You just never see me sulk,' I managed.

I was going to leave Plataea. I *loved* Plataea.

But I loved the islands, too, and I loved Briseis, and this was, apparently, the right thing to do.

I'd stared at the stars a great many nights, making this decision.

'How was Heraklitus?' she asked.

'Angry. He has some difficulties with his mother.'

She leant back and smiled. 'Most young men do,' she said with icy calm.

Well, he was in for a bad afternoon.

'How—?'

I was about to ask after my daughter, and everyone else in Plataea that I loved.

Briseis dragged me to the couch and sat suddenly, pulling me down.

'You will just take me and sail away?' she asked.

'I believe that we have to do this. For the good of all.'

She bit her lower lip, as she did when she was troubled.

'Now that it has come to this,' she said, 'I am hesitant.'

'You, Helen? Hesitating?'

She shuddered. 'Helen destroyed. In my youth, that was a flattering name, but now, I dread it. Arimnestos, I am happy enough here. And in Ionia ... what then?'

'Damned if I know,' I said. 'But I've looked at the game board, and the game is in Ionia. And I know that you and Archilogos have laid the groundwork.'

She nodded. 'When do we leave?'

She leant back. I wondered what she was thinking, as her voice was distant.

'My ship is in Piraeus. We have no time at all. So I'd say tomorrow morning. Leave Eugenios to pack what we'll need for a year or more and follow. He can take one of the cargo ships. Take only what you need, who you need.' I was stroking her neck, looking into her eyes.

She got up. 'Well ...' she said.

She summoned Eugenios and issued a battery of orders, fluidly running through a dozen different items, so that I knew what she'd been thinking as she sat with me on the kline.

I hoped that she hadn't stood in my house for six months, thinking of what she'd take when she left.

I followed her up the temporary steps to her rooms, where she stood for a moment, considering, surrounded by her handmaids. Then she issued them all orders on packing, and I followed her from room to room as she looked at things, until we passed into the room we shared.

The doors weren't finished yet, and we had heavy curtains for privacy. As she passed, she slipped the cord that held them, unpinned the shoulders and stepped out of her chiton.

'We'll be on a ship,' she breathed. 'with no privacy at all. And time,' she said, very seriously, 'is of the essence.'

Athens reflected my own inner turmoil perfectly. It appeared that every man and woman in Athens was working desperately on some project or another. Thousands of people, slave and free, men and women, worked away at completing the encircling walls. Even as I watched, huge drum columns from a temple destroyed by the Persians were being sectioned and put into the wall. The socle or base layers were all complete, and now the Athenians were embellishing the height and breadth and, in some places, putting in defensive towers.

Down by the sea, the new port of Piraeus was growing at the same rate. Between landing my trihemiola and returning from Plataea, the walls were higher, more ship sheds were complete, and what had been a strip of open land by the sea was already populated with a dozen new-built warehouses.

I left Briseis and my sister Penelope with Jocasta and went back to my ship. Penelope is married to Brasidas, and when I said we were going out to the islands for at least a few months ...

Regardless, I spent the afternoon gathering oarsmen from various 'establishments' on the waterfront. The speed with which an oarsman or deck sailor can run through a month's prize money is truly stunning. We sometimes placed wagers on how ridiculous the tales would be – excuses for joining late ran the gamut from stupid through pedestrian and into the utterly unbelievable.

There are few places on the face of the earth more squalid than an oarsman's brothel. So I went from loving husband to ruthless nautical tyrant in an hour.

I gathered Old Nestor and the two marines that I could find, Zephyrides and Kassandros, and they, with Styges and Damon, were my wake-up crew. We moved through the new-built alleys of the port, summoning our people out of their holes and promising to leave behind any lubberly bastard too lazy to be aboard at first light.

We earned a few imprecations and a whole string of blood-curdling curses from the hag who ran a particularly nasty 'house' behind the warehouses, a rickety construction of piled amphorae, old hides and a stolen Persian tent.

An hour later we sat to eat in Jocasta's garden on the slopes of the Acropolis. Such is life.

We sailed in a light rain. The sea smelt wonderful, and the gulls screamed, and despite the wet, it was a good day to be at sea, and we had a breeze over the starboard quarter as soon as we rowed clear of the harbour. The sailors had the mainsail taut before the sun poked through the clouds, and Briseis and Penelope came on deck and watched the waves.

A fine day, and it was followed by four more. We rowed for a day, coming into Naxos. I rowed, and all the marines rowed, and then Pen and Briseis insisted on rowing, although they didn't strip to the waist, despite some requests. We had a happy ship, and she moved along well, and I was starting to trust her trim and her steering.

I think I need to mention that I started the summer a little thick in the waist. It was easier to add and harder to take off, the last few years, and the summer of Plataea had trimmed me down a little. But as spring became summer throughout the Inner Sea, I rowed when I could, sparred with Brasidas and the other marines, and generally did what I could to make my armour fit.

At Naxos we picked up the *Ariadne* by prior arrangement. Briseis landed and we made some visits – a grandson of Lugdamis, the great tyrant of Naxos in the last century, as well as the daughter of the former Persian Satrap. There was an element of comedy to these visits, because ostensibly I was doing the visiting. Women, except in circumstances regarding religious festivals or birth or death, do not often visit among themselves.

That's not strictly true, but we'll discuss it another time, eh?

But in this case, I would lead our group to a beautiful house, be ushered in, sacrifice to the household gods, and slaves would take my cloak, bring me wine ...

And I'd be ignored until Briseis was through. Naxos had started the great Ionian revolt, back in my youth – they were the first to resist.

Right? You can see where this is going.

We left Naxos on another grey day and I landed on a lonely beach on Icaria and we spent the night. There was a storm somewhere off to the west, and I wasn't willing to make the long run straight to Lesbos, and I was proven correct by a two-day blow with a strong westerly, out of season. We ate fried fish on the beach and I snuggled up in my magnificent new cloak. Briseis went visiting with Penelope, because even little fishing villages mattered in her master plan.

In fact, we spent a few delightful days, despite the wind and rain.

So in the end, we were at the very end of spring when I landed the once and future Queen of Ionia at Eresos. I felt that I'd come full circle in sixty-odd days, but it was a year for circles. While Briseis went up Vigla to speak to her former teacher, I rode a borrowed horse into Eresos and found my local captains, Parmenio, Herakles and Helikaon.

'We're raising Ionia,' I said. 'This is the revolt as it should have happened.'

I outlined what I had in mind – gathering ships from Lesbos and Chios and Samos, and striking at Halicarnassus, mostly to show that we were active.

'By the gods,' Parmenio said, striking his fist into his open palm.

Herakles fingered his beard. 'Who's paying?' he asked.

I probably rolled my eyes. 'Didn't you make enough off your Phoenician captures?' I asked.

'Enough to buy a ship,' he sulked. 'Not enough to pay the rowers from my own pocket.'

I might have bit at him, but I could well remember that particular problem.

'I think we'll ask the cities that support us for a financial contribution,' I said.

So there it was. I had five ships – the nucleus of a fleet.

Briseis sent me a message that we had rooms in Sappho's palace. I rode wearily back down to the beach, and then trudged up the steep old road into the ancient fortress after I checked on my oarsmen and my sailors. As they'd spent all their money in Piraeus, there should have been limits to how much trouble they might cause.

I thought we were going to roll in a blanket and sleep, but when I'd been greeted and given wine, Cleis gestured, and my friend from Mytilini came in with Briseis – Alysia.

'Tell Arimnestos what you told me,' Briseis said.

Alysia shrugged. 'My husband says that there is a Spartan messenger in Sardis.'

Sardis. The capital of Persia's dominion over Ionia.

I felt cold. But I still didn't understand the riddle.

Alysia's revelation was damning enough, but it lacked details.

'He's a Spartan,' she said. 'Red cloak, arrogance ... all the outward signs. But the Satrap ...'

'That's Artaphernes, son of Artaphernes,' I said.

'Yes,' she said. 'Do you know him?'

'All too well.'

If you haven't heard all my stories, Artaphernes the Elder had been a mentor and a friend – indeed, soldiers of his guard taught me to fight in the Persian manner. When I went as an ambassador to the court of the Great King, I went under Artaphernes' protection. But he was dead now.

And Briseis had been his wife. His principal wife.

Did I tell you that the world was simple?

Artaphernes the Elder had been Satrap of Lydia, ruler of the richest part of the world that I knew, a wise, good man who tried very hard to end the Ionian Revolt with words and not murders.

But his son – a son by another mother, of course – hated Briseis. Initially, I think he fancied her, and intended to take her for his own. Among Persians, this is almost normal, whereas with us it would be a terrible impiety. Regardless, she spurned him, and he hated her for it. I have noticed that it is a signpost of weakness in men that they cannot abide the refusal of a woman, as if they believe that women should not be allowed to decide.

I'll note that although I am not always the greatest admirer of the Spartans, among them it is considered beneath contempt to resent a woman's refusal. But among their many glories, the Spartans have more enlightened views of women than most cities.

Bah – Artaphernes, son of Artaphernes. There are very few men I genuinely despise, but he is one. Next to Dagon, who was pure evil, he is the next worst man I've known. It is a mystery how he came to be such, as his father was as noble and wise a man as you'll ever meet. He was well-beloved of the Great King, and had been a Satrap several times.

My mind ran like horses in an Olympic race.

The Spartans had sent a Spartiate – not a messenger or a helot, but an officer – to Artaphernes the Younger, currently Satrap of Lydia. He was the nephew of Darius, cousin to Xerxes, and next to Xerxes, probably the most powerful man in the Persian empire.

'There are many reasons that the Spartans might have sent an ambassador to Artaphernes,' I said. 'From Pausanias? Do you know the man's name?'

Alysia nodded. A girl brought wine and water, and Cleis spoke to her quietly.

'Have you eaten, Arimnestos?' she asked.

I admitted that I had not.

She asked the girl for food, and left the room for a moment and then returned.

Alysia shrugged. 'I suppose that there might be many reasons for the Spartans to approach the Satrap of Lydia,' she agreed, although with more than a little sarcasm. 'But as to the rest, my husband insisted that the Satrap made every effort to keep the Spartan a secret, and that he only discovered the man's presence because his refusal to bow to the Satrap had become gossip even among the palace slaves.'

Phrynicus and Aeschylus, the greatest writers of my generation, were in agreement that the gods love irony. There was something as delicious as pomegranates to the notion that the 'secret' Spartan ambassador was revealed by his arrogance in refusing to bow to the very Persian tyrant that we were all supposed to be fighting.

Cleis came back, and directed two young women in laying a table. Then she turned.

'Do you know where this messenger originated?' she asked.

Alysia shook her head. 'I assume he came from Sparta,' she said.

'Did he speak Persian?' I asked.

Alysia flushed slightly. 'I doubt it.'

'As do I. And that means he has a translator and a staff.' I looked at Briseis. 'Leave this to me. I have friends ... I won't name them, even here. But—'

'You?' Alysia asked, and her tone was slightly derisive. 'You have friends in Sardis?'

I looked at Briseis. She smiled like a queen.

'I also have friends in Sardis,' she said. 'My immediate interest would be your other friend, husband. The queen of Sparta.'

Yes, that's fair. My wife had been the wife of the former Satrap of Lydia and Ionia, and I hadn't ... quite ... had the queen of Sparta as a lover. Or maybe that's all in my head. Who knows?

But Gorgo and I were old friends, and virtually co-conspirators. In the year before her husband fell at Thermopylae, she had involved me in Sparta's last attempt to wrestle peace from the Great King. Even then, there were forces in Sparta who sought peace. Even then, there was a faction who hoped for the survival of Sparta *and* the destruction of Athens.

And, I thought, there was the former Spartan king, Demaratus. He had been the Eurypontid king, until he was deposed in the year of Marathon. He had opposed Cleomenes in his attempts to support Athens against Persia.

Cleomenes, who was Gorgo's father. I hope you are following this. Spartan politics is every bit as complicated as Athenian politics, with the added spice of violence and murder at the highest levels. And I knew something that very few other men knew – that Gorgo and the exiled Demaratus maintained a correspondence.

As usual, Briseis had seen to the heart of the issue. Someone needed to talk to Gorgo.

Later that night, Briseis lay in my arms, and we planned my letter. The next morning, Cleis wrote to Gorgo – as the heir of Sappho to the heir of Leonidas, so to speak – and my letter went to her the same way hers went to the exiled king, Demaratus. I wrote mine on the wooden board of a tablet, and then Cleis poured wax over it, and wrote her letter in the wax. In her letter, Cleis mentioned that I was visiting and wished to send my regards.

That was all. I left it to Gorgo's native intelligence to figure out that a wax letter sent so far might be a message in itself.

At the same time, while Briseis and Alysia and a dozen other women wrote letters to their friends, I wrote other letters. I wrote to a rich woman in Babylon who might be dead, and I wrote to Cyrus in Sardis. I walked down to the beach and found Brasidas and took him for a long walk. We went along the beach, beyond Vigla and the old palace, and then up a steep volcanic plug that sat like a tilted table, high above the sea. We climbed without effort, because we were both of us in fine shape by then. When we reached the top, we were close to the sky, and the sea was a sparkling carpet at our feet, in magnificent blues tinged with green and white.

I poured a little wine from my canteen and we shared it.

'Trouble?' he asked in his Laconian way.

'I don't want to offend you,' I said carefully.

'About Sparta, then,' he said.

'About Demaratus,' I said.

Brasidas stiffened.

I have very few secrets from Brasidas, and in this case, I could see no reason to keep anything back. I told him the whole story. I even told him things he'd been present for, like my visits to Sparta and to Susa in Persia. I did that to make clear to him how carefully I'd considered the whole thing.

'You are like my right hand,' I said. 'But you are also the only man I know who can approach Demaratus of Sparta and get me an answer.'

He looked out over the magnificent sea and then looked back.

'Possibly,' he agreed.

'Brasidas,' I said, 'the Spartans have sent an ambassador to the Satrap of Sardis.'

He looked at me. 'Are you *sure*?' he asked.

That took me aback. 'There's a peer in a red cloak at Sardis who refuses to bow to the Satrap, but waits on him like a courtier,' I said.

He blinked. This time he didn't look away – only, for a moment, he looked like a man who'd taken a blow.

'Mmm,' he grunted softly.

'I assume that the ambassador is from Pausanias,' I said.

'Regents cannot send an ambassador,' Brasidas said. 'Only kings.' Then he paused. 'At least, that's how I understand the law.' He shrugged. 'You have been in the Vale of Sparta more recently than I.'

'Do you think ...?' I asked, as hesitantly as I might have approached my daughter about something personal. 'Do you think that there have been quite a few kings, lately? And do you not feel that the ephors are trying to increase their powers, as a body?'

Brasidas folded his arms. 'I never think about it,' he said.

I tried another tack. 'If the ephors are angling for a separate peace with the Great King, would Demaratus know about it? And would he be in favour, or against it?'

Brasidas looked at me, and the silence stretched away.

There are times, between people – good people, honourable

people – when the trust that underlies friendship can be stretched to breaking point. It happens between husbands and wives, between friends and friends, war comrades, people in the assembly, politicians, fishermen … It is universal.

I was pushing Brasidas to the edge, and I knew it. Whatever his relationship with Demaratus – whether they were lovers, father and son, half-brothers – I had no idea. But I was pushing into a place where I was not welcome.

Brasidas nodded slowly, as if I was still speaking. And then his eyes met mine.

'Demaratus was deposed by an illegal proceeding that involved many people,' he said, 'but he will never forgive the ephors. And he hates Leotychidas. So if he knew of such an attempt, he would not be able to be in favour of it.'

I nodded, refusing to allow my face to reveal the smile I felt building in my jaw.

'That's why I have to send you to him,' I said.

He nodded.

'And, if you can manage it, to Arwia.'

Arwia was a friend in Babylon. Brasidas had hatched a plot with her before. She was a very special woman, and a powerful one. I was a little concerned that she might not have survived the Babylonian revolt.

It says a great deal about Arwia that Brasidas, man of bronze, smiled suddenly, like the sun coming out from behind a cloud.

'Arwia,' he said, as if he'd forgotten her name until that moment.

'And I need to remind you that you are married to my sister,' I said.

Brasidas looked at me for a moment. He put a hand on my arm.

'Not all of us are the slaves of our appetites,' he said.

Ouch. A hit like that is a little like when you are sparring, and your friend slips through your guard, past your shield, and lays his sword on you, and you haven't even clipped him.

There was worse in store for me, though, because the next day, as Brasidas made ready to depart, Penelope, my sister, appeared before me with her hands on her hips.

'You are sending my husband to Susa!' she said.

'Quiet!' I spat.

'Susa!' she repeated. 'To die!'

'No,' I said. 'I believe that he'll be perfectly safe.'

'Really?' she asked, apparently mollified.

'I'm going to make him an ambassador from Plataea – from me. I'm sending a letter to Themistocles as well, so that Brasidas will be the League ambassador. He won't travel through Sardis – he'll go through Tarsus in the south. We know people there. He'll take the Royal Road all the way.'

'So there's no danger,' she said.

'None,' I said.

'Excellent,' she said. 'Then you cannot object if he takes me.'

Perhaps I'm not doing a good job of telling this story. Here's my point.

Every day of the new Ionian revolt seemed to raise my personal stake. I was certain that the future of my marriage depended on my decisions – I suppose that's always true, but more so when politics and war enter a marriage. Now my sister and the man closest, I think, to my heart, were both going away, at my orders, into the heart of the enemy lands.

I hadn't lied. There should not have been any risk to Pen or Brasidas. But I knew there was, and I knew that my sister was as stubborn as I am myself.

Sadly, I also knew that by sending Brasidas with his wife and a staff of attendants, I made it much more likely that they would be safe.

Preparing the nascent Ionian fleet for sea was a feast day by comparison. At some point I left the diplomacy to Briseis, kissed my sister, and took my little fleet around to Methymna on the north coast, with Alysia as a passenger. We were wined and dined by the oligarchs of that fair town, and I arranged for a 'subsidy' – never call it a tax, brothers . . . I found that there was another captain there, one of Parmenio's friends, willing to try his luck.

We sailed around to Mytilini. Alysia left to see what more she could discover, and I had another dinner, this time with the lords of Mytilini.

I already missed Brasidas.

It was unfair to Styges, another of my closest friends. But Styges had been a catamite, a slave, and then a free bronze-smith. What he'd never been was a rich ambassador, an aristocrat, a gentleman. His manners were fine, but Brasidas, in addition to being a terror on an enemy deck, was a man I could take anywhere. Indeed, he was obviously the genuine article, whereas I was sometimes a pirate.

And Styges felt it, which I never intended. But the problem was that being captain of my marines, that summer, was more about drinking wine with soft-handed merchants than about clearing an enemy deck.

But that was coming.

I did what I could to make Styges feel wanted and welcome, and settled to an exercise regime that might allow me to fit in my armour after a steady diet of too much wine and too many sweetened barley rolls. And just possibly, too many years.

My six ships sat on the beach for a few days. I went to three symposia, each with more flute girls than the last, and I learnt too much about the politics of my favourite island. The Ionian tendency to allow men to have sex with *porne* at parties was ... uncouth, at least to my Boeotian sensibility.

Regardless, the removal of the Persian governor and his garrison had left a power vacuum, and the early Persian retribution for the revolt had wiped out a third of the aristocratic families. Lesbos was at the brink of *stasis* – civil war. In this case, a civil war complicated by class conflict and abetted by Persian gold, or that's what I thought that I sensed. I realised that I could turn Styges' liabilities into assets, so I set him loose to see if he could find the Persian gold in the back alleys of Mytilini, a city twice the size of Piraeus and sometimes considered a rival to Athens.

The three cities – Eresos in the south, where Briseis was, Methymna in the north, where I'd just been, and Mytilini, the largest city – were in a perpetual state of competition. That's nothing new – that's all of the Greek world. But when you throw in a pro-Persian faction, a liberation faction, a democratic faction and an aristocratic faction, all with their own agendas and propaganda, you have a poisonous brew.

That said, I had an idea. And my idea was that if the long arm of the Great King was stuck out to play in the muddy waters of Ionian politics ...

I might grab it and twist it a bit.

On my fourth day in the beautiful double harbour of Mytilini, my wife rode over the mountains with an escort and almost instantly became the most desired guest in the city. Every hostess vied to have her, and she went from house to house, weaving with one woman, baking with another, or gossiping on the balcony over the garden.

A few times she was actually invited to dine with other women, usually her fellow graduates of Sappho's school.

Together we began to build a picture of the political situation on the island. Parmenio, Helikaon and Herakles helped, too.

There were almost too many factions for there to be a war. The pro-Persian faction was finding its progress heavy going in the face of everyone's memories of the sack of the island by the Great King's soldiers. But in Mytilini, Briseis found us a thread, and we began to wind it in.

Her thread was a wife named Perictione. I never met her, but I gather that she was young and mistreated and angry, and unwilling to submit to a much older and somewhat vicious husband. He beat her, and he beat his slaves.

She didn't invite my wife to dinner. In fact, my wife didn't meet her, at least not initially. But Perictione had attended Sappho's school, and Briseis met several of her friends and heard the same story over and over.

The spice to the story was that Perictione's husband – Ataelus, son of Laertes – had been a tax-farmer for the Persians during the occupation. And he'd claimed that he would be again. Apparently, when he was resentful of his fallen condition, he drank too much and hit his slaves and his wife.

Just gossip. Alysia helped, of course, and her husband was *still* a tax-farmer.

Styges slipped into the man's house the way a greased axle slips into the socket on a chariot. He represented himself as a travelling 'fixer', the kind of almost broken freedman who markets his day labour and can be trusted to mend a pot.

Ataelus was a miserly sod, and tried to cheat him on his wages.

Styges spent two days fixing every piece of bronze in the place, and got to know the slaves.

'No direct contact,' he said.

He was in my newly rented house, sitting upright on a kline, dressed like a poor craftsman. He even looked twenty years older than he was.

I shook my head. I didn't have all summer.

'No direct contact,' Styges said again. 'But I think I've got something. Fat boy,' that was rail-thin Styges' name for our target, 'only has one frequent visitor – a merchant from Samos. He's expected.'

'Samos,' I said. 'That would be perfect.'

I don't wish to give the wrong impression. Everything had to be done at once. So in there somewhere, I got my bleary-eyed rowers together and dropped down to Ephesus, carrying a surprise. I didn't want to go, but also I did … which characterised my entire life with Archilogos.

I swear I found him on the same couch that I'd left him.

'How's ruling Ephesus?' I asked.

'How's piracy?' he asked. He was working up to anger. 'When I heard your name announced, I had six emotions all at once.'

'Think of how I felt coming here,' I said. 'Look, Archi, will you feel better if I say that you were right?'

'I don't particularly care if you say it,' he said. 'I was right. And your precious Spartan navarch is failing to take Cyprus while Artaphernes gathers armies to crush the Ionian cities. There's a rumour—'

'There's a rumour that there's a Spartan ambassador at Sardis,' I put in.

Archilogos nodded. 'So you know that one. We're cooked if the Spartans allow Artaphernes to march on us, do you know that? I've committed my fortune to the freedom of Ionia, and the fucking *Spartans* are going to sell us to Persia.'

'Briseis thinks that if the Ionians stand together, they can stop the Great King. And that if they show signs of rallying, Athens will support them.'

'Athens is tied to this entente with Sparta.' Archilogos waved at a slave. 'Where are my manners? Get him wine.'

It was odd to be in that house, and not know the slaves. Not even a wink. I'd served wine to the Persian Satrap on the same couch – different coverings. And a much better Persia.

And one of the most beautiful rooms I'd ever seen.

But I digress.

'I believe that Athens is ready to lead an Ionian league,' I said. 'And more importantly, so does Briseis.'

'Then go and fetch her here to help me lead it,' Archilogos said. I realised he was a little drunk.

'Surprise,' I said.

Briseis walked past me and embraced her brother.

'You brought her?' Archilogos asked, stunned.

Briseis smiled. 'When Arimnestos changes his mind, he doesn't go for half measures,' she said.

And with that, I was committed absolutely – my fortune, in the shape of my personal warships. My closest friend, my sister, my wife. We were going to free Ionia, or die trying, despite the self-interest and division, the Persian gold, the malfeasance of some old men in Sparta.

I was deeply afraid.

But in my heart, I was glad, because I thought that all the adventures had ended when we stormed the Persian camp at Mycale, and I was wrong.

And listen, friends. This was *my* war. I first went to sea to fight for Ionia. My Long War started here, in this house, and here I was again, with Briseis and her brother. Because in a year of circles, this was the obvious one; to finish what we started, twenty years before.

I'm just not cut out for a life of ease.

Antaeus, you asked last night about Artaphernes the Younger, and I should explain. I'd certainly hoped that I'd killed him at Plataea – goodness knows, I was in the Painted Stoa with him at the point of my spear.

But of course, the wily serpent had got away. His bodyguard, which included some of my oldest friends, put his magnificent gold-embroidered cloak on some unlucky horseman. Even when they were prisoners in my house, Cyrus and Aryanam, my Persian friends, never revealed that they had, in fact, done their duty as oath-sworn nobles – they'd covered the escape of their master.

It was a year or more before I knew.

In a way, it made my role easier. I admire the Persians – in many ways, a noble race. But I loathe Artaphernes the Younger. Or the Lesser, as I think of him.

We spent two days in Ephesus and then sailed back to Eresos to find a big round ship, the *Zephyr*, with my son Hipponax at the helm and Eugenios with Briseis' household and furniture. I bought a house for us in Methymna on the north coast. After some discussion, it seemed the best place for our residence – for what might prove to be the capital of the new Ionian League, or so we permitted ourselves to imagine. In the short run, Methymna was traditionally an Athenian ally and didn't seem to have a pro-Persian faction.

I suspect I was much mocked by my oarsmen as we rowed back and forth along the coast of Lesbos, moving Briseis and politicking at Eresos, but it was a beautiful time. In early summer, the sun was warm and the sea calm, and Lesbos is one of the most beautiful places on all the face of the earth. The tens of thousands of tiny flowers had come and gone as they do every spring, but along the cliffs, the yellow flowers bloomed. There was jasmine in the deep valleys along the little streams, and green on the hillsides that would soon wither to a blond brown.

On one of our visits to Eresos, I ran across my former passenger Socrates and his daughter Gaia. Socrates was sitting on one of the terraces of Vigla, looking out over the sea.

'How is living in paradise?' I asked.

He gave me a twisted grin. 'Dull,' he admitted. 'A few days were restful. Now, I'm ... bored. My daughter and her friends speak of nothing but the freedom of Ionia, and I'm sitting here waiting for a ship.'

'Are you needed at home?' I asked.

I had a notion. Socrates was a plain-spoken man, strong, not too tall. He might well have passed for 'everyman'.

'Not in the least,' he said.

I sat down. The very air was perfumed. It's not for nothing that I refer to Eresos in spring as 'paradise'. I'm not sure that the Elysian Fields have more to offer.

'I wonder if you'd play a part for me,' I said.

Socrates leant forward and smiled. 'Tell me more.'

'I'd like you to play an Athenian metic.'

Metics are registered foreigners – important people in the business of shipping and trade. Athens has more metics than any other state that I know of, and more trade.

He made a face. 'But I'm a citizen,' he said. And then, reading my expression, he said, 'Ah. I understand. Sure. I know the trade, that's for certain.'

I laid out my plan. I'd made it up on the spur of the moment, but I liked it.

'I hate the aristocrats and old oligarchs in Athens?' he asked. 'That's not play-acting.'

I smiled. 'I know.'

Briseis began to hold court in Methymna, and people flocked there. Archilogos was out on the sea, moving along the coast, rallying support.

I was in a tavern in Mytilini, dressed as a slave.

Socrates, my new recruit, was well dressed. We'd commandeered Hipponax's half-cargo of alum-tawed hides from Athens to be his own, and he was meeting various merchants and factors, looking for a sale. He made it clear that he wanted to sell the whole cargo, and given the state of Ionia at that time, that made it almost certain that he wouldn't sell it for a while, which gave us a chance to watch him.

Socrates revelled in his role. He was the discontented, self-made man, a little pompous, a little difficult, but mostly a man who'd buy a potential client some wine and tell a good story. An easy man to like.

A man who wasn't happy with the government of Athens. Who despised Aristides and Themistocles, too.

'I don't know what's worse,' he said on his first day. 'A genuine blue-blood or a fake working man. They're both parasites.'

I'm not sure Socrates was acting.

Regardless, he attracted clients and listeners and debaters, and I served wine and got few tips and plenty of curses, and I wondered if this was a waste of time.

The second day was the same. I thought of Archilogos, out there on the beautiful early summer seas – good fellowship, easy prizes …

The third day was the same again. I was learning things. I heard a lot about how Lesbos had been treated by the Persians, and I only really understood the factions by serving wine to citizens arguing over everything from barley prices to planting times to the state of trade with Aegypt.

But late on the third day, Styges, also dressed as a slave – which was, in his case, in a filthy chiton and no sandals – appeared at the bead curtain of our taverna. He gave me a wave with three fingers – the signal that we were on.

I didn't pass the signal to Socrates. He knew that we had a target, but why make him nervous by telling him that the target was present? He was so good, so believable, so bluff and hearty and righteous …

Ataelus, Perictione's husband, brushed in through the beads. He looked around carefully, asked another slave a question, cuffed him, and went to the table Socrates had occupied for three days.

'I hear you hate Athens,' he said.

Socrates grinned, but shook his head: 'No.'

'Hate the government,' he said. 'Taxes to build a fleet, and for what? Persians are beaten. Let's all get back to work.' He smiled. 'You in the trade?'

Just for a moment, I was afraid that Ataelus would top it the nob, announce that he was too aristocratic to indulge in trade, and trap my friend Socrates into hating him. He seemed like the type.

Instead, he shrugged and sat without invitation.

'I hear you have a cargo of white hides.'

'I do. More like three quarters of a cargo. Four hundred and seventy-five hides, all white and glossy, without stain or imperfection. Temple sandals, women's shoes—'

'Armour,' Ataelus said.

'Wall decorations,' Socrates said.

'Armour,' Ataelus repeated.

Of course, the best Athenian white leather was what many of us used for spolas, the white leather cuirass worn by many marines. Tawed leather lasts a long time at sea, rain or shine. But then, so does bronze.

Socrates shrugged. 'Have it your way. I never tell a customer how to use his products.'

Wine was brought – by me. I poured it carefully and Socrates gave me a smile and a copper *obol*.

'Good pais,' he said.

Ataelus began bargaining for the whole cargo, which seemed remarkable to me, even if he was buying it for armour ...

Until it occurred to me that Athens had embargoed all of the Persian empire.

I'm slow.

Ataelus was probably buying *for Persia*. They, too, used the white spolas.

And Ataelus was a fool. Vain, arrogant, self-important – he had all the skills. He patronised Socrates, lectured him, and then *bragged that the hides were going to the mainland*.

It was all so easy that I ordered Styges to spend another day following Ataelus, to see if it was all some complicated double trap.

Styges wanted to grab him, but I suspected that would have ramifications in the local political scene unless we had more proof. Until Archilogos had visited all of the mainland Ionian cities, I didn't really need to be anywhere else, although there *was* the pull of my wife, just a few sea miles away ...

And my ship, with the rowers earning their drachmas on the beach.

I had a hunch, though. I asked Socrates to send for his daughter, borrowed from her school. When Gaia arrived a day later, Socrates introduced her to his new business partner, and the two of them were invited for further negotiations at the house of Ataelus. Gaia had orders to befriend Perictione.

I took a day off from being a slave and spent the day training with my marines, minus the three who were watching over Ataelus' house.

We'd paid local longshoremen to move the hides from our round ship into a warehouse. All of the longshoremen seemed to be looking over their shoulders through the whole move, but while I saw their apprehension, I didn't put my finger on the reason – more fool me.

And the very next day, like a gift from the gods, a heavy trireme of Phoenician manufacture came up the channel from Chios under sail and landed on the beach.

The captain was from Samos. My little network of slave boys on the beach got me that titbit before the ship's oars were dry from the landing, and I promise you that each of my little urchins made a handsome profit.

When Thrasybulus the Samian landed, he walked straight into a net of my informers. He walked up the beach, drank wine at a waterfront taverna, went to a brothel . . .

. . . and sent his helmsman to arrange a meeting with Ataelus. Gaia was still there, having spent the night. She was sitting in Ataelus's front room, weaving, when the kubernetes – one Euplainos by name – was ushered in by the steward. He delivered a message verbally that Gaia couldn't hear, and left, staying mostly to alleys.

Aten was having far too much fun leading the urchins and dock-boys and girls who'd become my spies, although he reported that they were surprisingly anxious. They were all becoming a little more prosperous on my two drachmas a day, but Aten said they looked over their shoulders when they took it.

He brought me word that Euplainos had visited and, later that day, word that Socrates had closed his deal and sold 'his' cargo. I was no longer pretending to be a slave. I'd moved to a different taverna, at the north end of the southern beach, near the best neighbourhood and not too far from the palaces and only a drunken stumble from our ship. While running a sting against a traitor is good fun, I was also negotiating the subsidy that Mytilini would pay to the Ionian League, or whatever we eventually chose to call it. I was trying to get them to volunteer some ships. I could count nine good triremes down on the beach – I was beginning to be annoyed.

I wasn't dressed finely, either – never look like a prince when begging for money. I had a good, plain brown chlamys with a dark border and a bronze pin, and under it an old red chiton – so old that pink was probably a better description. Good cloth, but not on its best day. It was a chilly morning. I was hoping for news about Thrasybulus, and I had my chlamys pulled around me for warmth. I had none of my people around me except Aten, who was, in his cheerful way, helping another boy wash dishes. I could see the Samian's ship along the beach a couple of stadia. His people were busy, and I wondered what he was up to.

Every day has surprises.

I was sitting on my bench, calculating the daily cost of keeping a warship with professional rowers at sea, making marks on a wax tablet with a long bronze stylus that I liked. Listen ... I was getting older, my fingers hurt every morning, and I'd had so many knuckles broken that everything was stiff. A long stylus is easier on an old man like me ...

I was rudely interrupted.

'Who the fuck are you?' the man said.

I looked up. I think all that saved me was that I looked so innocuous, writing with a stylus. A scholar, not a fighter.

I said 'What?', or something as insipid.

The stranger was big, and he was standing at the apex of a triangle of 'muscle'. Three big men. Bald. All three wore their chitons like kilts. None of them was hard like a farmer or an oarsmen – plenty of fat over the muscle, but lots of muscle, too, if you know the type I mean.

I had them in one glance. Criminal enforcers.

'We're going to take a little walk,' Apex said. 'You need to meet someone who is going to explain something to you. The boys on the waterfront are ours. All of them. If you want them to spy on people, you pay us.'

Very carefully, I moved my right foot. It had been stretched out in front of me. I moved it along the table's leg.

I smiled up at Apex.

'Don't,' I said. 'Just spare me the speech, turn around, and walk away.'

'Hey, cock,' said one of the other corners of the muscle triangle. 'Do as he says or we'll have some fun with you.'

Apex leant forward, put his hand on the table, and put his face close to mine.

'Count of three,' he said.

'Don't,' I said.

'One,' he said.

I slammed the stylus through his extended hand and into the table. He reacted as I'd expected, trying to jerk back, and I used his strength as well as my own to throw the whole big slab table into his face.

I assume it hurt, because he gave a choked scream.

But he hadn't become an enforcer by being weak. He ripped the stylus out of his hand and came at me with a bellow.

I took the sword out from under my chlamys and slashed him across the bridge of the nose. It was a deliberate cut, straight from the scabbard – something I practise and practise. It is a nasty move – one or both eyes, and the bridge of the nose, in one flick of your blade.

He fell back.

'Just take him and leave,' I said, 'or I'll . . .'

They were foolish.

This is something I'll never understand. If I faced someone who dropped, say, Aristides, or Cimon, or Styges, gods be with us, with contemptuous ease, I'd immediately reconsider my tactics. I might be enraged, or filled with a desire for revenge, but I'd also know that something was not as I had expected.

On the other hand, perhaps that's why I'm alive at my age and these men were second-rate enforcers in a small town.

They came at me. The one who'd spoken had a club, and he was fast. The club went up to strike, and he struck with a feint over his head, but it was all untrained stuff. I cut into his cut, and fingers sprayed, the massive advantage of the sword over the club. He got a piece of my left shoulder and he reached, left-handed, still probably unaware that he was short of two fingers. His feet tangled in the flipped table and I back-cut to his shoulder and chest.

And that was it, because Aten had deftly stabbed the third man from behind, right between the shoulder blades. He was dead before he hit the ground.

The tavern-keeper was horrified. I thought he was angry at the mess we'd made, but it turned out that he had other concerns.

Apparently, Mytilini had a gang who controlled the waterfront. Their tentacles even extended into nicer establishments like this one. Helios, the name of the freed-slave owner of this establishment, was terrified, and angry.

I felt foolish, because now I knew why the longshoremen had been skittish, and why Aten had said the boys were nervous about our money.

'They'll kill me and my entire family,' Helios said.

'Who's the boss?' I asked.

Helios shook his head. 'They call him Oinos. He sits in the Trident all day. That's where I see these men.' He looked at them. Two were still alive. 'After the Persian garrison left ... They're terrible, lord. They will kill you. They allow no opposition.'

'How did I miss this?' I muttered.

Of course, some lowlife had taken over the waterfront in the power vacuum. As I said, I felt like a fool.

On the other hand, it was a golden opportunity.

I sent Aten to the ship.

Before my innkeeper could panic further, Aten was back with Leander and Diodoros, Achilles and four sailors, all in armour, and a dozen oarsmen under Damon and Young Nestor, as well as Ka and our new archer, the tall old man, Vasilos. I can't remember why Nemet couldn't come. Sick?

Ah, the years. Regardless ...

Aten caught at my cloak.

'Message from the traitor's house, sir.'

'Later,' I said.

Aten shook his head. 'The Samian is moving.'

'Damn,' I said. Of course, everything was happening at once. 'Carry these two gentlemen,' I called to the oarsmen, and I led them to the Trident. It was a squalid place, with an outer door that had been sloppily whitewashed. Even from outside, it smelt of piss and spilled wine.

I surrounded it, putting men in the alley behind, and then I went in.

I paused just inside, to let my eyes adjust.

It was a dark place, and it smelt worse inside than out. The tables looked sticky in the grey light. The floor had bits of grapes – and worse – rotting away, and there were only a handful of tables.

Oinos was fat. He was the only man sitting in the place. There was a slave at a big table, and four bruised girls. One of the girls was gyrating, slowly and without feeling, on a wooden crate, in what was supposed to be a display of eroticism, I suppose.

It was more depressing than lewd. And her ankle was chained to one of the wooden supports that held up the roof.

'Oinos,' I said cheerfully. 'There's been a misunderstanding.'

I smiled and pushed deeper, and suddenly Oinos was *not* the only man in the room. There was more muscle, and some of the thin, dangerous men you always find attracted by violence and easy money.

'Fuck off, foreigner,' said one of the thin men. 'No one comes in here without permission.'

'Bring them in,' I called, still keeping my voice cheerful.

Four oarsmen dragged in the damaged muscle and dumped them on the floor.

Leander and Diodoros appeared, in armour, at my back.

'Stand up, Oinos,' I said. 'I want to talk to you.'

'Fuck off,' spat the fat man.

'Last time,' I said. 'Stand up, or we kill everyone here. I have all the exits – none of you even has armour. Understand?'

'You're fucking dead,' Oinos said, but he was standing, head bent under the low ceiling.

There was a shout from the back – followed by a grunt, and the well-known sound of a body falling.

'Clear,' shouted Achilles.

He appeared at the back, his sword dripping.

I stepped forward until I was two paces from Oinos.

'You're done,' I said. 'I own this waterfront now. I have marines and oarsmen – I can put two hundred armed men in the street. In armour. You have ... what? Ten? More like nine now. Understand?'

'You're fucking dead.'

I began to think that he was too stupid to run a waterfront.

'Kill one of his men,' I said.

An arrow buzzed like a wasp. The talkative thin man fell with an arrow in his gut, and started to make the terrible noises a man makes when he knows he's been robbed of his life.

'Now you have eight,' I said.

It was an odd situation and I was surprised at my reactions. To be honest, I'm an old pirate and almost nothing used to shock me. My initial reaction to the muscle had been that when I met their boss, I'd probably co-opt him for my own operations.

I think it was the girl chained to the pillar. I just wasn't as inured to human suffering as I had once been. I was angry, and there were other tyrants besides Artaphernes the Younger.

'You have no idea how badly you've screwed up,' Oinos said.

'I don't have time to discuss it,' I said.

I deliberately stepped in, provoking him. As if we'd rehearsed it, he swung at me – a good punch, and fast. He got a piece of me – the same shoulder the club had hit – and that hurt.

Then we killed him and all his people.

Sorry, friends. Sometimes, it's not very heroic.

We didn't have time to clean up the mess, because I only needed to go to the rickety door of the Trident to see the Samian's heavy trireme pulling away from the beach.

Aten, bless him, had already fetched Gaia. My first fear had been that somehow Thrasybulus had seen through my deception and grabbed her. But Socrates' daughter was a good deal smarter than that, and the Samian probably never even realised that she wasn't part of the household. But somehow, the Samian captain had made it into Ataelus' house without us knowing.

I have to hand it to Gaia. I was standing in the sunlight, cleaning the blood from my xiphos. Leander was flicking his spear point into the sand of the beach to clean it. Diodoros looked a little pale.

Gaia never flinched. And there was a lot of blood.

'The Samian came just after dawn,' she said. 'I was already up. I heard the steward greet him at the back, at the slave entrance. Then I went up to the women's quarters and waited there. On the *exhedra* I could hear most of what they said. The Samian wanted the hides – he left gold. And he left too much. Ataelus was afraid that if he was taken with all that gold, he'd be implicated. The Samian told him not to be a woman.'

She looked at me. 'Why do men think women aren't brave?'

I shrugged. 'No idea,' I said.

I ran it through my head, still a little high on the daemon of combat, and it added up. I had Ataelus' paymaster. I knew where the tax-farmer fell in the pecking order, and Ataelus' utility was done.

'Where's Styges?' I asked.

'Still watching the house with Kassandros and Zephyrides,' Gaia said.

I wished for Brasidas, or Styges, but Leander was growing on me.

'We'll take the traitor, Ataelus,' I said, 'and then put to sea.'

Leander nodded.

'You take the men here, and surround his house,' I said. 'Aten, go to the archon and tell him that I am moving against Ataelus, son of

Laertes, who has betrayed the city to the Persians, or tried to.'

I pointed at Damon. 'I need you to go back to the ship and prepare her for sea. We'll pursue the Samian, and she'll have a long lead.'

He grinned. 'We'll catch her,' he said.

Young Nestor looked at me sharply. 'I'd best go with the helmsman,' he said.

And there it was. My plans, such as they were, were laid.

'What do I tell the archon about the dead men?' Aten asked.

'They were selling the town to the Persians, too,' I said.

That seemed better than 'they mistreated their slaves'. And for all I knew, it might have been true.

I'm not always a good man.

Ataelus folded before I had a chance to threaten him.

To be fair, we took him to the Trident before the flies had even had a chance at the corpses, and that seemed to drain him.

It was a terrible performance, and it was painful to watch, even though the man was easy to despise. He wept, he blamed others – by Artemis, he blamed his wife for spending so much money that he'd *had* to betray his city to the Persians. He blamed everyone but himself.

And he'd tried to hide the money. He claimed that it had already been moved, and he lied, and lied – lied through his tears.

Gaia walked past me into the women's quarters, and returned in less time than it takes to mumble a prayer to Zeus. She walked into the kitchen, opened a pithoi in the floor that usually held unground barley, and hauled out a bag with almost a thousand gold darics.

Gaia was a very strong young woman. That bag weighed as much as my ship, or seemed to.

'Kill him,' Gaia said. 'Free his poor wife. Can you imagine being married to that?'

I had to wonder what had made this thing – this snivelling, miserly coward, afraid of everything, willing to betray his neighbours. But I'd had enough killing for a day – too much, really.

So I did the next best thing. When the archon arrived, I took him aside.

'He is a notable man from a famous noble family,' he said.

'If he is found guilty,' I said, 'the Persian gold can replace the subsidy the town fathers would have to pay. Neither you nor the other councillors will have to pay anything.'

And so I committed Ataelus to an ugly death. I have worse things on my conscience.

And I sent Cleis the value of Perictione's dowry from the Persian gold, so that she could make a new start, and Gaia took her back to Sappho's school to hide from the world for a while.

But that was all for the future. On the spot, I heard Ataelus' broken confessions and Aten wrote them down, filling six wax tablets with the man's ramblings. He accused a surprising number of prominent men in Mytilini, and he described a terrible mixture of smuggling and crime and Persian involvement.

If Ataelus was an example of the Persian spy network, they had some awful material to work with. And the speed with which he betrayed his companions suggested that no one should ever have trusted him with anything.

I had a different problem. My problem was the archon. I kept him outside by various excuses, but it was clear that he wanted to take possession of the traitor – he and a dozen of the city's 'gentlemen', including his son Dionysius, who seemed as large and capable as his father. By the time Aten had filled his first wax tablet with confession, and I understood just how many of the town's prominent men were accused, I realised that the archon would want Ataelus silenced. Immediately. Whether the archon's name was actually on the list or not.

And Thrasybulus was sailing away. Rowing away, to be more precise. For a while, we could follow the flash of his oars as he rowed south, even from the windows of Ataelus' house, but the Samian was gone now.

I was afraid.

I'd meant to catch a traitor and I'd kicked a hornets' nest. Mytilini was not loyal to the Ionian rebellion. It was rife with men who were more interested in keeping their ties to Persia. Before we curse them, let's remember that Persia was a good master in many ways, and that until recently, the nexus of trade had been east, into Babylon and south into Syria, not west to Sicily or Athens. Mytilini, like Athens, was a city of merchants, and the rich always have an eye on their money.

But I had thought better of them. Their sons had died at Lade, and they had joined the first revolt with a will – they'd fought to the last.

I wondered if I dared to sail away, and I wondered if I should cut and run as soon as I could. I considered grabbing the archon and his family as hostages. I considered a great many alternatives, and in the end, I decided to keep an outward calm and behave as if nothing was amiss.

'I really must insist that Ataelus be turned over to the city authorities,' the archon said.

I nodded agreeably. 'I have reason to believe that Ataelus was plotting against me and my ship,' I said. A lie, but a good one, in that it explained my high-handed actions. 'I need to know if he expected help beyond the Samian.'

'We can question him,' the archon said.

He was called Theo, for Theophilos – a big, friendly man with an orator's voice and a firm handshake. He was not displaying anything like unease. He hadn't even mentioned the word 'jurisdiction'. We were just two friendly magnates having a very slight disagreement. At some level, I liked him, and I very much doubted he was a traitor.

Traitor. Such an interesting word. They were Ionians, caught between many millstones.

I felt I could trust him, at least part way.

Styges brought wine. He was still pretending to be a slave.

'I understand your caution,' Theo said, putting an arm on my shoulder. 'But this has to be sent to the proper authorities before mistakes are made.'

'What sort of mistakes?' I asked.

'I wouldn't want this bloody-handed traitor to escape justice because of a legal quibble,' he said.

I nodded. 'I don't think he'll escape justice, do you?' I asked.

He looked away – the first trace of embarrassment.

I decided on my course, and I followed it. Life is risk – I had to risk something.

'This fine young man is your son?' I said. 'Dionysios?'

He looked surprised. 'Yes,' he said.

'I wonder … does he have a panoply?' I asked, looking at the young man.

Dionysios grinned. 'Have I, though!' he said. 'It's beautiful – almost as nice as yours.'

Not a traitor.

Well, I've certainly been wrong before in my judgement of men, so I tried to keep my thoughts off my face.

'Perhaps Dionysios would like to come with me when we sail to take the Samian?'

The young man looked at his father the way a boy does when he asks if he can have a puppy.

'How soon will you go?' the archon asked.

'If you'll lend me your son, I'll be gone in two hours,' I said.

Theophilos looked at me for a long time. But he never lost his dignity, and he never stopped smiling, as if everything was fine. Perhaps it was.

'Yes,' he said. 'Of course my son can sail with you. Make him row!' He laughed, as if he didn't have a concern in the world.

But he understood. And I understood.

With his son as a hostage, I was sailing away to catch Thrasybulus. But I was trusting that he would hold the town for the rebellion. Trusting that his love for his son, if not his patriotism, would mean that I wouldn't return to find that the nest of traitors had declared for the Great King. It was still a risk. They might kill Theophilos.

I didn't think so.

I leant in close. 'Ataelus has revealed a great many men as traitors,' I said. 'He may be lying. He may be telling the truth.'

He nodded.

I backed away. 'Dionysios! Get your armour!'

The boy set off at a run.

My marines delivered the wreck of Ataelus to the court. He hadn't been harmed in any way, but he looked ... smaller.

Aten copied out the names, and gave the copy to the archon.

'I'll be back with six ships,' I said. 'And several hundred hoplites. Just in case.'

The archon nodded confidently. 'It is not as bad as you think,' he said.

'Good,' I said. 'Because I think it's pretty bad. May I offer a word of advice?'

Theophilos smiled. 'I have found you to be a wise man.'

'Frighten a couple of them – the most dangerous. Or publicly arrest one or two. The rest will run. Or try to seize the city.'

The archon gestured towards the Methymna gate, where a dozen dark red cloaks could be seen on the walls.

'We have enough citizens to hold the city,' he said.

'Good,' I admitted. 'Because I can't spare my marines.'

In an hour, we were at sea. We had too many marines – I had all of my own, along with young Dionysios, and of course, Hipponax, who'd brought our round ship *Lotus* out with the hides and refused to be left behind.

I'd never had Hipponax and Heraklitus under my eye at the same time before, and I'm sad to say that I have nothing profound to offer. Young men are very similar, at least the good ones. These two were mostly steady, occasionally fractious, handsome enough, annoying, given to pointless boasting and ...

And all the other sins I'd committed. And how well I remember them ...

Hipponax had an edge on his half-brother. A season of commanding a round ship in all weathers, even with a crew of six, had rubbed a good deal of foolishness off him. Sailors are not slaves. Even with Sekla or Leukas or Megakles on the same deck, he'd had to win some authority.

And we had Achilles aboard – my cousin. I introduced him as such when I was introducing Dionysios around, and he glowed.

Quite an assembly of young men. They postured a little, and I noted that both Leander and Zephyrides had some of Brasidas' talents – a smile and no more attention for a young man's bragging.

Bah. You aren't here to listen to me prate about my sons.

We got to sea in no time, and we were rowing into a headwind as soon as we were off the beach.

I walked to the point, amidships, where all the oarsmen could hear me.

'This will be a long chase,' I called out. 'But I think our quarry is stuffed with Persian gold, and you'll all share, and it's double pay each day until we catch him.'

Poseidonos yelled, 'Then we should all row more slowly, eh, lads?'

The roar of laughter told me that my crew was sound and ready to play hard.

We passed down the channel between Lesbos and the mainland, and into the waters south of the island. Moira, or Tyche, gave us a little fishing boat out in the great blue sea, and we bought all his fish, and he gave us news from earlier in the day. The fisherman had been fishing in the deep water north of the Chios channel. Our heavy Phoenician trireme had not gone away south into the channel, but west around the island.

She had turned west. That meant the west coast of Chios, or somewhere to the south. But not by the direct route to Samos.

We tossed a purse of coins to the fisherman and turned to starboard, and now the wind was abeam, right on the port side, pushing us back to Lesbos. I could see Mimas, the Black Mountain, on the port bow before I turned, and it was so clear I could almost see into the Bay of Erythrae. That was a town on my list to visit, and I was, to all intents, sailing away from her.

We passed close to the black cape and opened the Chios channel. We could see the shipping all the way down to the town of Chios, and not a sign of our quarry, unless he was hiding behind the islands.

We pulled past, and coasted northern Chios as the sun set. I knew a nice beach under the great mountain, right in the northern tip of the island, and there was a small temple of Heracles there. I'd visited it several times, and I landed there and beached easily on the sand, and we grilled fish and ate like kings.

And we rose in the dark and slipped out to sea. There's often a north wind in those parts, with the dawn, and we got our mainsail up and ran off almost a parasang, thirty-odd stadia, in an hour. I had Ka aloft, watching the coast for campfires, but I didn't expect to find my Samian here. I thought that he'd run all the way down the coast and camped at Dynami, or one of the other deep coves on the southern side of the island.

How did he know he was being pursued?

Another hour, and we had sunrise in the east, over Asia. By the time we were looking into the little bays on the south side, the sun had been up for two hours and all we got was a hint of woodsmoke. The day's real breeze came up and the sails came down and the oarsmen grumbled, and we rowed on. By the height of the sun, my oarsmen were flagging, and I took a turn myself, as did every marine. I noted that young Dionysios didn't hesitate, but stripped and took an oar down in among the thalamites.

We rowed.

We rowed.

Three hundred and sixty stadia to Samos. If the Samian rowed all night, he'd be home in the morning. And my ship wasn't fast under oars.

It bothered me that he knew I'd been after him, although I admitted to myself that we hadn't had the best secrecy in our endeavours and that I, too, had hunches when I was pursued.

As we passed the southern end of the Chios channel, I began to realise how hopeless my pursuit was. If he now turned north into the channel, I'd have to look into twenty fishing towns to find him.

I was willing to wager all my gold that he was standing straight on to Samos, and I couldn't see how I was going to catch him.

I'm not usually beaten. I hate it. It makes me feel ...

Well, angry. And beaten.

Sunrise showed me Cercetius, the tallest mountain of Samos, rising high above the island, and sea marks for the city. Samos has a chequered history – queen of the sea less than fifty years ago, she's still a dominant sea power, but her triremes changed sides at Lade and killed a great many of my friends. I have a hard time seeing the Samians as allies, but they were the first to join us at Mycale, and they seized and executed the leaders of the great betrayal at Lade.

Like many great cities, Samos has a beautiful deep bay to protect her beaches and her merchant ships, and lines of ship sheds to keep her triremes over the winter. We rowed into the harbour of Samos cautiously, as I had no real idea what would greet me. The Samian captain at Mytilini had led me to suspect that Samos had changed sides again. It seemed all too possible, and my one ship was not going to redress the balance.

But as we got deeper and deeper in the bay, which is less than five stadia wide, we could see no sign of a heavy Phoenician trireme on any of the beaches on either hand.

I'd been suckered.

I'd chased Thrasybulus across the Ikarian Sea and lost him in the darkness. I had to assume he'd turned south, towards Patmos and Leros. Was he aware of my pursuit? Had he turned south in the darkness, with a laugh at my expense?

Or was he on some other mission? It occurred to me that he might have had an objective on the west coast of Chios – a visit, a drop of a bag of gold. And then away at first light, and he'd have still been ahead of us.

I'd had him in my hands, and I'd wasted my time chasing a small-time crime lord.

I gritted my teeth, landed in Samos, and paid for supplies. I raised the level of muttering aboard by telling my crew that there would be no shore-going, as we'd be away as soon as I had some information. I walked ashore, aware of the sound of two hundred angry oarsmen and sailors, and found a customs officer.

'I'll have to look at your cargo,' he said.

'I don't have a cargo,' I said. 'I'm an officer of the new Ionian League and I gave chase to a ship in Persian service.'

In the end I had to let him look at the empty holds to convince him. I didn't have so much as a document to identify me as a captain in anyone's service, and on Samos my name might well have been used to frighten babies. The customs officer and the local aristocrat, Polycrates, who came down to the beach, both suggested without much subtlety that they thought I was a pirate.

'What exactly brings you to Samos, Trierarch?' Polycrates asked.

'As I told this gentleman, I gave chase to a heavy Phoenician trireme that took on a cargo at Lesbos. The captain was Samian.' I smiled, as affably as I could manage. 'I serve the new Ionian League, and I have reason to believe that he is distributing gold for the Great King.'

'We all fancy a little gold, do we not?' Polycrates asked. 'I'm sure your crew were slavering in anticipation, but as you can see, there are no big Phoenicians here, with Samian captains or any other sort.'

No one likes to be patronised, which may be why I find the Samians a difficult lot. Their historical memory of being a major power has blinded them to the modern realities.

'We patrol these waters,' Polycrates said. 'I'll inform our captains of the ship you describe, but you understand that you cannot just attack a ship in our waters. This is not some little lickspittle town in Lesbos. This is Samos.'

I was very tempted to suggest that lickspittle was exactly the way I'd describe Samos' craven behaviour at Lade, but it's really never wise to prod a boar, as long as he has tusks.

I smiled a little. 'I'm an officer of the Ionian League,' I said again. 'I'll take him wherever I find him. Samos is not yet a member, I believe.'

'Samos *led* the Ionian revolt against the Great King,' Polycrates said.

Again, an opportunity to speak my mind on the role of leadership in the *last* Ionian revolt.

Maybe he read my thoughts on my face, as he flushed red.

'If there is to be a new Ionian League,' he said, 'it should start here, or Samos will go its own way.'

And this is why I should never be a diplomat.

'That would be a pity,' I said.

'You are insulting me!' the man said.

'I was at Lade,' I said. 'The last time Samos went its own way.'

Oh yes, I'm quite the diplomat.

By now we'd drawn a crowd. We were on the stone quayside, where the big ships and important visitors came alongside. The crowd was mostly prosperous people – women in conical sun hats, men in broad-brimmed straw *petasus* hats and chitons, and slaves, already naked in the brilliant sun.

No one was on my side.

Polycrates' face was mottled with rage.

'My father was killed by the Persians,' he barked. 'You are an arse.'

I looked around. Angry people make me relax. I assume it's a war instinct, but I change my posture, deepen my stance ... Consciously or unconsciously, I'm getting ready for violence.

'It's possible that I am, sir,' I said calmly. 'But I promise you that Samos is not going to lead any league in your lifetime. And I need you to understand that I am an officer of the league that is even now coming into being, and that, if I catch this ship, I will take or destroy her with no reference to you or the government of Samos.'

And that's what happens when I feel angry and defeated before I engage someone in conversation. I'd probably just endangered the whole of the league's relations with the largest naval power in Ionia.

I felt like an arse, I promise you. And yet it was true – Polycrates was living in the past, and there was no way that Briseis and Archilogos were going to accept the leadership of Samos.

I have to put it down to an ancient rivalry. Samos is the enemy of Miletus, and Miletus of Samos, and thus it has been for two hundred years. Ephesus is an ancient ally of Miletus, and so there is no love lost between my wife's family and the Samians, even before the treason of Lade.

Greeks. Take off the outside pressure for an hour, and we're at each other's throats.

The only sign of the fortune of the gods in the whole day was that we had rowed into the bay, but the steady wind from the south and east wafted us out with only our boat sail set, and we emerged from the bay before the sun was halfway across the sky. It was the edge of summer – long days and short nights.

I thought of lingering – of finding some fresh water and holing up on a tiny beach to see if the heavy Phoenician trireme would appear round the next headland. I'd look a proper flat if he sailed in an hour after I sailed out.

Against that, I'd left Mytilini at the edge of *stasis* and civil strife, and I had other duties in the north of Lesbos.

'Set the mainsail,' I said to Damon. 'We're for Lesbos.'

He was quick enough not to comment.

Old Nestor raised an eyebrow. 'Can't win 'em all, eh?'

I suspect that I growled.

When you have a reasonably new crew, as I did, impressions count. We'd got off to an excellent start, taking the Phoenician triremes off Lesbos, and we'd improved that by our raid on Tyre. But we'd just rowed over half of the Inner Sea and never even *seen* our quarry, and my oarsmen were fractious, to say the least.

And since I'd managed to anger both the customs official and the government, I hadn't stopped even to load a cargo of Samian wine – sweet stuff, delicious in winter. I've noted before that once you give way to anger and the darkness that comes with it, you often compound your errors through oversight and irrationality, and I had just done all of those things.

We landed just at the edge of darkness on the beach below Chios. I was in a foul mood, entirely of my own making. But I had enough sense to get my ship ashore, stern first, and to see my oarsmen ashore, under cover and fed. It was warm, and I wandered the beach in the darkness, looking for a place to be by myself and to think.

But I heard a stir by the fires – that sudden burst of voices that denotes incident or trouble – and I checked my sword and hurried back.

There was a little crowd of Chians who had come down from the town. It was almost like being transported back in time, and before I'd reached the fire I'd realised that this was the beach on which I'd recovered after Lade. And that the troubles of that past were so much greater than my present troubles, that my darkness was merely a re-enactment of the tragic past. I lived in the miraculous new world in which we, the Greeks, had won Salamis and Plataea. A setback was not a defeat.

But the memory of the past, especially the unjust defeats of the past, can be like an old wound that will not heal. Eh?

I knew the man before I came up to him, and it was like seeing a ghost – Stephanos, perhaps my first loyal friend and officer.

But of course, he was dead at Lade. And his brother Harpagos, dead at Salamis.

When he turned, I knew him – Neoptolimos, Stephanos' sister's son. With Melaina.

I embraced each in turn. They had known hardship and horror when the Persians came with fire and sword, and they had survived.

'How's bronze-smithing?' Neoptolimos asked.

I laughed. 'I haven't heard the sound of the hammer in half a year or more,' I said. 'How's fishing?'

Neoptolimos had brought his uncle's ship alive out of the victory of Salamis, where Harpagos had died.

He spread his arms. 'I caught all the fish,' he said. 'There aren't really any left.'

Melaina caught up the hem of her cloak, where it was weighted, and smacked him with it.

'He's bored,' she said. 'Take him away before he makes trouble.'

'Can you raise a crew?' I asked him.

'I wouldn't even have to raise my voice,' he said. And then, his voice tighter, he said, 'I thought … I thought you'd call for me. I hear you raided Tyre!'

A little bitterness.

It's an odd thing. I had thought of him before the raid. But I've been the death of half his family, and I wondered if just this once I shouldn't leave them alone.

Apparently Apollo, god of Chios, had other notions.

'I'm not exactly sure where to get you a hull,' I said. 'But I'm sure it can be managed. What happened to your uncle's trireme?'

He shrugged. 'The Athenians took it back,' he said.

I nodded. 'Surely Chios will be sending a fleet to support the Allies,' I said.

'We sent a dozen ships,' he said. 'I'm not enough of a gentleman to captain one, and I'll be damned if I'll serve as a sailor for a trierarch who wasn't at Artemisium or Salamis.'

'Fair,' I said. 'I'll find you a ship.'

I spent the night talking with Melaina and Neoptolimos, and in the morning, I sailed away a happier man.

Morning. A glorious pink morning with a chill in the air. I'd slept well, the whole last watch, curled under my cloak, with the night just cool enough to make me feel drowsy and warm and slow to rise.

Melaina came down and brought me a warm bowl of chicken soup. I drank it greedily.

'How's marriage?' she asked.

I smiled. 'Terrifying,' I admitted.

She looked out to sea. 'I've outlived two men,' she said. 'Not really sure what to do, now. I don't feel old enough to be a matron.'

'Neoptolimos no doubt thinks we're both older than the stones,' I said.

'Anyone under thirty thinks those of us over thirty are nigh to death,' she said. 'I've been nigh to death,' she went on. 'This isn't so bad. It's only that I'm as bored as he is. The sea is in our blood.'

'If you took a fishing boat and started fishing, what would happen?' I asked.

She looked at me. She sat on her haunches like a much younger woman.

'Perhaps nothing,' she said. 'I've been tempted. The sea is always interesting, at least.'

'Maybe when Neoptolimos is gone, you should take his boat and fish,' I said.

'Maybe no one would speak to me,' she said.

I lay back, sipping soup. 'Then maybe you should go as a colonist,' I said. 'You are young enough, and a colony needs solid women – dependable women who know their crafts.'

She smiled. 'You do know how to flatter a girl,' she said. 'What colony do you have in mind?'

I think it just sprang into my mind. I have these moments, and I ascribe them to the spirits of the air, or to a particular daemon, or perhaps to Athena or Artemis whispering in my ear.

But in that moment, with no preparation and no real prior thought, I saw this place. I don't mean that I saw it as it turned out to be, with Therick's hut over on the hillside. I mean, it suddenly occurred to me that I'd never really be a good Plataean any more than Briseis would, but I could found a colony in Thrace and live out my days with my friends. My wife would be close enough to Ionia to visit it in a long day's sailing ... or perhaps she'd be visiting me.

In many ways, it was the most powerful idea I've ever had on the spur of the moment.

Listen. Many ideas crowded in on me in that moment, on a beach, speaking to one of my oldest friends. I knew the war would go on – perhaps forever. And I knew that there were opportunities in the eastern seas – adventures and politics, war and peace, sailing, perhaps even exploration.

And I knew that Briseis would never be happy in Plataea.

I'd been planning a dinner – I've spoken of it elsewhere, but I'd taken some steps already to gather all my friends at my house in Plataea in the coming autumn. But now I could see a whole horizon before me, and I began to wonder why I hadn't considered founding a colony before.

'Perhaps I'll found a colony,' I said.

All that, in a blink of Melaina's dark-honey eyes.

She smiled. 'Well,' she said. 'I'd need a good word with the great man, I expect.'

'He's heard good things about you,' I said, trying for a lighter tone. But she looked away.

She frowned. I only saw one side of it, but I knew that look, the same as her brother's.

'You'll come back for Neoptolimos?' she asked.

'As soon as I get a hull for him,' I said.

She looked at me. She had magnificent eyes, dark yellow, and dark hair. A true islander. Her eyes held nothing of flirtation – only a little hurt, and some hesitation.

'Neoptolimos thought you'd never come for him,' she said.

I nodded.

She looked away and then glanced back.

'Do you remember making love to me, after my brother died?' she asked.

After the disaster of Lade.

'Yes,' I said.

She got up, and looked down at me. 'I suppose that I expected that you'd come back for me, then,' she said. 'Be sure and come back for Neoptolimos.'

I'd never even thought ...

'Melaina!' I said. 'I killed his father and his uncle, or near enough.'

She shrugged. 'Harpagos went the way he'd dreamt of going. He was never meant to be a Chian peasant fisherman. He died like a lord.' She shrugged. 'Stephanos loved you. You're easy to love, aren't you?'

I've been wounded a few times, but that comment cut deep.

'Yesterday, when he saw your ship, he was so angry he was going to ... Never mind. As soon as he saw you, all he wanted was your good grace. And I'm no better. When you are out of my sight, I curse you, Arimnestos of Plataea. But here you are, drinking my soup, taking for granted my nephew's adoration, hatching a new plan for a colony. And I want to go with you.'

She shook her head. 'I know you aren't evil, and I'm quite sure I'm no one's fool. So why do you have this power?'

Aye. And I can't deny it, either. Men follow me. I'd spent the day before in a rage, and they feared me more than they censured me.

'I'm sorry,' I said.

She looked at me. 'Well,' she said. 'That's not a bad start. Tell me when you found your colony.'

We made Lesbos at the edge of darkness. The sun was long down behind Olympus, but there was enough light in the sky for us to beach our ship under the walls. Theophilos, the archon, met us as soon as we landed, and I could see Socrates up on the wall, leaning out with an oil lamp.

'We saw no action and reaped no glory,' I said.

But I could tell that, for Theophilos, the glory of having his son back was enough. Dionysios was full of tales of living rough at sea, and sparring with Leander and Kassandros and the others.

'I'd be happy to have him again,' I said. 'A very good young man.'

His father glowed.

There's the deadly power – to take a man's son as a hostage, and make him like it. I'm careful of how I use it. It is charisma, pure and simple – the god- or goddess-given talent to win people's hearts. It won't surprise you that since my talk with Melaina I'd been thinking about it. It was a voyage for thinking of all my errors. Anger and its aftermath often has that effect on me.

Despite my fears – and I had plenty of them – we landed at Mytilini and the city was still loyal to Ionia. Theophilos was a cunning man, and he'd arrested only two plotters, both rich and deeply unpopular.

'We'll try them all together,' he said. 'We'll sequester their estates, and offer payment of a few drachmas a day for wall repair, which will ease some lives in the *thetis* class.' He shrugged, unashamed.

'As long as we're only punishing the guilty,' I said.

'No one likes to see how sausage is made,' he muttered.

We parted, his son waving goodbye in the last light of the day, the fitful red sky glinting off his polished bronze as it flashed from under his Tyrian cloak.

A dozen tavernas right up against the sea wall opened up. They were right to do so. I put a board across two Gaulish barrels and paid every oarsman ten days' back wages – thirty silver drachmas. The marines and sailors got more. Old Nestor marked them down as paid on a tablet against their names. The ship's book, as we called it, was a four-leaf wood and wax tablet set. On the back, the names of every sailor and oarsman were written in sepia – so far, none had lines through. It seemed odd that we'd fought twice, and rowed over the whole of the Eastern Sea, and not lost a man. I muttered a prayer to Poseidon.

Anyway, we paid them by torchlight, and let them go to their pleasures, and I wished for my wife.

Instead, I met Socrates, who waited while the men were paid and then took me for a cup of wine.

'There's news on the waterfront today,' he said. 'The grain ship from Athens touched in Cyrene. The captain says the siege of Amathus is a failure, and the Allied fleet is breaking up – pestilence and incompetence, sounds like.'

'Breaking up?' I said.

'Sounds bad,' he said. 'Sounds as if the Spartans dismissed Cimon and there's bad blood.'

I shook my head. 'Dismissed Cimon?' I looked at the bottom of my wine cup. 'Perhaps it's just a rumour,' I said.

'Athenian captain said he saw the Athenian fleet off the beach,' he said, 'and Xanthippus was coming out to take command.'

I shook my head. If this was true, it was very bad for Ionia.

In fact, it was bad for all of Greece.

I knew I was missing the sense of the riddle, but I couldn't find it. The Spartan ambassador, if he was real, must have been sent before the kings knew that Athens was rebuilding her walls. Or Pausanias sent him, and had no right to do so, and had now dismissed Cimon.

It didn't make sense. I could make up stories to explain it, but the stories still didn't really hang together.

Methymna remains one of my favourite places in the world, and we sailed around from Mytilini. In my memory we never touched an oar, which may be an old man's fondness for the place that might be belied by a cursing oarsman. But let's imagine that day. The pure blue of the sea and the lighter sky, the looming mass of Asia visible through the sea haze, the mountains of north Lesbos rising, mighty, jagged spikes, and then, suddenly, after you round the northern peninsula of the island, you see beaches – first the gravel beach at

Skiamandi, and the hot springs at Euthalou, called 'Thermi' like every other hot spring in Greece. Then you see the headland and the mighty fortress high above, and you think, 'How in the names of all the gods did Achilles ever take that thing?'

The fortress towers over the town, and it has heavy stone walls whose lower courses date back a thousand years. The town itself runs from the acropolis all the way down to the sea, with walls and towers that cover a dozen stone jetties and twenty ship sheds. The town has two beaches, like any good harbour town, so that ships can land in almost any wind on one of the two, and row off, too.

The town is mostly whitewashed mud-brick houses on stone foundations, with pretty red-tile roofs and paint. Even the poorer Methymnans tend to paint their houses like temples, with bands of bright red and even expensive lapis blue. The inner harbour and breakwater on the point date back to the time of the Trojan War, and that's where the fishing boats lie up during the winter. There are twenty or more warehouses, and stadia of drying racks for salt fish. The smell of fish is everywhere, but the position of the town on a northern promontory gives it the cleanest, most frequent breezes in Greece.

I landed on the west side of the point. I remember the landing well, because, perhaps as a result of four days of bad news and tension, I was determined to look flashy on landing. So, against Damon's advice, I took the helm myself, brought her in close to the beach where the water is still good and deep, We put the oars over hard to starboard while my oarsmen bit into the water on the starboard side, and my sailors, at a motion, dropped the mainsail.

We went from full sail to a near stop in five ship's lengths, pivoted end for end so fast that we took on water through the lower oar-holes, and came to rest with the stern perhaps a quarter of a stadion from the beach.

I grinned like a fool, because it was flashy and had taken perfect timing, and we'd pulled it off. The oars gave three strokes backwards, and the stern rode up the beach and we were in, neat as neat.

'Wasn't that pretty?' I demanded of Damon.

He shrugged.

Old Nestor smiled. 'Pretty is as pretty does, sir,' he said. 'An' we could had taken a minute longer and no danger to ship or crew.'

I could tell Damon agreed.

I grinned, and Poseidonos grinned back from his oar.

'But it was good fun to do,' I said. 'And it shows how good our training is.'

Poseidonos was still grinning. 'It'll make a pretty story,' he agreed.

Damon was still looking out to sea. 'But ...'

I realised that he was not happy and I changed my tone. I try not to be a despicable tyrant.

'Speak up,' I said. 'I won't bite.'

He smiled. 'One mistake by an oarsman – or the boys brailing up the sail – and we're bow first into the beach at cruising speed. Broken ram and hurt men.'

He had a point. And because I was no longer in a foul mood, I didn't have to be angry at being gainsaid. This is another aspect of anger that I note. In its absence, you deal with the world in a completely different way.

'Truth in what you say,' I said.

I could see Briseis coming down to the beach. She wore a light saffron chiton in the Ionian way, with glittering golden pins that I could see catch the sun a hundred paces away. She was walking down the long stone path from the fortress, so she was above me, with a dozen other women in attendance and as many men, one in armour. She had a broad-brimmed straw hat and a gauzy veil over her shoulders, so that her face was covered. I'd have known her anywhere, just by her shoulders and the straightness of her back.

As she came closer, I could see that she carried a magnificent silver *hydria*, the big water-carrying vessel they used in temples, and behind her were women with wine amphorae.

My wife was intending to welcome me in style, with a religious ceremony.

I shrugged into my best chiton, with the embroidered ravens, just in time to note that the shoulder of my bronze thorax had torn it.

'Aten, I need my armour,' I called out, and he was there, laying it on the deck, bless him. I remember when he was too scared to get the halves closed on my breast and back. Now he put it on while chattering at me, put the pins in and snapped greaves on my legs, while my oarsmen chattered their way down the twin planks over the stern.

So rather than first, I was nearly the last man ashore. Nearly, because Styges appeared in his armour. By Ares, he had all the marines turned out, so that we came down the planks like gods in bronze, and he formed them on the beach.

Briseis came forward. She is a woman of several personas – this was not Briseis my wife, but Briseis the priestess. She came forward at the head of her women, and she poured water and then wine over my shield. The other women did the same for the marines. And then she smiled at Aten, and he was handed a silver kylix brim-full of dark red wine.

'Welcome home,' Briseis said.

She gave me the cup to drink, and I poured a libation on the sand and took a sip and passed it to Styges. He raised it to Briseis, poured a libation, and handed it to Kassandros, who happened to be next in line. And then to Zephyrides and then to Leander and so on, until Achilles poured a little drop in the sand and drank the rest off.

Most of the oarsmen had lingered, and all the sailors. They'd more than lingered – they'd formed in four ranks on the beach. They weren't neat ranks, like soldiers, but they were there, without orders.

I smiled. 'I hope you have a lot of wine,' I said very softly.

One of the things I loved best in Briseis was her ability to change directions like a dolphin. She had come to greet me, but now, without a pause of a sign that she'd ever planned anything else, she began to serve all the sailors. When she and her women had passed them, they were presented a problem. The sailors all had shields. Many were pelte, or small rimless aspides, but they had something.

The oarsmen, on the other hand, had only their oars.

One of Briseis' women was a dark-haired local girl, perhaps thirteen years old. I didn't know her, but I guessed she was from one of Briseis' friends' families. She was smart, that young woman – she took her pitcher and blessed the man's oar. Of course it was old Poseidonos, first in the line. He, who had seen fifty fights and knew more curses and foul stories than any man I know, blushed with pleasure to have a fine lady give him the 'home' blessing.

The women continued along the ranks, blessing the oars. Everyone does it now, and I've heard men claim that the Athenians invented the blessing of oars after Salamis, but I think it was Briseis, and young Cleo of Methymna, a girl who could think on her feet.

It took a while. It was time well spent. There was a little ribaldry, and men shifted in their places, but it wasn't the sort of ceremony that men resent. It was more of the sort of moment that builds a team, that gives spirit.

Wars are won in odd moments – decisions about moving food, or about locating a well, or scouting a camp. I won't claim we won the Ionian war on the beach of Methymna.

But by the gods, I felt our luck change.

We spent almost a week in Methymna. There was a local sea festival, with a feast and sacrifices to Poseidon. There were some major repairs required to my new ship – or rather, completions, for she'd been taken in a state of 'near' completion. For example, her hull had never been properly pitched, nor her main deck completed. I wanted to use the festival to give her a naming feast, like a new-built ship, but Damon and Old Nestor convinced me to get her finished first. So she went into the beach and headed for the shipwrights. There was a lot of work to do, and that took up my days.

But in the evenings, sitting on beautiful terraces high above the sea, we heard news and plotted strategies.

Archilogos was there, with his own squadron. There were four ships from Ephesus and another two from once-mighty Miletus, as well as three more from the smaller coastal towns on the Asia Minor side of the strait.

Chios had ten ships prepared to serve with the Allies, and Mytilini five, but piracy – or its near-cousin, privateering – has a wide appeal. We had my three friends from Lesbos and the promise of at least Neoptolimos from Chios. Parmenio rowed away after the festival with *Amaranth*, one of our captures from Tyre, towed behind with a skeleton crew under Damon.

As is too often the case, I've left my oar and I'm gathering wool at the rail, so to speak, but it's difficult to discuss strategy unless you know where your ships are.

Most of my trierarchs wanted to raid Aegypt. It stood to reason, as Aegypt was the richest and most exotic land on the Inner Sea, and she was under Persian domination, and her merchants rivalled Ionian merchants in every port. But there were three problems, and I laid them out in front of all the captains and Briseis and Archilogos, and a dozen other local aristocrats who'd become the 'court' of the new Ionian revolt.

'First ...' I said, holding up my hand in the Greek way. 'First, Aegypt's navy is almost untouched. The Phoenicians are crippled and the Carians are gradually changing sides, but Aegypt can probably still put more warships into the water than all of the Greek states combined.

'Second, friends, let's try and remember that the poor bloody Aegyptians have revolted against the Great King almost as often as we ourselves. Striking their merchants will only serve to drive them closer to their overlord. Really, what we'd like is a nice Aegyptian revolt.'

That got a great many nods. Lesbos and Chios are centres of trade with Cyprus and Aegypt. Many aristocrats here had guest-friends in Aegypt, or long family associations. And we all knew, and had known since the dawn of the first Ionian rebellion back in the year of the battle at Sardis, that if only we could convince the Aegyptians to rise with us, we'd deny the Persians access to the sea altogether.

I raised my hand.

'And last . . .' I said. 'Last, but not least, Aegypt is a long row away to the south. We'd be taking our last line of defence and rowing ten days away. That would allow Artaphernes to raid Lesbos or Chios at will – to try a siege of Miletus, or even Ephesus.'

It was odd, but having lost the first Ionian revolt, we actually knew how certain strategies played out. We'd raided Cyprus – we'd fought a naval battle there, twenty years ago, and we'd won it. But we'd lost the land battle, and the Persians had laid siege to three mainland Ionian cities while our fleet was busy in the south.

Even aristocrats can learn from their mistakes, I find.

Archilogos had also been against the Aegyptian venture. Now he rolled off his couch and stood up.

'If we're not going to Aegypt,' he said, 'what do you propose?'

Agon, the senior trierarch from Miletus, raised himself on one elbow.

'I think we should stay right here,' he said. 'Arimnestos says the Carians are coming over to us, and that may be true, but we haven't seen much of them yet, and the queen of Halicarnassus was out early this spring, collecting tribute for Xerxes. We should patrol from Black Cape all the way up to the Dardanelles.'

'And how do we pay our oarsmen?' Herakles, the captain we'd recruited in Eresos, asked.

You get the gist. We debated two nights running, while the excellent Lesbian wine made the rounds and my wife sat in a woman's chair, watching, offering nothing.

And the third night, in the shared pleasure of the festival and all the rites we'd celebrated, and a good dinner of sacrificial beef, we voted unanimously to send our squadron down to Halicarnassus and along the coast of Caria. It was a typically Greek compromise – not too close, not too far, in the direction of the Allied fleet so we could get news of it, some chance of prizes among the Syrian and Carian coasters.

The only problem was that I'd been sailing around the Aegean in a ship that wasn't really completed, and I'd already begun to strip her and finish the pitch and the decking. There was nothing to be done about it. Old Nestor had already found worm in my new ship's planking, and we knew we'd have to come at it.

The Ionian squadron went to sea without me. In other circumstances, I'd have been worried. Command is a touchy thing, and command among peers and volunteers can be a nightmare. But Archilogos took command and I knew he'd do it well. I also knew that he was an Ionian – a true Aeolian – and they'd follow him anywhere. I worried that he'd be rash, still trying to prove himself to Xanthippus and Pausanias and Aristides – and I worried that he and Briseis had plots within their plots.

But there was nothing, and I mean nothing, that was going to get my ship to sea for another week. And I had my wife all to myself.

Well, after the sun set, anyway.

By day she sat in the cool of her porch, surrounded by other aristocratic women. One would read poetry, usually Sappho, and the rest would weave or embroider. In fact, my new house, about halfway up the hill to the fortress, had been purchased mostly for the size and beauty of that porch. There, the wives of the so-called leaders debated the strategies and watched the waters far below.

I was stripped as naked as a slave and spotted with black pine pitch, which burns, by the way, even as it sticks to your skin. Twenty of us were pitching the hull of the new *Apollo's Raven*. We'd done a poor, hurried job of it in early spring and now had to do it all again, and carefully, sometimes taking off the last pitch before applying the new.

We had her masts out and her hull turtled on the beach, and several hundred paces of local scaffolding all over her upturned hull, where it looked like half the timbers were missing. We'd had to take a third of the planks off her – a terrible job in the early summer sun. I'd paid two local shipwrights for the pleasure of using 'their' beach, and paid more for their workmen, but my sailors seemed to do most of the work, which may be the norm in these situations.

But we had the planks back on, and the pitch was from Thrace, and we had enough, thank the gods, because Thrace was really just two days away to the north. Pitch of this quality was ten times the price in Athens, and worse elsewhere.

I was thinking a great deal about Thrace in those days, because of my new dream of a colony. I'd been in the Chersonese with Miltiades, twenty years before, and, as I keep telling you, every day of the new Ionian Revolt seemed to put me in mind of something from the old one, so that I had the strangest feeling of reliving my own past. I kept expecting Miltiades to ask me to walk with him, or Epaphroditos to walk around the stern of my beached ship.

I was just contemplating how I'd once exchanged a bunch of Phoenician hostages on this very beach, with bloody results, when a small trading ship came round the breakwater. She seemed to appear by magic – which is just an effect of the long headland and the warehouses – but there was something dramatic about her entrance. She was under full sail, right close in, which seemed odd.

To be fair, it seemed odd, but I'd done the same a few days before, showing away like a pimply boy. Did I mention this? That night, as I lay with my wife's head on my chest, I asked, just a little put out, 'Did you see us land the ship?'

Briseis wriggled. 'Yes,' she said. 'If I hadn't seen you coming, I wouldn't have been there to greet you.'

I grimaced. 'Did you see the manner of our landing?' I asked.

She raised her head. 'It looked ...' She stared into my eyes. 'Was it something remarkable?'

I sighed.

Regardless ...

The merchant ship rounded the point. She shot up, head into the wind, and dropped her mainsail and her foremast sail, too, and dropped her anchor stone, and a swimmer leapt into the water. That was dramatic – they had news.

I walked, with as much naked, pitch-splattered dignity as I could muster, along the beach until I reached the point that the swimmer would land.

He was a slim boy, and looked more Aegyptian than Greek, but his voice was pure Aeolian.

'Persian ships at Samothrace!' he said.

The curious thing about people is when they panic.

You might have thought that, as we'd just sent our fleet away to the south for at least ten days, and we knew the allies were still laying siege to Amathus and my lovely *Apollo's Raven* was lying upside down with all her innards out like a dead bird on the beach, that news of a hitherto unimagined Persian squadron loose in the Thracian Sea would have panicked us all.

Especially as the news was worse than that. The actual news was that Tenedos and Lemnos had launched triremes to support the Ionians, and that they had met the Persian squadron and been taken. Four triremes had been lost, and two Chian wine ships taken as well, all in three days.

Did I say our luck was changing? I knew immediately that even small actions like this could threaten the whole Ionian revolt. It's not that the Ionians are fickle; it's that they're pinned between Athens and Persia. But a few Persians victories, some serious threats to Ionian merchants, and our whole rebellion would come crashing to a stop like a trireme under full sail striking a rock.

On the other hand, Poseidonos practically rubbed his hands together with glee.

'Oh, now we're for it,' he said.

And Young Nestor did a little dance, even as he spread hot pitch. 'Hades to pay, and plenty of pitch hot,' the boy said. That got a laugh from the crew, but everyone knew that this was bad.

We worked by torchlight on the beach, and we worked in the burning heat of the midday sun. We worked, and swam to take away the sting of the pitch burns, and then we worked again. Every man of my crew worked, and most of the nautical population of Methymna worked.

As we worked, we looked out to sea, watching the horizon for the mysterious Persian squadron. The town had a garrison of local men, and they would shout tidings down from the fortress, seven hundred steps above us. They could see to Asia, north and east and west, so that only the south was hidden, and we expected no foe from the south.

When we thought we were almost done, we found more rot – more teredo worm. That was a time to curse the gods, but no one did. We took more planks off, in places removing pitch we'd just laid on. And yet, in two days, working every tide, we'd closed up the hull, pitched her stem to stern, so that she was smooth and shiny and black from ram to swan's wing.

We rolled her back on to her keel and washed her clean and ran her into the sea. We finished the main deck planking and got her masts in at the stone pier that men had built in the time of the Trojan War.

I summoned the priest of Poseidon, because sometimes you have to know you've done everything that could be done. I called her *Apollo's Raven* again, and we painted raven's wings on the bow behind the eyes and the ram, which swept forward like a beak, and which we painted black to match the hull, with a thin line of expensive vermilion along the thranite oar ports. Briseis said the words, the priest prayed, we all sang the hymn to Poseidon ...

> *I begin to sing about Poseidon, the Great God, mover of the earth and the fruitful sea, god of the deep who is also lord of Helicon and wide Aegae. A two-fold office the gods allotted to you, Earth-shaker! You are the tamer of horses and the saviour of ships!*

And then, without wasting another prayer, oarsmen and sailors and marines were dashing up the long planks from the stern.

Briseis kissed me, the last man on the beach.

'I made you something,' she said. 'Because the only time you dress well is when you go to fight.'

She handed me a chiton.

The wool was scarlet, dyed in some eastern place, maybe with the fantastical 'grains'. The edges had fancy work, and the whole garment had enough embroidery to turn a spear point – ravens and sunbursts.

'I'll only get blood on it,' I said.

'See that it's someone else's,' she said. 'Anyway, that's why it's red. Get going, before Old Nestor says something unforgivable.'

I kissed her, the pleasure all too fleeting, and ran up the plank.

It was mid-morning – three days since we'd heard of a Persian squadron, perhaps five days since they'd taken the ships of Lemnos and Tenedos. Somewhere, there was a Persian officer who'd missed a chance to take me and mine, helpless on a beach.

Apollo's Raven was going to make him rue his error.

The thing that makes Lesbos so essential to any maritime strategy in the eastern part of the Inner Sea is the way it sits like a good neighbour, hard against the coast of Asia. The island is so close to Asia that you can swim there, on a good day, although there's quite a current in the channel, and if you aren't careful, you are dead.

But it's not just close to Asia. Lesbos is a day's rowing south of the Dardanelles, the strait that guards the entrance to the Euxine. A day south, and you are in the midst of the great Ionian city-states. Two days south, and you are in the Dodecanese, with Rhodos and Samos close at hand. With ten or more wonderful harbours, Lesbos offers refuge to every pirate, and a base to every invader.

The Lesbians didn't seem to celebrate the Thargelia, which we celebrate in Plataea and they also celebrate in Athens. A religious festival devoted mostly to the fruits of agriculture, it marks the end of spring and the beginning of summer – the 'birthdays' of Apollo and Artemis. We sailed on the fifth day of Thargelion, a day before the Feast of Artemis, and ran due north. This 'Persian squadron' puzzled me, because I couldn't see how it could exist. I was not surprised that there were still ships and men loyal to the Great King, Xerxes. Even after Artemisium, Salamis, Mycale, and our little raid on Tyre, I suspect the Great King and his allies still had more ships than we did ourselves.

But his ships were mostly from Phoenicia. We'd hit Tyre, but not Sidon, and they no doubt had a hundred triremes alone. And north of Phoenicia, Artemesia of Halicarnassus and her allies among the Carian cities had another twenty, or even as many as fifty ships. They'd been out early in the spring – canny captains and first-rate ships.

But up in the north? Lemnos and Tenedos were islands near the mouth of the Dardanelles, and north of them was the coast of European Thrace.

Boyhood had taught me to be a patient hunter. And I was after big game – to take four or five Ionian triremes had to be the work of at least three big triremes, and maybe as many as five.

I just had a hard time imagining where those five had come from. Which, in a way, was a tribute to my ignorance.

I knew what the merchant had said – the fight had been close to Lemnos. I knew that win or lose, a trireme needed to beach for the night, unless the trierarch was exceptionally daring. A squadron that had taken ships and their crews would need the beach all the more, to put a few reliable men aboard each capture.

I put up my mainsail and ran up the gentle south wind for Lemnos.

It was fully dark before we put our anchor stones over the side. We coasted into one of the open beaches on the Asian side of the island – huge beaches like half-moons sunk in the sea. We slept on our oars and ate honey and sesame and garlic sausage, and before dawn we were moving, prowling the coast, looking for a camp or a sign. Instead we found a fishing boat, out early – two young men more interested in giggling like girls than in keeping watch, so that we picked them up before they even knew we were there.

It was the feast of Artemis, and they weren't boys. They were two young girls, twelve or thirteen – the age when all women are sacred to Artemis. I took it as a sign. We were all courtly and gentle, as it was Artemis' day. The coarsest oarsman understood the importance of our 'capture'.

They had no fear of us, as young women often do, and we gave them no reason to fear us. After half a cup of watered wine, they joined in telling us that a Persian captain had bought sheep from the village, threatened their father and rowed away north with two ships badly damaged and in tow, leaving two hundred captured oarsmen on the beach.

We sent them on their way with a couple of gold darics as a reward.

I landed a little after dawn and sought out the recently captured oarsmen, and got the entire story – a brutal tale of bad luck and terrible mismanagement. The captains had quarrelled. They'd made separate landings and separate camps on separate beaches, and two were taken before the others even knew what had happened. The other two launched to make a fight of it, but were overwhelmed.

Oarsmen can be coarse, and they are often ignorant as pigs of anything on land, including how to spend a few drachmas. But when a hundred oarsmen tell you that the enemy has eight triremes, you have to believe them.

'Twelve now,' a slab-cheeked brute said. 'Oh, lord, it was tragic like a bad play.'

'Some o' ta' fewkin' marines just sat an' surrendered, like,' another oar called.

It surfaced that Lemnos had social problems. The oarsmen and the sailors came from a class that supported Athens, and thus Greece, but the hoplites and officers were ... less sure.

Let's be fair ... odds of eight to two might make me sit and surrender, or at least consider it.

So – my enemy had at least eight triremes, some of them damaged, and he'd sailed away north on much the same breeze I'd used coming off Lesbos.

It was shocking. Disheartening. We'd won every sea fight for two years – we'd thumbed our noses at them. I thought the Persians were cowed and hiding in their ports, and here was some bold sprite taking Ionian ships in the Aegean.

Couldn't be allowed.

At the same time, odds of twelve or so to one didn't really appeal.

On the other hand, it was the feast of Artemis. We fought Artemisium under the eyes of Artemis, and we fought Salamis while the Brauron girls prayed, and Artemis had always been more a friend to us than her brother. And as I said before, when Briseis and her women blessed our oarsmen, something changed – some feeling, some ... luck.

An hour later, we were running north for the coast of Thrace. I'd been on this coast a dozen times. I'd raided her with Miltiades and I'd sold slaves at Mesembria.

Young Nestor was watching the peak of Samothrace as we left the tip of Lemnos behind. He was nimble enough to go up into the leather basket, come down for a report, and climb back up.

'Behind Samothrace there's a dozen harbours on the Thracian coast,' Old Nestor commented from the port-side steering oar. 'One long beach.'

'Doriscus has a Persian garrison,' Damon put in from the starboard-side steering oar.

Doriscus. We'd always given it a wide berth, back when we were pirates of the Chersonese, precisely because the garrison was large, and well led. The governor was Maskames, a Persian noble and nobody's fool.

Doriscus had to be the lead suspect, then. The fortress itself was well up the local river from the sea – a deep river in a wide delta, more like a jungle than like the oak forests of European Thrace. I'd heard it was impregnable. I'd never actually laid eyes on it.

We sailed to Samothrace in two hours, pulled around the island, and then rowed on, even though we might have sailed. We were a lone Greek ship on a hostile coast. The Thracians would hate us as much as the Persians. Without sails, we were almost invisible.

From Samothrace to Doriscus is about three hours' sail. The coastline is low, with a long beach, but the birds give away the river delta before you can see the low-lying land. The Evros is a mighty river that rises far inland. It's only navigable for the first twenty stadia or so, but it is wide and deep that far.

When we were a dozen stadia off the coast, we could see the low land and the beaches.

'What do you think?' I asked my officers.

Damon looked out under his hand. 'You could hide a fleet up that river,' he said.

Old Nestor nodded. 'What I was going to say.'

I wanted to curse, but it was the birthday of Artemis and I had to trust her.

'Lay us for the river mouth,' I said.

'There's a sandbar,' Old Nestor said. 'It's like a half-moon off the main mouth. You have to row in with the land and pass into the river mouth hard by the land.'

I went forward and told Young Nestor, on lookout, to watch for the sandbar.

'You seem to know the place well,' I said when I was back by the steering oars.

Old Nestor shrugged. 'Been here twice,' he admitted. 'Running cargoes, like.'

That seemed fair. Believe it or not, there never was a law in Athens against trading with the Persians.

It was a little after midday. A terrible time to attempt to spy on anyone, as the bright sun lights on your rigging and shines off your oars.

On the other hand, with new pine pitch and the favour of Artemis, I was confident we could outrun any pursuit with a fair wind.

'Lay us for the shore,' I said. 'Hard by the river entrance.'

We ran a fishing net up the boat sail mast, and decorated it with some greenery as soon as we were in with the land. A net and a mast, with some green leaves, looks remarkably like a tree from any distance. And in a river lined with trees thicker than hoplites on a battlefield ...

We ran a second net up the mainmast, and Aten fetched us most of an oak tree.

The Evros is about two stadia wide in the main mouth, and stays that wide for twenty stadia of length. We crept upstream. I was already aware of the lateness of the hour, and how far we'd have to go to land safely on Samothrace, and how short of water we were. The whole thing was insane, anyway – one ship against ten or twelve, in their home territory ...

I had only the lower deck rowing. I was resting all my good

rowers, because I expected to have to run. And I walked down the main rowing deck, telling every rower what I was going to do when we were spotted. We would turn end for end, pivoting in place, the port-side rowers reversing on their benches while the starboard rowed forward.

I didn't have a plan. I just wanted to press my luck and see what Artemis would give me.

We rounded bend after bend, and each time, instead of a view into the enemy port, we'd see another stretch of muddy water lined with big trees.

Two hours past the middle of the day. We barely had steerage way against the current, and the river was cold – cold enough to make me wish for a cloak when we were shaded by the big trees. Snow melt from the mountains deep in Thrace.

We turned, and turned. There were mudbanks in the river, shadows like sharks in the depths, but Young Nestor called them out and earned a month's pay in an hour. And that's why we went so slowly.

Somewhere in the third hour, the boy in the tops missed a shadow passing under the ram, and we struck. It was a long, soft strike. That mudbank whispered under our keel for as long as a man might count to ten.

And then we stopped.

We were so well stuck on that bank that the ship felt as solid as if it had been on dry land.

I tried rocking her off by having Styges lead the marines up and down the catwalk, but that had no effect except to increase my frustration.

'Artemis!' I said aloud.

I moved all the sailors well aft, with the marines, so that the helmsman was crowded with all of them. The ship moved a little, but not much.

I shook my head, biting my lip. I was on a fool's errand, led by some belief in luck and the goddess Artemis, and my ship was aground in a Thracian river, even if this wasn't a Persian pirate base. The Thracians are not a joke. They'd come at sunset, or a little later. Three or four hundred. With fire arrows.

I felt deeply foolish. And all my people looked at me.

'Hush!' Styges said, with gentle force.

Most of the men fell quiet.

And there, somewhere upriver, probably quite close through the trees, even if several stadia away in the winding belly of the snake-like river, we heard voices. It was a timoneer calling the stroke on a warship.

An enemy warship.

My beautiful warship was stuck on a mudbank, and there was a trireme somewhere within shouting distance.

I leant down into the thalamite deck.

'Can you lads swim?' I asked.

Every man-jack raised his hand.

'Over the side,' I said. 'Stow your oar and jump. Fast as you can.'

Fifty-four men. At three talents each, I was getting rid of the weight of an entire cargo load.

Clear as day, in good Greek, I heard the timoneer yell, 'Sixteen, row dry or I'm coming for you!' in a voice like thunder.

'They're Greek!' said some young fool among my lower deck oarsmen.

'Over the side,' I ordered.

They went. The water was freezing cold, and they went, one after another.

'Nestor, ropes over the side. We'll want them back.'

As half of them went, I could feel the deck alive beneath my feet. Two thirds, and we were afloat.

I pointed at Poseidonos.

'Back water,' I said, as softly as I could manage.

About two hundred paces upstream, a beautifully painted trireme began to make the turn. Her ram-clad bow appeared from among the trees like an actor coming out of the scenery at the festival of Dionysus.

'We're clear!' Aten yelled.

A hard decision. A third of my oarsmen in the water, and we are bow-on to an enemy. Back water? Fight?

'Get them aboard,' I said.

I looked for Ka. Bless him, he'd already climbed the standing mast – he was hidden among the greenery. Nemet was replacing Young Nestor on the boat sail mast.

His former helots and Vasilos, the old man we'd picked up in Piraeus were all down the side.

'Hide your bows,' I said. 'Marines, lie down.'

Heraclitus used to say that most men see only what they want to see.

That trireme came downstream, turned neatly – and with long practice – to avoid the mudbank that had taken us, and *only then* did the command and helmsman see us. But then we were perhaps fifty paces apart, and he was moving at a fair speed – a little faster than a man walking – and we were perfectly still, our main yard in among the branches of a mighty oak.

By then the thalamites were mostly aboard. Half a dozen oarsmen were still in the water, but they'd all had the presence of mind to drop into the water on the landward side.

The enemy trierarch said something, and the helmsman turned, looked at him, and flicked the steering oar. We were close enough to see them clearly.

'What the fuck?' we heard their trierarch say.

I think he'd spent some long seconds assuming I was a friend, but the trihemiola build would have given us away. No one used them but pirates and Sicilians.

'Shoot,' I said.

A bronze-tipped sleet fell on the enemy ship, and there were screams.

None of our archers missed, at thirty paces.

'Back water,' I ordered.

I still had only two thirds of my rowers, because the thalamites weren't back in their seats yet, and the ship was listing sharply to port because that's what a light hull does when men are climbing the port side. It made it hard for the starboard-side rowers. Hard for everyone.

As a result, we backed water, but we bumped our stern into the shore.

And then Artemis leant down from the heavens and played her part.

Ka and Vasilos were loosing so fast that their arrows seemed to flow out of them. Nemet gave his high-pitched grunt every time he loosed.

Our enemy had a long, low trireme – even lower than usual, like my friend Epaphroditos had ... Come to think of it, that was a northern Aegean ship with all the fancy paint ... She seemed longer than most triremes. Her rowing frame was perhaps a tenth longer than mine, or more.

She was going downstream, remember, at a walking pace, and then the trierarch had ordered that the helm turn towards us. We backed water and slammed our stern into the bank.

The current caught our bow. Our oarsmen were facing a variety of problems, with men climbing into their seats, oars in a tangle, and some water coming in from the steep angle imparted by men climbing the side. But skill, practice, and perhaps a gentle nudge from the goddess, and we were turning rapidly, our bow following the movement of the enemy ship like a hunter's hand and eye following a bird on the wing before he looses his arrow.

And then our little advantages began to tell.

We knew we were in an enemy river. All our marines were in their armour. Our archers were armed and loosing arrow after arrow. Their helm was a bloody mess, and the trierarch was already dead. The helmsman fell across his oars, turning his craft to starboard, away from us, out into the current.

And his marines had other problems.

Something was wrong amidships. I couldn't tell for certain, but it seemed to me that his oarsmen were attacking his marines.

'Don't shoot the oarsmen!' I roared.

Then I looked back at Damon. 'Put our beak into her,' I said.

I motioned at Poseidonos. 'Prepare to row forward,' I said.

'Catch!' he bellowed.

Perhaps a hundred oars responded, going to the 'prepare' position, oar extended, high in the air, waiting for the order to dip.

I nodded to Damon and started forward towards the marines. Ka loosed up above me.

'Give way!' called Damon.

'Styges!' I called. 'Over the bow. Kill the marines and she's ours.'

Styges said nothing. He only pointed.

A second trireme was coming around the next bend.

We touched. It wasn't anything like a ram. Our ram slid under her keel, probably stripping away a layer of pitch. Our bow stopped on their oar frame with a deep creak as the good oak took the strain. We began to drift downstream.

An arrow whispered past me.

'Do it!' I ordered.

Styges leapt, followed by Zephyrites and Kassandros, Achilles and Kalidion, Leander and the rest.

I had meant to go with them, but instead I stood on my own small foredeck and watched the oncoming trireme. She was still struggling to make the tight turn in the river, her port-side oars backing, a number of oars crossed. That one observation told me everything – a scratch crew, or a mixed crew. Captured oarsmen? Something like that.

These were the captured Lemnian ships – I had little doubt. At a guess, that meant there were two more coming behind, or perhaps the whole squadron.

'Damon!' I yelled.

I ran for the steering oars. This was going to be close, and I needed the gods to keep the next trireme in a state of confusion for a little while.

'Giorgos!' I yelled at the thranite. 'You and Philokles there. Cross your oars and come up on deck.'

They obeyed, looking confused.

'Old Nestor! Choose four deckhands to go with Damon. Armour, weapons. You stay here. Steady, men, you hear me?'

'Aye, aye, sir.'

I ran aft to the oars.

'Hand over, Damon. Take the sailors and two master oarsmen, follow the marines and take that ship out of here.'

I was pointing at the ship next to us. We'd come together, bow to their amidships, just aft of the mast.

My marines had already cleared the enemy deck. As I heard later, the archers had done all the work – there wasn't a living enemy marine or officer. Styges was shouting at the oarsmen, and Leander stood behind him like an avenging Fury.

'Go!' I roared at my prize crew. 'Get under way and follow me!'

Damon waved, and made the leap to the enemy ship's bow, followed by the sailors and the two oarsmen.

I watched Giorgos leap – he was last.

'Back oars!' I called over Poseidonos.

They reversed their benches like veterans.

I nodded to Poseidonos, and he roared, 'Give way! And! Stroke!'

In one stroke we were away, our ram gliding out from under their hull even as Giorgos made the leap to their deck and rolled forward. The current was forcing the hulls together. The other ship was about to strike the far bank stern first, and I needed to be clear.

I looked back over the swan's breast of the stern, leaning well out. This is why the commander is usually amidships – the stern is well protected but offers very little vision.

'Aten, get to the bow,' I ordered.

I leant out, leaving the steering for a moment. That's a pretty dangerous thing to do in the middle of a sea fight, in a river with a current. But I had to see for myself. I needed to know ... all those things you can know when you look at your opponent.

So I risked it, and looked.

There was the second trireme, just at the end of her turn, her bow coming on, perhaps three hundred paces away. Her oar-loom was a mess. Tight turns are never easy, and it looked as if Athena or Artemis had aided me with a little chaos. Some poor bastard had broken ribs where his oar-shaft had caught a crab and slammed into him, panicking his mates.

Or so I guessed, in one glance. I caught the steering oars before they could swing on the current, and looked at the banks. We were backing upstream, slowly enough that we seemed to be standing still. The ship Styges had taken had struck the far bank now, stern first. It was starting to turn in the current just as we had, her bow being taken downstream while her stern stayed tight to the bank, the graceful forward curve of the overhang of her stem caught in branches, her stern lightly stuck in the bank's soft mud.

That was Damon's problem, now.

What I had to decide was whether to turn and fight the next ship, or whether I could run.

Sadly ...

'Prepare to "about ship" to port,' I said.

That would cause the port-side rowers to stay reversed and pull, while the starboard-side rowers rowed forward, until we'd turned end for end.

Poseidonos was down in the rowing frame and could see when all his people were ready. When he raised his hand, I ordered, 'About ship!'

'Stroke!' Poseidonos said.

And we started to turn.

Turning against a current is hard. Judging a turn as the current moves you downstream towards a turn and a mudbank is harder still.

I glanced over at the ship we'd taken. Damon wasn't even in the steering oars – he was amidships, bellowing commands.

Not good.

My next opponent was a hundred and fifty paces away.

'Pull!' I cried. 'Pull, my brave lads!'

I wished I had a really good singer to lead them. I needed the bow around *faster*. And the current was slowing us.

'Pull, you bastards!' Poseidonos called. 'And! *Pull!*'

The deck heeled slightly.

My bow was beginning to line up with the enemy ship. And she was coming on.

Ka was waving his hand for my attention. He pointed at his bow.

'Yes!' I called up to the masthead.

He turned away, already nocking an arrow.

Bow on.

Aten waved, and I waved back. It's not that easy to see the length of a trihemiola – the standing masts and rigging prevent good vision.

I called for one of the deck crew to take the port-side steering oar. We didn't usually put a man on either side, but if I stood at the starboard oar I could see the length of the starboard side – a much better view of the world, allowing me to watch the onrushing enemy ship and Damon as well.

I made my decision. Damon was all the way around, his bow pointing downstream, and he had all his sailors and marines poling off the bank.

It was too late for the enemy ship to change direction and aim at our capture – also suicide, in that I'd be able to oar-rake him at the very least.

Trireme combat is all about being fifteen to twenty heartbeats ahead of the action. Everything takes time – time to relay orders, time to row, time to accelerate or decelerate the sheer mass of the ship.

'Prepare to back oars,' I ordered.

We were bow-on to our opponent, but there was nothing to be gained by accepting a head-to-head engagement.

His marines were in his bow.

My archers were playing on them, at seventy paces.

'Back oars!' I called.

'Stroke!' Poseidonos ordered.

One stroke, and we were moving, because we were going *with* the current.

Fifty paces. Six archers, all of them growing tired because this was the second engagement. No enemy archers at all. Perhaps the Persian commander didn't trust these captured Ionians, or he didn't have enough real Medes to put on the ships.

Ka, shooting down into the enemy bow, was deadliest.

By the third stroke, we were moving quite quickly.

By the fifth stroke, it was unlikely that our attacker would strike hard enough to damage us.

We were passing the captured ship now, leaving her behind on the far bank. She did have her oars in the water.

A fourth ship appeared at the bend in the river. She was six hundred paces away.

I had other problems. I wasn't used to fine steering. It was years since I'd spent much time at my own helm, and I was about to try backing around a bend in the river.

My heart began to beat hard enough that I felt as if I was choking.

It's one of those things. I never remember feeling this way in combat – sometimes before, and occasionally after, but never during. But steering my ship with two hundred lives depending on my steering . . .

I leant out. The bend went to the starboard side and was not, thank Poseidon, terribly sharp. I leant in and looked at my fellow steersman, who was a young sailor I didn't really know at all.

'Nicanor, lord,' he said with a confident smile.

'You ready, Nicanor?'

He nodded, leant out, and leant back in.

'Probably a sandbank on the starboard side,' he said.

Of course there was.

Always have a sailor around when you need one.

I leant out again, saw the bank moving by a little faster than a walking pace. I looked upstream, and there was our attacker, now about twenty paces away. Nemet was not shooting. He was lifting the boards on the foredeck – out of arrows, I had to surmise – and going after the stores there.

I glanced back at the young man on the port-side steering oar. I had relieved Damon to go aboard the capture, but Old Nestor had been steering for hours and he looked tired.

'Ready?' I asked.

'Give her a little, sir,' he said. 'Little more. Going to turn like a right slug, she is.'

There I was, the terror of the seas, trusting someone else to judge the turn.

'Just there,' he said.

'Turn three points,' I called out, and leant on my oar.

It's very different, turning a ship from the stern when going stern first. Try turning any boat from the bow, when you're going forward.

"Starboard side, drag your oars,' I called.

Poseidonos repeated my order.

We turned. When we'd turned almost far enough, I told Poseidonos to stop. He had them lift their oars free, and we were around, the last degrees managed by the steering oars as we continued in the centre of the river. We had two stadia of straight rowing before the next turn – this a sharpish one, with a disorder of floating tree trunks in the hollow of the bend.

One crisis at a time.

'Back oars,' I repeated.

Poseidonos nodded at me.

'Steady,' I said to my partner at the helm.

Young Nestor was handing sheaves of bundled arrows to the archers, and Aten was sending four sheaves aloft on a line, to Ka.

Our opponent took the turn. He was going faster than we, and trying to make up distance. He cut in to the turn, shaving the bend.

Just for a moment he was too close to the bank . . .

Twenty or thirty oars caught on the out-thrust mudbank. Men screamed as their shafts turned on them. Some splintered.

She shot through the shallow water, losing some way but ploughing over the shallows with a muddy bow wave. As soon as she was into the deeper water she began to turn to my starboard, because all her port-side oars were dragging in the chaos after the self-administered oar-rake.

I was tempted. But I didn't have another prize crew – my deck was already thin.

We continued backing.

The capture came around the bend, bow first, rowing cautiously. But she got past the enemy ship, which was rocking as sailors ran to get spare oars into the mangled hands of the oarsmen on their port side.

I could see Leander in the bow, watching the enemy ship the way a sea eagle watches a salmon. Arios waved, and I waved back. Diodoros was leaning out of the far side, looking at something.

I had Poseidonos check our way, and the capture went past us, the rowing ragged. Damon didn't even glance my way.

'Young Nestor,' I ordered. 'Take my place.'

'Aye, sir,' he said.

'I think we should turn end for end,' I said.

'Thought you meant to back all the way downstream?' Old Nestor said. He raised an eyebrow. 'Yes, we should get the bow in front. I hear it's the sailor-like way to proceed.'

His sarcasm was wasted on me, and I leant down to Poseidonos and outlined my plan.

He gave the preparatory, and we coasted as the oarsmen changed seats. The next bend seemed to rush towards us, and turning end for end is not always the easiest manoeuvre.

But if you give your people time – if you prepare them for complex manoeuvres – they will respond. In this case, I counted to thirty, to make sure everyone was ready.

'About ship,' I ordered.

And around we went. Now the current was pushing to bow, not the other way around, and we turned end for end faster than I'd thought possible, with hundreds of paces to spare. Damon was just making the next turn, carefully staying in the deep water.

The river widened past the bend – I could see it already.

I had to think ahead. I knew where to find a friendly beach on Lemnos, but we wouldn't make it before darkness, and I didn't relish leaving Damon with a hostile ship and no food in a blue water voyage in the dark.

Samothrace?

I didn't know it. But it was the logical place to go.

Logical. But ...

I didn't really know the mouth of the Evros all that well, but I knew it was a delta, with five or six mouths.

'Nestor,' I said. 'Is there another mouth that's navigable?'

He made a face. 'I suppose,' he said. 'Tough in a big ship like this.'

'Can we get over the bar?' I asked.

I described my plan to him and he looked frightened for a moment, and then nodded.

'Aye,' he said. 'It's ... possible. And maybe ... Maybe we'll be inside the bar all the time. I think it's like a big half-moon, off all the mouths.'

'That'd be good,' I said.

I went forward to prevent the sailors from throwing the greenery over the sides.

Bow first, the bends in the river were nowhere near as challenging. I had to dissuade the sailors from laying the sails to the masts, a process by which the yards are brought on deck and the sails attached, preparatory to raising them.

We weren't going to raise our sails.

My next concern had to be Thracians. But way out in the delta, I suspected that they couldn't come – they'd have to cross two or three other deep branches of the river to reach us. We didn't have a lot of good – or clean – fresh water. The Evros was both cold and muddy, and who knew how many men and women had pissed in it this close to the sea? I liked to get my water in small creeks, or straight from a spring – common enough on Greek islands, sometimes smelling a little of sulphur.

There ought to be fish, though.

And even a fractious crew can get through a night without food. It's not a great option. Hunger and thirst and fatigue are the same thing as fear for most men, and fear turns quickly to anger.

We went downstream a good deal faster than we'd run upstream. We were less cautious and we had the current with us. The distance that had taken us all morning to run off, going upstream, was the matter of two hours downstream. I could see the sea over the last long neck of land – a low hump of sand dunes, treeless except for one lone pine tree – and I thought of the old pine forests along the beach at Marathon.

I hadn't seen a pursuer in an hour, except sometimes, as we raced along, we'd see the top of their boat sail masts above the low banks of the lower estuary – always two turns behind, and being cautious.

I waved a spear with a red chiton on it until I had Damon's attention, and he let me go ahead.

'Follow me,' I said.

Leander waved, and Styges pointed at something with his spear.

The water got deeper, and there was a touch of swell. The water would now be brackish, if not salt.

'East or west?' I asked Old Nestor.

He made that face. 'Ten years since I came this way,' he admitted. 'Lot can change in a river.'

I nodded.

'East,' he said.

We were only out on the sea for three or four stadia, pulling like heroes along inside the bar – the drifted silt and mud of a thousand springs, when the mighty waters would rush south from the Thracian mountains, and deposit their dirt at the mouth.

We stayed perhaps two hundred paces off the long beach. We passed two small openings, but the third was wide enough to take our ship and we turned, having overshot, and pulled in. We passed a long spit of mud and sand and then slipped along a narrow channel, just about twice as wide as our hull and her oars. We slowed to a stop as the vegetation closed in on both banks, turned our ship about while there was still room to do such a thing, and so that we were bow on if attacked, and dropped our anchor stones in water only about twice as deep as our hull.

Damon followed us in.

As soon as he had his ship turned and anchored ahead of us, I sent Aten and another boy, along with Arios and Diodoros, ashore on the south bank, to work their way to the sea and keep watch. I had the sailors redecorate our masts with greenery, but I was already confident that we were invisible from the sea side. I was conscious that I didn't know how much farther our arm of the delta extended. I decided there and then to get myself a *pentekonter* or a smaller ship to use as a scout.

The oarsmen lay on their oars, telling stories and complaining, no doubt. I served out a little wine and some honey and sesame seeds, and we waited as the spring *muops*, the biting flies, came out in shoals and bit us unmercifully. They were near to driving me mad, and I could move around on the deck, and I cursed several dozen times and wondered aloud what they ate when they didn't have Plataeans.

They got worse at twilight, which is when Diodoros came back.

'By Artemis,' he said. 'The insects are bad here.'

'I'm near a mutiny,' I snapped.

'No bugs on the beach,' he said. 'We saw their whole squadron – seven ships. They went south towards Samothrace, rowing hard. Rowing hard enough to make splashes. Aten told me to tell you.'

'And you say there are no insects on the beach?' I asked.

'A few. Not like this,' he said, swatting three.

'Nestors! Look alive,' I said. 'Warp us over to the seaward bank.'

Old Nestor used the last light of day to give me the kind of look the dog gives a cruel master.

'Nestor, dammit!' I snapped. 'There are no insects on the beach. We're safe – we're going to sleep on the sand.'

'Aphrodite's swelling . . .' He paused 'Aye, aye, sir,' he said. 'Come on, you lubbers.'

The moans and complaints didn't cease until they were asleep, but the beach, and its breeze, were a damn sight better than the innards of a ship in a cloud of midges. It was a warm night, and I was asleep in about as much time as it took to pull my cloak over my head.

We rose before dawn. I split the crews, taking half of the Ionian oarsmen out of the other ship, the *Winged Nike*, and replacing them with my own people. I divided my sailors, and put Leander in charge of Achilles and Arios and Diodoros. I gave them Vasilos, the old archer, and two former helots, so that they had some chance in a ship fight.

I took Damon aside.

'Don't fight anything,' I said. 'If we get split, run for Methymna.'

'We need food,' he said.

'Wind is from the north,' I said. 'We can be in Methymna tomorrow midday. They'll be hungry, but short of rising against you, there's not much they can do. We stay in with the coast of Asia and don't let them see Lemnos going by.'

Damon said, 'We could just run for Lemnos.'

'I don't want to tangle with this Persian squadron,' I said. 'Not yet. We scouted and got away alive. With a capture. Let's get away.'

Damon nodded.

And that, for the most part, is what we did. We sailed south and a little east, passing Tenedos on our starboard side. Before darkness fell we were in the out-current of the Dardanelles, and not a ship to be seen.

In the darkness, I turned west and stood out to sea a dozen stadia, mostly to weather the little islands up against the coast of Asia. We passed Troy, and I said a prayer to Heracles my ancestor. The Ionians aboard grew louder and louder in their complaints, until I sent Styges and Zephyrides down into the rowing frame – with a little wine – to explain to the oarsmen that we were fine and safe, and that any further complaints might get a different reception.

It was a clear night and the wind held, so I watched Asia coast by with the occasional fire or lighted house. When everything to my port side was dark, I turned a little to port and ran south by east. I alternated Young Nestor and Aten in the bow, watching like the sea hawks they had become, but this was a route I'd sailed since was a boy. I knew the sound of the sea and the shape of the current coming through the Mytilini channel, and I held my course with confidence. A little after the sun rose, I saw the red tiled roofs of Methymna and the fortress high above.

And there on the beach, bless them, were Neoptolimos and Parmenio and their ships, ready for sea.

It felt odd. I'd sailed against an enemy, taken a ship in a stiff fight, and never taken my sword from my scabbard. Other men had made the leap to the enemy rowing frame. Other men had risked their lives against bright iron and ruddy bronze.

It felt odd. It still does.

But with Parmenio and Neoptolimos, I had four ships. And at four to seven, I was willing to take on my enterprising Persian navarch and his squadron. I won't say I rubbed my hands with glee. I've certainly lost enough fights to fill a few graveyards, and nothing is certain. But Artemis had been with us on her day, and I felt that air, that indefinable sense that we could beat them and capture back the mastery of the northern seas from this interloper.

Once again, Briseis washed my shield on the beach, and her ladies blessed every oar. My new Ionian oarsmen stood in loose ranks to be served wine by Ionian ladies, and were too polite to grumble about their hunger.

But in two hours they were eating fresh bread – good tough barley bread – and fried fish and squid, and drinking good wine.

And Briseis was telling me that the siege of Amathus had failed, and that Pausanias had quarrelled with Aristides and Cimon, and that the Allied fleet – what was left of it – was at Samos.

We were sharing a single kline on a terrace above the sea. We could see past Antissa down the coast, and the last of the sun gilded and rouged everything in a holy light.

'Where's your brother?' I asked, tracing one finger slowly along her marvellous neck and shoulders.

'Quite possibly at Samos,' she said.

'So it's just us,' I said.

She rolled over to face me.

'Just us,' she agreed.

'I can cruise in the channel, keeping two ships on the beach,' I said. 'Until the fleet comes.'

'If it comes at all,' she said. 'But that's not what you want to do.'

I shook my head. 'No,' I agreed. 'I want to put to sea at dawn with four ships and go looking for them.'

She nodded. 'Because you trust your luck?' she asked.

I thought of that odd feeling – that I hadn't drawn my sword. Did I trust my luck? Luck is a dangerous concept for Greeks. We believe that luck is god-given, and usually deserts you in your hour of great-est need. But then, we're great gamblers, so perhaps we squander it. Anyway . . .

'No luck,' I said. 'After Salamis and Mycale, they should fear us. This one doesn't. I want to beat him because . . .'

'Because otherwise the others might lose their fear?' she asked.

'The Greek allies are kept together with catch and clay,' I said. 'And our reputation on the seas is greater than our number of ships or our successes warrant. So, yes. We need that reputation. It does more to protect the coasts of Ionia than twenty triremes.'

She leant in. 'That is a brilliant rationalisation for doing what you want to do.' She kissed me lightly, the way married people do, as punctuation. 'So do it. Just see to it that you win. And don't die.'

'I'll try not to,' I said.

'I would not forgive you,' she said.

I smiled into her eyes. 'Do you have any thoughts about Thrace? I asked. 'The insects are terrible, but I saw a good deal of prime farmland.'

'Are we founding a colony?' she asked.

'Maybe,' I agreed.

She smiled and lay back, watching the sun settle over Lesbos.

'I might enjoy Thrace,' she said. 'When Ionia is free, I suspect we won't be able to live here.'

That threw a little ice water on me.

'Why?' I asked.

She smiled, but it wasn't a happy smile.

'The very excellence that will take us to victory,' she said, 'will, in time, be poison to our neighbours. Is that not always the way, with Greeks?'

'We don't sound very nice,' I said.

I meant it as a jest, but in my heart, I thought of Pausanias – only a year before, the greatest man in Greece – and of Miltiades and Themistocles, and even Aristides. Miltiades was dead, Aristides just back from exile, Themistocles denied even an acclamation for glory.

'No,' she said, her head turned away. 'No. We don't, do we?'

In the end, we didn't sail at dawn. Old Nestor and Damon and two shipwrights convinced me that the apparently incidental damage our ram had done to the capture deserved a day's attention and a repair to the damage of the pitch, and the Lemnian oarsmen needed a day off and some food.

'They're soft,' Neoptolimos said, with all the arrogance and strength of size and youth.

I shrugged. 'They got here. They've been captured and released, and we need to make sure they prefer us to the Persians.'

'I can replace them all with Chians in four days,' Neoptolimos said.

I considered a variety of replies, as I was no longer a hot-headed youth. I considered explaining to him that these were men, as he was a man, with pride and dignity. And patriotism. And that they needed a day to pull themselves together.

But what I said was, 'I don't have four days.'

And he accepted that.

The Lemnians were, for the most part, excellent men. They were several cuts above Athenian oarsmen – socially, I mean, not as oarsmen. Athenian oarsmen view themselves as the very best in the world, and they are probably right. The overweening arrogance of these very lower-class men was probably what kept offending aristocrats like Aristides.

The Lemnians were from what might otherwise have been the lower ends of the hoplite class – young, patriotic men who'd decided that it was better to pull an oar for freedom than to stay home. Lemnos is a bit of a special case. Miltiades had taken the island for Athens in the early days of the Ionian revolt. It had remained, to all intents, part of Athens. Miltiades had moved most of his colonists, when the Chersonese fell to the Persians, on to Lemnos.

Regardless, the rapidity of their defeat had shocked them, and I suspect that there were some among them who felt that collapse of self that comes with capture in war. Our recapture hadn't really made them whole.

Others were like angry bears, roaring for revenge. That was no saner, although it made them more reliable in a fight.

I saw that they were fed – meat, and fish, and all the bread and honey they wanted. I 'strongly encouraged' the best of my Athenians to go among them and befriend them, and I paid from my dwindling resources for a couple of wine shops to open for business on the beach.

I had my marines in the citadel, three hundred paces above me, able to see all the way up the coast of Asia. I wasn't particularly worried about being surprised.

The day passed. I met a lot of nice young men who might be dead in a day or two. I contemplated my own many failings, and I lay cuddled with my wife, feeling like an actor who has forgotten his lines.

And the next morning, as the sun rose off to the east, a rim of fire over the blue-black sea, we left the beach and ran north and west, bound for Lemnos.

It was a very frustrating day. Neoptolimos in the *Amaranth* had trouble with his sailing tackle. The wind, so promising early in the day, veered round and came in our faces, forcing us all to row, and Parmenio's *Gad's Fortune*, the largest and heaviest of our triremes, didn't like the rising seas and held us back.

I spent the day signalling formation changes, which frustrated the oarsmen and the captains, too. Neoptolimos and Parmenio both had the Ionian mindset that they could take anyone, ship to ship, and had no need for complex manoeuvres. Dionysius of Phocaea had attempted to train that out of the Ionians before Lade, and failed. Twenty years later, we were still facing it.

And the oarsmen grew frustrated with the stop and go – the rowing soft, and then laying out – cruising speed, ramming speed, check your oars, wait, wait, go like hell.

Too bad. I'd seen more fleet actions than most men, and more ship fights than almost anyone, with the exception of Megakles and Cimon. I wasn't going to budge, and as it was plain to me that we weren't making Lemnos in a day, as we'd hoped, I didn't mind if we messed around in the open sea.

They weren't bad, but they weren't great, either. The station keeping was the worst, because we had four very different ships. My *Apollo's Raven* was heavier and stiffer than the others, and had fewer oarsmen, despite which I wasn't the slowest, but the second slowest – and the fastest under sail, and I could make sail in conditions where the others could not.

The *Gad's Fortune* was our largest ship – the hull newly touched up, brilliant vermilion red. She was tall and heavy, and even a capful of wind on her long, broad flank and she'd make leeway. She was slow, by Athenian standards. She carried more marines than any of the rest of ours, and I'd convinced Parmenio to add some archers, which was not the Ionian way. Archers weren't that easy to find on the islands – I'm guessing because they had no large animals to hunt.

The *Amaranth* was, as you'll recall, another Phoenician capture. She was a Tyrian design, so lighter and faster than the *Gad's Fortune*.

She was fast, and easy to handle, but she waterlogged easily. That is, if she was at sea too long, her timbers soaked up the water and she grew increasingly sluggish. She was also too narrow to sail in any conditions except with the wind almost directly astern.

The *Winged Nike* was a Lemnian ship, fast and fancy. She, too, was narrow, with no real deck at all, only an amidships catwalk. She was the older kind of trireme, where if there was any accident to the heavy rope binding the stem and stern, she'd fly apart, because she had no heavy upper deck to brace her. In short, a racing shell with a ram. She was better at almost everything than my other ships, but her limitation was sea-keeping. She was bad in a swell, and had none of the little storage areas that the others had. Every Phoenician ship was prepared to carry a little cargo – my own *Apollo's Raven* had a hold, some ballast, and a storage compartment in the bow behind the ram. The *Winged Nike* had none of those.

This is the huge advantage of Athens or Corinth or Aegina, who can build fifty triremes to the same designs. They all have the same limitations and the same advantages, so that the navarch can plan his campaign down to the details of supply, based on his own doctrines and his ships. I had four different ships in a fleet of four. We couldn't all sail well, and we couldn't all row upwind well, and station keeping, by which I mean forming a fighting line with the ships almost oar-tip to oar-tip, was brutal.

Well, that was long-winded. Let's just leave it here – we spent the day rowing about the ocean, trying to be better at the most basic manoeuvres. Towards nightfall I ordered the squadron to turn to port, and we fetched up on the beaches of the island of Philoctetes, sacred to archers. Vasilos was a devotee and wore the charm, the bow and arrows of Heracles, and he took Ka and Nemet and the former helots ashore to the shrine and initiated them.

The rest of us had a hasty meal and a surly sleep. We'd landed on the south side of the island and I doubted that our fires could be seen by the enemy, but I put up a hasty tower of four mainmast yards on the headland and manned it all night with marines.

Morning came, warm as true summer, and another wind change, this time from the east and full of rain. Some of Damon's sailors had rigged a net in the surf and brought us a breakfast of little whitefish, fried in oil – delicious, and a good omen. We cleared the gravel beaches in good humour and had the wind on our flanks. I might have been able to make sail, but it was a bad point of wind for the rest. The *Winged Nike* took water in through her lower oar-ports even with her mast down, while the *Gad's Fortune* sagged away to windward every stade.

I had Diodoros singing. He had a fine voice, and had desired to be a rhapsode and he knew most of Homer. We sailed along with a deep bass voice singing to us of wily Odysseus and the bow of Heracles, a story about the waters and beaches around us, and our oarsmen rowed with a will.

The rain came and went, and visibility was variable. I had the boys take turns high above the deck in the mainmast nest, but the horizon was close. Even as we heard the seabirds that indicated that we were close to Lemnos, we didn't see the loom of her mountains.

In my youth, a small island had detonated in a titanic explosion that could be heard for miles. It had happened just off Lemnos, and when the resulting waves had died away, the island was gone. Legend has it that the forges of Hephaestus are on Lemnos, and they certainly produce wonderful swords and some excellent armour as well.

The point is that Lemnos has a smell of sulphur – of activity in the ground. We could smell it, but the rain and the clouds hid the coast. I kept walking forward, looking through the mist, and hoping to hear the sound of waves on a beach.

After three hours, I finally heard what I sought, and I used my signals to order my ships to follow me. I turned to starboard and ran west along what I had to suppose was the south coast of Lemnos. I could hear the birds, smell the stink, and sometimes hear breakers, but I still hadn't seen the coast.

The east wind was dying – I had reason to hope the weather would clear. I'd just turned to Old Nestor to ask his view when, over the starboard side, I saw a trireme, clear as day. She was perhaps five hundred paces away, rowing serenely along the same course as mine.

I had a moment to think that Parmenio was far off his station, and then I leant out and looked back. I could just see all three ships behind me.

'Action stations,' I snapped. 'Quiet as you can.'

Rain struck us, and visibility vanished. I couldn't see a stade. Nemet was climbing the mainmast, and he was almost invisible before he got all the way up.

Aten was standing on the stern bench, waving a red chiton on a spear until he got an answering wave from astern. Then he raised my bronze-faced aspis and made the signal.

I saw the answering flash.

The marines were already in their armour. The oarsmen had their cushions set.

'Turn to starboard three points,' I said.

I appeal to all of you as huntsmen. You know that feeling, that time does not flow evenly, but expands and contracts to fit our needs? We often discussed it in my youth, sitting at the feet of Heraclitus. He would ask each of us to describe an occasion on which time ran very quickly, and another very slowly. In time, he led us to incidents where it ran slowly for one boy and quickly for another.

His point was that we cannot be sure that time, as we assume it to work, is even real. Or any more real than the rest of our perceptions.

I leave that to wiser men. But the five hundred paces that separated me from that other trireme were a clear demonstration of the way that time passes, because I believe that I lived a lifetime in those heartbeats, and I had the time to consider many things that I had done ill, and to regret them. Not my various failings as a man – not the way I treated a woman as a chattel, or killed men and took their goods. Those are thoughts for different times, dark nights under starlight.

What I thought about was all the mistakes I'd made in the last few days, and paramount among them was hubris.

In my haste to prove that we were better men than the Medes, at least at sea, I had dismissed any thought of defeat. And here I was, in a fog, committing my four mismatched ships to a fight with an unknown number of enemy ships, with the only intact squadron capable of defending Ionia. And I hadn't taken the trouble to send a messenger boat south for Archilogos, which, as we closed, seemed to me more and more foolish. I had taken a risk, and compounded it with foolishness.

Is self-doubt the coin of age? I never used to have these thoughts as a younger man.

The doubt was so powerful that twice my mouth opened to order Nicanor, who was now my helmsman, to turn to port.

I didn't. I still wonder what it might have been like, had I done so.

*

The fog – or rather, the low cloud – was so thick we could barely see the wave tops ahead of the ship. Sometimes I had trouble seeing Aten's signals from the bow.

I leant down to Poseidonos.

'Check the oars,' I said. I said it softly.

I had an idea. It was odd, how that idea cut through my own fog of doubt. I prayed, quickly, and watched the oars come up to the check, the top of their rotating motion as the rowers came back.

We glided silently in a world of ghosts. Somewhere above us was the sun. It was brighter above, and a puff of wind touched my face, moist and cold. I could smell the seaweed and the sea. Somewhere off to my port side, gulls cried.

I could hear another ship rowing. I could hear the timoneer, ordering the stroke, and another voice, cursing ineptitude.

And the crack of a whip, so loud that it sounded as if it was next to my ear.

I'll say again that my new ship had a different rig, so that the two steering oars needed two separate men; two skilled men. With Damon on his own ship, and Old Nestor effectively my first officer, I needed helmsmen and I'd temporarily promoted Archilaus, a very reliable deck had, and young Nicanor. I had the best ship in my squadron, but two new helmsmen made me unsure that I could win a complicated ramming fight.

However, as with my other fears, there was nothing to be done.

'Two points to port,' I said to Nicanor in a conversational voice.

I leant well out, looking astern.

There was the *Gad's Fortune*, glowing red in the strange light. I could see Ariston, now Parmenio's marine captain, in the bow, leaning on his spear, watching the sea. I felt another puff of breeze coming off the land and I heard the gulls. Based on these table-scraps of information, I made my guesses. I guessed that we were crossing the great bay that pointed like a finger up into Hephaestia on Lemnos – perhaps close in among the tiny islets of the east side.

I guessed that my squadron was bringing up the wind and the sun, too. I had mere heartbeats before the low cloud burned away. It was already lighter.

I guessed that my enemy was cruising in a column, or perhaps a double column – seven or eight ships.

If Artemis was at my shoulder, we were coming up behind the last ship.

If I was mad, and wrong, we were coming up behind the lead ship.

I made a motion with my hand – the knucklebones of fate were cast. It was too late to turn away. If I declined the engagement, I'd be pulling upwind to a potentially hostile beach.

I was in my armour. I took my spears from a stand by the helm.

'Nicanor, Archilaus, listen to me,' I said.

They both nodded, but their eyes never left the fog off the bow. Nicanor was a fisherman's son, in a position of immense responsibility. Archelaus was a veteran deck hand, and the promotion to helmsmen meant a great deal to him. There are many heroes in the world. Both looked full of concentration, and afraid, but they were both determined to succeed.

'In a moment, the clouds will break,' I said. 'Put the beak into the stern of the ship that will appear dead ahead.'

'Aye, lord,' Archilaus said.

Just that. No doubts that there *was* a ship dead ahead. I envied him that.

If that enemy ship had spotted me, he might have turned to port or starboard – he might be setting up to ram us this instant.

But I could hear him, and that whip-crack ...

The sky grew lighter directly overhead.

I ran forward. It was much easier on the new *Apollo's Raven*, with her solid deck over more than half the ship. I paused by Old Nestor on the command platform amidships.

'I intend to take the ship just ahead,' I said. 'The moment we board, you shear off and try for an oar-rake on the next ahead. It's your fight after that. Your ship, you hear me?'

'You—' he began, but I slapped his shoulder.

'I need to wet my spear,' I said.

A younger man's words, but true – I had already had my fill of sending other men to do my dirty work. I was not ready to admit to age.

My archers were ready, Nemet was high above, leaning into the slight breeze like a very intent cat, and Ka, in the bow behind the marines, was in much the same posture.

I had never ordered silence, and yet they were all silent. The grunting of the oarsmen as they pulled was less, too. I was almost to the bow, where Styges crouched, ready like a lion to leap on his prey. At his shoulder, Leander stood like the figure of Ares on a vase.

Dead ahead in the murk, I heard, 'I can hear the gulls on dog island,' and another voice, with a Persian accent, say, 'Very well.'

All doubt fell away, as it always does.

Another puff of breeze, and a flaw in the ever-present fog, and there she was, the stern arching high like the breast of a swan, and the helmsmen standing on either side. She was painted a dark red, and she wasn't Ionian. We were some degrees off a ramming course, but before I could say anything, Nicanor, true to his choosing, flicked the oars like Harpagos or Stephanos might have. Our bow settled in to line up with our enemy's stern as if we were both settled into the stone grooves of the old chariot roads. I saw Archilaus say something, and both men's heads dipped as they put weight on their oars. We were committed.

'Ramming speed!' I roared.

I stepped forward, taking my place behind Achilles, who shot me a glance and wriggled, as if to let me take his place. I had time to put my hand on his shoulder. I knelt.

I put my spear between the left side and right, splitting the marines in two sections. Heraklitus and Hipponax were on the right, with Arios. I had considered making them helmsmen, and then abandoned the thought. They wanted to be marines ...

'You stay here,' I told them. My mind was racing.

Heraklitus glared at me.

Too damn bad.

Our oarsmen may have got in four full-power strokes, and we struck. Bow to stern is a difficult strike, but the very safest for the attacker.

Poseidonos roared, 'Starboard-side oars in!'

Next to me, Ka rose to his full height, grunted as he pulled his heavy bow, and loosed, all one beautiful, fluid motion, his black skin glowing with the first kiss of the sun.

I flipped my helmet down over my face and settled the hinged cheek plates.

The ram strike went in just forward of the stern, to the port-side aft corner of the enemy rowing frame. Because both ships were moving forward, the impact was minimal, initially. We scraped down their side, but we were moving faster – almost twice their speed. Our bow was crushing the oars against the hull and splintering them against the softer flesh and bone of the humans who drove them, and the ship seemed to scream.

I was scarcely paying attention by then. Ka's first arrow took the nearest steersman under his outflung arm, and he was dead before he fell, the whole arrow through his unarmoured body. Achilles and Leander were already on the helm platform. Leander killed the other helmsman before I made the leap.

I landed well, got both feet under me, my only wound the bite of my left greave into my instep as I landed. I went forward on to the deck, having kept enough balance to kneel, wager a glance forward, turn, and go, with Diodoros at my shoulder. There was a long catwalk, almost a central deck, down the middle of the ship over the rowers's heads – a Sicilian or Carthaginian design.

I started along it. The oarsmen were mostly African – I could see them under my feet, even with my helmet closed – but there were some who looked like islanders. Slaves? Captives?

On the port side, men were writhing in agony or screaming as their oars were ripped from them or into them, the bow of my *Apollo's Raven* ripping through their oar loom like an angry horse through a pile of twigs.

No time to think.

I ran.

I have a bad wound, an old one, and I don't run too well. Sometimes, though, when the gods allow, or the spirit of a fight is on me, the lameness seems to fall away, and I run like I ran as a young man.

In a ship fight, there are two ways to win. One is that you fight your way through the ship, an exhausting slog, the agony of repeated combats wearing you down. You hope that you and your friends are stronger, because in a ship fight, there are usually only winners and dead people.

The other kind can only be achieved in the first clash. It has to be as if Zeus threw you from his hand, a thunderbolt of steel and bronze, so that men who ought to make a fight of it simply drop their weapons.

I ran.

It is really the only part of the fight that I remember perfectly – my bare feet slapping against the trim, almost white planks of the catwalk, my breath coming in long, slow bursts. Like the approach in the fog, it seemed to last a very long time.

The Mede, or Persian, officer amidships had a long spear in both hands. He stepped out to meet me with the confidence of the well-trained man, and the spearhead stayed low as he watched me run.

I threw my javelin.

He tried to bat it down – a flick of his long spear – and too late he realised that it was too high for him.

I took the head of his spear on my shield, already slowing. I remember that it punched through the bronze face and stuck. By then I'd seized my second spear from behind my shield. I swept it across the face of my aspis, head down, snapping his spearhead clear of the bronze, sweeping the spear to my left. I powered forward with my right leg as I rotated my shorter spear, so that the *saurauter* went in just over the top of his beautiful scale corselet. It skidded along his neck bone and through the skin and muscle where the shoulder and neck come together. I slammed my shield rim into his head and down he went, sliding off my spear. I went past the Greek trierarch, who sat against the mainmast bolster with my javelin in his guts. I killed him with a flick of my right wrist and went to the bow side of the command platform.

The enemy marines were frozen in the bow of their ship. We'd just killed the entire command crew.

'I am Arimnestos of Plataea!' I called. 'Surrender now and you will live.'

Sadly, this was not the day for the thunderbolt.

The marines charged me.

That's the part I don't remember – from the moment when I realised from one man's facial expression that he had to make himself charge, to the moment when I realised, in a good deal of pain, that I'd fallen halfway off the catwalk, and it felt as if I'd been kicked between my legs.

I remember an impact, using my spear to fend off blows, the relief as someone's aspis pressed into my back, the stinging pain as I took a spear through my foot, the fall, and then ...

And then it was over and I wasn't dead. Again. I just had a spear wound straight through the top of my instep, and my foot had already swollen like a melon. How does the skin do it? It looks tight enough ordinarily, and then ...

Zeus, I remember the foot, swollen and feeling like it belonged to someone else.

And Leander leaning down, his face a mask of fatigue under his helmet.

'Now what?' he asked.

'Get me up,' I muttered, or something like that.

I got an arm over his shoulders and went aft to the command deck, and leant out over the rail, all my weight on my arms.

Below and to my left, just at the edge of my peripheral vision, I could see the heads of the port-side oarsmen. A lot of heads were hanging slack. There was a lot of moaning.

Out to port, it was almost a clear day. How long had we been fighting? To starboard there was a retreating wall of cloud, but above me the sky was blue and the sun was bright.

My foot hurt as if I'd dipped it in molten bronze.

I suspect that I swore a good deal.

But ahead, on the port side, the *Winged Nike* was just passing us, pulling at ramming speed. Just beyond, but to the starboard of our bow, was another ship, not one of ours, with no oars out on its port side, drifting, its bow rising and falling on the swell. And beyond that ...

An island and a long line of rocks ... towards which the fresh breeze was pushing us. Not fast, but inexorably, like the hand of a god.

I sagged. For a moment, the will to fight on left me, and I just sagged over the rail, unable to even contemplate the next step. I looked back, saw that all my marines were looking at me. Styges was straight as an ash tree. Leander was cleaning his spear.

They weren't done.

The problem was that most of them, good men as they were, were not actually sailors. If I'd had Hipponax ...

What I needed was sailors.

I took a few deep breaths. I remember thinking of Briseis. Men claim they think of their loves in a fight – I think they're liars. But it did occur to me that if I didn't move myself to some serious action, I'd be dead, and that made it unlikely that we'd ever make love again.

Call it what you will, it got me moving.

'Styges,' I said. 'Leander. I need you to sort out which of our oarsmen is dead or badly hurt. I need new oars served out to the men who can wield them.'

I leant out from the catwalk, and my foot screamed. Maybe I did, too.

'There are spare oars,' I said, pointing to a narrow space under the catwalk.

Styges nodded.

'Don't be gentle,' I said. 'We don't have time for a mutiny.'

I leant down.

'Listen to me!' I shouted. 'If you don't row, we all die. If you row, I promise you your freedom. Simple choice.'

Some faces turned to look at me.

Some didn't.

Some of those men had already had enough. Some wanted to kill me.

I looked at Ka.

'Anyone here speak your language?' I asked.

Ka shouted something.

No one twitched.

'No,' he said with a shrug. Then he tried again, rattling off something staccato. Many heads turned to him.

He looked at me, and shrugged.

'I don't know, Ari. I only speak a little. It's a trade tongue that the *mgeni* use. Far from my home but—'

'Tell them that if they row, we all live and I'll set them free.'

Somewhere behind me, a hollow pounding began. It wasn't my ship. It was . . .

Close.

Ka shook his head. 'I don't even know the word for "row".'

He shook his head again, and barked something.

Two of the oarsmen shouted back.

Ka raised a hand. He ducked down into the thranite frame, which was no small trick for a man as tall as he. He spoke very carefully, enunciating each word.

The two men shouted back, and then fifty men were shouting, insisting, every one trying to speak at once.

Ka took his long knife off his hip and slammed it into the oar frame and left it there, vibrating.

Silence.

Leander chuckled. 'Well played,' he said.

Ka spoke the same words, one more time.

I looked over the side, and the line of rocks was much closer. The ship ahead of us was already on them, pounding rhythmically against the islet. Men were screaming.

'Give them oars!' I yelled.

Leander pushed past me. Ka picked up a spare oar and thrust it, not very gently, at one of the two loudest men.

The man took the oar and started to feed it out through the frame.

Poseidon. I had no oar master, no sailors, and no helmsmen.

I still remember trying to walk aft. I had time to see that my Persian wasn't dead – time to pull my spear out of his neck and use it as a crutch.

I needed them to reverse their oars. That is, I needed them all to turn around, settle on the bench behind them, and pull.

I had heard the timoneer, who lay dead just forward of the helm, call out to them in Greek.

I prayed to Poseidon. That's mostly a lie. I cursed, and almost fell, twenty times.

But by the time I'd wiggled and hobbled and cursed my way to the steering oars, Leander and Ka and Styges had pushed oars into fifty pairs of hands.

I could barely see and I wasn't sure my voice would hold, but there wasn't really anyone else just then ...

Except my useless cousin Achilles. Not really useless. He was good at killing.

And he'd apparently been paying attention for three years at sea.

'Want me to beat the time?' he asked.

'Good lad,' I said.

I grabbed the steering oars, as much to hold myself upright as to steer.

'Reverse your oars,' I croaked.

Thank the gods, Achilles repeated it in a young man's braying roar.

'Tell me when they've done it.'

'They're doing it!' he called.

I went out for a moment. I swear it – it all went black. The pain just ate me.

Achilles screamed something.

I pulled myself together. I looked forward as best I could.

'Stroke,' I muttered.

Achilles called 'Stroke,' and slammed the butt of his spear into the deck.

Our bow struck the dying ship ahead of us, and Achilles' saurauter bit so deeply into the deck that he couldn't pull it out.

Bad luck. He wrestled with the spear instead of calling the stroke. Our rowers fell into confusion, and the current began to pull us into the rocks.

We were *so close*.

'STROKE!' I roared. It came from within me and left like a lion pouncing.

The oars rattled along, as ragged as new ephebes at their first spear drill. I don't think the ship even moved.

'Check!' I called. I could only really see the port-side rowers. 'Pull!' I called when most of them were up and ready. At least the poor bastards were obedient.

Achilles had it. He left his spear in the deck and leant down.

'Pull!' he called, on time.

I motioned to Diodoros.

'Sing!' I called.

'What?' he asked, and then realised it didn't matter. I thought he'd sing Homer, but what we got was a drinking song.

> *The girl in the golden sandals*
> *Has hit me with the sloppy grape of her love.*
> *I was drunk at a party*
> *and I couldn't even move.*

See, I can still sing it. It was quite popular then, a play on old Theognis.

You don't care. Anyway, he sang. And the rhythm picked up.

For ten strokes, nothing much happened. We bumped the wreck again, and we were right in the kelp. There was a rock the size of a house an oar's length off the stern, and we were done.

And then we weren't. Suddenly we were sliding away backwards. We were, if anything, gathering way, and I had to steer, and suddenly ...

Suddenly I realised that I was aboard a captured ship in the middle of a battle.

We weren't done yet.

It is an axiom of sea fights that captured ships cannot be trusted to fight. There are dozens of reasons, and we exemplified them – angry oarsmen on the verge of open revolt, unfamiliarity with the ship and rig, insufficient prize crew to fight and hold the oarsmen down.

And that made me a spectator.

As it proved, my captains had all read my last moment plan brilliantly – or perhaps each of them innovated from what they were given, as I had.

So, as the low cloud cleared, we took the last ship but one in a long column. There was, it turned out, another ship behind us, as the *Amaranth* discovered. Neoptolimos was last in our column, and he guessed at where he was supposed to turn, and ended up passing the stern of another ship in the fog. At the last moment he realised it was not the *Winged Nike* and turned, coming up on her starboard side in a hail of thrown javelins.

The lifting of the murk showed me the *Amaranth* and another, lower ship, long side to long side, their marines locked in combat.

Forward, over the bow, was like a different world.

Old Nestor had oar-raked the ship ahead of the one we'd taken, leaving her to be sucked into the rocks where we'd rammed her inadvertently. She was being pounded to death against the shore, and there were already men crawling like seals out of the water on the islet. That was a stade ahead of me, and slightly to port, and the whole of the bay beyond was appearing as the sun burned off the last of the morning fog.

By the grace of the gods, Nicanor had turned the *Apollo's Raven* to starboard. Judging from where I could see my ship, three stadia away and south, she must have missed the rocks by an oar's length.

And she'd tackled another ship. They were locked together in a death grip, so close they looked like one thick hull, turned half away from me.

Parmenio had done something extraordinary. He'd apparently turned to starboard earlier – perhaps he'd crossed our stern in the fight. I had no idea. But he'd come in from the south, from the starboard side, and rammed a ship. I could see its hull, upside down, with swimmers clinging to it, and the long vermilion hull of the *Gad's Fortune*. At first she appeared motionless. A moment's attention suggested that she was backing away from her kill, and her oars flashed in perfect unison.

If I had almonds, I could show you more clearly. In short, my little squadron had attacked the rear of their column, and the front half of their squadron was turning back on us, oars flashing in the new sun.

The enemy ships were all spread out over stadia of ocean – it's very difficult to keep station in fog.

But we were in a great deal of trouble. Two of my ships were still locked in their fights, and win or lose, they weren't going to be fit for more. Only the *Gad's Fortune* was untouched, her marines just visible crouched in the bow. The *Winged Nike* was close in to the islet, pursuing a fleeing trireme. I cursed because Damon was headed the wrong way to help the rest of us, but he was also new to command, and I'd expected a great deal of my trierarchs that day.

I had five marines and a good archer. A great archer.

And spirit is everything. Sometimes, you can break men's spirits without fighting to the death.

It seems like a very long story, but in fact, I took it all in one long glance, and it took me as much time as a man would sing the hymn to Artemis to make my decision. I know, because Diodoros sang:

> *I sing of Artemis, whose shafts are of gold,*
> *Who cheers on the hounds,*
> *The pure maiden, shooter of stags, who delights in archery,*
> *Own sister to Apollo with the golden sword.*
> *Over the shadowy hills and windy peaks she draws her golden bow,*
> *Rejoicing in the chase, and sends out grievous shafts.*
> *The tops of the high mountains tremble and the tangled wood echoes*
> *   awesomely*
> *With the outcry of beasts: earth quakes and the sea also where fishes*
> *   shoal.*
> *But the goddess with a bold heart turns every way destroying*
> *The race of wild beasts: and when she is satisfied and has cheered her*
> *   heart,*
> *This huntress who delights in arrows slackens her supple bow*
> *And goes to the great house of her dear brother Phoebus Apollo,*
> *To the rich land of Delphi, there to order the lovely dance of the Muses*
> *   and Graces.*
> *There she hangs up her curved bow and her arrows, and heads and*
> *   leads the dances,*
> *Gracefully arrayed, while all they utter their heavenly voice, singing*
> *   how neat-ankled Leto bare children supreme among the immortals*
> *   both in thought and in deed.*

I wanted to go to the *Apollo's Raven*, but she was past the rocks and the islet, and the drift of the hulls and the wreck of the dead trireme combined with my fractious crew to render that too far and too hard.

The *Amaranth*, on the other hand, was perhaps ten ship's lengths away.

I leant on my port-side oar to take all the weight off my wounded foot.

'Prepare to turn the ship to starboard,' I called out.

Achilles repeated as if he'd been born to be a timoneer. He even raised his hand in the air, showing me that he was watching the oarsmen to make sure that the starboard-side oars were reversing.

I watched as a wave of nausea came over me. The pain in my foot was remarkable. I'd fought with worse wounds, but the amount of pain, and its pulsating nature, was making me unsteady.

I leant on the oars.

Achilles waved his hand.

'Turn to starboard,' I called, and Achilles ordered the oars into the water.

It was pitiful, compared to the old *Lydia,* or the *Athena Nike,* or even my new *Apollo's Raven.* I swear that no two oars struck the water together – the hull was full of curses. Do you know what happens when oars cross in a trireme? If you catch a crab, or mis-row, you risk slamming the butt of your oar into the man in front, or your own head. Oars are heavy and neatly balanced. Throw that balance off on the thole pins, and the oar becomes either a terrible labour or a weapon the sea can use against you.

We had seats for a hundred and eighty oarsmen, more or less, but at least twenty were dead or too badly injured to row. Of those remaining, almost all the starboard-side rowers were alive with intact oars – call them eighty.

But on the port side, where the *Apollo's Raven* had raked her way down the side, there were perhaps forty oars in the water, and they were ragged and poorly handled.

We turned well enough. It wasn't pretty, but we got around in good time.

It was when I ordered us forward that the wreck of the oar loom showed. We immediately began turning to port instead of going straight. Even leaning the steering oars all the way, I couldn't compensate, and we swayed like a drunken man.

'Cease rowing!' I called out. 'Rowed of all!' I didn't have the energy or the two healthy feet to climb down into the hull. 'Achilles! I need the same number of oars each side. Pair them – the men able to row on the port with someone on the starboard. Everyone else must stow their oar.'

Achilles looked at me with a little fear and a fair amount of incomprehension.

Why hadn't I brought Hipponax? Or Heraklitus? He might be a

soft-handed Ionian boy, but he'd been brought up with ships. Achilles was a Boeotian bumpkin like me.

We were beginning to drift.

'I need the oarsmen to be balanced,' I said, as slowly as I could make myself speak. 'We can't have more oars in the water on the starboard than the port side.'

Achilles blinked. And nodded.

He went into the oar frame, already snapping orders. Ka joined him. Thanks to the gods, Ka, the archer, knew what was needed.

I looked out over the port side, towards the enemy ships. They were coming straight at me, bow-on – four of them.

Well. I had my aspis, dropped when I took the oars.

I had sunlight.

I hobbled to my aspis, and lifting it was like Atlas taking the weight of the world on his shoulders.

I flashed it.

No answer.

I flashed again.

Nothing.

Come on, Parmenio!

But why should he look as us? A capture? He'd be looking to the *Apollo's Raven* for orders.

Flash.

Wait.

'Ready, cousin!' Achilles shouted.

I turned back to the job at hand.

'Give way, then,' I said.

It was still pitiful. It took ten or fifteen strokes to feel the bite of my steering oars, and to have enough way to develop any confidence in the ship.

We were now headed due south, because of the false turn – almost tangentially away from the line of ship combats.

'Prepare to turn to starboard,' I called, and the rowing was no better. We turned very slowly – worse, if anything, than before.

Was that a flash from the east?

I took the chance and picked up my aspis again. I flashed it, and the *Gad's Fortune* flashed back immediately.

Flash-flash-flash: *Form line.*

Pause. We had finished our turn.

'Prepare to give way!' I called.

An answering flash from Parmenio: *Understood.*

I held up the heavy aspis again. Flash-flash. Flash-flash: *On me.*

Another answering flash from Parmenio: *Understood.*

I dropped the aspis as if it was hot, because my left shoulder has taken too many hits over the years and I was about done. I got back into the steering rig. I could see the thranites looking at me expectantly.

At least they weren't in revolt.

'Give way, all!' I called.

Diodoros began to sing, and he slapped his hand on his aspis for rhythm.

We began to move – a wounded water insect creeping over the waves towards where the *Amaranth* and her enemy were locked in a deadly embrace. Ten ship's lengths – no distance. You could walk it in the time it takes to put a bridle on a horse.

Now, time hobbled like a man with a wounded foot.

But we had steerage way, and I pointed the bow at the open side of the enemy trireme. There was a huddle on her deck – men fighting. It was Chians against some other Ionians. Every man had his own device on his shield, and I didn't know any of Neoptolimos' marines well enough to know who was who. Or who was winning.

We limped along, closer and closer.

When we were two ship's lengths away, I called Leander and the rest on deck. Zephyrides and Kassandros, who was wounded, Achilles and Diodoros, Leander and me. Ka as an archer. That's all we had.

I nodded to Ka and he spat over the rail.

'Who do I shoot?' he asked.

He had a point. I was used to Ka's archery making all the difference in ship fights – not here.

'We have to look dangerous,' I said.

Six tired men. And me. Kassandros had had a spear straight through the muscle of his left bicep, over his shield – a wound I've taken and given. I was hobbling like an old man, and I couldn't imagine getting from ship to ship, although the swelling was less.

'Oars in!' I called. 'Look sharp, there.'

They did that well enough, pulling their oars aboard and stowing them under the opposite bench. Every oarsman fears that moment of impact.

We ghosted along. Leander turned, straightening.

'Go,' I said to Achilles. 'Kassandros, stay with me.'

Close in, I could make out the fighting. Neoptolimos had rammed bow to stern, as we had, and cleared the helm and fought his way down the ship to the command platform, but this ship's marines were better trained or just better led. The fighting was right there, at the stump of the unset mainmast. Neoptolimos had emptied his ship. I could see him, the helmet back on his head, directing his sailors. They were working their way down the oar frame, trying to envelop the enemy marines, but the enemy ship had some fighters, and their sailors were fighting back.

I touched my steering oars. I wanted to kiss their bow, just where the rowing frame started. I pointed, and Leander nodded. He had three marines. But he was going into the *back* of the enemy.

I hate sending other men to do something I should do myself.

Hate it.

Just then Zephyrides smiled, tossed me a casual salute with his spear, and popped his helmet down over his face. He looked like a rested athlete, ready for a run.

He said something, and Leander laughed, and Achilles laughed. In the bow, the sun sparkled on their bronze, and they looked like gods, and *I wasn't going with them.*

I missed my mark by six feet or so, because I'm not Harpagos. But glory to the gods, my new ship's oar frame caught on theirs, and the two ships began to drift together. Achilles tossed a grapple and so did Ka, and they had no men to spare to cut themselves free.

Leander leapt.

No one was there to contest his leap, and then they were all three aboard. Men were looking over their shoulders, and Ka, standing amidships, loosed his first arrow, sure of his targets now.

Whether it was the man pounding down the gangway at them, or the arrow that had just punched through an aspis to send an enemy marine gasping to his knees, it was the end of the fight. The enemy turned – there was shouting . . .

Neoptolimos, bless him, was not in the thick of it, not in the battle rage. He told me later that he'd fought from the first, taken a wound, and fallen back, as men do. He was clear of the action, and he saw when the enemy sailing master motioned that he would surrender.

Neoptolimos roared for his men to fall back, and they did. Puzzled, like dogs pulled off a dying stag, they fell away. Their ferocity dissipated, so that from my distance I could watch the change from killer to tired man – the slump of the shoulders. Ariston, in the thick of it, shoved an adversary, shield to shield, making the man stagger into his fellows, but Ariston kept his head, flicked his sword in a kind of salute, and held his ground.

The enemy marines were down to five – two on their knees.

For as long as it took to watch that, my foot did not hurt. Make of that what you will.

'Neoptolimos!' I croaked.

Kassandros had handed me his canteen, full of wine. I took a long pull, and felt immediately better. I poured a little to Poseidon and drank another mouthful.

'Neoptolimos!' I managed, louder, and he turned his head.

'Form line on me!' I called.

I pointed at the four warships coming down on us. Parmenio was coming up like a racehorse. Behind him, on the far side of the rocks, because of wind and current, the *Apollo's Raven* was locked with her opponent.

'Prepare to turn the ship about!' I called. 'We will turn to port!'

No one to repeat, now.

And I had no marines. None.

The gap was already too wide for Leander to jump. He stood at the side, looking at me. Achilles was at his shoulder, and the three of them watched as we poled off and turned away. The rowing was better, and I wished above all for Diodoros and his singing.

Instead, I picked up the splintered shaft of a spear and tapped the rail with it.

And we turned.

Behind me, Neoptolimos was already back aboard the *Amaranth*. He was shouting.

I was turning to port, away from his capture.

But he'd left someone competent aboard the capture. There was a lot of yelling, and my three marines vanished like something in the machine in a play in Athens.

We were turning.

Did I mention that in trireme combat, everything is about being twenty heartbeats ahead of the action?

My bow came on line with the onrushing enemy. The first of them was alone by about five hundred paces. He'd already passed the *Apollo's Raven* and was headed for us.

Parmenio and the *Gad's Fortune* appeared to be flying from him, but Parmenio was at a good cruising stroke, and would reach me first. Not by so very much.

We were bow-on.

Ka picked up his quivers and walked forward, the only fighting man left on the ship. If the rowers chose to rise off their benches, we were dead men.

'Prepare to give way,' I called.

It was a very small miracle. But as I later discovered, a little group of starboard-side oarsmen had moved to port-side benches, laying their wounded mates in the centreline. They took spare oars, or starboard-side oars, and as a result, I went from about forty oars a side to about sixty, and it showed.

We began to creep forward from the first stroke. At the time, I assumed that it was because I had the wind at my back. Or Athena, her hand on my stern.

We went forward.

Behind me, Neoptolimos had the *Amaranth* turning away from his capture, using the force of poling off to turn her bow to the north and get her around as his well-trained Chian fishermen reversed her from the starboard side. She turned like a shark scenting blood, much faster than we had, and started forward ...

And slowed, tucking in an oar's length from the tips of our oars, as we'd practised.

Parmenio was flying at us, and I thought he was cutting it too fine, but a hundred paces away his starboard-side rowers backed oars. His whole ship turned so fast that the sides churned the water, the red ship bobbing unnaturally and leaning as she turned, and she began to slide backwards from what had been her original momentum.

It was one of the nicest pieces of ship handling I'd ever seen. As the *Gad's Fortune* glided to a stop, we came up to her, and she went from backing to rowing forward smoothly, and we were a line of three facing one opponent, with me in the middle.

He turned away.

We continued to creep forward. I couldn't raise sail and leave my own ship alone to them. The *Apollo's Raven* was still fighting, three stadia away upwind.

We had to get past the islet and the rocks, as well.

I turned a little, cheating my bow seaward, to the south.

We kept our line.

This is why you practise.

South and east, the foremost adversary who had turned away met up with his companion and they formed on each other.

I looked aft.

Neoptolimos' capture had a low hull, painted a grey-blue the way pirates often paint their ships. Trickles of blood were showing amidships, dark stains on the pale hull.

But she was turning.

We crept forward.

The third enemy ship joined their line.

And the fourth.

We went at them at a walking pace.

The new capture began to come up. She was rowing as few oars as I was, and not with a will. I had to assume that my marines and Neoptolimos' marines were in her oar decks, inducing unwilling men to row. Ugly work.

It was all ugly work.

I kept my little group at our slow pace. Slow, but direct – we were now going straight at the other ships, bow to bow.

The capture caught us up. However unwilling the oarsmen, she was beautifully handled. Neoptolimos was not short of helmsmen. They joined our line and slowed to our ponderous pace, and there we were, ten stadia south of Lemnos, the mountains of the island rising like the shoulders of gods behind me, the sky clearing, the sun beautiful on the water. Our opponent now had the wind on their starboard bows, and we had it on our port sterns.

At about a stade, Ka stood up and loosed an arrow. He didn't shoot at the ship directly opposite, but diagonally downwind so that he had the wind directly behind him. He loosed a flight arrow, very high – a short arrow like a dart launched off a sort of stretcher, a wand carved to fit.

One tiny arrow.

It vanished.

I won't try to convince you that he hit something at a stade. Perhaps the little arrow fell into the sea, unnoticed. Perhaps it struck the enemy navarch in the eye.

Actually, I'm sure the latter didn't happen.

But what did happen is that before I could draw another breath, all four enemy ships began to turn, end for end.

I admit it. I fell to my knees and gave thanks.

★

And we still weren't done.

Parmenio went dashing south, the moment we were sure that our opponents weren't going to return. He went to rescue the *Apollo's Raven*.

I hadn't had time, since the first shock of combat, to consider all that I had risked until then. But as we lay alongside the *Amaranth* and she sent a helmsman and three competent sailors aboard, *then* I had time to consider. Time to think about what we'd won, how close we'd come, and what a fool I'd been to engage at all.

I might have considered that Heraklitus was there with Hipponax, in the thick of the fighting, with Old Nestor and the rest.

My gut churned. My joy in victory abated and was replaced with dread, and I wasn't even thankful when the *Amaranth's* third helmsman took the oars from me. All I could do was watch.

The *Gad's Fortune* had killed her prey with her ram, and her marines were untouched, and so Parmenio went for the enemy ship on its unengaged side. But the enemy ship didn't wait for them.

I could see them moving. The shivering of their hull, even at that distance, showed that men were running on the deck. And then they were poling off, leaving the *Apollo's Raven*.

I'd taken half the marines out of my ship. And Ka.

The gap between the *Apollo's Raven* and the enemy ship grew, and the enemy got their oars out. The *Apollo's Raven* just rocked on the waves.

Parmenio had elected to turn, to come up on the enemy's unengaged side, and that cost him time. The enemy ship was under way and pulling well – an excellent crew.

The *Gad's Fortune* came about, brought her bow into line ...

And coasted to a stop by the *Apollo's Raven*.

It was the right decision. I agreed with all my heart. The enemy ship rowed for as long as a priest might recite the morning hymn, and then suddenly her boat sail went up, opening like a flower, and she was running downwind, due south.

None of us were going to catch her. I was already sitting on the helm-bench while one of Neoptolimos' sailors with a good repute as a leech was cleaning my foot wound, manipulating it and making me howl.

That feeling just wouldn't leave the pit of my stomach. Part of it was from watching that last ship run, and I worried that the luck had shifted. I kept turning, despite the pain, to look south, wondering if they were coming back – five fit ships to five tired ships. Worse than that, actually, as two of our ships were captures.

But by the time Parmenio was alongside the *Apollo's Raven*, I could also see the *Winged Nike* nosing around the islet with a third capture. And now, five to seven, I no longer thought our opponents might come back at us.

I ate some sesame and honey, and drank too much neat wine, and it went to my head, and didn't make me feel better.

I knew where there were two hundred good oarsmen to make up my crews, and a beach where it was safe. I only needed to know whether the *Apollo's Raven* was fit for three hours' rowing. I lacked the necessary signals. We only had six.

So I watched as my marines came back from the recent capture. I watched as a dozen borrowed seamen from the *Amaranth,* good boys from Chios, threw the dead over the side on my new ship, and then went below to fetch the dead oarsmen.

There was some shouting.

Oh, Zeus, here we go, I thought.

Ka and Achilles went below into the oar frame, and Ka came back. 'They want to bury their friends,' he told me. 'At least, that is what I think they say. They say, not in water, no spirits. I think.' He shrugged his long-armed, eloquent shrug. 'Ari, they make no trouble. They rowed for you. Can you give this?'

'Yes,' I said.

Somehow it animated me, and I've seen this before, too – the troubles of others give me the spirit to help them, even when I'm too tired to help myself. I looked at the middle-aged man who'd just finished swaddling my right foot and was lacing a sandal to the bandages.

He met my eye.

'Will you see to my oarsmen?' I asked. 'I have some injured men down there – broken ribs, broken heads.'

He sighed. But he got to his feet.

'Yes, sir,' he said in his Chian accent.

'Double share,' I said.

His face became animated.

'Now ye're fewkin' talkin', mate,' he said. He trotted forward and went down into the rowing frame.

I tried putting weight on my foot and it was better. Much better. Almost incredibly better. I knew he'd poured water and then wine on it. He'd cleaned it, and he'd put some sort of resin or pine-sap on it, but . . .

It just hurt. Just a normal hurt.

My oarsmen were no longer muttering. The day was looking up, and I leant back, took another mouthful of wine, and then shouted directions to Neoptolimos, who told me to suck eggs. I was giving navigational instructions to a man who lived just over the horizon.

Parmenio was returning, and the *Apollo's Raven* was getting under way behind, her oars moving competently – better than mine were likely to manage.

It is an oddity of war at sea that if you fight with your ram, you tire your rowers but your marines are untouched, and if you board, your marines are exhausted but your oarsmen are untouched.

I got us under way even as Simonides, the leech, worked on injured men. Ka and Diodoros were lifting men up and bringing them up to the catwalk.

I was having a look around this ship. It wasn't Carian, and it wasn't Phoenician. The commander had been a Persian. I'd forgotten him, but now I whimpered my way forward and found him, still lying in his beautiful corselet, at the structure in the deck that held the mast, when it was up.

I put a hand on his forehead, and then leant down, reminded myself that I'd taken a blow to the groin by trying to crouch too fast, and then I saw his chest go up and down. There was fresh blood at his neck. He had a good sword, a Greek sword, and I took it, just in case he awoke and was tempted.

My borrowed sailors were quite adept. No one needed me, and I sat beside my wounded Persian. I gave him some shade with my chlamys, and then I rigged it to cover him, and woke him for a mouthful of water.

'Good day to you,' I said, in Persian.

'The blessing of the sun on you,' he said. And then groaned.

I got Simonides for him when he came up from the oar decks. With Leander to help, they stripped his armour and his robes and washed the blood away.

We had rounded the great southern headland of Lemnos and we were already coming up on our friendly beaches – hardly even a voyage on a normal day, twenty-five stadia all told.

I liked that the Persian had lived. I liked Persians. And I liked having a prisoner, who might tell me something about why there was suddenly a Persian navy in the northern Aegean.

I took no part in the landing except to make sure that my prisoner was treated carefully and taken to a boat sail awning ashore. I was trying not to fall on the rough sand when I saw Hipponax, shoulders down, his right arm crusted in dried blood, and they were carrying Nemet into the shelter.

Damon came up with them, his eyes like bruises in his shockingly fatigued face.

'Sir,' he said.

I was watching Nemet. He'd taken three bad wounds, any one of which might be a death blow, and he was being laid gently by my Persian. Then Ka burst past me to see to him.

'Give me a moment, here,' I said. 'This man has been my archer and friend for years.'

He was going. It was obvious from the way his skin was losing its lustre, turning almost grey. But he reached up to Ka, and they clasped hands.

Ka knelt by him. I'd bought them all on the docks in Sicily – Nubians from south of Aegypt. I'd freed them, of course – slaves don't fight well, for obvious reasons.

It occurred to me then and there that I had once offered to take them home. And now Nemet wasn't going home, or he was going very fast, depending on what you believe.

I fell to my knees in the warm sand by Nemet. He'd always been the silent one. I knew he didn't speak much Greek. I knew that he was expert at anything to which he turned his hand.

I hadn't lost a good friend in a while, and you forget too quickly.

'Ari,' he said. He sucked in some air, looked at Ka as if to say something, and he was gone.

Ka sat on his haunches for a moment. Then he took his knife and laid it on Nemet's chest, and took Nemet's knife and put it in his own belt.

Then he sat back and gave a yell, a ululating scream not unlike the ancient war cry.

Two of the helots were carried in.

'They grabbed spears with their hands,' Damon said. 'They tried to fight with bow staves against spears.'

Hipponax sank to the ground by me. I went over his body. He had cuts, and they needed to be cleaned, but no serious wounds.

Damon said 'sir' in that exhausted tone.

I realised that Heraklitus wasn't there.

I looked around for him. I saw Nicanor and a young oarsman carrying Arios. They had him on a cloak between two spears, and his right leg looked as if it had been shredded by some horrible machine.

He managed a smile through the pain.

I looked at Damon. 'What happened?'

'They had a deck *full* of marines,' he said. 'Twenty? Thirty?' He shrugged. 'Our sailors fought, and fought well. Old Nestor held the amidships and we ...' He looked away. 'We held the helm. In the end, the oarsmen were coming off the benches to save the archers.'

Arios gave a choked scream as someone poured a canteen of watered wine over his leg. There was an older woman with iron-grey hair – probably the healer from the village, or a midwife. She wasn't afraid of blood, or giving orders to men – midwife, then.

She was organising the wounded.

Damon wouldn't meet my eye.

'All my fault,' he muttered.

'No one's fault but mine,' I said, and I thought, *But where is Heraklitus?*

The iron-haired woman knelt by Arios and poured more water on his leg. Now I could see that it had been hacked. Blows had gone *through* his greave, as if someone was using an axe.

'You should see the other guy,' he managed in a croak.

The woman glanced at a sailor by her side and started talking to Arios, and he sat up a little to answer. He didn't see the sailor, who – suddenly, and with real strength – pulled the ruined greave off the leg.

'Oh, *gods!*' Arios screamed.

The woman had his hand.

'I can save your leg,' she said to him. Perhaps five times, she said it, until he was calm.

Damon looked back at me. 'When Parmenio came for us, I knew we'd make it. More and more oarsmen were joining in, and the enemy were slipping away. I think we killed their captain, or one of their heroes. Arios here put a sword in him, and the others broke.'

'Well struck,' I managed, or something like that. There was bad news coming. I could tell.

Hipponax looked at me. 'Heraklitus fought like a daimon,' he said. 'And then ...'

Damon shook his head. 'They gave way, and Heraklitus said, "We can board them!" and leapt on to their deck.'

'Oh,' I groaned, like a defeated man in a play.

'They were poling off.' Hipponax looked at me. 'Pater, I was too far from the rail to jump. I was! Zeus, I . . .'

A young man's guilt.

'No blame to you,' I said. 'Or you, Damon. They killed him?' I asked, with a calm that surprised me.

Damon shook his head. 'No. No, I don't think they killed him. I think they took him.'

That feeling in my gut sharpened to pain. Briseis' son, in the hands of the enemy.

'Well,' I managed. 'We'd best take care of our Persian, then.'

One of the very worst aspects of leadership, and one that is seldom discussed by philosophers, is how hard it is to sit feeling sorry for yourself.

I wasn't immediately panicked by my son's capture. He was rich and well armoured. If he survived the combat, I was sure we could trade him for something or someone. I was far more concerned that he was simply dead, and I was having a hard time imagining facing Briseis and telling her that I'd lost her son – our son.

That I had, in fact, lost him without a thought, because . . .

One of the things that makes me effective as a killer of men, is what I don't think about. There are a great many things I don't think about in action – and it's not as simple or foolish as being 'without fear'. Fear is good. Fear keeps you alive. I've also come to think, over a life of conflict, that fear is the salt on the meat. If you weren't afraid, then survival and success are not as delicious. Is that a terrible thought? Yet it is the overcoming of fear that makes for courage, not its absence.

As usual, I'm rowing away from my port. At the point of action, I don't consider who is my son and who is not. I don't reckon on how long I've known Nemet, and whether I like his silence better than Ka's humour. I don't reckon who goes to the most dangerous post, and who stays behind, beyond the simple needs of the moment. I mean, I have – I have done such a thing. But I needn't. When I wear the persona of the commander, it is like one of the actors at the gods' festival wearing a mask. I put it on, and those other things are no longer my problems.

So I had left my two sons, and Nemet, to fight on the *Apollo's Raven*, and I'd taken Leander and Diodoros and Kassandros and Zephyrides to follow me, in a sweep of my spear. And now I was paying the price, and I could never explain to Briseis why. There was no why. I had given an order ...

I might have sat in the sand and drunk too much and thought of all the things that I'd done wrong, but then, as I said, no one gives you time to wallow in self-pity when you are in command.

I was trying – and I was leaning on a spear. Not my beautiful spear, the Persian spear I'd taken at Plataea, inlaid in gold – that was gone. My new spear was light and comfortable in the hand and had a pattern-welded head, and someone had loved it. I'd stuck its end into the gravel and I was leaning hard against it, and trying not to weep. I'd wandered away from the beach fires to sulk like Achilles – not my cousin, the one in Homer – but I didn't get far enough.

Of course, the man who had the courage to follow me was Styges.

He put a hand on my shoulder, spun me around, and said, 'I'm sorry.'

I shrugged. 'Not your fault.'

'Maybe it is,' he said. 'I lost sight of them.'

I remember sighing, or maybe forcing a smile. What I said was not too bad.

'You can't be everywhere, Styges, and even you can't kill all the enemies.'

He nodded. 'I'm not really here about Heraklitus. I'll pray they took him prisoner. I'm here about the ... Africans.'

'Africans?' I asked.

Nothing was really penetrating. I find that one of the earliest effects of age is this inability to change topics, to adjust suddenly. *Africans? What Africans?*

'You captured that ship.'

He pointed. You have to imagine Styges, covered in cuts, with brown-black stains and his fighting chiton all but glued to his hips by dried sweat. He actually swayed when he talked. But he was still performing, still an officer.

I remember that I actually had to turn my head and look. I was that tired.

Right. That ship. That ship over there. Half the oarsmen were Africans. Right, right. Got it.

'They don't speak much Greek,' I said. 'Ka managed to communicate with them.'

Styges nodded. Looking at him, I knew what he'd look like when he was old. As I, in the arrogance of middle age, still thought of him as a 'youth', it was shocking to suddenly see him as my own age or older, with deep lines in his face. The man was at the end, and still functioning.

I was twenty years older than Styges, and I didn't yet feel like I was at the end. I think this is why we Boeotians don't put the best ephebes in the front rank, the way the Spartans sometimes do. Age brings a different strength to men – and to women, too, I think.

Styges shook his head as if to clear it.

'They're angry,' he said. 'I'm ...'

He met my eyes. We'd been through a lot together, and his lover had been Idomeneus, who was the greatest killer of men I'd ever known. Mad as one of the god-struck, brave as a Titan. But the advantage of my having known Styges since he was a small boy was that he didn't have to prevaricate.

'If they make trouble,' he said, 'the marines will kill them. We're too tired to ...'

'Too tired to negotiate.'

How well I knew what he meant.

I turned away from my own daemons out there at the edge of the beach, and went to meet the Africans.

One of the most interesting aspects of life with triremes is that they have big crews – two hundred men each – and it's an old and painfully accurate joke in Athens that in the hull of a trireme you can find almost any skill and almost every crime.

We had four crews on the beach, and another of stranded oarsmen from the original defeat, which felt as if it had happened in the ancient Trojan War, for all that it had only been a week. So we had almost a thousand men on two big beaches, and it turned out that among them we had not one but four men who could communicate well with the Africans.

None of us could speak their language, but most of the Africans could speak at least some Aegyptian. Demotic Aegyptian, that is.

Of course, one of the men who could speak to them was Aten.

They had three representatives, or leaders. They were all tall. You could see why someone had purchased them as rowers – long limbs like Ka or Nemet ... Gods, I was going to miss Nemet, for all he was usually silent.

They didn't stand like slaves. They stood like gods, heads high, all but looking down their noses at us, one hand on the hip, the other loosely by the side – an orator's pose, or a warrior's.

One of the men who spoke Aegyptian was Bastos. A half-Greek, half-Aegyptian captured at Artemisium, and now a free oarsman, he'd apparently married a Chian girl and rowed for Neoptolimos. He and Aten were engaging the Africans, while Neoptolimos and Parmenio and I listened and talked among ourselves.

'Where is that ship from?' I asked. 'Carthage?'

'I think she's a privateer out of Cyrene,' Parmenio said. 'With a Persian commander.'

'They're buying pirates?' I asked, and realised that I had absolutely no right to moral outrage. The whole original Ionian revolt had been directed by pirates of one flavour or another.

'Whereas the ship you helped me take,' Neoptolimos said, graciously, 'is a pirate from Skyros.'

'And the ship I sank was Carian,' Parmenio said.

This may surprise you, but this was the best news of the day. A scratch squadron cobbled together from the desperate men of three nations ... that was much better news than some bottomless well of naval manpower that the Great King had suddenly tapped. In fact, once I looked at the evidence, it was obvious.

At that moment, Aten beckoned me.

'You will want to hear this,' he said, and he was excited.

'Lord, this is Rigura,' he said.

The broadest-chested man inclined his head. I bowed mine. Courtesy never hurts.

'This is Mera,' Aten said, and again, the bow – a shorter, very powerful man.

'This is Ole Llurin.'

Ole Llurin looked like ... a Titan. His face had a slight cast to it that made him look inhuman. He was as black as night, and his muscles shown like polished ebony, or black iron. I don't think I've ever seen a man with such a superb display of musculature, even among Olympic athletes.

I inclined my head again.

Aten turned to me.

'Lord, I have heard you say, many times, that you wanted to go south from Aegypt. To coast the Red Sea.'

I nodded. 'There's good iron and steel down that coast,' I said. 'I met traders ...'

In the course of speaking, I used the Aegyptian word for worked iron – *bia* – for no better reason than that's the word you use when buying it.

All three Africans turned their heads at the word.

I had assumed that Rigura, who looked every inch a prince or king, was their leader. But Ole Llurin smiled.

'Ah,' he said '*Bia*.'

What I had not seen, when I looked at his muscles, was the gleam of his eyes. Under that strange face was brilliance – as soon as he spoke, I could see the intelligence. It burned there.

'I think Llurin may be a title,' Aten said in his sing-song voice. 'I may be wrong. But they are iron workers. Or traders. Perhaps both.'

He said something to the three of them – not a sentence, but a long speech in Aegyptian. And Bastos added, using different words. I didn't know what they were saying, but I could tell that Bastos was co-operating with Aten, smoothing out his sentences. I heard later that Aten spoke a very formal, priest-bound version of the language from the Nile Delta, and of course these men spoke a southern, inland dialect.

'They are steel makers,' Aten said. 'Or rather, Ole Llurin is a steel maker. Rigura is perhaps a trader. Or a soldier.'

I nodded. I *was* fascinated, but at the same time, I was too tired for all this.

'Listen, Aten,' I said. 'Ask them what the problem is right now. Tell them that we are tired, that food is coming, and that there will be wine.'

Aten translated.

Rigura nodded to me, a good nod. A man-to-man nod that said, without language, 'I see you have problems of your own.'

But Ole Llurin was not to be put off. He said something with force, all but spitting into Aten's face.

Rigura put a hand on his shoulder.

Mera looked around, as if looking for help.

Aten didn't back away – the measure of the man he was becoming. He managed a smile – good, I had taught him something.

'Ole Llurin says he is prepared to fight to the death right now, right here, on this beach. He will not be a slave again.'

On the one hand, that seemed like a ludicrous threat. There were five armoured men close by, and more within call. On the other hand, most of us were dead tired, and many had stripped off their panoplies, and it is very difficult to summon the spirit of war once you have let it slip. And Ole Llurin looked very dangerous indeed.

Sometimes, as I probably say too often, you have to take things at a rush, or very slowly indeed.

I walked right up to Ole Llurin, and handed him my new spear. I put it into his hands, and then I was unarmed and he was armed.

'Tell him he is a free man,' I said. 'Tell him that it is my custom to ask captured slaves to row for one summer in my service to cover their ransom. Tell him he can find fifty men on this beach who will speak for me, that I am a man of my word.'

Ole Llurin was looking at the spear with something akin to lust.

So was Rigura.

Curiously, it was Mera who was unimpressed.

Aten translated, and I waited.

Then I raised my hand.

'Tell them I have been a slave,' I said. 'I have rowed for the Carthaginians. Tell them I will speak to them a length. Tomorrow. That now I have fought a battle and I am too tired to be ...' I was out of words. 'Too tired. To negotiate. Let the spear make them free men.'

Aten spoke it all. I'm guessing he spoke it twice, because he went on too long, and Mera said something, and then it seemed to me he said it again.

Ole Llurin nodded. And then, with immense dignity, he kissed the spearhead. And with no more words, he turned, carrying the spear, and walked back to the circle of his people.

'That man is an iron-smith?' I asked. 'Crap. Somewhere, that man is a king.'

Styges, at my side, put an arm around my shoulder.

'And you are a bronze-smith,' he said. 'Perhaps we'll start a guild.'

The next day, we filled our benches from the men of Lemnos and Tenedos still willing to volunteer, and moved our wounded to houses in the easternmost town. Alexanor, Polymarchos' brother, had taken two wounds, one of them quite serious. Across the fleet, we'd got off lightly, because victory never costs as much as defeat, but we'd lost a dozen marines dead, and as many more wounded, and we had the usual butcher's bill of wounded oarsmen and sailors as well. We did our best to close our ranks with Lemnians, but I balked at taking their upper-class men as marines, and left those billets empty.

I promised the new oarsmen Athenian rates of pay. We were short on marines and archers, but not deck crew or officers, and I felt that it was enough for what I had in mind.

I made sure my Persian officer was receiving the best medical treatment, but he was withdrawn and anxious. He turned his head away when I spoke to him in Persian, and answered only in grunts.

I called my captains together on the beach, well after dawn. I didn't see any reason to keep pirate hours when men were so tired. Thank the gods, I hadn't lost any important officers. I had Parmenio and Neoptolimos, Damon, now a trierarch, and Hipponax, who I'd promoted on the spot to command my new capture, whose name, according to the Africans, was *Apollo's Serpent*. It was a good name for her – she was so long and low – and the pale grey-blue of her hull made her seem even more serpentine.

By the time we'd crewed the captures, examined our oarsmen, and looked at the state of our ships, we only had six. One of the captures had cracked her keel in the fighting, and without a complete rebuild in a proper yard, she was firewood. That's what she was going to be the moment we sailed away – the local shepherds were already eyeing her.

Our other capture that was still afloat was a fine, if somewhat heavy, Greek trireme. The *Theseus* was from Skyros, with a heavy deck, almost but not quite a trihemiola like my *Apollo's Raven*. The Skyrians are notorious pirates, who will serve anyone for silver. When questioned, the oarsmen, who were for the most part free, told us they were fishermen from Skyros. I knew I couldn't trust them at sea and replaced them with Lemnians. Neoptolimos put in some Chians, as he'd taken the ship, and he put his cousin Ion in command. Ion and Hipponax were of an age, and I suspected there would eventually be drama, but for the moment I had six good ships under my command.

The only good thing I learnt from those Skyrians was that the ship that had escaped us – with, I devoutly hoped, my Heraklitus aboard – had also been Skyrian.

So, the morning fire crackled, burning driftwood with that salty tang that driftwood fires have, and there were clouds over towards

Asia, but otherwise the world was beautiful. I looked around at my captains. Parmenio was tall and blond and calm, and Hipponax was all but bouncing on his toes in pride and nerves. Ion was constantly touching his face, as if to make sure it was still there. Neoptolimos wore a tired smile, and Damon had dark circles under his eyes and probably hadn't slept.

As my teacher Heraclitus used to say, *War is the king and master of all; some men it makes kings, and others, slaves.*

Never more true than the day after an action.

'When everyone has had some bread and *opson*, I said, 'We're going back north, to scout the estuary and look into Doriscus.'

Parmenio nodded, but Damon looked away, and Neoptolimos looked ... thoughtful.

'Let's run the numbers,' I said. 'The Persians had ten ships—'

'Or eleven,' Damon cut in.

'Or eleven,' I said. 'We've taken three and sunk two. At best, they have six. We have six.'

Damon nodded. 'You intend to fight again today?' he asked.

'No,' I said. 'I intend to watch any enemy we meet scuttle away. There's no way the three ships that escaped yesterday are back in Doriscus. They sailed *south*.'

Neoptolimos nodded. 'And at least one will run for Skyros,' he agreed.

'That leaves the Persian captain three ships. If they can't take us nine to four, they can't take us three to six.'

Damon nodded slowly. 'Some of us have done enough fighting for a whole summer,' he said.

I looked them over. 'I agree,' I said. 'And the marines have it worst of all. Despite which, it is my intention to put to sea this morning and scout the enemy coast, if for no other reason than to rub his nose in his defeat.'

I wasn't saying what I really thought – that the other 'three' enemy ships were shadows. I suspected that they were either badly damaged or full of worm or had mutinous crews. Otherwise, they should have been at Lemnos the day before, facing us in Poseidon's dance. I would be surprised if our adversaries had any more ships.

I've been surprised before, though.

We came off the beach in sun, but a light rain came off Asia and the breeze died, and we rowed north along the coast.

I didn't try for Doriscus in one day. Instead, with our limited supplies, we landed on Samothrace and bought sheep and bread, and ate well. The rain continued long enough to soak through my cloak, but it was going towards high summer and it was merely uncomfortable.

The next morning, we launched as soon as there was light enough for a man to see his oar. We pulled away into a deep fog. The oars squeaked away against their thole pins, the ships 'speaking' as the rigging and the wood moved with the movement of the sea.

The rising sun brought us a brighter grey light. The sea was almost flat calm, and the sun seemed very distant, an odd day, and not one to raise the heart, except for the magnificent sight of Samothrace behind us, rising from the cloud like a god.

But it was an easy day for oarsmen, as the flatter the sea is, the easier it is to row. We whisked across the seventy or eighty sea-stadia at cruising speed, and we were in the estuary, seabirds and land birds filling the sky around us.

I left the *Apollo's Raven* and the other triremes on the beach outside the estuary, with a watch kept on the little sand bluff to watch the last stretch of the river. I went aboard my capture, the *Apollo's Serpent*, because she was shorter and lower and probably more manoeuvrable, and we went upstream, rowing only one deck at a time to save energy, because we were all aware that we might have to run in a hurry if we discovered that my guesses were wrong.

But we needn't have worried. We rowed slowly with the mainmast up, and Ka perched high above us, on constant watch for movement from the other side of each long spit of land as the river proceeded, itself a writhing serpent, back and forth, back and forth. We passed the landmarks of the former combat, and found the charred remnants of a trireme, burnt on a mudbank – abandoned and burnt after we'd damaged her, I hoped.

It was almost evening when Ka warned us that he could see smoke, and we could all smell the town. We crept closer – we heard the alarm ringing off the hills to the north. We'd been spotted.

But they should assume we were a friendly ship.

We turned the last sharp bend in the river and found ourselves in a bay, or perhaps more properly, a small lake. It had a muddy, reedy shore on the south side and a line of wharves and a town on the north side, climbing away up a hill that grew increasingly steep until it rose to a fortified acropolis at some height. It lacked the majesty of Methymna, but it looked very strong. It was far larger than I'd anticipated, and there were tilled fields stretching away up the river valley.

There was a fine sand beach right against the town, and on it were two military triremes and a third under construction.

Only now that we'd turned the last bend in the river could we see the camouflaged tower that stood among the trees. I glanced back at it, and then at the citadel high above.

'Prepare to about ship,' I said to Hipponax.

'We could burn the triremes,' he said.

I nodded. 'Except that we don't have a fire lit,' I said, 'and they have a garrison, and probably a system of coded signals we were supposed to—'

I was still speaking as the first arrows began to fall.

Hipponax leant forward.

'About ship!' he called.

The rowers knew their parts. We were turning before he was done with the order, turning like a water insect, on the spot.

The arrows were well launched, plummeting almost straight down – heavy bows, more than two hundred paces away. An oarsman, a Chian veteran acting as the number two, died instantly when one of those plunged right through his head.

I dragged him clear of his oar, laid him in the middle space, and pulled in his oar in lest it foul the next man.

More men were hit, and the sailors rushed to get the heavy canvas screens up, but we were around, our bow pointing towards the exit from the little lake, and Hipponax had the stroke. We received five or six more arrows, and we were away. Two dead, six wounded, for a few seconds in full view of the town and fortress of Doriscus.

Two men had died so that I could look at the charcoal fires burning on the hearths of the town. But I had seen a great deal in the few minutes we'd been in the basin. I'd seen the size of the town, the wealth of its agriculture. I'd seen the ships and warehouses, and the sheer number of Thracians gathering at the waterside, immediately identifiable by dress, by posture, by the sheen of distant tattoos.

Worth men's lives?

I can't be the judge. But ignorance kills more people than knowledge, and those three triremes didn't trouble us that summer.

That's another story, as you'll hear.

Part Three
Byzantium

SUMMER, 478 BCE

But the violence of Pausanias had already begun to be disagreeable to the Hellenes, particularly to the Ionians and the newly liberated populations, These resorted to the Athenians, and requested them as their kinsman to become their leaders and to stop any attempt at violence on the part of Pausanias ...

Thucydides, *The History of the Peloponnesian War* Book 1, 95.1

We call Samothrace 'the Island of Winds', and there are some old sailors who believe that all winds originate there. Certainly, the next morning, when we came off the beaches of the Evros, we caught a fine wind blowing out of the Thracian mountains, and it wafted us south, hungry but safe, across the Dardanelles.

Between the straits and Tenedos we found a clump of grain ships waiting for the wind to shift – big round ships like the *Poseidon* I'd ordered built the winter before, carrying Euxine grain and probably fish oil, too, homeward bound for Athens or Sicily. I boarded the largest with Leander at my back, and the captain was obsequious, assuming we were pirates.

I was tempted. I was a rich man by then, even by the standard of Athens, but I was spending enormous amounts of my own money on the Ionian war, making Briseis the most expensive bride in Plataean history, I suspect. It was tempting, but all five ships were Athenian, except for one Corcyran, and I've never stooped to seizing allied ships.

Almost never.

I did hear their tales, though – that there were Carians in the straits, and that they feared the Persian squadron at Doriscus. I gave them reassurances and sent them on their way unplundered. Grain is the lifeblood of Athens. She needs grain from Aegypt or the Euxine – or preferably both – to keep prices low at home. Attica doesn't produce enough grain to feed Athens at the best of times, and in the summer after the battle of Plataea, there were burnt homesteads and fallow fields everywhere in mainland Greece.

Then we turned south, taking the wind with us, and sailed for Methymna, which we raised the morning of the second day.

This time, there was no Briseis waiting on the beach, no ceremony of welcome, and no feast. I was landing, full to the brim like a bride's wine cup, with news and victory, and Methymna was virtually empty of listeners.

They'd all rowed around to Mytilini.

Because Pausanias, Cimon, Aristides and the whole Allied fleet were on the beaches of Mytilini.

I stayed the night, despite my various causes for anxiety. I paid off my rowers out of the funds Briseis had left at Methymna. I saw to it that all the former slaves got a wage, and I sat with the Africans under the trees by the beach and heard their tales of sailing coasts I'd never seen or even heard of, with Aten and Bastos translating and drinking my wine. As you will hear, if you sit another night, these conversations bore fruit.

Rigura, especially, was good company.

And I was putting off having to tell Briseis.

It was the work of a few hours to row around from Methymna to Mytilini, and our reception there answered all expectations. I had time to think while we worked our way around the long headland at Sykimenea. Time to wonder what it meant that the Allied fleet was here. Had they taken Cyprus?

Had they failed?

As soon as I saw Cimon on the beach I knew they'd failed. He embraced me, hugging me hard, and Aristides was practically at his shoulder, pounding my back. This sort of reception is the result of men who'd been shaken. I could read it, from the slight frown on Aristides' face to the raucous cheers of Cimon's oarsmen.

And there was Archilogos. He didn't look happy to see me, but that turned out to be a misinterpretation. In fact, he just had bad news to deliver.

'I hear you swept the Medes from the sea,' he said.

I shrugged. 'We did all right,' I said, wary of his look.

'We're to disband the Ionian fleet immediately,' he said.

I rolled my eyes, but there was a great deal going on and I was busy embracing other captains and enjoying praise, which, I confess, I'm prone to do.

There was Lykon, one of my few Corinthian friends, commanding the *Penelope*, and there was the Aeginian navarch, Polycritus.

He managed a thin smile, pointing at my little squadron.

'I hear that you captured them all by yourself,' he said.

'Not quite by myself,' I said.

'Better than we managed,' he remarked with some bitterness. 'Half my oar-benches are empty.'

I looked back at Aristides.

'Was there a sea fight?' I asked.

Lykon looked over his shoulder.

'No,' he said.

'The furious arrows of the Lord Apollo,' Cimon said. 'We were hit with disease. We had to abandon the camp, it was so bad. My oarsmen got it, too.'

'All told, we lost a thousand men or more,' Aristides said.

Let that put our casualties into perspective. Win a naval battle, lose thirty men. Scout a fortress, lose two men. Rot on a beach in a siege, lose a thousand men to disease.

'That's bad,' I said.

I could see from their faces that they had a great deal more to say.

'Where are the Spartans?' I asked.

'Camped on the other beach, other side of the town,' Cimon said. He didn't sound angry, just tired. 'The beach with the better breeze, and the better access to water.'

'And Pausanias negotiated for a market, and grain, for his ships,' Lykon said. 'But not, apparently, for ours.'

'I can get you food,' I said.

I found the man I sought on the waterfront – my friend Socrates.

'I think we need Theophilos,' I said.

Socrates scowled. 'Nice to see you, too, Arimnestos,' he said with a little sarcasm. And then, because he really was the most helpful man I'd ever met, he said, 'I know where to find him. Good to have you back. Some of these folk don't know what they're doing.'

I was drinking bad wine in the shade of Aristides' awning when Theophilos sent word that I could meet him in the agora.

'He's overseeing a law court,' Socrates said.

I rose. Aristides raised an eyebrow.

'Of course, you know the archon,' he said. 'But is this wise?'

I shrugged. 'You gentlemen need a market, and grain,' I said. 'Don't you?'

Cimon was looking out to sea. 'We do. But we don't need to further antagonise Pausanias.'

'The man's impossible,' Lykon said.

'Not impossible,' Aristides said. 'Just shockingly tyrannical, even for a Spartan.'

'It's as if he's afraid,' Cimon said. 'The victor of Plataea. What can he be afraid of?'

'Are you gentlemen coming?' I asked. I gathered my stool and Aten, and finished my wine. It was mid-afternoon, which in summer is just the time the law courts reconvene. 'If not, save me a space.'

Aristides frowned. 'I'm trying to decide whether it is better for me to attend you, and keep you from some polemic speech, or to remain here, so that I'm not involved.'

'Zeus,' I spat. 'All I'm doing is requesting a market on your beach. At your request, or so I thought.'

Aristides nodded.

Cimon shrugged. 'Fucking Pausanias has made us all cowards,' he said.

Aristides looked at the town.

'Listen, my friends,' he said. 'Athens and Sparta, yoked together, can defeat the Great King. Not alone. We cannot afford to provoke the ephors or Pausanias.'

Cimon looked as if he disagreed, and Cimon was a great admirer of Sparta.

Aristides picked up a chlamys and threw it over his shoulder.

'Very well,' he said.

So it was Aristides, Lykon and Cimon who came with me to the agora. I sent Aten to find Briseis with directions for Socrates, because it was clear that there was a great deal wrong, and I was already in over my head. And Briseis was to politics as I am to a phalanx fight.

But it hadn't taken me an hour to lose my taste for the Allies, and remember fondly the pressures and loneliness of command. Loneliness has a great deal to recommend it. No Spartan tyrants, for example.

I got some of the latest events on the walk from the waterfront into the twisting streets of the town, up and through the grubbier residential area, with mud-brick houses and wooden structures to hold merchandise and some cheap wine shops for sailors.

The longer they'd been on the beach at Amathus, according to Cimon, the worse Pausanias and the Spartans had behaved, demanding the first fruits of any raid, taking the fresh water, demanding the best spots on the beach for their ships.

'Pausanias has taken Agamemnon as his guide,' Cimon muttered.

Socrates led us, greeting people as if he was an old citizen, but he was an easy man to like and he'd no doubt already made a place for himself.

'And why does he continue to disband every Ionian squadron?' I asked.

'He maintains they are untrustworthy and illegal,' Aristides said. 'He claims that all these islands remain the property of the Great King, and that the only acceptable solution is that the people who wish to be free of the Medes must sail west and found colonies in Magna Grecia or Iberia.'

'That's insane,' I said. 'I can form a larger Ionian fleet than you have right here.'

'I don't doubt it,' Cimon said. 'Pausanias says it will turn on us as soon as it is superior.'

'Mad,' I said.

By then we were shouldering through the gathered spectators at a civil law court. Aristides' eyes flicked to me.

'No,' he said. 'I think he has his orders.'

Cimon frowned – I could tell there was something between them.

I was worrying about Briseis. Fleets and armies and Spartans and disease are all very well. I had a report on a Persian outpost, I had won a nice little victory ...

None of that would matter to Briseis. Or, actually, it would *all* matter to Briseis – but in the market-scale of our lives, the loss of Heraklitus was likely to outweigh everything else.

That's what I was thinking when Theophilos' long staff slammed down three times on the marble paving of the law court stoa, just ahead of me, and declared a case complete.

I met his eyes across the heads of two prosperous fishermen who were, neither of them, happy with the verdict. The archon was not happy – nor could I expect him to be, with sixteen thousand oarsmen and marines wandering his waterfront, looking for wine and trouble.

'Navarch,' he said.

I bowed. 'Archon,' I said. 'May I have a word?'

I felt as if I was an actor playing Miltiades, because he remained my model of how to do this – threat, bluster, praise and flattery. And a little bribery when required. Miltiades had all the old skills.

We stepped back under the portico into the deep shade among the columns.

'How can I help you?' he asked, his formal mask giving way to an equally false look of beaming delight in seeing me. 'I gather that you have won a famous victory.'

'A very small victory,' I admitted. 'But better than defeat, and the shores of Lesbos are safe, at any rate.'

He nodded, his eyes on the law court. I didn't blame him. The court was an immediate problem, and the Medes were far away. Politicians have to live for the moment, like a swordsman in a desperate fight.

'I gather that the Spartan navarch asked for a market over on his beach,' I said. 'On the north side.'

'He did,' Theophilos said. 'And I suppose you want your own?'

'Well, the Athenians do,' I said. 'I thought you were allied with Athens.'

He shook his head slightly. 'We are,' he said. 'Your fool of a Spartan tried to give a speech yesterday, ordering the people to move to Magna Graecia.'

I ran my fingers through my beard.

'I'll do my best to get you a market when the law courts close,' he said. 'I'm sure the farmers want your business. I'm just not sure I can afford to have my town be the base for the Allied fleet for very long. Can you help with that?'

'Perhaps,' I said, because that was the sort of policy commitment I wouldn't make without Archilogos and Briseis to advise me.

Theophilos leant close. 'Remember what I told you about factions in this town?' he asked me.

I nodded.

'The aristocrats are distinctly offended by the tone of the Spartan,' he said. 'And his demand that we disband our squadron was a direct insult. Some of our people lost their whole families to the Persians.'

I nodded. 'I need the market,' I said. 'You need the Athenians.'

He had already taken a step back to his law court, but now he paused and looked back.

'What are you saying?' he asked

'You need the good graces of the Athenian fleet,' I said.

'You think they'd leave us?' he asked. 'Perhaps that's best. We can defend ourselves.'

'Perhaps,' I said. I kept the sarcasm out of my voice and I didn't say, *You did such a good job the last time.* Instead, I said, 'But ideally, it would be the Spartans who sailed away, and left you with the Athenians and the Aeginians.'

He nodded. He may even have nodded enthusiastically.

'Yes,' he agreed.

'So help me,' I said.

I touched his shoulder, and turned away, looking for Cimon and Aristides. And I saw them – they weren't twenty paces away.

They were talking to Pausanias. He had four Spartiates at his back, and there was a circle around them.

I looked back at the archon. He was staring angrily at Pausanias.

'Because he's armed?' I asked Theophilos.

He used a very derogatory term for the Spartan navarch. He was flushed with rage. To walk about armed in someone else's city – and by armed, I mean in your panoply with a spear – is tantamount to declaring yourself the conqueror. In fact, it is literal hubris.

By contrast, Aristides and Cimon and I were dressed like country gentlemen, in chiton and chlamys. I had a sword under my chlamys, and anyone who wanted to see that probably could, but it wasn't obvious and it wasn't going to scare a housewife.

Pausanias looked at me.

I smiled with as much meaning as Theophilos had offered me, and pressed forward to Pausanias.

'I'm quite certain that I dismissed you from my fleet,' he greeted me.

I shrugged. 'But now you are in my city, Navarch.'

'Your city?' he asked.

'I am a citizen here,' I said.

It was true – I'd been a citizen of both Methymna and Mytilini since the first revolt. Unless they'd revoked it. It was the reason I could trade hides here, among other things.

Pausanias paused, looking at me.

'Very well,' he said. 'I gather that, against my orders, you raised a rabble of pirates and attacked some locals who support the Medes.'

It's very difficult to be civil when you don't particularly like a man, and think he's a fool, and he is actually trying to provoke you. On the other hand, I'm a contrary man at times, and Pausanias and I had at least shared a battle and some politics. I thought I knew him.

'My rabble managed to defeat a squadron provided by the Persian governor at Doriscus,' I said.

'Oh, now it's a Persian squadron,' Pausanias said. 'By which standard, the pebble in my sandal is a great mountain.'

I shrugged. I was aware that shrugging has the same effect on a

Spartiate as it does on a parent. Do you recall, when you were an ephebe, how your father felt about that shrug?'

'Zeus,' he spat. 'None of you so-called Greeks has the least sense of discipline or obedience.'

I leant in close to him, ignoring his soldiers.

'You never ordered me to do anything except leave your camp,' I replied.

'You were ordered to go home!' he said, growing truly angry.

'I went home,' I said. 'I went home and fetched my wife, and we came back—'

'Damn you, Plataean!' Pausanias was literally spitting his words, his anger unchecked. His Spartiates looked distinctly uncomfortable. 'You have made a great deal of trouble.'

'On the contrary, Navarch, I have saved northern Lesbos from a major raid that would have been an embarrassment to the Allies, and would have set you back ...'

I was in mid-sentence when it all came together for me. The boldness of the Persians. The anger of the Spartan. The gold and the Samian spy. The Spartan emissary.

Someone had promised the Persians a free hand here.

I understood it – or rather, I read it in his anger. Pausanias knew that I had won a victory, and that victory wasn't just a personal affront. Pausanias just wasn't that petty.

My little victory had spoiled a piece of Spartan diplomacy.

In one moment, I saw the strategy and its fruits. I saw that Brasidas was doomed to failure in Babylon.

I saw that the Spartans were no longer attempting to save Greece. I suppose I'd suspected it before, but now the proof was on the face of a man who'd won the greatest victory in Greek history, but lacked the depth to wear the laurel well.

'Disband your ships,' he snapped. 'And silence your wife. You should be humiliated that a woman of yours speaks so much.'

'Does she remind you too much of Gorgo?' I asked.

The knuckles on his spear-hand grew white.

'You dare?' he said.

Aristides attempted to stop me, but I was through with Spartans.

'I dare, Pausanias. Get you gone. And don't return to this place in armour, or with weapons, like a conqueror.'

'All these islands are either slaves to the Great King or spear-won,' he spat. 'I will go armed where I please.'

I shrugged. 'You lie from ignorance,' I said. 'But you lie. These islands are free. They have fought to be free since you were born.'

Pausanias was at the edge of unreasoning rage, but as at Plataea, he held himself back. He glared, and then he mastered himself.

'You are like some insect created to disturb me, Plataean,' he said.

I nodded. 'That may be fair, Navarch.'

He took a deep breath and let it out. 'Rumour is you took a Persian prisoner,' he said.

I nodded agreement.

'Give him to me,' he said. 'That is a direct order.'

I considered a number of alternatives in less time than it takes Father Zeus to flash his lightning, but in the end I concluded that my son – if alive – was on Skyros, not in the hands of the Persians.

'Very well,' I said. 'As long as you admit that this Persian indicates that I fought a Persian squadron.'

'Do not provoke me, Plataean,' he said.

Aristides took me by the cloak.

'Come away, Arimnestos,' he said.

Pausanias shook his head. 'The three of you think you are a different fleet,' he said. 'Trust me in this – I will teach you to obey. Aristides, you and Cimon claim to admire Sparta, and I say this – our greatness is based on obedience. You will learn to obey me. Only then will we be allies.'

I smiled. 'That's funny, Navarch. "Ally" has a very different meaning in Plataea. It implies equality, and shared risk.'

'Sparta commands and others obey. That is the only form of alliance that Sparta tolerates.' Pausanias nodded, and turned away.

The people of Mytilini made a road for the armed men, a tunnel through the crowd, and the Spartans strode away, their red cloaks vaunting behind them.

'I'm sure you meant well,' Aristides said.

'What's wrong with you?' I asked him.

Aristides started.

I realised that I couldn't make my accusation without backing, in a public market. And anyway, I was in Mytilini. I needed to see Briseis, and I needed to talk to my princess of spies, Alysia.

'Meet me for dinner tonight,' I said.

I clasped their arms, and then went to tell my wife what had happened.

*

Telling Briseis that I'd lost her son – our son – went almost exactly as I'd imagined, because I knew her so well.

No tears.

No recriminations.

She looked away, her face carved beautifully of iron.

'I see,' she said quietly, her voice firm. Not disinterested. I knew that this was Briseis in deep emotion.

'I'm sure that—'

'I have friends on Skyros,' she said. 'I'll send letters.'

She glanced at me. It was not an unfriendly glance, but neither was it what you might call 'loving'.

'We will ransom him,' I said with a confidence that I felt. Mostly. Except in the dark moments when I thought ...

'We may have to outbid Artaphernes,' she said. 'By quite a bit. In one purchase, he can avenge himself on us both.'

I had thought of this.

'I doubt he'll even know for weeks. We should have the boy home and dry before the Satrap even knows ...'

'He'll know,' she said. 'I assume he has a spy in this house. And a spy in your crew, and a spy – a dozen spies – on Lemnos. Artaphernes pays gold for news. His father always did – that's how he did so well as Satrap.'

I looked at my sandalled feet.

'I'm sorry.'

'You should be,' she said. 'And then, I'm utterly unfair, am I not?' She smiled, and she was the mercurial woman I'd known as an adolescent. 'It's not that you lost him, my dear. It's that this is what women dread every time our sons, our lovers, go over the horizon – that you will not come back, or you will come back forever changed. Wounded, angry, sad, in love with someone else, or dead and rotting ...'

She lowered her head and pulled her veil of fine wool over it to cover her face.

'I was better at this when I was young,' she went on. 'I told myself that I cared nothing for any of you. Believe me, it's a better choice for a woman than giving *love*.'

I sat on her kline and put my arms around her. She leant back against me. I could feel her pregnant belly, which seemed to be growing every day.

'I'll be old soon,' she said. 'This will be my last child. And then I won't bear you any more. I want a daughter.'

'I approve,' I said. 'Daughters are the best.'

'I want a child who won't go off to dip their hands in blood as soon as they're old enough,' she said. 'Perhaps she'll be a poet or a priestess.'

'Perhaps she'll be the Helen of Troy of her generation, like her mother,' I said.

I felt her stiffen.

'No,' she said, fiercely. 'Perhaps you think that was funny, but it wasn't. It's no life for anyone.'

But as if to give her words the lie, she snuggled back against me.

'I don't mean now,' she said. 'But there have been some trying times.'

The silence went on a bit.

'I drove him away, didn't I?' she asked.

'No,' I said. It was a bit of a lie, but I did it well. 'He wanted to be fighting. He leapt on to an enemy deck without his friends. That's not on you.'

Silence. No weeping.

After what seemed to me a reasonable length of time, I said, 'I have invited Aristides and Cimon for dinner.'

There was a pause, and I heard her take in a great breath.

'Of course you have,' she said, and rolled to her feet, still graceful despite the lateness of her pregnancy. She was due in early autumn, and she was just getting to the hard part.

I realised that I had offended her.

'I'm sorry,' I said. 'But there's a great deal going on.'

'I know,' she said. 'And we have a house. And someone has to feed the richest two men in Athens their dinners, or the poor things will starve.'

'You *like* Aristides!' I said.

'I like his wife,' she snapped. But then, in a much nicer tone, she said, 'I'll go and arrange dinner.' She looked at me. 'How many did you invite?'

'Cimon and Aristides,' I said. 'But I'd like to have your brother, and perhaps Parmenio, and Lykon.'

She nodded.

'We need to talk about Ionia,' I said.

She nodded again. 'I'm finding that the freedom of Ionia may be too expensive,' she admitted. 'I'm going to go back to Plataea for the birth. I don't ... trust ... everyone here.'

I nodded. 'They're afraid,' I said. 'I have another favour to ask.'

Briseis sighed. 'Yes?'

'I need you to invite Alysia,' I said.

'She's not a dancing girl,' she objected. 'You can't order her to perform for men.'

'I need her views on the Spartan herald at Sardis.'

Briseis nodded slowly. 'I'd hate to think of her being tortured by Artaphernes because one of your friends spoke too widely.'

'Put her in a veil,' I said.

Briseis didn't join us for dinner, and we sat on our kline in a fine, mosaic'ked room, eating red snapper freshly caught that day, and drinking too much wine. It wasn't a pleasant meal, for all that. Courtesy kept us at it without discussing the war, but we all knew that as soon as the dishes and side tables were cleared, we'd be at it.

Briseis came in when the food was being cleared. A pair of slaves brought her a heavy chair, almost a throne, and set it by my kline.

She sat, swathed in wool veils.

Archilogos, her brother, came and sat on my kline, beside her.

'So,' I said. 'Let's get this started.'

Aristides lay back, looking at the beautifully coffered ceiling and holding his wine cup on his chest.

Lykon rolled over and propped himself on his elbows, hands under his chin.

Parmenio took a barley roll, spread honey on it, and smiled.

Cimon lay back and nodded.

'I'll start,' he said. 'Pausanias has to go.'

Aristides winced, but didn't disagree.

'He is no more popular with the Corinthians than with the Athenians,' Lykon said. 'Which, considering we are Peloponnesians and members of the league, is perhaps the more telling.'

Archilogos nodded. 'He humiliated the Ionian squadrons that went to join the fleet,' he said. 'And he referred to my ships as "pirates and rebels", as if our being in rebellion against the Great King was something of which he disapproved.'

'It's not Pausanias,' I said. I looked at Aristides. 'I'm sorry. But what you are up against is the policy of Lacedaemon. The ephors. Pausanias is both conservative and very much a member of the Sparta First faction. But he would not be misusing the allies unless he had orders to that effect.'

'You think that he has orders to misuse us?' Aristides asked.

'Far worse than that,' I said. 'I believe he is supposed to see to it that the Great King regains Ionia.'

Archilogos started.

Aristides almost spat his wine, but he was a veteran symposiast, and he swallowed.

Cimon sat up.

Lykon cursed.

Only Briseis was unmoved.

'What's your evidence?' Aristides asked.

'A month ago, there was a Spartan herald, a Spartiate, at the court of Artaphernes, Satrap of Lydia,' I said. 'More recently, there was a squadron in the northern Aegean, acting with confidence against Lemnos and Tenedos, as if they had every reason to believe that their activities would not be contested. There's been quite a campaign of Persian gold seeping into these islands. The Great King is trying to brew a counter-revolt, and Sparta wants to see to it that this happens.'

'Why?' Cimon asked, but I suspected he already knew why.

'Because Themistocles got the walls rebuilt,' I said. 'Taller and stronger than ever before, isn't that so? And now Athens has Piraeus, a larger port than Phaleron! And the navy is also larger. Athens is recovering from the great war, and is now preparing to have an empire. *Of course the Spartans want to stop you.*' I looked around the room. 'There was a party in Sparta, even as the Persians pushed into Attica, who were cheering them on! There were always voices in Sparta supporting the Great King, or at least praising the results. The ephors felt cheated over the Long Walls. In Sparta, they no doubt say the walls could only have been built to secure Athens from siege ... by Sparta!'

Cimon nodded. 'I have heard those very words,' he said.

'And so the ephors feel justified in reaching out to deprive Athens of Ionia,' I said.

'Athens does not own Ionia,' Archilogos said.

'That's how Sparta sees it,' I said. 'So Pausanias took the Allied fleet to Cyprus to further the policies of Sparta's Cretan allies ... and to keep the Greek ships in the south. But we've been active and lucky. We burnt ships at Tyre, and defeated a squadron in the northern waters, and so the Persian threat to Ionia has not materialised.'

Aristides shook his head. 'I find it difficult to believe that Sparta would enter into negotiations with the Great King less than a year after the death of Mardonius.'

I pointed at Eugenios, and he stepped out of the room and returned with a figure shrouded in blue-grey wool from head to foot – beautiful weaving, an enormous veil six feet wide and as long as a boat.

I recognised Alysia from her walk – and I had sent for her, after all.

'Despoina,' I said, 'these gentlemen find it difficult to believe that the Great King is negotiating with Sparta.'

She shrugged. 'I cannot prove the Great King is negotiating,' she said. 'But the Satrap of Lydia has had Spartan officers at his court for almost two months.'

Aristides lay back as if he'd been hit in the head.

Cimon sighed. 'And the cream of the jest is that this evening, Pausanias ordered us to prepare for sea, because we're going to lay siege to Byzantium.'

'Byzantium!' I said.

Lykon laughed. 'Not even part of Ionia,' he said.

'Ah,' I said, thinking of the grain ships. 'Brilliant.'

'Brilliant?' Aristides asked.

'A Spartan tyrant sitting in Byzantium can close the Euxine grain trade at will,' I said. 'Thus starving Athens.'

'Athens has Aegypt,' Cimon said.

'Not if the Great King chooses to impose the embargo that he's long promised!' Parmenio said. 'I see it now, Ari.'

Cimon rubbed his beard. 'I'm worried that I also see it now.'

Archilogos asked, 'What can we do?'

Aristides shook his head. 'Nothing. If Pausanias goes on like this, the Alliance will collapse anyway. And that might be best for everyone.'

'Best?' I asked.

Aristides nodded at me. 'If the Spartan-led alliance collapses because of actions the Spartans take, then something can be built on the wreckage, like using old temple foundations after an earthquake.'

'You are suggesting we do nothing?' Archilogos asked. 'You are suggesting that we just beach our ships and let the Carians attack our islands?'

Cimon ate a barley roll. It was still bulging in his cheek when he spoke.

'I suggest,' he said thickly, 'that you beach your ships and overlook half a dozen privateers who can cruise your coasts. Launch them yourselves and pretend you have no idea who they are. Otherwise ... I hate to admit that Aristides is right, but he is. Pausanias was the most famous man in Greece last autumn, and before his year is out, his reckless hubris will have cost him all he gained. Stay by your ships.'

I leant over. 'If you put twenty ships in the water after Pausanias is gone, there's nothing he can do to stop you.'

'And in the autumn we'll make a different set of alliances?' Archilogos asked.

Aristides looked at him, and then at Briseis.

'Yes,' he said. Just one word.

'Yes.' Briseis spoke softly. It was the only word she said.

Archilogos looked at his sister, and he intended to protest, but for the first time that evening she spoke. Her voice was quiet, and throaty.

'I see a different future,' she said, and she sounded more like a Sibyl than my wife. 'Keep your ships near to hand. Watch the coast of Asia. And if the Just Man says that we should wait for Athens, then let us abide.'

She sounded unearthly. And more to the point, later she claimed not to have spoken at all, and when I told her what she'd said, she tried to deny it.

'A woman doesn't speak in such a situation!' she said.

'You did,' I chided.

In Croton and other cities of Magna Graecia, and on Sicily, and other places I'd been, women sat with men. I took Briseis' advice all the time – possibly more often than she took mine.

But then, she doesn't spend as much time laying siege to things as she might. I'm good at siege work. As you'll hear.

In the morning, I walked my Persian prisoner across the peninsula that held the acropolis and citadel of Mytilini, and walked down the steep street to the beaches that the Spartans and their allies had taken. My Persian was a little more garrulous that morning, and I pointed things out to him. Mytilini is a beautiful place with two remarkable harbour-beaches, and the fortress is as old as time himself.

'Do you feel better, going to the Spartans?' I asked.

'Oh, yes,' he said. 'I'm sure that they'll see me home.'

Then he looked at me as if he'd said too much, but I looked away and began to prattle about the fineness of the homes. In fact, you could see fire-charred timbers where some of the best homes had been burnt by the Persians back in the year Philippos was archon basileus of Athens, but I didn't point that out.

I tried to get him to admit that he'd expected to land on Lesbos, but he shook his head.

'I really can't say,' he said, and other evasions.

I was conducted directly to Pausanias, and met him in a fine – probably captured – Persian tent. He had one side rolled up and he was seated on a camp chair, gazing out to sea.

'Ah, Plataean,' he said.

'I brought you a Persian, for good measure,' I said.

He nodded, and a helot handed me a wine cup. He gave another to my Persian, who took it and bowed.

Pausanias accepted his bow like a man to whom other men bowed every day.

'So,' he said. 'Are you prepared to obey me, Plataean?'

Sometimes, it's better to just lie. So I lied.

'Yes,' I said.

'Well, then,' he said. 'You may rejoin.'

This is the 'artfulness' of Pausanias. He assumed, in his arrogance, that I wanted nothing more than to be back with the Allied fleet. And he assumed that, when I rejoined, the fledgling Ionian fleet would collapse without me.

Ionians have had fleets since the Greeks went to Troy. Archilogos most certainly didn't need me.

But I didn't tell him that.

Instead, I said, 'Are you aware there's a Persian governor at Doriscus?'

'Where's that?' he asked, and I explained, with the help of some almonds.

I watched him very carefully. I also watched my young Persian. Sadly, either I'm easier to fool than I thought, or there was nothing to see.

'Interesting,' Pausanias said. 'But not for me. We'll go to Byzantium, and if you and the Athenians will obey me, we'll take it.'

I had been offered a seat. Now I took it, and leant back as if Pausanias and I were old comrades – which, in a way, we were. Comrades are not always friends.

'Perhaps this time you'll ask us how to conduct a siege?' I said.

He made a face, as if there was something strong in his wine. But after a long pause, he said, 'Perhaps so. If I do, it won't be in public and I won't be humiliated.'

I nodded. 'Ask me to your tent, then.'

'You're not my type,' he said.

I was tempted to make a Plataean comment about Spartans and their small boys, but I let it pass.

'Speak to Aristides or Cimon, then,' I said.

'Would you believe,' he said slowly, the way Laconian gentlemen usually speak, 'that I prefer you?'

It was my turn to make a wry face.

He smiled. 'Thanks for bringing the Persian without a fuss,' he said. 'There's more going on than any of you know.'

That day, it was hard to see him as the scheming nemesis, the tyrant of Greece. He seemed much more like the competent Spartan prince who'd won the Battle of Plataea. Angry – and mistreated. Pausanias wasn't the mastermind of a plot to defraud Ionians of their freedom. He was the tool, and he resented it, even as he obeyed.

I nodded and rose to leave, and he spoke.

'And Plataean,' he said. 'Silence your wife, before she does harm.'

And suddenly, it was not so hard to see him as the tyrant.

When I tell a story, I always tend to make it sound like a salmon line stretched taut behind a boat, the big fish already hooked, so that when you listen, you say, 'Yes, we're listening to a tale that will end with the Battle of Marathon' or suchlike. And when I tell a story that way, there's a way in which the stretched line is a lie. When you are in the story, you have no idea whether there's a salmon hooked on your line, or a piece of kelp. And there are many lines – in fact, there's a net of lines, and no man or woman can easily tell which little line will yield a fish and which will come back empty, or wrap around your ankle and pull you in . . .

I think that my allegory is getting away from me. Suffice it to say that while this is a story about the Second Ionian Revolt, there were other lines in the water, and I was involved with them.

So, for example, while we were in Mytilini, I had the first of many conversations about a voyage down the Red Sea and along the east coast of Africa. Indeed, then and for a year after, I was almost as interested in hearing everything Rigura and his friends had to say as I was in following up on various leads from my Mytilenian traitor.

It was difficult to find the time to talk to them, because the political meetings were constant. Generally I find assemblies a waste of time, but when we, as the 'leaders' of the nameless faction that found itself opposed to the ephors' policy ... When we had, as I say, decided to take no immediate action, we then had to convince fifty trierarchs and ten times that many marines and officers that we were right in taking no action.

It was interesting, from a political point of view, that Pausanias, by his arrogance, had united the Corinthians, who generally loathed Athens, with the Athenians and the Aeginians. The men of Aegina had been brilliant at Salamis and at Artemisium. Their navy was second only to the Athenian navy, and they were old enemies of the Athenians.

Bear with me a moment. Just consider that if you were Aeginian, in three summers you'd passed from a state of war against Athens, to an alliance with Athens against the Great King, to a loose coalition with Athens against Sparta, or near enough.

My point in all this is that I had precious little time to sit under an awning with a cup of watered wine and hear about the navigation of the Red Sea, despite that being one of the most interesting tales anyone could have told me. And these Africans had not only done it, but were good sailors who knew the technical details.

First and foremost, as we paid off the Ionian ships or consolidated them into a secret 'privateer' squadron under Archilogos, I kept the Cyrenian ship for my own, and crewed her, too. I promoted Rigura to helmsman – he was obviously capable of command. I left Hipponax as the trierarch and provided him with the best marines I could find.

Damon kept our first capture, mostly crewed by Ionians, but, by some careful manoeuvring, and using the departure of Xanthippus's ship and three other Athenian triremes as an excuse, we had him listed as an 'Athenian' ship. It's not done today, but in those days, there were private ships serving Athens. You know, Miltiades' entire fleet was his personal property, and even at Artemisium, Cleinias son of Alcibiades had a private ship, and so did I, and so did Cimon. Most 'private' ships were little better than pirates, which is why the big city-states were inclined to build national navies.

But the Athenians were still flexible, back then.

And the *Apollo's Raven* was now a stout ship with a good crew. I moved some oarsmen about ...

You don't care. But these are the things that occupy you in the face of action. So I had precious little time to talk to Ole Llurin and Mera and Rigura. But as all three were now deckhands or officers, all of the Africans seemed more satisfied, and a few drachmas and some wine went a long way towards evening various scores. I heard their stories. They'd brought a cargo of worked iron up the Red Sea to the Aegyptian ports, and then been convinced by a pair of priests to take their cargo overland to Memphis on the Nile.

No one had dealt fairly with them, and at Memphis the priests had seized their cargo and enslaved them and their entire crew. After several revolts and the death of their captain in captivity, they'd been sold to a slave merchant in Cyrene.

They'd been rowing for a year, and only a little good fortune amid all the ill had kept them from Salamis.

What could be worse than to die, a slave, in someone else's battle for freedom?

But as day led to day and there was no open revolt, even when Pausanias released my Persian prisoner to be rowed across the channel to Asia, I spent more time with Rigura and his friends. Rigura's Greek was already better, and I suspected Ole Llurin had more Greek than he let on, but Mera was the most fluent. With Aten and Bastos to translate and support, we managed to stumble along, and the challenges piled up. It was, in effect, impossible to sail the Red Sea without the support of the Aegyptians, with whom we were presently at war.

I mention this because, when I heard that my Persian had been released, I seriously considered leaving Pausanias and trying Africa then and there.

But the very next day, things began to move in ways that suggest that the gods do take a hand in the affairs of men. First, my son Hector sailed into the harbour in a deeply laden round ship, full of Aegyptian grain, which he and Sekla had negotiated and purchased despite all the bans of the Great King. They'd already made the run to Athens, back to Aegypt, and into Mytilini. The fleet had paid ready cash and bought the entire cargo, which did a lot to restore our fortunes and allowed Pausanias to declare a sailing date.

Hector and Sekla brought us Leukas, who had been my oar master after the death of Onisandros, a great man; I'd last seen him on the beach at Delos. And with him was Polymarchos, the athletics trainer and sometimes one of my marines.

I had to tell Polymarchos that his brother, Alexanor, had been gravely wounded at Lemnos and was there in the care of the local people.

I also tried to reach Pausanias to ask that something be done about Doriscus, but no one was interested.

Regardless, when he set the sailing date for Byzantium, spirits rose. Every man in the fleet knew that they had been beaten at Amathus, and they were eager to make something out of the summer. We had three days to prepare, and we spent those days in a flurry of cleaning and polishing, loading food stores, and arranging resupply. For my part, I sent fifty oarsmen into the hills above the town with permission of the town council, and they cut wood.

The wood they cut, we sharpened into long stakes and heavy crosspieces – an easily erected palisade, with all the parts numbered. I'd seen it done by carpenters in Athens, and it worked well enough, in the end. We filled half the round ship with our palisades and we filled the rest with water, wine and grain.

I left the round ship to Sekla, although he looked longingly at the *Apollo's Serpent*.

'That's a nice ship,' he said.

'You can have her when we've taken Byzantium,' I said.

He nodded. 'Good,' he said. 'Except that I can't afford to keep a trireme.'

I leant over. 'When this is over, we're going to sail the Red Sea.'

His eyes moved slowly around the horizon and then met mine.

'Now ...' he said, 'Now you make me smile. I'll have to fetch Doola, though. The Red Sea? When?'

I shrugged, and introduced him to Rigura.

I'm sure I'm leaving out a hundred details. Trying to prepare for a major siege with an overall commander who is completely uninterested in the preparations is challenging, to say the least.

I think this deserves a little explanation.

As a group, the Spartans look forward to war as a contest. I suspect that they are as prone to fear as other men, but their whole way of life is directed at subjecting that fear to nobler virtues of loyalty to comrades, and fear of the humiliation of failure.

But despite all that, the war for which they train is a contest – their strength and prowess against that of an enemy. I think this is why they detest a siege. Sieges aren't won by prowess or strength – they are won by cunning and luck. The best way to take a city is to suborn a traitor inside to open a gate. The traitor's hand is the most effective weapon. Second to that is disease. The poisoned arrows of Lord Apollo have settled more sieges than any other cause, and it is a matter of Moira, the fortune of the gods, which side fails first under that deadly barrage.

The two virtues most likely to succeed in siege warfare are cunning and patience, both of which the Athenians have. And I'll add to that another element, a sly one. Athens is a city of tekne, of craftsmen, great and small – and from marines to free oarsmen, the crews of her triremes are a cross-section of her crafts. Carpenters and miners, stonemasons and iron workers are all essential in a siege. Sparta has all these skilled craftsmen, but they mostly disdained to bring them to war. In fact, the only 'Spartans' in our fleet were a hundred or so Spartiates with Pausanias. The rest of the Peloponnesian force were men of windy Pilos and sun-drenched Mycenae, Hermione and Corinth, and the other sea-girt cities of the Peloponnese.

Hector and Hipponax were inseparable, and had endless questions about the siege, its expected duration and the needs of the fleet. They were intelligent boys and they'd already worked out that Byzantium would be like Troy – that is, we'd have to keep the fleet and marines supplied for weeks from Lemnos, Lesbos and Chios.

Having heard them out, I sent to Athens and Plataea for Megakles and Leukas, asking them to come out with round ships and to pur-chase grain. At the same time, I suspected we could get grain from the trade passing down out of the Euxine. That inland sea was ringed with golden grain, a byword for wealth in Athens. If I couldn't have a life of piracy, I could at least make a healthy profit selling the Allied fleet their grain.

And wine, which I recommended that one of my merchant cap-tains should load in Sicily.

Neoptolimos, now 'dismissed' from service, offered to take all my messages to Athens. He was going to run a cargo of mastic to the city – just the sort of high-value cargo that a trireme could make a profit carrying. Mastic only grows on Chios, and everyone uses it.

The last night, Briseis arranged a dinner. We had Cimon and some of his officers, and Lykon, but for the most part it was my people, all gathered. Instead of lying on couches, we sat on benches in the courtyard of our rented house under the spreading olive tree, and ate tuna and wild boar and stacks of bread and salted oil, and we drank twenty big amphorae of wine. Leukas had brought us word of all the preparations in Plataea – of temples being rebuilt, and our house nearing completion.

'I'm going back,' Briseis said. She began to outline to me her plan to gather all of our friends that autumn, for a great dinner in Plataea.

'You are needed here, surely,' I said.

She shrugged. 'Until the Alliance rejects Sparta,' she said, 'there's little I can do. I want to get news of Heraklitus. Then I'll gather my household and go to Plataea.'

'Pausanias will think that I silenced you,' I said.

She leant over and brushed my lips with hers, something that has always inflamed me.

'Let him think what he will,' she said. 'Pausanias has become a character in tragedy. He is the tool of his own destruction. As he might have been a great man, the process is sadder than I had expected.'

Then we passed the wine bowl and told tall tales.

And the next morning, we sailed for Byzantium.

Byzantium stands in one of the strongest places in the world, on the European side of the Dardanelles, with a high acropolis for defence and two fine beaches, as well as a separate deep bay where an entire fleet can anchor.

The location sticks out from the European shore like a left thumb at full stretch, if you turn your hand so that your palm is up and your fingers are pointing back towards your body. I agree that this posture might hurt your wrist, but now you can see the shape of Byzantium. The city is just where your thumbnail is.

Storms can work their way up the Propontis, but never into the spur of the sea that runs up the northern shore of the thumb. That's where we wanted to land, but that's not how it came out, as you'll hear. We didn't come in one mighty fleet, either, for a variety of reasons, none of them pretty.

First, at the appointed hour, the fleet left its beaches at Mytilini. But the Peloponnesians, leaving the northern beach, caught the breeze from Asia immediately and sailed away, leaving the rest of us to row around the acropolis-citadel for an hour before we could raise our sails.

There was worse to come. At Artemisium and Salamis, we'd had days to practise leaving our beaches and forming in lines for fighting. Even with that, Salamis was a dreadful spectacle of broken oars and poor communications. Among the veterans, and by that I mostly mean Aeginians and Athenians, there were perhaps a dozen crude, shared signals, but the small states, the Ionians and the Peloponnesians had no sort of signals. Back in Miltiades' time, we – and by 'we', I mean the loose coalition of pirates and idealists who carried the flame of the Ionian revolt – became so used to operations at sea that we developed some formations that we employed ... well, all the time. We sailed in double columns, and we rowed in double columns. We even practised deploying rapidly from those columns into fighting line. Dionysius of Phokia, who's now living out his old age in Marsala with Doola and Giannis and other old friends, trained us hard in the months before Lade – so hard that many ships defected, or refused to train.

I was not a great friend of Dionysius of Phokia, but I'd learnt almost everything I know about sea tactics from him.

Athens and the Ionians had been fighting at sea for forty years or more, not just in great fleet actions like Salamis, but in deadly hit-and-run raids, commerce raiding, and avoiding the tender attentions of Carian pirates, among others.

The Corinthians had kept up to date, and the ships from Hermione were at least aware of the new tactics and the notion of keeping a formation while cruising.

Pausanias apparently despised such tactics. It's remarkable, when you consider that Spartans have a great reputation as tacticians, and when you consider that the other Spartan king, Leotychidas, the Eurypontid king, was familiar with all of our columns and lines ...

It really appears that Pausanias was a very petty man. Or worse.

Apollo's Raven was off the beach and rowing, with the familiar voice of Poseidonos coaching the oarsmen, Nicanor and Young Nestor steering, and all appeared right with the world. I was just settling down to enjoying the perfect blue of the sky and sea, the magnificent mountains rising in Asia just a few stadia away, and the spectacle of the Athenians coming off their beaches. I had the honour to be first in our line, with the *Apollo's Serpent* tucking in nicely under our stern, and Damon's *Winged Nike* came third, with a dozen Athenians just coming off the beaches behind us and filling in. We were the left-hand column, on the island side. On the Asia side, a little farther out in the strait, Cimon's mighty *Ajax* led.

Leukas was watching the *Ajax* without any reference from me, making sure that we kept pace, and we rounded the promontory at

Barbalios together, perhaps a stade apart, each of us with another twenty or so ships behind us. We could feel the wind change. On my deck, Giorgos already had the sails laid to the yards, and the oarsmen were taunting the sailors, as they usually did.

As we prepared to make the turn and raise our sails, we caught our first sight of the Peloponnesians. The Corinthians were all together in two short columns, but the rest of them were spread over twenty stadia of the channel, in no particular order, the fastest ships pulling ahead, the slower ships lagging.

I tried not to think of what a dozen well-handled ships – Carians or Aegyptians, perhaps – would make of that tangle. Even as I watched, one of them went aboard another, her ram smashing into the oar-frame, and even five stadia away we could hear the shouting and the curses.

It was already late in the morning when we launched, and as I watched the Allied fleet straggle across the ocean, I wondered if we were likely to make Lemnos in one leg. I closed to shouting distance with Cimon.

'Methymna?' I shouted.

He flashed an aspis twice, meaning *yes*.

So the Peloponnesians sailed off into the evening, and we landed on the beaches of Methymna. I slept alone in my own bed, and started a wax tablet with a long letter for Briseis, mostly because I already missed her.

So you can imagine my pleasure, an hour later, when she came in, accompanied by her women, and Alysia.

She smiled. 'I hoped you'd be here,' she said.

It appeared that Archilogos, as well as Parmenio and Herakles and Helikaon, had followed us from Mytilini. They were going to make Methymna the base for the Ionian squadron. Thanks to our efforts and the good merchants of Lesbos and Chios, they had a small treasury and five good ships. Neoptolimos would join them with two more ships from Chios after he'd run his cargo into Athens.

So we had one more pleasant evening, and Alysia told me everything she'd gathered about Byzantium.

'I have a good friend in the city,' she said. 'Someone I trust absolutely.'

'Someone I could meet with?'

'Absolutely not. But if I receive anything useful, I'll pass it along.' Alysia smiled, and when she smiled, she really could melt your heart.

It was a smile of such surpassing innocence that, even knowing her as the most effective spy in the Ionian revolt, I almost trusted her.

Regardless, we got off Methymna's beaches in good order the next day, and we rowed all morning, until the 'Point of Asia' and turned out into the open ocean. From there, we started seeing Peloponnesian ships immediately. Some had landed on islets and some on the coast of Asia itself. They were putting to sea with no order at all, and we bore on, our two long columns raising sail in order. In the evening we landed on Tenedos, and we purchased food and oil. By then we had most of the ships of Hermione with us.

The next day started with rain, but Cimon and Aristides got us off the beaches just after dawn. The clouds were breaking as we dropped our sails and turned north and east into the Dardanelles. There's a current coming out, although even that is tricky. Oarsmen say it's a long, bitter pull, like walking uphill, to row a big ship all the way to the Euxine.

We landed at Troy, and made sacrifices to the shades of the Greek heroes. The triremes lowered and stowed their mainmasts. But it was still midday and we were in hostile waters.

We rowed in two long columns up the Dardanelles. We were a stirring sight, and the straits themselves were beautiful. I was in the middle of the Europe-side column that day, with Aristides in the lead. Cimon was somewhere on the Asian side, because Eumenes of Anagyrus, one of the heroes of Salamis, was leading the Asia-side column. We camped on an island in the Propontis. The whole trip up the gut of the straits, Cimon and I rowed along, side by side, shouting recollections to one another. Our youths had been spent here, fighting Carians.

The Propontis has its storms, as I well remember, but it is for the most part as calm as a pond – a huge salt lake between Asia and Europe, surrounded by little fishing villages, and with the town of Byzantium on the north shore, where the inlet from the Euxine comes in. We hadn't seen Pausanias for days, and I'd begun to hope that perhaps he'd sailed home.

The evening of the third day out from Methymna, we raised Byzantium at mid-afternoon. We had the breeze, and we were sailing in, and there was the town, and there the acropolis.

'Tough nut to crack,' Leukas said, and Old Nestor spat thoughtfully over the side.

'An' this from a bunch that couldn't take a soft city on Cyprus,' he said.

We lowered our sails and beached along the coast of the Propontis, south of the town and in relatively open country. Styges led the marines ashore at last light and occupied the headland above us, and we felt secure enough to beach stern first. We put all of our marines ashore under Cimon's captain, and we cooked dinner, looking at the citadel of Byzantium a few stadia east, down the coast.

No one attacked us in the night, although when morning came, Tekles, the captain of Cimon's marines, sent runners to wake us.

Off to the west, making no effort to hide themselves, were Thracians. There were at least fifty of them, all mounted on steppe ponies.

'Double the guard,' Cimon said.

'Let's see if they'll talk,' I said.

Cimon blinked slowly, and then narrowed his eyes.

'My father held a large portion of these straits for years,' he said. 'Thracians don't talk. They fight.' He shrugged. 'And they're all Medizers, anyway.'

I was watching the Thracians. Several of them flashed with gold – Thracian aristocrats wear a lot of gold. There were at least two women, and several young people, or very small warriors.

That didn't have to mean anything. Thracians took the very young on raids, and there were women among their warriors. But they weren't alarming us with wild yells, or beating drums, or riding about raising dust to hide their movements. I'd seen all of these things. They were sitting quietly on a low, wooded hill, in full sight of our outposts.

'Aten, get Styges and three marines,' I said.

Lucky Aten got to climb back down the low bluff to the beach and fetch sleeping men who'd stood a night watch. But show is important, and I wanted to look important.

'If they kill me,' I said, 'I recommend that you murder Pausanias and have Aristides take command.'

'That's good advice,' Cimon said. 'But don't die. I'd miss you, and anyway, Styges won't take orders from me.'

He smiled, but he didn't volunteer to come along.

Half an hour later, the Thracians were still there, and Styges came up the low cliff at a jog, with Leander, Kassandros, Kalidion and Zephyrides at his back.

I pointed my spear at the Thracians.

'We're going to walk towards them,' I said. 'If they charge us or shoot arrows, we stand our ground and die. Otherwise, we walk right up to them as if we haven't a care in the world.'

Leander glanced out over the sunlit hillside. Then he smiled.

'Sure,' he said. His tone conveyed a little disappointment, as if he'd expected either a better plan or more adventure.

Cimon smiled. 'He's almost as Laconian as Brasidas,' he said.

We set out. It was only two stadia or a little more, but there was a valley with a little watercourse in the bottom, and we had to jump from rock to rock before climbing the far side. The last three hundred paces were across grassy, open ground – perfect for horses.

I was looking around. I knew Thrace pretty well. Most of it is better pasture and farmland than anything mainland Greece has to offer. The trees are bigger and the grass is greener. The winters are colder, too.

The Thracians sat on their ponies and watched us climb, as still as statues or Spartans. The horse moved a little – nipped grass, tossed their heads because of flies – but even they were very still.

We kept walking.

There was a big, red-faced man with grey-shot black hair and a long beard, who had not one but two big gold armbands and a fine helmet. He and I locked eyes early on, and I walked towards him, my spear back on my shoulder except when I needed it as a walking stick.

He sat astride his horse, impassive.

When we were within fifty paces, another Thracian pushed in front of him. She had the same jet-black hair, but she was younger. Not much younger – perhaps my age – with tanned skin and lines around her eyes, and a long scar across her face. Her eyes were a lurid green, and she had tattoos over most of the skin that showed, but she also had a beautiful scale corselet and a scarlet kaftan.

I halted perhaps five paces from her, trying not to breathe too hard.

I nodded.

She nodded.

'I'm Arimnestos of Plataea,' I said in Greek.

'I'm Katisa of the Melinditae,' she said. Her accent was not too barbarous, and she managed a slight smile. 'This is my land.'

'Do you claim Byzantium?' I asked.

'Are you here for Byzantium?' she asked.

Here we go, I thought.

'We are at war with the Great King,' I said.

'Everyone knows this,' she said. 'The birds in the trees and the bears in the hills know that the Great King was beaten by the Greeks, and now you pursue his ships.'

Right. Important advice here – never assume that barbarians are stupid or ignorant just because they wear trousers and speak badly.

'We intend to take Byzantium,' I said.

She looked at the distant town, which, from her hill, could be seen quite clearly.

'You took a walk,' she said, indicating the beach from which I'd come.

'Yes,' I said. 'I don't have any horses here.'

She nodded. 'You can ride?'

'I can,' I said.

She nodded again. 'My people have not held the town in two hundreds of years,' she said. 'But that changes nothing. Seasons change. Wind changes. The Melinditae do not change.'

The big man with the black and grey beard grunted an affirmative, and a younger man gave a yip of agreement.

'Our enemies are in that town,' I said.

'Will you hand it to us when you take it?' she asked.

I shrugged. 'Probably not,' I said agreeably.

She looked at me, one eyebrow slightly lifted. In that moment, she looked just a little like Briseis, when I say something untoward.

'Well,' she said. 'That no doubt counts for honesty, among Greeks.'

'I don't suppose you'd like to sell me some horses?' I asked.

'I'd like nothing better,' she said. 'How many do you want?'

'Ten?' I asked.

Why not ten? I had in mind the ability to ride around the town and scout it, every day. And also to get away from Pausanias when I wanted to.

She nodded, and then we were dithering away, like two farmers on the high road from Plataea to Thebes working out the price of a lamb. It wasn't unpleasant, for all that I suspected that she thought she could steal my horses back whenever she felt the urge.

We settled on some minae of silver, and I sent Kassandros back to camp for a roll of drachmas.

'The horses will be here before the sun is a hand higher,' she said. 'How much would it cost me to buy the town from you?'

I shrugged. 'I'm not in command. I would be selling something that isn't mine.'

'Ha!' she said. 'This is almost wisdom. Of course it isn't yours. It's mine!'

She seemed to think that was quite funny, and she was still barking her barbarian laugh as she rode away.

But that's how, an hour later, I came to be riding along the outwalls of the city of Byzantium. It was already two hundred years old – older, if the Thracian tale that they'd had a town there was true. The walls, as I could observe, were mud-brick atop a socle of good stonework that rose about the height of a man above the rolling ground, and the mud-brick went up another two man-heights, slightly slanted back. The base of the wall was thick with brush for most of its length, and the towers were too infrequent to protect it all. In places, ivy or some other creeper had overgrown the whole wall. In two places the mud-brick had eroded or collapsed in the spring rains.

The walls ran across the 'thumb' – the whole peninsula – right at the 'nail'. There were warehouses and small farmsteads outside the walls, and there were lower walls along the waterfront. Cimon took the *Ajax* to sea and coasted the whole town, looking for landing sites, while I rode abroad.

We met again in early afternoon, in the shade of his stern. Aristides was there, and a dozen other captains. So far, the Peloponnesians had landed further east and had their own beaches.

'Pausanias landed while I was scouting,' Cimon said.

No one had much to say to that.

'I like the little hill where we met the Thracians,' I said. 'There's water in the stream, and the hill is just steep enough to be held.'

Cimon nodded. 'I thought that, too.'

'I think we should take our palisades and fortify the hill, and make our camp there,' I suggested. 'Then run two lines of palisades, or at least felled trees, all the way to the ships.'

'Like the long walls in miniature,' Aristides said.

'Exactly. Then we have water, forage, and access to retreat.'

'And Pausanias?' Cimon asked. 'I say we take a tip from Themistocles. We build it all today and tomorrow, before he can stop us, and then we decline to move our camp.'

Aristides nodded his assent.

'Do you think we can take the place?' Cimon asked.

I shrugged. 'It's strong,' I said. 'The towers are badly spaced and I see a couple of places for an escalade, but we won't have surprise and they have a garrison of Persian regulars.' I shrugged. 'Starvation or a traitor.'

Aristides nodded again. 'Athens has some friends in the city,' he said. 'Half our grain comes past here. I'll see what I can do.'

Cimon nodded. 'I can't see a really good landing place,' he said. 'But I see three or four that are too small for a main landing, but could cause lots of confusion.'

'We agree that our first try is an escalade on the outside wall,' I said, 'after you start a diversion by landing on the sea wall.'

Aristides pointed with his cornel-wood stick.

'First, we build our camp,' he said.

So we did.

Remember, we'd cut hundreds of palisades. We emptied the round ship first, and then cleared all our decks and holds, and at the top of our little cliff, crews of oarsmen and marines dug post holes and drove them in. Other groups cut brush from the wood line, covered by archers in case the Thracians got ideas. When the palisades were up and dug in, the brush would be woven in among the uprights for stability and a little more protection.

The work moved with astounding speed once we got it organised. Almost eight thousand men can do an incredible amount of work in just a few hours, and by my second trip up the hill, the palisades reached the base of the hill and had started up the slope. Cimon was laying out a camp, assigning each ship the space to set their mainsail and boat sail as huge tents, and Aristides, always the thoughtful man, was laying out latrines which oarsmen were digging in the fertile soil.

Tekles and Styges and I laid out the little fort at the top, encompassing the camp but not the latrines. We laid out a main gate, facing the town, and a second gate to the latrines and a third so we could deploy to face a Thracian threat. On the beach, they were emptying the round ships and piling up the grain and wine and olive oil. I wondered if my new friend Katisa would sell me cattle or sheep.

In late afternoon, I was riding across the open ground behind our little fort, hoping to meet a Thracian who wouldn't kill me. Instead, I found a dozen Peloponnesian officers walking along the cliff top path, headed for our ships.

I reined in. They'd just caught site of our camp.

Pausanias nodded to me.

'Plataean,' he said. 'Why must Athenians always build walls? Is it part of their religion?'

I chose to act the Laconian part myself, and say nothing.

He nodded. 'That is not where the camp will be,' he said mildly enough.

'I think that is where the Athenians have chosen to make their camp,' I said.

He nodded, and kept walking.

I rode along, and Sparthius grinned at me.

'Do you have a horse for me, Ari?' he asked.

'I do, if you want one,' I said.

Spartans are not, for the most part, great riders. Neither was I, but Sparthius and I had spent weeks riding over western Asia with Persians, and we had learnt from masters how to ride in all countries in all weathers.

Aten, on the other hand, was in a state of very near revolt. He was not fond of horses.

I rode along, exchanging gossip with Sparthius, until Pausanias beckoned me.

'Go and tell those men to cease work,' he said.

I shook my head. 'No, sir,' I said. 'I think you'd best discuss that with Aristides and Cimon.'

He looked at me, eyebrows arched.

'There is nothing to discuss,' he said. 'I am the commander, and this is not where we are placing our camp.'

Sparthius winked at me.

I had no idea what that was supposed to mean.

Soon enough, we were all under Aristides' stern with wine in our hands.

Pausanias said, 'This is not a council. Just obey. The camp must be where I landed.'

I smiled, because smiling usually works better than frowning.

'Sir, your ships are seven stadia from the walls,' I said. 'Too far for daily raids. Do you have good fresh water?'

'Don't presume to question me!' he snapped.

I shrugged.

Cimon said, 'Pausanias, we are well suited here. And we know how to take a city.'

'Any body of men too cowardly to come out and fight can scarcely be fearsome opponents,' Pausanias said.

'Cowardly?' Cimon asked. 'They are many times outnumbered. I think they have fewer than a thousand fighting men.'

Pausanias looked at him with unveiled contempt.

'Even accepting your archers as soldiers,' he said, 'we have fewer than a thousand ourselves.'

'We have fifteen thousand oarsmen,' Cimon said. 'And two thousand deck crew.'

'Surely you can't mean to arm that rabble and call them soldiers?' Pausanias said. 'That would be shameful, like putting helots in your battle line.'

I was very tempted to say, out loud, *How on earth did you beat the Persians at Plataea?*

Instead, I said, 'Most of my deck crews are better armoured than most hoplites.'

Pausanias smiled dismissively. 'Sailors,' he said, as if to say 'useless slaves'.

Cimon continued to be polite. 'Regardless,' he said, 'no Persian garrison will come out and fight when so hopelessly outnumbered.'

'You burden me with all these useless oarsmen,' Pausanias said. 'If we win, people will say we had the numbers, and if we lose ... why, we must have been fools.'

No one said anything.

'From the hill we've taken,' I said, 'we can watch most of the walls. We have already cut the town off from any further supplies. And even if you have contempt for their fighting potential, you'll find that the oarsmen are very useful in a siege. Digging, building ...'

'Are you planning to lecture me on the conduct of war, Plataean?' Pausanias asked.

'I'd prefer that we did a little better than we did at Amathus,' I said.

Pausanias crossed his arms.

Aristides nodded. 'Let us handle this,' he said quietly. 'We know how to take a town.'

Pausanias shrugged. 'So you believe that this is the correct place for the camp?' he asked.

Aristides was firm. 'Yes,' he said. 'The hill, the beach, and the fresh water.'

Helpfully, I said, 'I've ridden the whole length of the city wall and all the nearby beaches on both shores. This is the best site.'

Pausanias managed a very slight smile.

'Excellent,' he said. 'Please vacate it, then. I'll put the Peloponnesians here.'

It took us five days to change our camp.

Aristides convinced us to do it after Pausanias walked off, as arrogant on foot as a Persian on horseback.

Eumenes, one of the trierarchs, spat.

'I say we pack up our oarsmen and leave,' he said. 'That impious bastard is an affront to the gods. Let's just leave him.'

Cimon's face was red with anger – possibly rage. His hands were shaking slightly, and his voice was very soft when he spoke, but his words were clear.

'That's what Pausanias wants,' he said. 'He wants us to sail away.'

Aristides nodded. 'I don't know whether he intends to take Byzantium for Sparta, and cut Athens off from the Euxine,' he said, 'or whether he simply wants the glory of driving the Persians from Europe ...' He looked at me.

I looked around the circle of captains.

'There's an excellent beach on the north side of the thumb,' I said. 'It has a fresh spring that's probably not enough water for all of us, but it's a start. We send four ships upstream to cut wood for more palisades. We can have a new camp in three days.'

Cimon looked at the sky and the shadows.

'Midsummer is here,' he said. 'How long do you expect the siege to last?'

I shrugged. I had been on the receiving end of a siege at Miletus, but I wasn't really an expert.

'Most cities fall to starvation,' I said. 'So over the winter.'

'Over the winter,' Cimon said, as if spitting a curse.

Most Athenians – most Greeks, in fact, including the Peloponnesians – only serve for the summer. We're all farmers, at some remove, even the richest men, and planting and harvest are sacrosanct. It's very difficult to get Greeks to stay in the field over the winter, and I wondered if Athens was paying for a long siege.

'The longest job is the one never started,' Aristides said. 'For whatever reason that Pausanias is playing the part of the tyrant, we want an alliance with the Ionians, and I'm willing to stay here to get it.'

'And as long as we're laying siege to this vital town,' I said, 'it's unlikely that the Great King will make a stab at any of the Ionian cities.'

I won't pretend there wasn't grumbling when Aristides gave the order – worse than grumbling. And some outright refusal to work.

Despite our own anger, the captains and navarchs remained calm ... and forgiving. We aimed at patience and light discipline, because the oarsmen had every reason to feel ill used.

But Aristides prevented them from leaving excrement in the streets, or flooding the stream with a salt-water canal, or any other slighting of the works or camp. We sailed away leaving it intact. Cimon and I had chosen the new camp with repeated visits, and we'd already filled the round ships with palisades and begun our new fortifications.

Our new camp was four stadia upstream on the northern arm of the water surrounding the 'thumb', called the 'Chrysokeras' – or Golden Horn – from its shape and colour in the setting sun, like a sheet of burnished gold rolling out under the prow of your ship. Our new camp did have the advantage of allowing us to close the whole peninsula to a relief force, and our fleet was by far the largest in the local waters.

We built our new camp with less will and less effort, but it was well laid out, and in some ways better fortified. I demanded that a watch be kept all day and all night, and there was some spectacular grumbling, even from officers.

'Let the Spartans keep watch!' Eumenes said.

I forced a smile. 'If the Spartans keep watch,' I said, 'you know that they will only warn other Spartans.'

Eumenes laughed, a good sign. 'Too fucking true,' he said.

On the second day after we moved, I was laying ropes and stakes to mark the position of the new works. It was late in the day, just after midsummer – really, late evening, but the light was good and I wanted to get it finished. We needed the wall to protect the ships, and Ole Llurin, who clearly had a head for such things, was laying out a complex gate area, when the Persians attacked our work parties. It was the first sign of life from the garrison, and it caught us by surprise, but it did not catch us unprepared. We had our archers at the top of our new hill, secure behind our first palisade. They covered our work lower on the hill and saw the Persians coming, shouting alarms.

The Great King's forces were both cavalry and infantry – almost twelve hundred men, at a guess. They came on quickly, driving in the oarsmen, who ran for the ships and their weapons.

Two hundred archers may not sound like a great many, but the moment their first ranging arrows struck into the Persian cavalry, the enemy soldiers stopped and deployed their great shields, the *sparabara* barricade.

And then, before Aristides could even bring Tekles and the marines off the beach, the Persians were withdrawing. It was the right decision – the commander had risked his entire garrison on a raid, and Ka and his archers had been alert enough to stop them. He couldn't afford a stand-up fight, even with cavalry. He slipped away, his horsemen raising enough dust to cover his retreat – a deliberate tactic, I believe. Night fell before we could mount a pursuit, and we had no cavalry. Our opponents knew their business – their timing had been precise.

Pausanias and his Peloponnesians were not in sight, as a low ridge runs down the peninsula like a spine. I determined on the spot to put an observation post at the top, or better yet, a fort.

The ships came back with another load of palisades, and we drove our works forward.

As I say, it took five days to move the camp and make the new place secure, but when we were done, we had more and better ground than our first camp, and some of the spirit had been restored. We still had to send ships away for water, because there wasn't enough, and a week into the siege, we needed wine and oil.

I left that to others, because I was determined to place a fort at the top of the spine, where it could see the Spartan camp and the city walls. And I wanted to start pushing our people into the ground in front of the walls. There were farm fields there, and while we built our camp we saw people harvesting fodder and some grain, and we really couldn't let the Persians have the farms.

So, over the next week, Cimon burnt the farms and I built a fort. My oarsmen sweated rivers into the parched ground while they carried heavy logs up the face of the ridge, with no cover, so that even the brownest man was burnt red. The ridge top had a forest of scrubby wild olive trees and we used these to form an abatis, and laid up a drystone wall, set our palisades and wove grape vines in among them to make them stronger. Then we cut the best timber we'd taken and raised a tower – really just four sticks and a platform – so that we could see into the city's acropolis, three stadia distant.

That night, the Medes tried us in the dark. They don't like fighting in the darkness, but then, who does? And they came with the moon, moving silently.

But I'd played all these games at Miletus. I had pickets out in the darkness, well in front of my new walls. Unfortunately, the Medes overran Giorgos' post, killing two oarsmen, but he raised the alarm and got away.

I had Styges and twenty marines inside the palisade, and I led them out at the trot. We spread out a little at the edge of our abatis, which is nothing but a line of felled trees with their branches entwined. It's a very noisy barrier, and you leave a few trails through for moments like this.

I led the way down one little alley, clear in the moonlight, while Styges led the other file along to my right.

There was movement in front of me, right where the brow of the ridge fell away, and there were big rocks. I turned that way in time to take an arrow on my aspis and get showered with cane splinters to remind me of my own mortality.

Fighting in the dark is a game of odds. Armour helps. Armour keeps you alive when you make a mistake, but a spear thrust will go right through bronze, and so will a well-directed arrow.

The man who came at me threw a javelin. I had very little warning, as I was facing the wrong way, and I can only guess that the head clipped the rim of my aspis instead of passing into my gut. But the shaft slammed into me, the butt clipped my chin, and I stumbled.

Leander threw his heavy *dory*, and it caught the man under his throwing arm and killed him instantly, and my marines surged forward. Remember that at this point, I didn't know whether we faced ten men or five hundred. I wanted to be cautious, but darkness either robs you of volition or makes you foolhardy, and you can guess which of the two applies to me.

Ignorance goes both ways. We charged, scattering our opponents, who were too lightly armed to stand in close combat. As the little knot of shadows in front of me broke, I saw movement across the whole hillside, like an ants' nest disturbed. I couldn't move fast – my various hip and leg wounds made a flat run untenable – but Styges' group caught a dozen men. Leander led the rest of my file, his loping run identifiable as he went down the hill, leaving me to watch.

The whole enemy force was running.

I raised my horn to my lips and blew the recall.

The next morning, Aristides met with Pausanias, who requested – well, indeed, demanded – that we turn over the prisoners, who were all lightly armed Thracian mercenaries. I wasn't there, but Aristides sent for the prisoners and handed them over. Later in the day, Pausanias released them.

He released them. I still shake my head.

Polycritus, son of Crius, who had commanded the Aeginian contingent and fought so well at Salamis, might have been accounted a Spartan ally. Ordinarily he hated Athens only slightly less than he hated the Medes. But that afternoon, he shook his head, spat in the sand, and looked at me.

'Whose side is he on?' he said, and walked away.

He spoke for us all.

But I had other problems. In the aftermath of the fight on the hillside, I sent Hipponax and Hector down to the main camp with the Thracian prisoners. And the next morning, while I felt the bruise under my beard where the spear had clipped my chin, Sekla came up the ridge and sat down in the fort, facing me.

'Out with it,' I said.

I was expecting he would want to leave. Sekla liked to be at sea.

'Your boys ...' he said.

'What of them?' I asked.

'Last night, they took the round ship,' he said. 'And set sail.'

'What?'

He handed me a tablet. 'Someone sly slipped this under my neck-rest,' he said.

I opened the wax tablet. It was neatly printed in well-formed Greek letters, all in the Cretan style, so Hipponax's work.

'Pater,
We've gone to rescue Heraklitus. We have a plan.'

I probably rolled my eyes. I know they filled with tears.

Of course they'd gone after Heraklitus. And there had been signs.

'How many men went with them?'

'Just the sail crew,' Sekla said. 'Leontos and Kephalos. It's an easy rig.'

I nodded, looking out to the Propontis to my right. There were several sails.

'You cannot leave,' Sekla said. 'I can. Give me the *Apollo's Raven* and I will follow them, support them if I can.'

'Take the *Serpent*,' I said.

He nodded – even smiled. 'You trust me in this?' he asked.

'You are like a brother to me,' I said. 'And what have I given you?'

'Freedom? Wealth? The respect of men like Cimon?' Sekla nodded. 'This is nothing. Let me go.'

'I should go myself,' I said.

'You are, in effect, directing the siege,' Sekla said. 'If you leave, many things may happen, none of them good.'

'Aristides and Cimon can direct the siege,' I said.

'Aristides spends his day keeping the Allied contingents from rowing away. Cimon is leading the aggressive patrols.' Sekla rolled his hand. 'Perhaps they are fine without you, but they are most definitely fine without me. Send me.' He looked out to sea. 'I feel guilty, anyway. I let them go last night, when I should have been suspicious.'

'You have nothing to worry about,' I said. 'They are young and bold, and perhaps they are only doing what I should be doing.'

'You are a commander,' Sekla said mildly, but I heard the sting in the tail of his sentence. *Behave like one.*

So I did.

The next day, as much to cover my apprehension about my sons as for any other reason, I put an Aeginian garrison into my fort and pushed my own people forward towards the city, three stadia distant. We linked up with Cimon. I had several mounted men and Cimon had almost a dozen, as he'd been purchasing horses, too. We'd armed our oarsmen and we had them out in front as *psiloi*, and we covered the ground thoroughly, right up to the walls.

A quarter of an hour at the walls taught us a great deal. We learnt that the Medes were mostly Thracian mercenaries with a handful of professional Persian infantry – not enough bows to keep us off for long. But the Persian commander was bold. He threw a mounted sortie at us from a side gate, and Ameinias of Pallene took an arrow in the leg, right through his greave, from the very first shaft loosed. He was perhaps ten paces to my right, watching the walls, and that's all the warning we had.

You'd imagine that horses can be loud, but they can be very quiet. I was mounted on one of my steppe ponies, and I had no shield, just a pair of javelins tucked under my leg. We were well back from the wall, perhaps three hundred paces, having made one feint to see what they had for archery. I was at the back of my little phalanx, because, being mounted, I was more likely to draw arrows and could do less about them. I had Styges and Achilles mounted with me.

My pony was as calm as if he was nipping grass on the great plains. His ears were up, but he was otherwise undisturbed by the screams of the wounded man.

The Persians had worked around into a stand of trees to our right rear, and we'd missed them. I saw a flash there, as someone's cap caught the sun, or perhaps a spearhead.

'Tekles!' I yelled. 'Close order – then at them.'

I chanced it, and trotted across open ground to Poseidonos, who was naked as his namesake, standing with a pelta and a pair of javelins and a big petasus and no more.

'I need you to harass their cavalry,' I said.

Arrows were falling around us, but the range was long.

'They'll eat us in the open ground, boss,' he said.

'Stay close to the hoplites, then,' I said. 'But push that way.'

He looked doubtful, but he called to them in his deep-sea voice, and they came.

Tekles roared for the hoplites to form close. When hoplites lap their great shields over one another in the closest order, there's not much for an archer to shoot.

I turned my pony's head and rode west, up the ridge and in among the wild olive trees. I saw Cimon off to my left, and I knew I had Styges and Achilles right behind me.

I reasoned that if they saw the hoplites come at them and knew we had cavalry – however inept – sweeping the hillside, they'd run.

They *should* have run. Perhaps they were tired of running. Perhaps, as the vaunted Persian cavalry, they were tired of running.

I used my knees to get my small mount to detour up a gully, and there, at the top, was a Mede. His horse was bigger than mine and he was above me, and throwing a javelin up from horseback is a miserable task.

He was watching someone else – Cimon, perhaps. His bow was up, an arrow laid to the string, the string tense but not at full draw.

He heard my pony a moment after I saw him. His head turned, and then his bow.

I threw. It was a terrible throw, and it tumbled, and smacked his horse's rump, and his horse leapt forward, spoiling his arrow.

My game little pony got its forefeet up on the top of the gully and sprang. For a moment I was in the air, fumbling under my left leg for my second javelin.

There was a second Persian behind the first, and I'd missed him because his dun-coloured horse matched the sandy soil and the rocks. He came at me with a yip, and his arrow slammed deep into my pony's neck, but I got his head around. I leant out, and stripped the Persian from the saddle with my left arm around his neck as he tried to ride by. He hit hard, his head making a hollow melon sound on a rock, that sent a chill down my spine.

I turned my pony, watching the first man. A third Persian burst from under an olive tree, and the tree's intertwined branches caught his bowstring and stripped his bow from his hands even as he tried to loose.

He drew his short sword, an *akinakes*, and cut at me, but I was already two paces too far, and he went horse to horse with Styges. His horse won the fight, but Styges killed him with one precise spear thrust even as his poor pony was toppling from the assault of the larger horse.

Styges hit hard, and screamed.

I turned my pony again. He was still game, despite an arrow standing out of his neck. The first Persian was somewhere in the rocks behind me, and only the gods knew how many of their cavalry had come to contest the hillside with us.

Achilles shouted his war cry at the bottom of the gully, and I saw a flash of movement. A riderless horse came up the gully, and there was a scream – whether derision or pain, I couldn't tell.

I didn't have the strength in my thighs, thanks to recent wounds, to lean down and pick up the bow or the javelins that the man I'd thrown from his saddle now had spilt all around him. I wanted them, but I wasn't sure I could remount if I dismounted. I had one javelin, and no more.

No point in waiting, then.

I let my pony pick his way north. His ears were pricked and so were mine. I could hear Cimon's riders, not so far away, but a little higher on the hill. I could hear two sets of bubbling moans from injured men. My pony was pouring blood from his neck wound, like barbarian paint, but didn't seem to notice.

Somewhere close was my Persian.

Behind the big rock was a large stand of fennel stalks. Fennel grows wild all over Greece, but in Thrace it grows in dense patches and then dries out in the summer to become almost impenetrable, like a wall. More important, anyone riding through it would break the stalks and make noise.

So my opponent was not in the fennel. He must have ridden around it.

He was waiting for me to ride out from the shadow of the rock.

Time was on my side. Cimon's skirmish line was closing in, and all I had to do was wait.

But I'm not good at waiting.

Despite my earlier hesitation, I slipped from the animal's back and readied my javelin. Then I gave a slap to my pony's hindquarters and he leapt away in a burst of wounded vanity.

I screeched for good measure, and then forced my way into the fennel stalks.

My Persian had been crouched over the neck of his horse, waiting. He rose, arrow to bow, and drew.

I threw my javelin.

He turned his head, warned at the last moment, and his horse bolted – perhaps frightened by mine, perhaps by my javelin.

I missed, and he missed.

The ground underfoot was treacherous – small rocks in sand, with larger rocks just the right size to turn an ankle, hidden under the fennel stalks. But I couldn't stay where I was, so I charged him.

He pulled his reins, intending, I think, to ride away, but my pony was close to his horse, biting at it. My Persian was unable to control his mount and manage his bow at the same time. It only lasted an instant, but in that instant I'd crossed the fennel and I was on him, my sword cutting at his unarmoured thigh.

He cursed and got at his own sword. I cut at his horse – the only target I had – and tried to throw him from the horse's back by his leg. He kicked at me, but the kick was weak, and there was blood everywhere. My cut to his thigh had opened something.

He looked down, clearly appalled at the blood, and then he slumped. The last look in his eyes was a sort of calm acceptance – the realisation that he was no longer in the fight.

Then he was dead, bleeding out in less time than a prayer takes, and I had his horse, who did not like the smell of the blood or the death of his rider.

By the time I collected his weapons, laid him out on the rocks, and calmed his horse, the fight was over. The Persian cavalry finally ran, having lost more men than they had any business losing. We'd lost four hoplites wounded and one dead, as well. By some miracle, or the whim of Hermes, we didn't lose an oarsman, although they prowled almost to within arm's length of the enemy cavalry.

We had one prisoner – the man I'd thrown from the saddle – and Styges was laid up with a broken hip where his horse had fallen on him. We had four good Persian horses, the most valuable loot we'd taken so far, bigger and faster than our steppe ponies, although not as tough.

But my steppe pony was the king of tough. He'd taken an arrow in the neck, and later that afternoon, a horse leech from among Cimon's oarsmen came and pushed the shaft through, and in an hour he was cropping grass.

My hips hurt, and my leg hurt, and my shoulder hurt. Everything hurt.

And before I could question my prisoner, Pausanias had released him.

The next morning, after a poor night's sleep in heavy heat with too many insects and not enough air, I mounted my new Persian gelding and rode out to check our lines. We had the camp's headquarters in the little fort where all the archers were camped, on the hill above our ships. There were two limp bundles on the packed earth, and all the archers gave them a wide berth – corpses, I assumed.

They had two men in the tower and most of them were up and about, and I noticed with pleasure that all of them had their bows strung and their quivers to hand.

'Anything to report?' I asked Ka.

Ka was drinking something hot – closer up, it smelled like mint tea. He sent a boy to get some, and showed me the day's tablets. We only kept a wax copy, showing what ships had what duty.

He pointed at one line.

'Two Thracians. Slaves, I think.' He shrugged. 'Vasilos heard them, and Phorbas and Myron ran them down.'

Vasilos was our old archer. It was really quite unfair to call him old – he seemed to be made of rawhide and steel, and he pulled a heavy bow. But he had a long white beard, and most of the archers called him 'Grandfather', with some respect.

Myron was a small, wiry man, made of the same rawhide. He was a former Spartan helot, who'd run off with his friends and been taken aboard by Moire and Ka some seasons before. Phorbas was another – taller and wider. He had long legs and was known as a runner.

'We need prisoners,' I said.

Myron smiled. He had the slave's habit of offering a pleasant smile to any comment.

'Yes, boss,' he said.

Phorbas looked at me. 'Never a word of praise, eh?' he snapped. 'Why take prisoners? Our former masters just hand them back to the Persians.'

I sat down on my haunches and sipped my mint tea.

'You're right, Phorbas – right twice. Thanks for catching these bastards. You did well. Now, next time, get us some alive.'

I laid two gold darics on the packed earth.

Phorbas raised an eyebrow.

Myron laughed. 'He won't know what to say for days,' he said.

I shrugged. 'Just take the money,' I said, looking at Phorbas.

I made him smile. He was a hard man – he'd been ill used. The ship-wide rumour was that his father was an important Spartan, and his mother had been a slave, and he'd been beaten with extraordinary frequency.

I looked at Myron.

'Do you two hear things?' I asked him. 'From the Spartan camp?'

Myron didn't even blink, nor did his pleasant smile change.

'Boss,' he said. He met my eye, and held it a long time. 'You've been good to us. No troubles.'

I took a sip of my mint tea and handed it to him, and he took a sip and handed it to Phorbas.

'Better with honey,' he said. He handed it back.

'I'll try it that way, next time,' I said.

Myron looked up the ridge – in the direction of the Spartan camp.

'There's friends over there,' he said.

'Kin,' Phorbas said.

'And deadly enemies,' Myron added. 'Men who'd gut us because we ran, and never a word about how we fought at Plataea, or Mycale.'

We looked at one another.

'I don't need your secrets,' I said. 'I just want to know if you'd know if something ... went wrong. There's a lot here that could go wrong.'

'We hear things,' Myron admitted.

Phorbas met my eye boldly – maybe with some anger.

'Listen,' he said. 'Let us talk to the others.'

It occurred to me, as it often does, that every man is the hero in his own tale, and that these escaped helots had their own tales of heroism, murder, oppression, and perhaps revenge. I really only knew them as competent archers – as Ka's archers. But of course they had their own lives, their own troubles.

'That's all I ask,' I said, rising. I left the gold darics. 'The money is for catching the Thracians. Not for informing on your friends. I don't want your friends harmed. I just need to know what in the name of all the gods is happening in the Peloponnesian camp.'

Myron nodded pleasantly. 'Thanks, boss,' he said, in a tone that might have meant anything.

I rose, cursing the pain in my groin and hips as I got up – cursing age and wounds and war, and the disunity of Greece.

'Got any more tea?' I asked Ka. He fetched me more and then went back to the tablets.

Cimon had come in while I was talking to the archers, and he looked over my shoulder while I reviewed the duty roster.

'We need a hospital,' he said. 'More than twenty wounded, and we're a week in.'

I nodded. 'The little stand of pines by the beach, 'I said. 'It's coolest there.'

He nodded. 'We need more water.'

'I agree,' I said. 'Let's send a few ships to fill their holds. We ought to have the amphorae to get it done.'

He nodded again. 'I want to try an assault,' he said. 'I know we'll probably fail, but I'd like to pin their ears back.'

'I agree,' I said. 'But ...'

'Here it comes.' He smiled, but there was annoyance in his tone.

'Every day we fight them in the middle ground, we're bleeding them and sapping their morale,' I said. 'Every time we assault them and fail, we take the casualties and bolster their confidence.'

Cimon fingered his beard thoughtfully. 'Put against that, we're still fresh now. We might just do it.'

'You just want to blacken Pausanias' eye,' I said.

'Zeus, don't you?' he replied.

I sat back. 'I think we can take a lesson from the Persians and take the town in a month,' I said.

Cimon brightened. 'How?'

I looked over the water, and wondered how my sons were faring, and why I was not with them. But Sekla had a point. I was not a young hero. I was an old commander.

'I propose we visit Pausanias,' I said. 'I'm guessing you were planning to do so, as well.'

Cimon smiled a hard smile. 'You have got me there,' he said.

'Depending on that interview,' I said, 'we'll try my plan.' I pointed at the corpse-bundles. 'Thracians,' I said. 'My archers say they were probably slaves.'

Cimon narrowed his eyes.

'What does that tell you?' I asked.

'That our Melinditae friends are trying to get a message into the town,' Cimon said. He scratched his shoulder, where the weight of his cuirass crossed his neck muscles. We all had sores there.

I thought of Katisa of the Melinditae.

'I'm not sure,' I said.

Cimon shook his head. 'Neither am I. There's dozens, if not hundreds, of Thracian tribes, with ever-shifting alliances and hatreds. Katisa may be willing to back us – there could be another. My family has held this region for fifty years. My mother was Thracian – she'd have known who was who around here.'

I looked west, towards the distant hills.

'I suspect we need to know,' I said.

Cimon nodded.

'Let's go and see Pausanias,' I said.

Pausanias was sitting in a grove of sea pine, on a plain camp stool, and nonetheless contrived to look like a king. He was doing a commander's usual work, holding a meeting of his officers to give out daily duties, no more tyrannical in that moment than I had been earlier.

I could see friends in that command circle – Lykon of Corinth, Medon of Hermione, who'd given all the Plataeans shelter in the year of Salamis, and Sparthius, with whom I'd travelled to the Great King's court. But there were also men with whom I had real trouble, like Adeimantus of Corinth, and others, like Amompharetos of Sparta, with whom I'd certainly had my differences.

On the other hand, Cimon was the closest thing the Spartans had to a good friend in Athens, and I had certainly done Sparta several services. Let me put it this way ... Imagine what it is like to have a close friend, some of whose behaviour appals you, and with whom you sometimes have hearty disagreements. I have several such friends.

One of them is Sparta.

We dismounted a fair distance from the command meeting, and helots took our horses, and I looked at them more carefully than was my wont. The taint of slavery and servitude is on all of us – although I disapprove of the way the Spartans treat their helots, I fully confess that in my many trips among the Lacedaemonians, I had never learnt the name of a single one, and had not, until then, spent much time even looking at them. It is too easy to not see what you'd rather didn't exist.

So I said 'Thank you' to the four helots who took our horses.

And they all gave me the false smiles and theatrical inferiority that they assumed I craved, bobbing their heads and cringing away.

Cimon glanced at me.

We waited on the fringes of the meeting, leaning on our spears for some time, until Pausanias finished with his assignments.

He glanced up, saw us, and then smiled thinly at his officers.

'Dismissed, gentlemen,' he said.

They nodded, and walked away. I caught Lykon's eye and mouthed 'later', and he nodded.

Sparthius waved, as if that were the most natural thing in the world.

And then we were alone with Pausanias. Truly alone – not even a helot was within earshot.

'Cimon,' Pausanias said. 'Greetings. And the Plataean.' He nodded.

'The blessings of Zeus, god of kings and commanders, be with you,' Cimon said, formally.

Pausanias nodded. He put his chin in his hand. 'I will discuss whatever you wish, Cimon, but let me say that I negotiate with all of you through Aristides, and I cannot be expected to regulate each and every one of you.'

'Negotiate?' I asked.

'Are you not in rebellion against my authority?' he asked.

Cimon shook his head. 'Not that I know of, Strategos.'

'Then why are you not in my former camp, as I ordered?' he asked.

I shrugged, and cut Cimon off. 'Never heard that you made such a ridiculous demand. Please stop giving orders that will not be obeyed. It's bad for the Alliance.'

'Let me understand,' Pausanias said slowly. 'You, as the commander of a city that can field perhaps six hundred men, are going to tell the Regent of Sparta how to issue orders?'

'Only if I must,' I said.

Pausanias looked at me under his heavy brows. He had a thick head of curly hair which he wore long, like a younger man, and which was nonetheless bald at the top – invisible until he put his head in his hand and leant forward. He was well-built, and had the air of authority that is essential in a commander, until he lost his temper. Most of us seem like fools when we lose our tempers. I know what I'm saying here.

He didn't explode at me. Instead, he looked, first at Cimon, and then at me, and said, mildly enough, 'You have no idea what it is like to command this force.'

'That may be true ...' Cimon began, but then he halted and looked at me.

We'd discussed how to approach Pausanias on the ride over, but not exactly who would play what part. Now he hesitated, perhaps from respect.

I'm aware that I have characterised Pausanias as tyrannical and petty. And he was. But remember that he led us to victory at Plataea. There was more there than the inferiority that great events had revealed.

Remember, too, what Briseis said. We Greeks tend to devour our heroes.

I leant on my spear.

'I think I do,' I said. 'I think I know that you have orders from your ephors that are utterly at variance with your own inclinations—'

'If you know such things,' he snapped, 'then you should keep them between the gates of your teeth.'

Cimon glanced at me again – this time, I guessed, to take the bit in his teeth. I nodded.

'We know that you have an ambassador going to the Great King,' he said.

Pausanias writhed like a serpent. 'Not I,' he spat. 'Not I, you prying interlopers.'

I won't say it hit me like a thunderbolt, because I'd lain awake considering the various scenarios that might have brought us here. So, the ephors had sent the embassy to the Great King. And because Leonidas was dead and Gorgo could not hold power, there was no representative of the policy of supporting the Alliance in the murky world of Spartan politics.

Pausanias had always been a leader of the faction that wanted Sparta to rule alone, but he had once been open to other ideas. I had to try.

'Pausanias,' I said, raising my hand, as if in supplication. 'We are not prying interlopers. We are Greeks, like you. With you – behind you, if you like – we faced the Medes at Salamis and Plataea. You are not here as a Spartan commander, or as regent. You are here as the commander of the forces of the Alliance, and your first duty is not to your ephors and their machinations. Your first duty is to us. To all of the Free Greeks.'

For a moment, I thought I had him.

Then he looked away.

'Thank you for sharing your thoughts, gentlemen,' he said heavily. 'Did you have something more concrete to discuss?'

'I want to assault the town,' Cimon said.

'If there's any fighting to be done, I will see to it,' Pausanias said dismissively. 'That's why I am here. I defeated the Persians at Plataea. I will defeat them here.'

Cimon's eyes narrowed. 'You know ...' he said. 'You know, Pausanias, when my father defeated the Medes on the field of Marathon, he requested the right to wear a wreath of laurel on public occasions, like an Olympic victor.'

Pausanias nodded. 'Yes,' he said, as if utterly uninterested.

'A man named Sokares of Dekarea rose in the assembly,' Cimon continued. 'He'd fought as a hoplite at Marathon, and he was no enemy of my father's. You know what he said?'

Pausanias shrugged.

Cimon stepped forward until he was very close to Pausanias.

'He said, "Miltiades, when you have gained a victory against the Medes alone, instead of having ten thousand of us at your back, then we'll vote you the sole right to a wreath of laurel."'

Pausanias flushed with rage.

'What a typically *Athenian* insult,' he spat. 'Get you gone,' he added, his voice thick with rage, spittle flying.

'I accuse you of not acting in the common interest,' Cimon said. 'I accuse you of putting the petty politics of your state above the needs of the Allies.'

'I accuse you of wasting my morning,' Pausanias said. 'And I accuse you of crass hypocrisy, Cimon, son of Miltiades! Perhaps you fool the Plataean, who seems in many ways to be an honest man. Indeed, the men of the little states require allies. They favour these associations, and honestly expect them to function. But you and I know better, do we not, Cimon? You accuse me of putting forward the interests of my state – of Sparta. But only Sparta has protected Greece. Only Sparta has the armed might to stop the Great King. And yet, who brought the Persians down on us like wolves on unprotected sheep-folds? Your father and a dozen other Athenian pirates, supporting and provoking the useless Ionians into revolt. Who endangered all of Greece by rising above their station? Athens. Always Athens. Always fucking Athens, where worthless little men scheme and pretend to politics and rattle their ineffectual spears at their betters. And when we Spartans had defeated your foes at Salamis and at Plataea, what did you, Athens, do to thank us? You prepared for war against Sparta and built new walls to protect you, so that you could go back to stirring the troubled waters of the Great King's empire. You want Ionia, Athens. And you will happily sacrifice the rest of Greece for it. You profess to love for the Ionians, but all you want is hegemony and empire. Your walls told us everything we needed to know about the future. So don't prate to me about Greece. If I choose to put first the will of my ephors and my king – if I choose to place Lacedaemon above all – how dare you task me with it? You are Cimon, of the Athens First faction of Athens. Except that Athens, which lacks all the great-heartedness of Sparta, has no other faction!'

By the time Pausanias was done, he was shouting his face a hand's breadth from Cimon's, and Cimon didn't withdraw, so that he was spitting in the Athenian's face with every word.

They glared at each other like rival lions over a corpse.

But the corpse was going to be Greece.

I took Cimon by the shoulders and dragged him back a step.

'Gentlemen,' I said.

They both looked at me.

'Athens is not without guilt in this matter,' I said. 'But you know yourself, Pausanias, that your tale is full of hubris and breezy assertions as hollow as old trees. The Athenians defeated the Medes without you, some years ago, at Marathon. At Salamis, you didn't provide one ship in ten, and Themistocles did most of the commanding. At Plataea, you had the noblest part, and both of us honour you for it – but Sparta alone would never have triumphed. Cimon and I, as ambassadors, know how close Sparta came to refusing to come at all.'

Both of them were breathing hard, like men locked in a fight.

'In this much you are perfectly accurate,' I said. 'We men of little cities, we need allies. And perhaps because we always need them, we see them with clear eyes, no matter what they say. When Athens sent Miltiades to us, in my youth ... Myron, our archon, was not fooled by the fine promises made. We knew that Athens was using us in a larger game. That is who you all are, frankly. Any state with the strength to imagine empire, reaches for it.' I shrugged. 'So. Perhaps there is some justice in your accusations, Pausanias, but we know more than you think about the politics of Lacedaemon. We know what your ambassadors are saying to the Great King. We know why you are returning the prisoners. You are playing a dangerous game.'

Pausanias sat for a moment.

Again, for a moment, I had swayed him. He opened his mouth to speak. I think the fact of the ambassadors angered him and gave my argument leverage, even while I lied about knowing what they were sent to say.

He looked at me ...

'It's not a game,' Cimon spat. 'It's treason.'

Pausanias' face closed.

'Go, before I lose my temper,' he said.

That close ... Or not. To this day, Cimon says that we were never close to changing his mind.

But I say, poor Pausanias, trapped between his duty to his useless, craven old ephors and his own ambitions and vanity.

He could have been the saviour of Ionia. And let you all remember that the treason was not his. Not Pausanias'.

It was the treason of Sparta.

I went to Lykon's ship, and there he was, in his armour, eating a bowl of oats with cheese grated into it.

'Having fun yet?' he asked me.

We embraced. He offered me a bowl of his gruel, and I started eating it. Cimon paced.

'Do you have your friend Philip, son of Sophokles aboard?' I asked.

He smiled. 'Captain of marines,' he said.

He turned to one of his oarsmen and said, 'Fetch the *taxiarchos*.'

Philip was a handsome man by any reckoning, with his mother's and grandfather's blond hair, and sea-green eyes. He was Lykon's best friend, and permanent war companion, and one of my sister's favourite men – actually, they both were.

'Philip,' I called. 'How's your Thracian?'

He shrugged. 'Tolerable,' he said. 'My mother and my nurse spoke it. I'm not bad.'

I told them the story of the Thracian slaves who'd tried to infiltrate our lines, and Philip understood the politics immediately.

'Care to come and be my translator?' I asked.

Lykon glanced at me. 'Is Pausanias going to burst into flames when he hears of this?' he asked.

I nodded. 'Almost certainly. I'm about to make an embassy to the local Thracians without consulting him.'

'Excellent,' Lykon said. 'Even Adeimantus is sick of him.'

'Gods, the sun must be turning green,' I said.

Cimon glanced at me. 'He has other problems than this siege,' he said.

I think that some of what Pausanias spat at him had hit home. He was very thoughtful.

'I know,' I said. 'But I don't have to care. I want to take this place and get back to Plataea. I'm building a new house – I've invited a great many guests for the autumn. You, for example. I don't fancy a winter siege in Thrace.'

Lykon shivered.

Cimon nodded. 'Nor do I. I assume you don't want the assault to go in until you speak to your Thracians.'

'If I can find them,' I said.

Sieges plod.

Greeks are good at fighting, but not particularly good at war. It's actually something of which we can be proud. Most of us think we have better things to do than fight wars, and so we've pushed war around until it's something agonistic, like a competition at the Panathenaic Games, or the Olympics. We dedicate a few weeks to our campaigns, march out to a place chosen by heralds, put our aspides on our shoulders, get it done, and go back to farming, or making sculpture, or enjoying fine wine.

It's really not that hard to be a strategos under those circumstances. Assuming basic competence, which is sometimes too much to assume, a man has only to see that his neighbours and members of his tribes and phratries are in their ranks, formed correctly. Sometimes there are little complications, like cavalry and psiloi, but for the most part, you line up your phalanx and go at it. Most campaigns, at least in my father's time, we settled in the time it took a man to eat the rations he brought from home. No need for markets or baggage wagons or latrines.

Cyrus, one of my Persian friends from boyhood, once told me that all Greeks are amateurs at the art of war, and being a snippy adolescent, I replied that war was a stupid thing to make a profession.

Now, the Great King and his empire have made thousands of Greeks into professionals – my whole generation has known little but war. Yet the traditions of our forefathers linger, and our amateurish efforts at logistics are based on the practices of the past.

Sieges are the antithesis of everything my father's generation believed about war. They last a whole summer, and sometimes through the winter. Most of them are settled by disease and starvation. And leadership, in a siege, is the constant response to events over which you have no control – disease and enemy action, but also boredom and its close friend, mutiny. And the daily grind of a siege has just enough military risk that under the boredom, around, it, shot through it like the veins in a oak leaf, is fear. Toss in hunger and fatigue, and both soldier and commander become locked in a grapple with themselves and each other.

Very few strategoi excel at these extended conditions. I can't tell you how often I've heard men – good men – tell me that they are 'good in a crisis', as if that excused all the other days of the year where they were indolent or impatient or incompetent. But the siege shows up every fault, because it rolls on and on, tempers fraying, impatience peaking, indolence leading to work stoppage, abuse leading to mutiny. Nothing in the commander's personality can be hidden – not the girl in his tent, not the extra cup of wine before bed, or the smell of his farts. The sort of magical charisma that makes a capable young man into a new Achilles won't last two weeks in the shit-choked trenches of a siege.

As I said the other night, the Athenians are much better at sieges than the Spartans. That's odd. Let's face it, Spartan discipline is much better than Athenian, and you'd expect them to excel at a long staring contest, which is what my old friend and helmsman Paramanos used to call a siege.

But there's one form of Greek warfare that does prepare you for laying siege to a city, and that is war at sea.

Sea warfare is all about food and water, campsites, landing places, leadership in storm and calm, good weather and bad. Leadership at sea is always, not occasional, and naval campaigns go on for months, or even years.

If you have followed this whole story, you know that even the Athenians and the Aeginians, masters of naval warfare, had lots to learn about the conduct of large-scale fleet operations. The Allied fleets at Artemisium and Salamis barely held together. Food was short, and latrines were terrible. In a single generation, we all went from 'fleets' of ten triremes to fleets of three hundred triremes – from two thousand men to sixty thousand – and all of the complexity that follows from such a huge multiplication. War was never going to be the same for anyone.

But all things being equal, by the high summer of the third year of the seventy-fifth Olympiad, the year after Plataea, if anyone was going to crack a nut like Byzantium, it was Cimon, son of Miltiades, Aristides, and me.

I've wandered off my road here to explain this, because while I was burning to talk to the Thracians, and to start the Allies on my little plan to take the city, none of that happened for days. It might never have happened except for a crisis in our logistics brought on, at least in part, by my sons taking one of our precious round ships.

My initial trouble was that we couldn't find the Thracians. That is, scouting found Thracians, north and west of the city. They weren't hard to find, as there were a fair number of them. But they weren't our Melinditae. They were, as Philip hastened to tell me, Odrysae. We lost half our mounted men in one skirmish, ten stadia from our camp, and we spent the next three days making certain that we were covered from our landward approaches as well as from the city.

Styges was recovering, and the irony that he had been too badly hurt to go and get killed scouting was not lost on either of us.

Regardless, spirits tumbled and the men assigned to picket duty grew unruly, I chose to lead three days' worth of patrols myself, from the back of my spear-won Persian gelding. Aside from some blue-blood Athenian cavalrymen who were serving as marines or officers, we had very few men who were really good at riding. I knew that Ka could ride, and a little investigation found three Scythians or half-Scythians serving as archers on other ships, as well as two coastal Thracians, and all of them could ride. With our captured Persian horses we could mount a patrol of ten men, most of them archers, from five races.

I offered them a gold daric for every patrol. That was very good for morale. I led them myself. Also good for morale.

For a pirate, I was bleeding money.

My ten men had, among them, three hundred years of mixed-culture cattle-thieving experience, and I leant on them heavily. We didn't accomplish much, but then, we didn't die.

After three days, during which Cimon took the aggressive patrols right up to the city walls every day and Aristides took four ships and harassed the seaward defenders to keep them in, I had learnt enough about the Odrysae to report to Aristides.

'There's thousands of them,' I said.

I was out of shape for horseback riding, and three days of tension and exercise had left me exhausted. Riding isn't restful. It's slightly better than running everywhere yourself, but only slightly. And a spring at sea had not prepared me for a summer on horseback.

I was out of shape and didn't want to admit it to myself.

Aristides nodded, motioning for more water in his wine.

'How many thousands?'

I shrugged. 'Based on horse herd and contacts and guesswork, five thousand,' I said.

'Or ten?' Cimon asked.

'Or twenty?' Aristides asked.

I nodded. 'They have a thousand mounted men and we have ten,' I said.

Aristides smiled. 'No one doubts you, Arimnestos.'

Cimon stroked his beard. 'You think they'll try to break the siege?' he asked.

'I think they're trying to make a deal with the Persian governor,' I said, 'in return for which, if a deal is made, they'll try to break the siege. We have one advantage – I don't think we were even supposed to know they were there.'

'What does your friend Philip think?' Aristides asked.

Philip had been wounded in the initial cavalry disaster, and was trying to recover from a trilobate arrowhead through his calf.

'Philip thinks that the Odrysae are here to reclaim this territory from the Melinditae,' I said. 'That's pure guesswork ...'

Cimon nodded. 'Sounds right. I grew up here. I don't remember the Melinditae here – but Pater might have dealt with them. There's always been a lot of conflict over the straits on both sides. And the Odrysae have been coming up with bigger and bigger confederations for as long as we've been around.'

'Maybe you should go and meet the Melinditae,' I said.

Cimon shook his head. 'Thracians are all about personal contact. You met the chief – you go and parley with her.'

It was all very well to say that, but we couldn't find the Melinditae, and that was a bad sign.

We were also running low on grain. We'd built a long line of ovens from the clay near the beach, and we could bake bread and barley rolls. I've mentioned before that a trireme is an endless source of skilled manpower, and we found more than a dozen competent bakers in the fleet, and just the smell of their bread was heartening. And ovens burn brush, which proved providential. The men assigned to cut brush to clear our new, landward-facing fortifications worked harder when Cimon let it be known that they'd get first place in the bread line, and their work was directly supporting the ovens.

We also had a few veteran charcoal burners, and they began to produce charcoal for cooking from smoking mounds like artificial hills. Trees are abundant in Thrace, and the charcoal burners were essential, because most of our cooks cooked on charcoal, not wood – we used clay braziers.

Aristides' crew was building a small wooden temple to Athena. The midsummer festivals were past, but the Panathenaea Megala, the great festival of Athena, was due in both the Athenian calendar and the Plataean and Aeginian calendar, beginning on the twenty-third day of Hekatombaion, a week after the full moon of the new year, at least the way the Athenians counted years. It reminded me that I was Archon of Plataea, and the Daedala would be celebrated without me – not a great Daedala, but a small one that might have been my own.

My point is that we were building a small city with temples and industry. In truth, with the Peloponnesians, the besiegers probably had more people in their camp than the citizens had in their town.

I've digressed far enough. We needed grain to feed the ovens. The production of good bread was essential for morale. We'd lost a round ship when my sons took mine. Two of them were permanently engaged in shipping amphorae of water from the springs up the coast, and we guarded them with a pair of triremes just in case.

But my trihemiola had more cargo space than most military triremes, and she could sail closer to the wind. And it was my sons who'd taken our other merchant ship.

'Lesbos will have grain to sell,' Aristides said.

'That's five days, at least,' I said. 'Two there, a day to load, and two back, and that's if everything goes well.'

It was the morning of the fifth day since we'd harangued Pausanias in his camp. The night of the full moon. A week until the great festival of Athena was to begin.

'Go tomorrow and we'll have bread for the feast days,' Aristides said. 'Better to fast now and feast then. I can explain that to the people.'

'And he will,' Cimon said, with his amused smile.

It was an expression that had been missing all too often – the three of us were growing worn like old chitons, fraying, tearing away. I snapped at Aten too often when a kind word would have sufficed, a process made worse by my knowledge that he was getting old enough to be a soldier and not a servant. Two years of constant warfare had worn away his slavish cowardice, the cowardice taught by bullies and overseers. He was as interested in fighting as any other young man.

I remember thinking *And then I'll just have to train another slave* which, when you get down to it, is as ignoble a thought as a man can have.

Regardless, Aristides looked at me. 'Someone has to explain,' he said.

'Cimon meant no insult,' I said. 'Are you two certain you can be at peace with each other while I'm gone?'

Cimon shrugged. 'Two more weeks of this and I'll hate you, him, and the Great King with equal intensity,' he admitted.

'We need the feast of Athena,' Aristides said.

That gave me an idea. I put it with my other idea about the siege and left it there to rattle around.

'I'll sail tomorrow,' I said.

Cimon followed me out of Aristides' awning.

'We should double the guards tonight,' he said. 'Full moon. If the Thracians intend to have a go at our lines, this would be their ideal night.'

And then we had some good fortune.

At sunset, Cimon and I mounted our horses and made the rounds of all the pickets – the sentries on our new walls and the men stationed in the dangerous places, well out from camp. We were both veterans of this kind of war. We left our horses and crept into our forward pickets, so as not to give their position away to watchers in the far hillsides.

At every post, we explained that the night would have bright moonlight and that we expected a Thracian attack.

In the very last light, Styges, mostly recovered, led our little mounted band all the way along our landward defences and then out onto the plain, where we'd cut all the brush, and along the far tree line. Dawn and evening patrols let us know if there was a build-up of troops preparing an attack.

Styges found nothing.

I was awakened in total darkness by Aten.

'Spartan camp is under attack,' he said.

I was up immediately and moving in the darkness, and Aten put me in my panoply. I mounted more by touch than sight, ignoring the pain in my hips and groin, and Aten got up on my steppe pony. The little beast was now fully healed.

We collected Cimon, Styges and the horse archers at the gate of the camp, as well as fifty marines under Tekles.

I wished I had Brasidas.

'I need you to run all the way,' I said.

Tekles tilted his helmet back on his head.

'Yes,' he said.

We went up the stony ridge behind the camp, up towards the fort, where there was a signal torch burning. We got a report there from Phorbas, that there were 'hundreds' of Thracians in the valley on the Peloponnesian side of the peninsula.

I didn't take any of the archers from the fort's garrison. Archers aren't that useful in a night fight, even in a full moon.

The moon was very bright, and when we went over the crest and down the other side, we could see the Thracians were carrying torches – at least some of them.

Cimon tapped my armoured shoulder.

'I'll take the cavalry to the left, towards the walls,' he said. 'You bounce their centre and I'll come up from the left like a thousand men, and they'll run.'

'Do it,' I said, and we were off. I stayed with Tekles, who didn't need me to tell him what to do.

I could see that the Thracians had broken into one of the Peloponnesian palisades that we'd started. They were putting fire into a warehouse or a wooden temple.

Or a ship. That would be a bad sign.

We went down that ridge, making what I thought of as far too much noise, but the Thracians were busy fighting and looting. How they failed to watch their backs when they knew there was another Greek camp, I have no idea.

You may remember that we'd fortified a low hill separate from the ridge, and the Thracians were trying to take it. Pausanias had his own camp there. The Thracians were not a match, even in the dark, for the forty Spartiates Pausanias had by him. The fighting had become desperate and personal – a clump at the gate, and another where the first attack had apparently axed through the palisade.

We crossed the little gully with the fresh water stream at the bottom, and started up the other side, undetected. We were coming up on the rearmost Thracians, who were pushing at the men in the axe-cut breach.

The Thracians were betrayed by their own arrogance. I know that at least one of them heard me and my horse picking our way up the trail that helots used to get water, but even in moonlight, a mounted Greek and a mounted Thracian have a lot in common.

My Persian gelding made the top, and I put my first javelin into the man who'd glanced down and then ignored me. I had a little bucket of fine javelins – five of them – from the man I'd captured. I threw the second at an officer, by his armour and sheer amount of gold he had on him. My spear bit through his bronze and into his back, and his choked scream was terrible.

I answered it with my war cry. I wanted panic. I wanted them to run. And I wanted the Peloponnesians to know we were coming to help them.

At my cry, all of Tekles' marines belted out theirs, screaming like gulls – *eleueleueleuelue*! – the Ionian war cry. The Thracians turned, caught between a rock and a hard place. I put another down with a javelin, a man so close that the weapon never left my hand. Inside the palisade, a deep voice ordered a push, and the moonlight shone down on the ferocious images painted on the bronze faces of the *aspides* of the Spartans. They struck hard.

The marines flowed past me. I saw Polymarchos killing his way through a crowd like the consummate professional he was, and Achilles, happier on foot than on horseback, and Arios and Leander, Kassandros and Zephyrides. They flowed around the Thracians, no formation, yet fighting like teammates in a game, or hunters in at the kill.

The Thracians ran.

The men who'd been trying to force the gate and the men already overrunning the lower camp – what proved to be the Corinthian camp – heard the fighting and the war cries. That might have proven our undoing. Someone rallied them in the darkness and they came at us, just as I was clasping sword-hands with Sparthius at the breach.

But fifty Athenian marines and forty Spartiates and a dozen desperate helots made a difficult foe, and we held our ground. I remember none of it, except the deadly sparkle of the steel in the moonlight, the glitter as an arrow flashed through the vision allowed by my helmet, the thrown spear passing like a comet, the brilliant reflection of a sword blade catching the moonlight, colourless, as sudden as the thunderbolt of the god.

You can only take so much of it. That's why the lines come together and then fall back – and the dark is even more shot through with terror.

It seemed as if we fought all night. I know it was not much longer than it would take to plough a furrow on my farm.

And then there was no foul breath in my face, no pressure against my horse.

Cimon had come out of the darkness from the direction of the city, our little cavalry screaming like savages. They'd broken the Thracians before they hit home – one last deadly surprise in the darkness, just as Lykon brought the Corinthian oarsmen en masse against the other flank.

When the sun rose, we saw that we'd killed a hundred or more of them, and Pausanias directed that they be stripped and the gold shared. But he didn't stop to thank us.

I think I hated him most that morning, because I was off my horse, sitting in the bloody dirt, Aten's head in my lap as he breathed his last. A Thracian's spear had pierced all the way through his guts, and there was another long cut on his thigh above his greave that, mercifully, killed him by bleeding out. For a boy born to slavery in Aegypt, I think he had a lot of love at his death. He'd proved himself worthy fifty times, and now I sat with him and wept, as much for all the mornings I'd snapped at his perfect service as for his death. We always weep first for ourselves – Heraclitus told me that.

But I felt unworthy. Bad. *Only yesterday I snapped at this boy and thought that he should remain a slave ...*

Do I weep for you, Aten, or for how I treated you?

The sun rose in the east, the first bright rays breaking over Asia across the straits and turning the calm water to a rosy gold.

'Oh, how beautiful,' Aten said.

And he died.

Cimon was there, and Styges and Leander.

'I didn't like him at first,' Leander said.

Styges blinked away tears. 'I did,' he said.

Cimon didn't say anything at first. But he put his hands on my shoulders, held me for a moment, and then said, 'He's gone, Ari.'

Aten's death didn't leave me with a desire for revenge. Instead, it put into me that traditional Greek idea about war.

The desire to get the gods-damned thing over.

We had a dozen prisoners, men too badly wounded to run. Thracians don't usually surrender, otherwise. From them, Cimon and Sparthius learnt that the Melinditae had lost a battle to the Odrysae and retreated towards Doriscus and further west, and that the point of the raid had been to distract us while a messenger got into the town.

'We're fucked,' Cimon said. 'Damn.'

It was full morning, and the weight of Aten's death was on me as if I was carrying his rotting corpse around in the sunlight.

'No,' I said. 'No. We're going to win this, because the price of losing just got too high. Listen. I'm going for grain. Aristides is correct – the promise of a proper feast will keep the laggards at the plough for another week or two.'

'I'm not at all sure we can win a stand-up fight with the Thracians,' Cimon allowed.

Lykon answered him. 'We beat them last night,' he said. 'Now Adeimantus is going to insist to fucking Pausanias that we complete our fortifications and link a palisade to yours on the hilltop.'

'That'd be nice,' Cimon muttered.

I pointed at Lykon. 'If we all pull together, the Thracians are no threat,' I said. 'Five, six thousand peltasts? We have a thousand veteran hoplites and ten thousand oarsmen.'

Cimon made a face. 'I know,' he said. 'But we have to stand to-gether.' He looked over at me. 'I'll take the cavalry patrols. I used to be a cavalryman.'

'I know,' I said.

Let me be blunt. I was in a bad place.

Look, my sons were gone, and I wasn't really as confident in them as I claim. I was looking at the possibility of all three being captives. It could happen.

And Aten. The boy had got under my skin. He was ... like another Hector. A good boy, becoming a good man. Dead. And for what?

What was it all for? Fighting at Plataea, we'd fought for our farms and our freedom.

At Byzantium, we were fighting for someone's idea of empire.

Before I left with the *Apollo's Raven*, I met again with Cimon and Aristides up at our fort on the ridge.

'I have a plan to take the place,' I said.

I laid it out. It was basically the plan we'd made the first day, with one or two little wrinkles.

Aristides nodded slowly, frowning over the complex, hard work wrinkle.

'Maybe,' he said.

'Everyone will work harder in the expectation of a feast,' I said. 'Or ... that's what you said.'

Aristides nodded. 'Perhaps,' he admitted.

But Cimon was smiling broadly. 'I like this,' he said. 'I suppose I'm a deceptive bastard, because I really like doing this.'

'And the Corinthians have already started extending their palisade to meet up with our fort,' I said. 'Look!'

Sure enough, below us, like purposeful ants, we could see long lines of oarsmen carrying stone and cut wood up the slope. You could actually watch the line of entrenchment grow.

'The Thracians will see it, too,' I said.

Aristides nodded. 'It might work,' he agreed.

The *Apollo's Raven* rowed down the Golden Horn and turned into the current of the Bosporus, and then we got our sails up, because the yearly northeaster was blowing right down the coast of the Propontis. We had to row down the gullet of the strait, but then we ran before it, keeping Archilaus and Young Nestor busy with the steering oars all the way and resting the oarsmen.

We left at dawn on the day after the full moon, and we arrived in the harbour of Methymna the evening of the next day – a fast passage by any count. Athena was with us. And Philip improved miraculously, as if a day at sea was all he'd needed to complete the healing of his wound. I've noted before that wounds at sea seldom sicken as they do on land.

Briseis met me on the shore with her women, and we enacted our ceremony only after I tasked Eugenios with finding me a full cargo of barley and wheat.

As these were the primary exports of Lesbos beside olive oil, he didn't expect too much trouble.

'I prayed you were not coming with news of a defeat,' Briseis said quietly. 'I saw your sister's friend ...'

'Philip.'

'Philip, and I thought, Oh, by Artemis, a ship full of wounded men, we've had a disaster.' She shook her head.

'You might now pray for our sons,' I said quietly. 'And a wind change. I need a zephyr from the south and east.'

She was big with child, and I rubbed her feet and heard the gossip of Ionia. Archilogos was at sea, cruising the channel off Mytilini and paying visits to Chios and other Ionian cities.

'I need to send a messenger,' I said.

But before I could organise one, Helikaon brought the *Morning Star* around the point from the channel. I sent him back to the Ionians with a message – really, a little more like a plea.

Too many balls in the air.

I told Briseis that I needed to talk to Alysia.

And then, that my two boys had gone to rescue her son ... our son.

She shook her head. 'I've already sent a ransom offer,' she said. 'I think you should call them off.'

'I can't,' I said.

We sat together on a long summer evening. I told her about Aten's death, and she told me about the comings and goings of Ionia.

'Will it ever end?' she asked. 'I'm tired of being afraid.'

'Not in our lifetimes,' I said.

She made a face. 'When people like my first husband prate about freedom, I wonder if they think of how many generations of suffering it takes to win a war like this?'

'Your first husband was an arsehat of the first dimension,' I said, or something even more to the point.

She laughed. 'You were a red-handed killer of men,' she said. 'Girls just don't find that as attractive as boys seem to think.'

'You seemed to find a use for me when I was around,' I said.

She smiled. 'One does not discard something beautiful just because it has a little blood on it,' she said.

I spent some time trying to puzzle that one out.

In the morning, as we put the grain into the *Apollo's Raven*, Alysia came on Archilogos' trireme.

'I'm coming with you,' she said. 'I have ...'

'An army camp is not the place for a ...' I paused, considering. 'A woman not used to an army camp.'

'I'll be perfectly safe,' she said.

'Will you, then?' I asked.

'Yes. I have a famous bodyguard.' She indicated the cloaked figure standing at ease near the helm.

It was Brasidas.

'Later,' he said, with a wave of his hand.

I embarrassed him with a long embrace anyway.

'Perhaps my sister will forgive me,' I said.

He smiled. 'Perhaps,' he agreed.

Alysia brought me the last link in my plan. And let's face it – it was never 'my' plan. It was the plan I'd made with Aristides and Cimon, and then altered and altered and altered as circumstances went for or against us.

Because that's how you win a war. Or a siege.

The presence of Brasidas banished the ghost of Aten. Perhaps that sounds terrible, but what I mean is that the sense of loss and failure that came with Aten's death evaporated in the face of the Laconian strength of my taxiàrchos, and the relentless and somewhat matronly strength of Alysia. And I saw, in the return of Brasidas and the providential arrival of Alysia, a change in our fortunes, or perhaps the hand of the goddess that had been on us since the first victory at sea.

And when the wind changed, first to southerly, and then a touch of south and west, I knew it was the wrong wind for the Dardanelles. But the right wind for another plan altogether. It was the right wind for the estuary of the Evros, where the Persian squadron was based at Doriscus. And where, according to a dying Thracian, I might find the Melinditae.

So I prayed to Athena and Poseidon and the winds, and took the *Apollo's Raven* to sea – another flight, as if all the Furies were behind us. We had a full load of grain, and enough oil and salt fish to keep the crew for a week, and I didn't intend to touch land until I could see the seabirds over the Evros delta.

It was midday before we put our oars in the water, but we were in with Samothrace when the sun rose. We landed a little north and west of the estuary, where the open plains come all the way down to a sandy beach, and there are hot springs just inland from the beach.

I was preparing to send Brasidas ashore with some sailors – all my marines were serving in the siege – but I needn't have bothered. The first Thracians came down, curious, perhaps looking to trade, while a dozen of my sailors were taking on a little more fresh water from a stream that emptied into the bay across the sand, as clean as clean.

But as predicted, Philip found them to be Melinditae. And before the sun was far down in the sky, Alysia was sitting under my boat sail with Katisa of the Melinditae. We shared wine. Alysia gave Katisa a necklace of lapis. Katisa gave her a fine steel knife in a red leather sheath decorated in hammered bronze.

We all drank a little too much.

I had no time for niceties beyond the exchange of gifts. But Philip smoothed over my gaffes, and I cannot pretend that Alysia's smiles didn't help the process. Thracians make less difference between men and women than Greeks, and they find our rigid demarcations alien, as we find their fluidity, I suppose, but with Scythians or Thracians, having a woman along is more than useful. It might be said to be essential.

The gist of what I said, through Philip's mouth and Alysia's eyes, was this.

'You have problems with the Odrysae. They are preparing to attack us. If you'll support us, we'll support you against them. We won't promise you the city – that's not on the table. But with an ally in the city, you can hold the Dardanelles.'

Katisa considered what we'd said for a long time, and drank two cups of unwatered Chian wine.

'I don't have enough spears to lose another battle,' she said. 'I might just have enough spears to win one.'

'Are you saying you will join us?' I asked, cautiously.

'I'm asking what guarantee you will give me that you will win,' she said. 'I will take a big risk, going back into the Chersonese with my tribe. If the Odrysae catch us before we join you, we'll be beaten badly.'

I knew in my heart that all I needed was for the Odrysae to look the other way – her way – for two or three days. But I believe in allies. Perhaps what Pausanias said is true – we men of the little cities know that we depend on others.

'Can you come up on Byzantium on the fourth day from today?' I asked Katisa.

'The Athenians will all be feasting,' she said.

Perhaps we all looked surprised, but she laughed, her tattooed eyes dancing.

'You think that we're so barbarous we don't have eyes and ears?' she asked. 'You build ovens and a temple. I have spies among the Odrysae. You will have a great feast.'

'You can be our guests for that feast,' I said.

She smiled slyly. 'I see now. You want us to cover your feast. When we come out of the hills, the Odrysae will look to us and not to the sleeping, drunk Athenians.'

'Perhaps,' I admitted. 'But they won't be able to concentrate on you. That I promise.'

She looked at me for a long time, and then at Alysia.

'These two men and this woman,' she said, pointing at Philip, Brasidas and Alysia. 'Your brothers and your wife?'

I shook my head. 'My sister's husband, my sister's friend, and my wife's friend.'

'Oh, sure,' the barbarian said with a knowing smile. 'And this is a picnic, eh?' She got up and looked at me. 'I see how close you are, all of you. So leave them with me. If all is as you say, well and good. If not, I sacrifice them to my gods on my own funeral pyre, and you learn not to lie to Thracians.'

Alysia stood up. 'I accept,' she said, before I could say anything, and then gave me a withering stare.

I looked at Philip, who shrugged.

'I'm game,' he said. 'It's only a two-day ride.'

Then I looked at Brasidas, who already knew the whole plan.

The real plan. Not the plan I'd just mentioned to the barbarian queen.

He smiled. 'Delighted,' he said.

He sounded as if he meant it.

Just north of the beach where the *Apollo's* Raven rested, stern first, her bow moving slightly with the ripple of the waves, there is a long ridge, crowned with a hill like the acropolis of a city, and just below that crown is a hollow, perhaps thrice the size of my father's farm.

I had time, while I waited for Katisa's final answer, to walk up the ridge, and into the hollow, and to imagine ...

Well, you all know what I imagined. But I felt then, and I still feel, the hand of Artemis, or perhaps Athena, at my shoulder, guiding my steps, pointing. When I stood at the edge of the hollow, I felt as if I was at the edge of a curtain between worlds ... Have you ever had this feeling? For a moment, I thought I could see Aten, aye, and Idomeneus and Harpagos and Euphoria.

It's a beautiful scene in a perfect location. There's arable land almost as far as the eye can see, and easy access to the Aegean, which lies at your feet. Samothrace rises before you, a mountain in the sea, home of gods. You can see your friends – and your foes – coming a long way off. The Dardanelles are less than a day's sail to the east. Lemnos, Lesbos and Chios lie almost literally at your feet.

I walked back and forth, and thought of Briseis, worried about my sons, and considered Aten – the life I'd given him, and perhaps taken away.

It was a thoughtful time – a few hours snatched from a long war. But in that hollow and on that hillside, I felt a sense of peace and a sense of ... fitness, perhaps, or belonging.

I'll never know why – there's nothing of Boeotia or Green Plataea in those rolling hills and oak-capped ridges. Thrace is colder, and even the stones are different. But, on the other hand, I've been stomping back and forth across Thrace since I was a boy. I lived in the Chersonese for almost three years, fighting for Miltiades.

We were perhaps two days' ride from Byzantium. We were less than a day's ride from the Persian fortification and palace at Doriscus.

So when the armoured riders appeared in late afternoon, and we gathered to swear oaths, I clasped hands with the Thracian queen.

I pointed at the hill and the hollow.

'I could live here,' I said.

She frowned, then smiled. 'Perhaps, if we are alive, and victorious, some days hence, I would have you as a neighbour,' she said. 'But you Greeks always say you want only a little land, and then ...' She shrugged.

To Brasidas I said, 'I could live here.'

Brasidas looked around. 'We're founding a city?' he asked. 'Excellent.'

I walked over to Alysia, where she stood by a horse. She and the horse were looking at each other with a certain mutual curiosity.

'You are sure you are willing to do this?'

She smiled. 'Actually, I'm terrified. I've never ridden, and I know the odds.' She shrugged. 'But I came to have an adventure, and I'll be damned if I'm turning back now.'

'Your husband must be a very good man indeed,' I said.

She smiled, then. 'He is,' she said. 'Sadly, at the moment he has no idea I'm here, and thinks I'm with my sister in Eresos.'

'I'd best get you home alive,' I said.

'I'll certainly be in less trouble if I get home alive,' she said.

'If it is any reassurance,' I said, 'you are the key to a plan that has been made by Aristides of Athens and Cimon, son of Miltiades, the wiliest fox on the seas.'

She nodded. 'I'd be happier with a plan made by Briseis,' she admitted.

'She, too, played a part,' I said.

We got off the beach at eventide, after a good meal of fish with the Thracians. I intended to sail at night – my crew had had a spring and most of a summer to grow used to my ways. We rowed a few stadia and then raised the sail and went across the wind, our worst point of sailing, and one that frequently required me to order all the sailors and some of the oarsmen to the leeward side to stiffen the ship lest we be knocked down, even in a light wind. It was hard, and dangerous, but a trireme couldn't have managed it at all.

I thought the risk worthwhile.

Due south all night. Dawn of the twenty-first day of Hekatombaion – two days until the great Feast of Athena – and we were running into the Dardanelles against the current, but with a fine light breeze filling the sails from the west, a proper zephyr that brought fine weather, and was the visible grace of the gods.

When I looked south, I could see a line of warships, low against the horizon, visible only by the flash of their oars in the morning sun.

We were heavily laden with grain and a deck-load of Thracian sheep, but I didn't think that the warships would catch us, for a variety of reasons. Still, as we completed the sharp turn into the mouth of the Dardanelles, I breathed a sigh of relief.

All day, we ran up the channel. Before darkness, the narrow straits widened into the Propontis, and we were almost alone, the siege having emptied the seas the way news of a crime can empty the streets of a town.

We were on time – just. And it is remarkable how, when one has tried very hard to accomplish something complicated, the mind dwells on the tiny details that could still go wrong. What if we hit a submerged rock? What if the Thracians were discovered in the hills west of Byzantium? What if there was a traitor in our ranks?

What if the ovens had failed?

What if the garrison had stormed the fort on the ridge top?

What if Pausanias had discovered our conspiracy to do what we'd said we would do?

What if Archilogos disobeyed his sister?

Never, I think, had I been so dependent on my friends. Never had I been part of a plan wherein every person had a role to play, like an actor in the Great Dionysium. Interlocking wheels, as complicated as the movement of stars.

I had plenty about which I could worry, and I did. I'm aware that we had a day of beautiful sailing, and then a night with the gods, the stars wheeling above us in a magnificent procession, the lights of the little towns on either side twinkling where a few matrons, perhaps, sat late over their wine. I envied them.

Eventually, I slept, with Nicanor at the steering oar, whistling to himself, and Archilaus beside him, silent, looking at the stars.

Old Nestor woke me with an ungentle toe in my midriff. I rose, cursed, and tried to enjoy the dawn around the protests of ageing fibres whose rest on the hard boards of the starboard helmsman's bench had not been the best. Already then, my hands hurt every morning, as if every man I'd killed had come to haunt the bones that did the deed.

I hobbled around the deck until I felt better, and looked at the rising sun, and thought of my hillside in Thrace.

Perhaps, some day.

Before me, in the pale pink light of dawn, the city of Byzantium rose atop her acropolis, perhaps twenty stadia away. It was dawn on the eve of the Great Feast of Athena in the third year of the seventy-fifth Olympiad, and I was almost home. And with my friends at my side, and many pairs of hands, a shipload of grain, some sheep, and some Thracians, we were about to take one of the greatest cities in the Greek world.

Or not.

The preparations for the first day of the festival were probably visible to everyone in the town. We landed our grain at the improvised jetty that the Athenians had constructed in our absence. Every one of the twenty-four ovens that had been laboriously laid up and dried and slowly fired was brought into action again, and the mountains of cut brush continued to dwindle as the bakers made the cakes and breads for the long-awaited feast.

The sheep came off our ship and went into pens behind the wooden temple, and the wine went into a guarded area. I was probably more popular that morning than I'd ever been as a mere war hero. Probably a hundred men came to congratulate me on finding the supplies for the feast.

A really observant man might have noticed that some of the sacks of grain were far too heavy, as if they were full of iron. Of course, he'd have had to be where he could see the ships unload. And he'd have had to be very observant indeed, as Ole Llurin and his men unloaded those sacks and were careful not to appear to struggle with them.

Athenians take the feast of Athena very seriously. And they were already tired of the siege, and it was only a month old. How did the Greeks manage ten years at Troy? Perhaps that's why Agememnon was such a little tyrant ... I'm sailing away again, eh?

Evenings were already a little cooler – autumn was coming. But the siege had many months left in it, and everyone wanted a few cups of wine and a little oblivion.

I made a great show of checking the sentries and ensuring that the smaller contingents had the defence of the long line of palisades running up the hill to the fort, where our combined archers held the pinnacle of the central ridge.

We held a muster of every man in the camp, preparatory to the feast. We counted noses for food and wine distribution, but while Cimon and Aristides reviewed the troops and harangued the oarsmen, Styges and Leander and I went through every tent, every shelter, every pile of brush, making sure that we knew the whereabouts of every man.

I slept a little, and at dusk, Cimon took the cavalry out on a long sweep about a bowshot from our palisade. His efforts were perfunctory – his men rode too fast, and the whole patrol had the look of men in a hurry to get to their dinners. But they raised a lot of dust out there in the open ground we'd created by cutting all that brush for our ovens, and the dust hung there until the sun set over the hills to the west.

I tried not to pace.

I drank a cup of my own wine in the fort, watching the stars come out, and Orion rising. Far out on the Propontis, a ship lit her stern lantern.

I tried to sleep again, and failed.

Everything kept me awake. The barking of the dogs – how do armies attract so many dogs? – and the lowing of the sheep in their pens, and the sound of our horses cropping the remnants of the grass on the hillside. The night birds, the shouts of nervous sentries, the crackle of the watch fire in the middle of the fort. The endless sound of the rigging of the ships slapping against the wooden masts below me, a constant tap-tap-tap like the pitter-patter of rain on your roof.

Why do men remember war as anything but anxiety and torment?

I lay there, thinking of all the things that could have gone wrong, and all the hostages I had given to the Fates. I reflected on my sins, and thought of Brasidas, and Alysia, and how ludicrously elaborate our so-called 'plan' was. How one spy, one deserter, would wreck it.

Some time deep in the darkness of early morning, there was a scrabble at the fort gate. I was instantly out of my cloak, walking across the packed earth of the fort's ground to where a sentry was quietly and professionally exchanging the complex passwords of the night with someone outside.

'Come ahead,' the sentry said, very quietly.

Kassandros and four marines waited inside, knuckles white in the moonlight on their spear shafts.

Ka came through the gate with four archers at his heels, all covered in mud, smeared with the stuff.

His grin was as wide as a sickle moon.

'I saw Brasidas,' he said. 'And the Thracian woman sends her greetings.'

I didn't need to ask any more. The former helots were tired, done in, and Ka's smile had a limp to it. They'd been out for almost twenty-four hours. They'd moved out in the darkness the morning before, shortly after our arrival, and then, while Cimon 'performed' his patrol to cover them, they'd slipped off to the west.

There were still too many things that could go wrong. But I could breathe, and as soon as I lay down, with Ka warm against my back, I was asleep.

The morning of the great feast.

Twenty-four ovens throw out a great deal of heat, and it was still summer in Thrace. And with the heat comes smoke, the bitter, clinging smoke from burning brush, much of which was still green. Come, friends, you know me ... I'd love to pause here and explain to you why it is brush and not solid wood that makes the best bread, but take my word for it, eh?

And because Athena's bread must be fresh, the very men who'd lagged for the last ten days at building entrenchments now fed the ovens with a will, and the smoke rose over the camp in a choking cloud, especially in the early morning.

As the sun rose, sharp and brilliant over Asia, Aristides began the sacrifices. He was, by right, a priest of Athena. I remembered the first woman I'd ever seen with an army – the priestess of Athena who'd prayed for my brother after my first battle – and I rather wished we had one of the great priestesses with us. I believe that women have a tie to the gods that men often lack. Somehow, in my own life, it is priestesses who have shaped my belief more than priests. But that's another story. Here, on the day, we were an army without even a prostitute, much less a great lady from one of the priestess families. So Aristides led the first ceremonies.

In Athens, the Panathenaea goes on for a week, and is perhaps the most important celebration of the whole festival cycle. There is a magnificent procession up the Acropolis – women and girls participate in a way that they seldom do the rest of the year. If you've never been, you should go. It is one of the most uplifting things I've ever experienced, but then, I admit, I have the honour to be a citizen.

One of the most important aspects of the Panathenaea is the games. They are not as famous, perhaps, as the Olympics or the Nemean Games, but they do get the very best competitors. They have a slightly more military flavour than the Olympics, too, as befits a more military goddess.

We began the day with a procession. It was vastly scaled down, but it had many of the elements of the greater Athenian version. The magnificent captured cloak of my Persian officer had been cleaned and rigorously repaired by the two professional embroiderers we found in the fleet – I'm sure I've mentioned before how a fleet of warships seems to have every profession under the sun. The cloak was magnificent in vermilion and gold, carried by no less than young Pericles, Aristides' young friend and follower. After the procession, led by every marine and officer in polished panoply, and followed by all the Athenian oarsmen, we went to the temple and the magnificent cloak was placed on a wooden statue of the goddess that had been made by two ship's carpenters with a talent for such things. She was a very buxom Athena, and her face had a trace of a leer that you don't commonly see on her portrayals, but her eyes were brilliant. 'Bright Eyes' was her epithet in the *Iliad*, but she was the brilliant goddess nonetheless, and the cloak and the aegis became her wonderfully. We loved her.

We sang some hymns, and went out into the early morning air to celebrate the games in her honour.

Here's an odd aspect of my own hubris – I think it is hubris, although it is not really treating another person as a slave. But, here we were, praising my favourite of the gods on her own day, and behind that festival I was playing a very dangerous game ...

And yet, I wanted, more than anything, in that hour, to be running with the athletes, fighting with my shield in hand, competing against the best that Athens and Aegina had to offer.

And instead, I sat in a himation, unarmed, unarmoured, and judged contests like an old man.

And I hated it.

Oh, they were all gallant. Young Pericles, who thought far too much of himself, was nonetheless a brilliant fighter. Nor was he alone in his brilliance, and there on the sandy hillside I saw a dozen feat of arms and athleticism that were more than worthy of the goddess.

Perhaps the most remarkable thing is that Cimon and Aristides had opened all of the events to any participant from the fleet, so that many oarsmen ran in the stadia and two stadia races. Remember that it is an honour to participate, and that it also gives honour to the goddess. In Athens, those games had been the prerogative of the aristocrats, but on a beach at the edge of Asia, any man could run.

Behind us, towards the palisades, the line of ovens continued to belch smoke, and the smell of baking bread was everywhere. Some of the runners complained that the smoke slowed them down, and there was coughing.

But at the Panathenaea, every man was supposed to make a sacrifice at Athena's altar – every free man. And by tradition, instead of a mass slaughter of animals, there would be enough animals killed to feed everyone and please the gods, and the rest of the sacrifices would be symbolic offerings of bread.

The baking went on.

So did the sport.

A particularly observant man might have noted that there were more chimneys than ovens – chimneys that ran on charcoal, and not brush. And he might have noted that there was activity on both sides of our palisade wall running up the hill, but he'd have had to be able to see through all the smoke.

But I digress.

I was judging the Pankration – a big oarsman from Sounion was coasting towards victory, vigorously applauded by Polymarchos, who was suddenly his coach – when Ka appeared at my side.

'The wood edge is full of Thracians,' he said. 'They're trying to hide, but we can see them from the hilltop.'

I nodded. 'Watch them,' I said, uselessly.

Ka smiled, and was gone. There was no archery contest to captivate him, at least where other men could see. Later I learnt that Vasilos had sponsored a contest in the fort for a golden coin and the right to be first to make sacrifice at sunset, and then won it himself.

In the full heat of the day, we went back to the 'temple' and sang, and in mid-afternoon, we prepared for the feast. I climbed the hill, having changed into a chitoniskos and a good broad petasus hat, and borrowed a marine's aspis. From the top of the ridge, I climbed the tower, carrying the aspis like a snail with his shell on his back, just so that, having reached the top, I could wave it a few times and climb back down.

Late afternoon. Trestle tables and rough shelters had sprung up across the whole of our camp, and men were waiting by the temple to make their sacrifices. The priests – Aristides and Cimon and I among them – began to kill the sheep, sacrificing them as fast as we were able, and sending the meat to be cooked on the long trenches of open fire. There were neat piles of bread shaped like animals on tables by the temple. Volunteers were laying out bread and oil and cooked meat from the sacrifices on the improvised tables in the camp, and others were keeping the dogs off.

As soon as the last sheep went to its just reward, the first marine came forward with his bread-sheep and tossed it on the fire, and the veneration began. Man by man, the crews of every Aeginian and Athenian warship made their sacrifices and then went to their tables, where slaves and volunteers poured them wine, and the feast began. At last, the ovens had ceased belching smoke, but for the moment, the roasting of meat and the massive smoke of the altars to the gods seemed to replace them. The smell of roast meat was everywhere, and my stomach grumbled.

An observant man, or perhaps a woman, might have noticed that there was a veil of smoke all the way from our line of ovens to the city wall. It wasn't as thick as it might have been, but it was deep.

The first cup of wine hit the stomachs of the feasters, and they grew so loud you could have heard them in Asia. One more time, they sang the hymn to Athena.

I begin to sing of Pallas Athena, the glorious goddess,
Bright-eyed, inventive, unbending of heart, pure virgin, saviour of cities,
Courageous, tritogeneia! Wise Zeus himself bore her from his awful head,
Arrayed in the warlike arms of flashing gold ...

They sang, and they drank, as the sun climbed down the sky.

At full dark, Cimon stood next to me, as sober as a man who feared a major attack.

'You said dusk,' he said.

I shrugged. 'Now I say dawn,' I said. 'I can't force the enemy to dance to my tune.'

Cimon made a face. 'I want to get this over with,' he said. 'What if you're wrong?'

Just nerves. But he'd said what I most feared, and it hurt.

I shrugged, looking out over the ocean and trying to will a fleet into existence.

'Maybe it was all for nothing,' I said.

'Aristides will kill us,' Cimon said. 'He's already worried that the whole ruse is an impiety.'

I glanced out to sea again. 'I'm a Plataean,' I said. 'Our Athena is a lot more understanding. And besides,' I said, suddenly, inspired, 'She was the patron of wily Odysseus, eh? Athena loves a good, complicated plan.'

The men feasting drank the night away, and the wine flowed. I had two cups myself, and sang a few hymns and a couple of frankly obscene doggerels, moving from table to table, checking on the oarsmen and the sailors. Again, a particularly observant man might have noted that there really weren't enough men sitting and drinking. Except that it was dark, and they were loud.

Oarsmen are loud, when they drink.

Men wandered off into the darkness to vomit up their devotions, and we steered them towards the city and away from our palisade. Another thing that an observant man might have noted, if he could see in the smoky darkness.

I walked up the hill to the fort on the brow – a long walk. I gave the passwords and went in to find Ka alert and both of his former helots by the low fire, clearly just coming off watch, or just going on. I approached, expecting a last cup of wine, but a man suddenly flinched away from the campfire and threw his ragged chlamys over his face.

I looked at Myron.

'New recruit?' I asked. I wasn't worried yet, but I had a sour feeling.

'Lord?' he said in his deep Lacedemonian accent.

I pointed at the man with the hooded face.

'I don't know you, friend.' I said

He let the chlamys fall and nodded, a sort of bob of the head that might have been servile, or a salute, or anything in between. He looked at Phorbas and then back at me.

'Tharpys, lord.'

'No need to call me lord,' I said. 'How can I help you?'

Then I really looked at him. He wasn't one of my former helots. Messenians is probably politer. Phorbas and Myron had been with us for a while, and Tekles and Gamon had been wounded and were on Lesbos, hopefully recovering.

Myron walked around the fire and joined Tharpys.

I gave him a long look.

'Are you recruiting?' I asked.

Myron clearly wanted to be anywhere else. But after a pause that went on far too long, he said, 'Tharpys is my wife's brother. I couldn't leave him with the Spartans.'

I pursed my lips. 'If the Spartans catch him, we're all dead.'

Even by firelight, I could read Myron. His face said, *If the Spartans catch us, we're all dead anyway, Plataean.* Messenian helots are, in their own special way, every bit as arrogant as their masters.

Phorbas leant forward, looking concerned.

'Listen, lord,' he said. 'He has news you will want.'

'I can go back,' Tharpys said. 'Just as easily as I left.'

By then, I'd seen the mess someone had made of his back – bloody weals on top of old scars. He was naked under a chlamys because his back probably wouldn't take a chiton, or it would simply adhere to the blood.

'Tell me your news, Tharpys,' I said. 'And drink a cup of wine. I'm not sending you back.'

Tharpys nodded. 'Do you know that there are two ephors in the Lacedaemonian camp?' he asked.

That was a little like a punch in the gut. I confess it is difficult to explain, knowing what I knew then, how it felt like a betrayal, or perhaps a new betrayal. Pausanias had met with us, had spoken with us, and yet he had ephors, the old men who made the *real* decisions for Sparta, *in his camp*? They had never attended a single meeting of the war council. They had never taken part in a single discussion.

The presence of two ephors explained a great deal. Keeping them hidden explained more. And, of course, ephors often accompanied Spartan kings into the field. But Pausanias wasn't with us as a Spartan king, or as regent. He was with us as the commander of the Allied force.

'The ephors told him to make any excuse he wants,' Tharpys said. 'But to end the siege as quickly as possible.'

'Tell him the part—' Myron said.

'I'm getting to it, ain't I?' Tharpys said.

'How did you hear all this?' I asked.

'We hear everything,' he said.

I shook my head. I didn't necessarily believe that helots heard everything. When I want to talk about secrets, I know how to make sure there are no ears to hear me.

But perhaps Pausanias doesn't know.

Tharpys looked at me. 'The Persians have your wife's son?' he asked me.

Just the question shot a chill through me.

'Yes,' I agreed slowly.

'The ephors said things about him, and about silencing "the

Plataean's woman."' He looked at me. 'And Myron said you'd want to hear it from me, straight, like.'

And there I was, blustering about recruiting.

I clasped his hand.

'Welcome to Plataea,' I said. 'I'll make you a citizen in the morning.'

He smiled – a little grim, but pleased, for the most part.

'I won't get caught,' he said. 'I ain't been caught these twenty years.'

Around midnight, I went to sleep. I might have lain awake all night, worrying about Briseis and my sons and the ephors. I didn't.

I should have had some terrible dream.

I didn't.

I slept the sleep of the just. No idea why – I just lay down, slept for four hours, and awoke to Ka's hand on my shoulder.

'I think we should light the beacon,' he said. 'Here they come.'

I got up on the fort's wall, and looked out, where ant-like Thracians moved across the open ground.

I gave him a sleepy nod.

He put an arrow into the fire that burned in the middle of the fort, and shot it up into the tower, where a bale of resin-impregnated brush stood. It burst into flame – a roaring flame twice the height of a man, visible, I suspect as far as Asia.

Off to the east, over Asia, the sky was just getting pink.

The Thracians had finally decided that we'd had enough to drink. I could see them more clearly now, coming over the open ground we'd cleared days ago, getting brush for the ovens.

It was now too late to worry about my plan. Our plan. Any plan.

The beacon was lit.

When the beacon burst into flame, it was visible for fifty stadia in every direction, and it was most certainly visible to the Thracians. Someone waved a shield, and they gave a deep-throated roar that echoed up and down their line, flowing and crashing like waves on a sea.

And then they charged.

From our vantage point far above them, as they began to come up our part of the ridge they appeared at first to be ants, and then foxes, colourful and low to the ground in the early morning pinkish light, and then ...

And then they appeared as men – men with big half-moon shields, and glittering spears, colourful tunics, armour of scales or leather, glittering bronze and iron helmets, their faces shadowy at first, until the shadows were revealed as tattoos that appeared the very essence of barbarity. They came at us in what had started as a line, perhaps four deep, but by the time they neared the palisade, they ran in clumps, or packs, like wolves pacing a wounded deer.

About three hundred paces from the palisade, men began to fall, screaming.

From my vantage point, I could see the guard being turned out in the Peloponnesian camp. Their palisade ran all the way to our camp and even had a tower in the middle, and they had guards out all night. Now the Peloponnesian marines and the Spartan hoplites began to emerge from their camp to man their wall sections, but the Thracians ignored them. It looked to me as if the Thracians had thrown three or four thousand men at our camp in the first light of dawn. There was cavalry and more infantry back there in the wood line, the rising sun catching their armour and their spear points.

The running men began to slow, and the little packs were shredding. A surprising number of them were down, and their screams were terrible, even to a man who has heard as many screams as I have.

About one hundred paces from the walls, the charging Thracians hit the first pit traps. The men who went into them died spectacularly, cruelly, and the whole mass ...

Stopped. They'd crossed a hundred paces of ground strewn with all the caltrops that Ole Ilurin and his iron-smithing apprentices could make, their smoke covered by our bake fires. Sharpened stakes, twigs, and iron against barefoot Thracians.

The pit traps were not elaborate. Nor were they deep. But they had stakes in the bottom, and the first runner died, and the mass slowed, as men – even brave men – will do. It is one thing to face fire, or enemies – another to face traps.

Ka slapped my shoulder and pointed back, towards Byzantium. We could see the garrison deploying from two gates, moving with the smooth precision of long practice and good drill.

'Stop the Thracians,' I said. 'Leave the rest to me and Cimon.'

Ka nodded, and went to the other wall, and the archers began to deploy themselves, moving out of the fort and on to the high ground in front of our entrenchments. In the time it had taken us to sing the hymn, they'd formed a line, two hundred archers long, no depth at all.

They began to loose arrows into the Thracians, who'd come to a stop just seventy or eighty paces away.

I leapt on to the back of my steppe pony. Very well, I confess that I climbed up on a mound of dirt and wriggled on to his back, because mornings are not the best time for middle-aged men to do anything dramatic. But I got aboard, so to speak, and we rode down the hill even as the Thracians bellowed and came on, thrusting before them with their spears, trying to find our traps. And truth to tell, the traps were hastily made and not so very effective, once the Thracians weren't running flat out. On the other hand, the slow-moving Thracians were a fat target for archery.

None of that was my problem any more. I turned my back on it; not as easy as it sounds.

At the bottom of the hill, there were some drunken men being shepherded aboard their ships. We'd had plenty of volunteers to be the feasters.

I dismounted and picketed my pony carefully, because we still had time.

My marines were waiting with all of the other marines, and Cimon at their head – almost four hundred men in panoply. Added in were the well-armoured sailors from the more piratical – or let us say, experienced – Athenian ships. Altogether, our 'phalanx' had almost a thousand men, and not a hangover among them.

What do you think all that smoke was for?

We had a thousand hoplites, give or take, against twelve hundred of the Great King's provincial regulars and perhaps fifty of his professional cavalrymen.

Of course, we also had several thousand oarsmen. The better equipped were proper peltasts, with small shields and a pair of javelins. Many were merely naked men with rocks.

The thing is that the Athenians remembered Marathon, and the days before Marathon. And they remembered Salamis, and they remembered Plataea and the fight on the left flank, and the olive grove. The little men – the kind of thetis-class citizens who served as oarsmen and psiloi – knew better than most light infantry how much damage they could do.

Here's a military secret for you younger men bent on glory. If you must have a field battle, it's best to have far more men than your opponent, if you possibly can. The whole reputation of Sparta is based on their ability to bring their Peloponnesian League into the field and outnumber everyone else's hoplites two or three to one. It works.

We had four thousand oarsmen.

Behind us, the Thracians were coming to a long line of palisades, and finding more pits, more traps, and a constant rain of arrows.

When their axe men cut through the palisades, they found out why we hadn't allowed drunks to go that way in the dark. The pits continued on our side ...

And then they were finally in our camp. It took them far too long, and by the time they were there ...

We weren't.

We were out on the plain between the city walls and our camp. We didn't hesitate, as this had always been one of the possible outcomes of the plan. Indeed, we jogged across the plain towards the Great King's regulars like men running to a prize.

One of the most difficult things about being a commander is making a decision in a hurry that will have consequences. One of the whole points of surprising an opponent is to force the enemy commander to make *his* decisions quickly, because that's when men make mistakes.

The Persian commander saw us coming and deployed.

His satrapal regulars, probably Carians and Lydians, formed a line from their column and immediately began to deploy their big shields, huge wicker-and-hide things that would protect them from arrows.

We had no arrows.

About three hundred paces from the rapidly congealing Persian line, we halted and formed our phalanx. We formed from the centre to the flanks, if you've ever done that. It was the only manoeuvre we'd practised the last three weeks, because we hadn't wanted to look too competent to our opponents on the city walls, who could see everything we did. Frankly, even with practice, it was a little chaotic, and if the Persian commander had released his cavalry right there, they might have made hay.

But he'd decided to form his battle line and prepare to receive us, and he held his cavalry back.

Cimon trotted up, magnificent in his panoply, like Achilles and Hector rolled into one. He was grinning from ear to ear.

'Poor Spartans,' he said. 'They'll miss the fun.'

I could see Styges, and my cousin Achilles, and Leander and Zephyrides and Kassandros and Arios and Diodoros. In fact, there behind them were Young Nestor and Nicanor and Damon, and all the sailors with a good panoply with Old Nestor at their head, worthy of his namesake in sun-gilt bronze.

I glanced at Cimon.

'There's no need to fight at all,' I said. 'The Persian commander has made the wrong decision, and he's already lost.'

Indeed, out in the brush, thousands of oarsmen were loping along like the Thracians, closing in on the flanks of the small Persian force.

'No one needs to die at all,' I said. 'If we charge them, some of us die, and then they all die, pretty much.'

Cimon frowned. 'Fuck,' he said. 'Of course.'

Unfortunately, the Persian commander had finally woken up to the danger our oarsmen posed to him. He had a volley of arrows loosed, and his little cavalry force burst from the cover of the sparabara line and went at our left wing.

Cimon smiled grimly. 'He made his choice,' he said, and we went forward.

At Marathon, we ran at the Persians and they shot at us, and we bested them. We didn't know we could do it, but we did.

At Plataea, the Spartans stood for volley after volley from the Persian Immortals, and then charged them, and beat them.

By the time we stood on the sun-drenched ridge at Byzantium, with the walls of the city towering above our left flank, we had the measure of facing a Persian line. It was painful, and Greeks would die, but we were sure we could take them.

And we did.

We marched in good order for the first hundred paces of their archery range, and they lofted arrows and hit us hard. They probably dropped more than fifty men in that first hundred paces.

But when we were about one hundred paces from the line of wicker shields, Cimon's spear came down sharply, and our whole front moved to a run. I was at the left end of the phalanx, with Kassandros to my right, and he ran much better than I – I was virtually hobbling. By the time we were on them, I was well back, as deep as the middle of the phalanx, and many men had passed me.

The front crashed into the line of wicker shields and pushed them along the ground, in some cases flattening the Medes behind them.

Enemy spears popped through the wicker as the enemy tried to kill us through the shields, but our push was unstoppable. Their line couldn't hold us, and they began to give way. The big shields fell, and we could see them. A few brave men stopped to loose a deadly shaft at point-blank range, Achilles took a shaft in the foot, almost in front of me, deliberately aimed by a Saka archer.

But the Sakje died on a dozen spears, and the Lydians were swept back, flayed when they rallied.

All that while, I began to work my way back to the front of the line. Men tripped and fell, or stopped to loot, or stopped to fight or kill, and I caught up – I was not fast, but I was relentless. We'd pushed them back a hundred paces or more, and I assumed the Persian commander was going for his gates, and I had no intention of letting him back into his city.

I was also on the left side of our phalanx, and I kept moving to my left. Phalanxes, like mobs, take on lives of their own – they are that monster with one hundred heads and two hundred legs, or more. We'd drifted to the right, not because of our shields, but because of our position on the ridge. The ground was not flat, and there were olive trees and the burnt remnants of farmhouses and byres and stone walls, and the result ...

The result was that we'd struck the right centre of their much longer line, because they were not as deep as we were. To my left, there were still lots of the Great King's men, and suddenly, instead of running, they all wanted to kill me.

The positive aspect – although I can't pretend that we stopped and thought this out – of a drift to the right, is that the enemy is closing in on your shielded flank. When you carry a giant round shield as big as a woman's sewing table on your arm, it's reassuring that your enemies have to come at that and not at your open side. And I had my Plataeans around me and behind me, and without much in the way of orders, we'd formed a tight mass of perhaps a hundred men facing to the left.

All of us would like to be heroes, but the sad fact is that Lydian satrapal levies are not a match for hoplites, on open ground. They weren't much better armed than our oarsmen. They had almost no armour, and besides their bows they had a long dagger, and a few of them had spears.

So as soon as we turned and faced them and killed a few, they broke off. They had to. They couldn't last in a fight. They turned to run, and our oarsmen fell on them from behind, which was ... grim.

I went back to my original direction, pushing up the left flank, hobbling along as quickly as I could manage. Over to my right-front, I could see the enemy commander – a Persian in a high-crested helmet with a fine scale shirt, mounted on a beautiful white horse. I wanted that horse – he looked like Pegasus. The commander had a guard of Carians armed very much as I was – perhaps a hundred men equipped as hoplites.

Cimon and his marines, led by Tekles, struck the Carians first, and drove them back a few paces.

I looked around, but we were in the rage of Ares. The dust cloud was all around us, and I couldn't see our psiloi, or the Persian cavalry, or signals, or even Leander.

So much for being a commander.

And once that was gone, I had no responsibility beyond getting home alive to Briseis.

My sword was undrawn, my spear unbloodied.

I led the twenty or so men who were following me around to the left, outflanking the Carians facing the best of the Athenian marines and aristocrats. Aristides was leading the defence of the ships. He had a thousand sober men, and we'd pushed most of the hulls out into the water to prevent them from being burnt if the plan went wrong. But Aristides' marines were with Cimon. There were men there who'd been fighting since Marathon – who'd been at Salamis and Artemisium and Mycale, and a few who'd been at Plataea, too.

The Carians were excellent. So they didn't break. They held their ground, or gave it up, pace by pace, and they died, facing their foes.

Well, most of their foes.

We came at them suddenly, from our left, which was, of course, their right. The shield-less side, if you've been paying attention.

We came out of the dust and we were on them, without a shout, without rage. I didn't intend to lose a man. To me, the whole fight was pointless. The Persian governor had made his mistakes and should have surrendered.

I put down a man in a fancy double crest. He was well armoured, but I rifled my heavy spear into his helmet and it went through his temple.

In the next few heartbeats, every one of my marines downed his man, and the Carians knew they were destroyed.

And they still fought on.

What a waste.

Their flank turned to face us and the Athenians flayed them. When they tried to fight the Athenians, we killed them, or pinned their spears back, or hampered their shields. It was close, for a moment, and a Carian tried to wrestle me, and my spear was broken – no idea when that happened. All I could do was bludgeon him with the stump of my spear while Arios stabbed him from behind me. He got inside my shield and died, almost dragging me down.

And then I could see the Persian governor. He was a body length away, trying to get his big stallion out of the press.

I threw the stump of my spear at him and missed. Someone else threw a spear and got his beautiful horse. The spear went in deeply and the horse whirled, all legs and teeth. The haft of the spear hit my aspis with a heavy blow, and I had to writhe to avoid a hoof, but there were too many of us to fail. Men went down, but more weapons bit into the magnificent, creamy-white of the horse, and he died, cut a hundred times, his hide all blood, and his master went down, trapped under him.

Styges rammed his spear into the ground by the Persian and covered him with his aspis – perhaps the calmest man in the phalanx.

I dragged my horn around from my back, stood over the Persian's legs, and blew as hard as I could. I got a sort of squawking noise the first two times, like a sick cow, but the third time I got a nobler sound, and then I blew again, and again.

And the fighting died away. Men died before it could be stopped – Lydians and Carians and Athenians and Aeginians ... and Plataeans, too.

But it stopped.

Men broke apart. Men who'd hacked at each other with faces set in the killing glare of hate now stumbled back – looked away. Their faces changed. A wounded Lydian was given water. A wounded Greek was allowed back into his own lines by the surviving Carians.

The man at my feet was unwounded.

'Kill me,' he said, in Persian. 'I will never surrender the town.'

Brave words from a brave man.

I offered him my hand to pull him to his feet.

'No need,' I said. 'Unless I miss my guess, it's already ours.'

Then, without explanation, we gathered our men and left some hundreds to watch the disarmed satrapal levy, and, with all our psiloi, we went back towards the camp. Here and there, isolated Persian cavalrymen had ridden clear of the fighting and loosed arrows at us. A dozen or more rode free, slipped past Ka's archers and tried to join the Thracians.

But the Thracians were running.

Some time in the last hour, while we'd fought the Medes under the walls of Byzantium, Katisa and Brasidas had crashed into the rear of the Odrysae. I gathered later from Brasidas that it wasn't much of a fight. One thing a life of cattle-raiding teaches you is when to run, and the moment that the hillside was full of Melinditae, the Odrysae vanished like Thracian snow in an Athenian summer. Later I saw a great many bodies, though – the trap had been well set.

I was almost too tired to keep going, but I managed to climb the hill to our fort, with Cimon, fifty marines, and the Persian governor, who was still trying to declare his courage.

Ka had brought his archers back inside. The Thracians had been too old in the ways of war to have a go at the walls, and Ka hadn't lost a man.

I reassured the governor that he had no need to give his life. I even jested to him, in Persian, that Pausanias would no doubt restore him to his office as soon as he could. No one found that funny.

We climbed up on the walls, and looked out over the low ridges and plain to the walls of the city.

There were hoplites on the walls, and a bronze aspis flashing from a tower.

I pointed at the men in bronze and motioned to the governor.

'Somewhere over there,' I said, 'is my brother-in-law, Archilogos of Ephesus.'

'The traitor,' he spat.

Archilogos and the Ionian squadron had landed out of the golden sheet of the rising sun, while the garrison fought us.

All along, it had all been a ruse for this – so that the Persians would attack the siege from the inside as the Thracians attacked from outside, while we appeared weak, drunk, with our guard down. All so that the Ionians could slip in from the sunrise, lost in the golden haze. I admit that both Briseis and I found it particularly sweet to have the Ionians take the town.

I shrugged. 'I think he served the Great King bravely and well for some years,' I said. 'But I think you should, when released, go back to your lord, and tell him that Ionia is Greek.'

'The Great King is invincible,' he said loyally.

I waved my hand. From the height of our fort, you could see well down the Propontis, and across to Asia, and north, into the hills of Thrace.

'Does it truly seem so, to you?' I asked.

We stood there in companionable silence for as long as a man might pray to a favoured god.

Then Cimon slapped my shoulder.

'Come on,' he said. 'I want to see the face on Pausanias.'

We went to the Peloponnesian camp with Aristides. We took no hoplites, as we suspected that Pausanias would react badly, and we saw no reason to make it public.

We might have saved our efforts. Pausanias refused to admit any of us – guards at the gate of his fort barred even Aristides from entering.

We trudged back to our own camp, and then began the process of occupying the town. The town had a population of ten thousand citizens and as many slaves, and rather more citizen women and children. The Ionians had, thanks to the gods, taken it without much violence, so that there had been no looting and no rape. In fact, as we heard later, Archilogos had led his men on to the piers and in through open gates in the sea wall – gates that were opened, I suspect, by money and persuasion. I believe there was more to the taking of Byzantium than I was privileged to know. My wife and her brother had secrets.

I was coming to terms with that.

The Persian governor had, apparently, every reason for the desperation of his last attack with his entire garrison. The town council had, in effect, demanded his surrender. He was in a difficult position, with insufficient food for a siege and a virtually hostile Greek population that was not going to stay silent for long. It made his behaviour more understandable.

Regardless, the town was ours. Archilogos allowed Aristides to take possession of the citadel, and we created a watch to patrol the walls and streets. We had a remarkable number of Persian and Persian-allied prisoners, from the governor himself and his entourage, captured intact in the citadel, to the dozens of Phoenician and other Syrian merchants, as well as toll collectors, tax men, scribes ... the apparatus of governing a satrapy. We had captured the capital of the Satrapy of Skudra. We had dozens of high-ranking Persian officers and nobles and their families.

They were rich men bent on growing richer. It was, after all, the rapaciousness of this very class that had sparked the Ionian revolts, and Persians didn't come out to the barbarian fringe of their empire unless they were bent on improving the family fortunes. Listen, there are many fine, noble Persians, as you know if you've listened to me tell the story of the Ionian War and Marathon. But there are also many bastards who run the Persian empire, and they would sell their own mothers for another daric.

Aristides and Cimon conferred about the prisoners while I was busy making sure that we had a strong garrison and patrols to prevent random looting, because Greeks are no better than other soldiers about other people's property.

Cimon divided all of the loot taken, which constituted the Persian, Phrygian, Lydian and Phoenician prisoners and all of their belongings. He divided them into two symbolic groups – the purple robes and gold ornaments of the Persians, and the prisoners, stripped of their possessions.

He offered the Ionians first choice, as they had taken the city.

Archilogos shook his head. 'This is a ridiculous division,' he said. He pointed at the chief scribe of the former Satrapy of Skudra. He was fat, jowly, and altogether a fairly ugly figure of a man. 'What is he worth as a slave?' he said. 'An obol?'

Herophytus of Samos, who commanded the ships from Samos that Archilogos had recruited, shook his head in wonder.

'Don't argue, my friend,' he said. 'We'll take the gold and the silver.'

Aristides smiled. 'And you have earned it all,' he said. 'Use it well, not just to enrich yourselves, but to rebuild your cities.'

We cleared the temple precinct at the top of the acropolis and put all the prisoners in the Temple of Hera.

The next day, Pausanias sent for Aristides.

We discussed, the four of us – that is, Aristides, Cimon, Archilogos and me – we discussed going to Pausanias as a group. We sat in the courtyard of what had been the governor's palace. Even stripped of gold and silver and fine wall hangings, it was a pleasant place, and it had good folding stools, better than anything I'd seen in Greece. The statues and wall carvings were not as good as those in my own house in Plataea.

Anyway, we were served wine by our own people. We didn't trust the Persians we'd taken – the Carians, brave men, had already tried twice to escape.

Aristides looked us all over.

'Pausanias will make demands,' he said. 'I would expect that he'll demand that we hand over the town, and all the prisoners.'

Cimon smiled at Archilogos. 'Which is one of the reasons we gave you the loot.'

Archilogos swirled the wine in his silver cup and sat back.

'Briseis has sent to Queen Gorgo,' he said, 'demanding the recall of Pausanias. We are accusing him of Medizing, and of behaving dishonourably, of bringing discredit on the name of Sparta. Ask any of his hoplites how they feel about being held back from yesterday's battle.'

Cimon looked around, as if we might be overheard. And he lowered his voice.

'Do you think that Gorgo has the power to unseat Pausanias?'

Aristides looked pained. 'As for me, I pity Pausanias,' he said.

'Pity him?' Cimon asked. 'That despicable whelp has betrayed Greece!'

Archilogos nodded.

But I knew what Aristides knew. Our eyes met.

'If the ephors recall Pausanias,' I said softly, 'it will only be to make him the scapegoat for their own failed policy. Pausanias has spent the summer trying to follow the impossible orders of his government.'

'My sister said much the same,' Archilogos said. He nodded to me. 'But she said, if Byzantium falls, so will Pausanias, because their whole strategy of containing or eliminating the Ionians will have failed.'

'I think Pausanias imagined, when he came here, that if he lost, he'd serve Sparta,' I said. 'And if he took the city, the ephors would accept a forward policy whereby Sparta could choke Athens' grain supply. I don't know that. I merely think it. But nothing has played into his hands all summer, and now we hold the city and there's no Spartan relief fleet and nothing to suggest that the ephors will back him in choking Athens of her grain.'

Aristides sighed. 'Themistocles, who I mostly dislike, nonetheless called this correctly. He said in the winter that the Spartans would do everything they could to hamper Athens and the Allies, *short of war.* Pausanias was willing to provoke war, but I don't think the ephors will support him.'

'And yet you pity him?' Cimon asked.

'Last year he was the saviour of Greece, and this year, because of the cowardly old men who have a vice-grip on power in Sparta, he is their tool, behaving basely. He is young, and malleable. Admit it – he has greatness in him. Instead, they will use him as a tool, and discard him.'

It was Cimon's turn to stare into his wine cup.

'You are taking all the fun out of this victory,' he said. 'I'd rather hate him.'

I drank off my wine. 'I believe that it is time to build an alliance against the Persians that will last,' I said. 'And that cannot be done with Sparta at the helm. At least, not the Sparta that we currently have.' I looked at Cimon. 'But I'll tell you a thing that I know, and it will . . . confuse you more.'

Cimon shook his head. Aristides looked a question. Archilogos made a face I'd known from childhood, that said, *Get on with it.*

You have to understand, you young people . . . I smile at you, all of you, my guests. It is odd, to have lived so long, after so much strife. But I wander like the old man I am. In those days, Sparta was looked up to as the leader of the free Greek world. Sparta had the institutions to command a military force, and veteran leaders. It had better drills, better dances, the finest body of hoplites with the best armour, and for the most part, the best officers. It was the "immemorial custom" of the Greeks to place the Spartan kings in command of any alliance.

It was virtually a sacred trust.

To suggest that the Alliance should change fundamentally – that the Spartans would have no place in the Pan-hellenic war against the Persians – was heresy. It was almost unthinkable. So when I made my proposal, *even though Aristides and Cimon expected it* it hit them like a bolt of lightning from Zeus.

Aristides frowned.

But Cimon looked at me across the table, and tugged on his beard. And nodded.

'Yes, by Zeus,' he said. 'Let's be rid of them.'

Aristides shook his head. 'It won't be that easy,' he said. He looked at me. 'And I fear it. I fear that pushing Sparta out of the Alliance is the first step on a path to . . .' He looked away. 'To an unthinkable war.'

Archilogos locked eyes with Aristides.

'Sparta wants us to pack our belongings and go to the west,' he said. 'Sparta wants us to give up our fledgling democracies and have oligarchies. Sparta wants to destroy Ionia and replace it with new colonies in Magna Graecia, close to Sparta and under her thumb. We decline the "honour". As we have fleets as great as Athens and far greater than the Peloponnese, we are as good an ally as Sparta – perhaps a better ally.'

Aristides nodded. 'I understand the logic,' he said bitterly. 'I'm merely far-sighted enough to see where it goes. Long walls, Ionian empire, war with Sparta and Corinth.'

Cimon finished his wine and slapped the cup down on the table so it made a sharp noise.

'The alternative is Athens under the constant threat of Sparta, a weak Ionia, and a strong Persia,' he said.

Aristides nodded. 'Yes,' he said slowly. 'Yes. But I say to you all, that the very best outcome here would be for Pausanias to take command of the effort to save Ionia, and for Athens and Sparta to make an unbreakable alliance against Persia. This would be best.'

Cimon nodded. 'You know I love Sparta,' he said. 'You know that I always speak for them in council! I am their proxenos...'

Aristides nodded.

Cimon sighed.

Aristides nodded. 'I'll go and meet with Pausanias and attempt to contain the immediate damage, so to speak. But we *will* give up the prisoners and town to him. Because the alliance with Sparta says that we must, and we are honourable men. And because that is the *only* way we preserve the League.'

Cimon smiled his father's smile, and said nothing.

An hour later, he rowed away with all the Lydian and Phrygian prisoners on his deck, leaving the Persian governor and his immediate family as a sop to Pausanias, and Aristides could do nothing but shrug.

Two very nervous weeks passed. The Peloponnesians moved into the town and we returned to our camp. Pausanias dismissed the Ionians and ordered them home.

A nasty incident then occurred. Pausanias, for whatever reason, decided to move his ship around from the camp where it was beached, to the harbour of Byzantium, a distance of eight or nine stadia by sea. After he'd got off the beach, two ships appeared and came up on either side of his trireme and began to crowd it, something only very expert captains would dare to do – their oars thrusting in among his oarsmen. His timoneer ordered his oarsmen to stop rowing and pull in their oars. Pausanias himself came to the rail and began shouting at the two triremes ranged up on either side of him.

They were Ionians, of course – Uliades of Samos, a veteran of twenty sea fights and the whole of the Ionian Revolt, and Antagoras, Neoptolimos' cousin from Chios.

Supposedly, Pausanias threatened them, saying that he would flatten their cities.

Supposedly, the Ionians answered that they'd had enough of his crap, and next time they wouldn't be so gentle. Then they rowed away.

Aristides sent me to Pausanias to try and smooth this over. I have never thought of myself as a diplomat, but I agreed that whatever bumps we'd had, Pausanias and I generally respected each other.

I was wrong.

I stood before Pausanias where he sat in the palace of the former governor, on the satrapal throne with two winged lions.

'Why are you here, Plataean?' Pausanias asked.

'I'm here to speak for the Ionians,' I said.

'The Ionians are womanish fools who deserve what will come to them – the disestablishment of their cities,' he said. 'They will receive no more support from the Allies. I have spoken.'

I nodded. 'But you are wrong, Pausanias, and you also lack the power to make good your threat.'

Sparthius, who stood in armour to the left of the throne, winced.

'Pausanias,' I said, 'I know what orders you received from the ephors. I know how difficult this has been—'

'Be gone,' he said. 'No one speaks so in my hall. You have always been an arrogant upstart from an upstart state of no account, Plataean, but to imagine that you can speak familiarly to the Regent of Sparta—'

'I've spoken so to the Great King himself,' I said. 'At the request of the kings of Sparta, I might add. Your time here is short, Pausanias. Rule wisely, or be remembered as a man too arrogant to maintain his reputation.'

'Seize him,' he ordered.

'I know you have ephors in your camp, Pausanias,' I said. I was angry – angry at the whole thing. 'I know that you have orders separate from the Alliance. Your ephors are old men—'

I was seized. And thrown into a stone cell.

*

Sparthius came to visit me on the first day, bringing good wine and tough bread and some unremarkable cheese. We exercised together, and talked about the weather, and he left.

The second day wasn't very different. He came to visit, brought good food, and we ran around the citadel together, struck shields with sticks, and lifted stones. The only thing I remember him saying, that day or the next, was, 'I'll bring you a bow.'

Bows, especially Scythian bows, being better for exercise than just lifting stones.

And so it went.

I didn't need a soothsayer or the Oracle of Delphi to tell me that the presence of a Spartan officer visiting my cell was all the comment the man would ever make.

I was bored, though. I had lots of time to think about my life, about the Spartans and the Athenians, about the Alliance, about the Persians. About my wife, my sons, and women. About cause, and consequence. Don't imagine I was not worried by the absence of my sons, or the threat of the ephors. I accepted the risks of war, but I wished them turned away. I'm human, like that.

I thought about war, and death, and the effect of the population of helots on the best, or what might have been the best, men in Greece.

After perhaps a week – I cannot be sure, but I remember a feast of Artemis in there somewhere ... Anyway, after a few more days, there were three Spartans visiting me. They all came together, and Sparthius introduced them – Labotas and Charylaus. Both were young – too young to have died at Thermopylae. Labotas had been at Plataea, and Charylaus was so young that this was his first military expedition.

Both of them were very angry, under their Laconian facade. They were angry at being robbed of glory by Pausanias, who had held them back from every action, every battle. It didn't take me three exercise sessions to see how angry they were.

I held my tongue.

I was two full weeks into my captivity when Sparthius came in, beaming with goodwill.

'I am to tell you that your sons are in the camp,' he said.

We did our exercises with joy.

'How many sons?' I asked.

'Two,' he said. 'I really am not sure. Aristides sent a note and said you'd want to know.'

'I'd like to know if I have all three back,' I said.

'Three sons?' Sparthius said. 'You have three sons? What joy!'

'And a daughter,' I said. 'I have a lovely daughter.' And then I smiled. 'My wife is very pregnant,' I said. 'Perhaps I'll have another.'

Sparthius smiled. 'Ah,' he said, as if his outburst about sons had exhausted his loquacity.

The next day, he told me that only two were in camp.

That gave me a crop of worries and no mistake, but I reminded myself that two was better than none.

Labotas admitted that the Athenians were demanding my release every day, and that Pausanias almost never left his rooms in the palace. I could see from his reactions that the Spartiates were feeling humiliated by his actions.

I didn't know what to make of that. Pausanias was behaving badly, and that worried me. The longer I sat in that prison cell, the more likely it seemed to me that he'd have me killed. In retrospect, I see that as an irrational fear, but you sit in captivity for a few weeks, watching the ships coming and going through your tiny window, and tell me that you don't begin to fear for your life.

And the ships were leaving. The Ionians were already gone, back to protect their own cities and their shipping, but now I could see that the Athenians were leaving as well. It was late in Metageitnion, as the Athenians reckon it, past the Feast of the Heroines, and while the sailing season had months left in it, autumn was knocking at our door. Farmers would be thinking of the wheat and barley crops at home. Merchants would want to get at least one voyage in before winter. War is not just expensive to states, it is disruptive to citizens.

I wondered if Aristides would really just sail away and leave me.

And then Sparthius came without his two young friends.

'It is very bad,' he said.

I couldn't imagine how bad it actually might be.

'What is bad?' I asked.

He looked away. We didn't exercise, and he left hurriedly, and I began to fear that all my fears were justified. 'It is very bad' may be Laconian, but it allows a man a good deal of latitude in his fears.

The next day, I was taken by guards to a room prepared for me to bathe. This happened from time to time, but on that day, I contemplated making a run for it. I confess that it seemed unlikely that I could take two armed Spartiates with my bare hands, but I was beginning to imagine that I might be quietly stabbed or choked in my cell . . .

Except that for all my anger at Pausanias, I couldn't really see the peers executing me, and what did that leave? A helot? A hired Persian with a bowstring?

I didn't really believe it. I'm just trying to give you an idea of what was passing through my mind. So the next day, when Sparthius came, I finally gave voice to my fears.

'I am afraid that I am to be killed,' I said.

Sparthius looked at me for a moment. 'No one here would kill you,' he said, choosing his words deliberately.

The guard on the door nodded silently.

Mutinous Spartans? Was that even possible?

'It is very bad,' Sparthius said again.

This time, I realised he didn't really mean me. He meant the whole situation.

And more time passed.

And then one day, when it was cool enough that I wanted a thicker cloak under which I could sleep, because the nights were longer and cooler, Sparthius came to my door in his panoply.

'Go free,' he said.

I was taken to the baths, washed, massaged and shaved.

I was given a fine chiton. I hate to think where it had come from. And a chlamys with a pin of silver, and my sword and staff were returned to me.

And I was escorted to the palace hall.

Pausanias was nowhere to be seen. The throne was empty.

Instead, an old man sat at the foot of the throne on a stool, alone. He had no guards, no supporters, no Spartiates. Not even a slave.

'Arimnestos of Plataea,' he said. 'I am Zeuxidamus, son of Anaxilas.'

I nodded. 'You are an ephor,' I said. 'Of the Lacedaemonians.'

He nodded back. 'Correct,' he said. 'I have ordered you released. But I wanted you to know that of all the acts of Pausanias, your arrest is one of which I approve wholeheartedly. He struck at you blindly, perhaps, but you are our foe, and we know it. You and your wife are enemies of Sparta.'

'No,' I said.

I think it is Spartans who bring out the Laconian answers in me.

'You deny it, but you act against us at every turn.'

'No,' I said. 'May I go now?'

'You would do well to restrain your wife,' he said. He glared at me like the angry old man he was. 'We have your whorish wife's son, and we will keep him against her good behaviour.'

I admit that just for a moment, I thought of killing him.

'You are emotional,' I said. I was pleased at how much that angered him. 'But I could no more restrain Briseis than stop a thunderbolt. Nor do I so desire. And if you harm her son ...' I'm very proud of my calmness while I said this. 'On your head be it. I would recommend that you restore him.'

'Let me tell you ...' he began in that tone that patronising old men get when they know all the answers and you are required to listen to them.

I turned and began to walk out.

'Arimnestos!' he said. 'I can have you put back in your cell.'

'No,' I said, and continued through the door.

I picked up my staff and walked out of the palace, saluted Sparthius and his two young friends, of whom you'll hear again, if you stay another night, and started for the gate.

Sparthius put a hand on my shoulder.

'I'll walk with you,' he said.

Aristides was there, and Hector, and Hipponax, and my *Apollo's* Raven was one of only fifteen ships still resting on the sands. The whole camp stank of urine and faeces – men can only camp in one place for so long. The ovens were cold. The little temple had been pulled down, and our pretty Athena was gone.

I hugged Hector and Hipponax, and then, after a brief and embarrassing pause, I shrugged.

'I know,' I said.

Hector flushed a deep red. 'We almost rescued him,' he said, 'but ...'

Hipponax was blonder, which made his flush redder.

'But Briseis had already paid his ransom.'

'And we ... decided to wait another day ...'

I stared out to sea. But in the end, I managed a smile.

'They moved him?' I asked.

'To Sardis,' Hector said. 'It's my fault,' he said. 'Hipponax wanted to attack, and I had heard that he was ransomed, and I was afraid we were messing with something too delicate for our spears.'

'You were,' I said. 'And you did right. We'll get him back, if I have to burn all five villages of Sparta.'

'Sparta?' Hipponax said. 'The Persians have him.'

Aristides gave me a look that begged me to keep my tongue between my teeth, and I took a deep breath and bit down on my rage.

'We'll get him,' I said again.

Both boys all but slunk off, they were so downcast. I had one ray of sunlight in my anger – that they loved their brother. And Hector *had* made the right decision. And Heraklitus was safe in Sardis.

After the boys had gone to their ships, I sat with Aristides.

'I'm sorry,' he said.

I sat looking out over the Golden Horn for a long time.

'I'm sorry, too,' I said. But I wasn't really sorry. 'I'm sorry for Sparta,' I added.

Aristides nodded. 'It's worse than you think,' he said. 'While we were here, their king Leotychidas was in eastern Thessaly, trying and failing to conquer. And now the ephors have arrested him.'

I looked at him.

'He took a bribe,' Aristides said, and shrugged.

'A Spartan king. Took a bribe.' I didn't smile.

'It makes me wonder about Demaratus,' Aristides the Just said.

'And Pausanias?' I asked.

'He murdered a girl,' Aristides said. 'A terrible business. A local girl he'd taken as a bed-warmer.'

'You mean, after we prevented our troops from raping—'

'Don't imagine that thought hasn't made the rounds of our campfires. Anyway, he thought she was an assassin coming into his bed, and he put his sword through her. And in the morning, one of his Spartans said, "'First blood to the strategos.'"

I nodded. Black Spartan humour. Meaning that the Spartans had gone the whole summer without bloodying their swords, and their leader had killed a girl in his bed. Spartans are very well versed in summing up complex thoughts in simple sentences.

'So,' I said. 'We're done here?'

'Yes,' Aristides said.

Epilogue

I was home in Plataea before the second harvest was in. Those of you who were present for my daughter's wedding have heard all this before – how it was Plataea's golden summer, how my second daughter was born, and my house was built, and I managed to preside over a few ceremonies as archon.

And as I said that night, I gave thanks to the gods every day, and I prayed, made my sacrifices, changed my daughter's diapers, and in general, was the happiest I had ever been. And perhaps will ever be. That autumn will always be golden – the smell of fresh-baked bread, the jasmine and mint of Briseis' head by me on the pillow – my spear only a decoration at last – the heady smell of new wine and new babies, and the glorious carpet of the land of Boeotia alive with new growth.

But in my head, I was in Thrace, imagining a colony, or in Sardis, arranging for my son's release. And in as much as I was a political man, with a political wife, we plotted a new alliance for Ionia even as she recovered from the birth. Of course, I told her of the threats of the ephors.

She smiled. 'The arrogance of those old men is astonishing,' she said. 'That they think their reach is longer than mine, who was the wife of a Satrap. Heraklitus will be well tended, and he may even learn something.'

I sent my invitations over the mountains. We laid Persian rugs from the tents of Xerxes, Mardonius and Artibazos on our floors against the cold. I spent my loot, and I was not ashamed to receive my share of Cimon's take. He hadn't sold the Lydians and Phoenicians as slaves, but ransomed them back to their families, and he divided the money fairly, and promised that he'd bring it to our dinner.

And a new year came into the world – the fourth year of the

seventy-fifth Olympiad, at least by Boeotian calendars. As the snow melted, it was difficult to even find the scars of war. Already Plataea was built anew. A small – but rich – city nestled at the foot of Cithaeron. We held a muster of our spears, and we had almost two thousand hoplites, because we had freed virtually every slave and replaced them with our Persians and Medes and Cilicians and Thracians.

War – some men are made kings, and others slaves.

We celebrated the Anthesterion and feast of my ancestor Heracles. There were thirty men and women in my house, and we were nymphs and satyrs, and the laughter drove out the darkness, as it should.

And the date of my dinner drew closer.

When the first flowers blossomed, I took a handful of my friends and rode over the mountains, and fetched Leukas and my father-in-law, and Aristides and Jocasta, Phrynicus and his wife, and Aeschylus, and Archilogos and his new bride Anthea, and Briseis' two sons, as well as Cimon and his insipid Thracian wife, and young Pericles, who'd spent most of the winter with Cimon. We rode like a procession of kings back to Boeotia, and there was Lykon from Corinth, waiting for us on the road with a veiled lady, and Sparthius, from far-off Sparta, and Megakles and Doola from farther still, and Gaius, who wept when we embraced.

And from Ionia came Archilogos, and Neoptolimos, and Dionysios of Mytilini, with greetings from his father and further words about Thrasybulus of Samos, with whom we were not yet finished. But that is also another story.

And there were plenty of guests from Plataea itself. Styges, of course, and Leander and Alexanor and their wives, and many new friends from both sides of Cithaeron – Damon and both Nestors, Ole Llurin and Rigura and Mera and Kassandros and Zephyrides and Arios and Diodoros and Philippos, still bouncing up and down, and Sebastos. But there was no shortage of hands to lay tables or set them, either.

I've told you all this before. But I repeat myself, as old men do, because really, of all my battles and wars, this was the high point of my life.

And as we rode down the pass into Boeotia, we gathered friends like the triumphal procession that in fact we were. Penelope from her farm, and Styges, as I said, from his forge and Tiraeus and Sekla and Alexandros and his wife, Gelon and Hipponax and Heliodora and Hector and Iris, Ka and Sitalkes and Polymarchos and Moire and Giannis, who had his own ships now. We went to the new Temple of Hera, where the statue of Mater Hera was my mother almost to the life – sober, one hopes. And there stood Brasidas to receive his bride, and Neomi to receive her groom, and Leukas and Brasidas were married, side by side, in fulfilment of promises made.

And that night, in the courtyard of our house, we lay on every kline from every house in Plataea. And wine flowed like the blood of heroes. We ate a whole tuna that took eight men to carry, and enough bread to have fed our phalanx at Plataea.

And the sober Spartan lady was Gorgo, and she lay between Jocasta and Briseis while they plotted the end of the dominion of the ephors, and Brasidas and Sparthius both looked shocked and went outside – and shrieked with laughter, and played with you, dear *thugater*.

It was Gorgo who told us the truth, as she saw it – the truth that no peer or Spartiate would share. The ephors were attempting the de facto overthrow of the kings. Oh, they'd leave the kings in place. But after sending two into exile, and allowing Leonidas to go to his death, it was Gorgo's view that their actions were intentional. They intended to be the rulers of Sparta, and leave the kings as figureheads.

And very quietly, she said to me, in between my little daughter's screams at her tickling, that she, too, pitied Pausanias.

'They had to bring him down,' she said. 'They brook no rivals. They rule by secrets and have no time for heroes.'

Poor Pausanias. Although there is more, and sadder, to tell.

But not that week, and not then. In that week, we were with the gods, like Miltiades in the day after Marathon, and only the fate of Heraklitus lay like a cloud on the distant horizon, when you are sailing with the wind on your quarter, all your rowers laughing on the benches, and everything seems right with the world.

I will leave them all there. In victory. In happiness. A little drunk, and beautiful. Brasidas with his crown of ivy askew, my sister gazing into his eyes. When he made the libation to begin the dinner, Brasidas mentioned that Antigonus lay with Leonidas.

Yes. I told it all to you before.

But what I didn't say was why we'd all come together – why Aristides and Cimon had come from Athens in the midst of a political crisis, and Gorgo, the very Queen of Sparta and the leader of her

Pan-hellenic faction, from Lacedaemon. I told the story as if we were gathering to have a party.

But what we gathered to do was create the League. Nowadays we call it the Delian League, but it was made at Plataea, by Aristides and Cimon and Archilogos, according to the historians. But what I remember is a roomful of women, their spindles rising and falling like children's toys as they made wool thread, Gorgo as precise as Jocasta. And as the drop spindles turned, they talked about the world, and in my memory, they settled as many things as Archilogos and Cimon.

And when they were done, Cimon rose, and we toasted the Alliance, and the war with Persia. And Briseis and I announced that we would found a colony in Thrace.

And Doola and Sekla discussed a voyage to Africa with our new friends. And I agreed. First, because I wanted to go – I've *always* wanted to go. But second, because a colony in Thrace would eat money the way a fine horse eats hay.

Leave us there, in the hour of bliss.

But no story is ever over, and if you come hunting again with me when the stags rut, why, perhaps I'll tell you what happened in the fourth year of the seventy-fifth Olympiad, when Cimon took the war to Persia, and I began to build our ships for the Red Sea and Africa.

Here ends *The Treason of Sparta*
which is part one of the 'Broken Empire' series, continuing the
'Long War.' It will be continued in *The Longest Voyage*.

Author's Note

When I sat down to read Professor Mary White's brilliant article *Some Agiad Dates: Pausanias and His Sons* (written in 1964, by the way), nothing in my knowledge of classical history had really prepared me for the evidence that Sparta wilfully worked against the Greek Alliance in the period immediately after the great Battle of Plataea in 479BCE. It seems impossible, if you were raised on the movie *300* and Steven Pressfield's brilliant *Gates of Fire* that the magnificent, warlike, honourable Spartans were in fact venal, selfish, and typically Greek political animals capable of working for their own interests against the needs of other Greeks, and especially the Ionian Greeks.

And yet, once I realized the reality of the situation, I also realized that it's all there, in Herodotus, and Herodotus is the basis of all of the stories I'm telling in the Long War series. Herodotus tells us that the Spartans tried to leave Athens to its fate after the Greek Alliance failures at Artemesium and Thermopylae. Herodotus tells us of the contention between the Athenians and the Spartans even the night before Salamis. And Herodotus tells us the story (with which this book opens) about wily Themistocles building the Long Walls of Athens to make her secure from Spartan attack while the Spartan ambassadors were fobbed off with promises.

All historical fiction is fiction, and this book covers dangerous ground, trying to tell the story of fractured alliances and devious politics in Athens and Sparta without departing too far from the historical record. And let me note here that the word 'Treason' is really too strong. Sparta had the foresight to realize that Athens would rise to empire by ruling the Ionians, and sought to prevent that, just as she had sought to prevent Athens taking over all of Attica, or becoming a democracy. Sparta's problems with Athens went back to the sixth century BCE and would continue through the Peloponnesian

Wars. Sparta simply acted in its own interest, and in the process betrayed the Ionian Revolt (of which Sparta had never approved) and her own regent, Pausanias, who was left trying to implement an impossible policy. To me, it is a genuine tragedy, a real-life Greek tragedy that deserved to be told as a story. But, in broad outlines, it really happened as described, and most of the details, including Pausanias abandoning sieges, releasing Persian prisoners, and being, in the end, recalled in disgrace, are all from period sources.

There will be two more books in this, the new Arimnestos series (which I call the *Broken Empire* series). As I have long promised, Arimnestos will travel to Africa and India and, if I have time to write it, found a colony in Thrace. I love writing Arimnestos, and we still have a long way to go. Also, we just performed the reenactment of the Battle of Plataea in 2022 and the hobby of Ancient Greek reenactment is growing, and my own interest in the period remains strong. If you want to have a look at what Plataea was like, visit https://plataea2022.com/, and if you want to participate, contact me through my author website at https://christiancameronauthor.com/ and put the word 'Plataea' in the subject line. I do try to answer all reader mail. We're reenacting Plataea again in 2024 ... and we don't just need hoplites, we need Persians, and civilians, and the whole ancient world ...

Thanks for reading. More Arimnestos to come.

Christian Cameron
Toronto 2023

Acknowledgements

As I put the finishing touches on the first of a new 'Arimnestos' trilogy, I would like to thank the many people and institutions who have made these books possible. I pride myself on my research, and that research is enabled by great libraries, especially the Metro Toronto Public Library, the Robarts Library of the University of Toronto, and the University of Rochester, my alma mater.

I dedicated this book to my friend and fellow ancient reenactor Giannis Kadaglou, without whom these books would either never have been written or would have been much worse. Giannis is the most thoroughly well-read person I have ever met on the world of Ancient Greece; he is not an academic, but a brilliant craftsperson, and yet his knowledge of the details of ancient life, ancient material culture, and current museum holdings or vase art representations is encyclopaedic. The number of times I have called on him (literally via phone or Zoom) to ask 'what's the best representation of a 5th c. woman's loom? What's the likely costume of a Spartan ephor?' and on and on ... and he always leaps into the breach and offers the best advice, usually solving my research query with photos from his own collection. Last year, at the re-enactment of the Battle of Plataea (in Greece, at Plataea, and supported by the Archaeological Museum of Thiva) he played the role of Pausanias to my Aristides ... so you can imagine how I envision my novels. Anyway, my hat is off to you, Giannis. I could not write these boos without you, and sometimes I imagine I'm writing them for you.

And while I'm discussing the Battle of Plataea, let me thank the contributions of every man and woman who attended, roughly a hundred and thirty-five participants from all over the world. Together, we did some excellent experiments and did a little to portray the reality of war and peace in Ancient Greece. If you are interested in looking at our photos, visit https://plataea2022.com/ thursday-morning-march/ for example. Prowl around the site. You'll see why I love re-enactment so much. By the way, we're doing it again in 2024 and probably moving on to other sites in 2026. Still time to make kit or just come and visit!

Let me also thank my daughter, Beatrice, who has been a reenactor whether she wanted to or not since age two. She was fantastic at Plataea.

While I'm thanking researchers, let me thank Aristotelis Koskinas and his wife Ilia Iatrou, both archaeologists and researchers, and good friends, as well as Evi Tsota of the Archaeological Museum of Thiva, whose support has been essential and whose comments on the roads of Boeotian slotted neatly into this book (and future books).

Finally, thanks to my wife Sarah for her patience with my passion for Greece, to Steve O'Gorman, the world's finest copy-editor (he's really really good) and the staff at Orion, especially Celia Killen, without whom this re-birth of Arimnestos would never have come to fruition. There's more to come folks! Two more.

Your Author,
Christian Cameron

About the Author

Christian Cameron is a writer and military historian. He participates in re-enacting and experimental archaeology, teaches armoured fighting and historical swordsmanship, and takes his vacations with his family visiting battlefields, castles and cathedrals. He lives in Toronto and is busy writing his next novel.